Five Nights of Yes, Ma'am

Mercy Denton

CONTENTS

AUTHOR'S NOTE   V

1. THEO   1

2. CALLIE   9

3. THEO   30

4. CALLIE   43

5. THEO   59

6. CALLIE   75

7. THEO   89

8. CALLIE   103

9. THEO   118

10. CALLIE   128

11. THEO   144

12. CALLIE   158

13. THEO   171

14. CALLIE   181

15. THEO   195

16. 16 CALLIE   208

17. THEO   218

18. CALLIE   226

19. THEO   235

20. CALLIE   244

21. THEO   252

22. CALLIE   263

23. THEO   273

24. CALLIE   283

25. THEO   298

26. CALLIE   311

27. THEO   326

28. CALLIE   340

29. THEO   355

30. CALLIE   365

31. THEO   375

32. CALLIE   391

33. THEO   401

Acknowledgements   414

AUTHOR'S NOTE

Welcome back to the Sinful Delights Series. If you're new here, welcome, welcome!

I hope you enjoy Callie and Theo's story, this book is very special to me and I hope you love it as much as I do.

Before you begin, I wanted to let you know that like the other books in the Sinful Delights Series, this book takes place in Canada and is written in Canadian English.

Some words may look different to you.

If you find what you think is an error that my editing team missed, you're welcome to drop me a screenshot here: mercydenton@gmail.com

Five Nights of Yes, Ma'am is about two people meeting at the wrong time and trying to make it work, anyways... because it's never always the right time, you know?

So grab on and hold on tight... because love is worth the leap.

Not every book is for every reader, please read the following content notes:

The MC has an alcoholic, abusive ex

Brief mention of addiction (FMC's parents)

FMC's sister has a brain injury, her recovery plays a central role in the story

Kinks: Male chastity, temperature play, light bondage, prostate play, cum eating, orgasm tease and denial, public play, including public sex, light impact play

Five Nights of Yes, Ma'am is a book that has my whole heart and I hope you enjoy it!

Thanks for reading,

Mercy Denton

1

THEO

DECEMBER 21

I could have booked a vacation. Anywhere in the world.

Somewhere warm and tropical.

Somewhere I could get my cock sucked—and then *locked*—because it's been a while.

I'm a patient guy.

But still... *It's been a while*.

Instead, I'm at this small winery in the Okanagan Valley that belongs to the little sister of my ex.

As I step out on the creaking porch, surveying the twenty-five acres of this winery and the view of the mountains in the distance through the light cloud cover, the tension eases, and I unclench my jaw.

I needed a change of scenery from skyscrapers and banks of monitors.

My dad likes to remind me that there are only so many hours you can sit at a computer before you forget that the sky exists.

But that justification is weak.

"You can stay for dinner if you want," Izzy says, but I hear the hesitation in her voice, even though the shy smile she gives me tugs at my memories of when things were good.

"I have to get back to the city."

They are hosting an investor breakfast tomorrow. David asked me to skip it.

Izzy pushes her wide-framed black glasses up her nose. "Our rooms are comfortable. You could stay the night. There's supposed to be snow, at least closer to the city."

I don't want to hurt her feelings, but being around Izzy leads me down past roads of heartache I don't want to spend a lot of time on.

"Let the man go, Izzy. He didn't have to come and get the wine, I'm sure he has a guy for that who could've delivered it to his brother." David wraps his arms around his wife and pulls her close to him. David isn't happy about my being here.

Or about all the times Izzy has texted me to help her.

Izzy's face crumbles.

Her brown eyes ringed with gold remind me of her older sister.

As much as I love Izzy, there's only so much of their similarities I can handle before the memories start to overwhelm me.

"Of course I was going to come myself." I pick up a crate of wine. "I've missed you, Izzy."

That much is true and the bright smile on Izzy's face makes me glad I said it.

Sometimes I'm quiet and stingy with my words but this almost little sister of mine has a need for reassurance.

"Let me load these up for you." David takes the crate out of my hands, reaches down, and picks up another one like it's cotton candy and not twenty pounds.

"Do you think Evan will like our wine?" Izzy bites her lips.

I shove my hands in my pockets, stepping out of David's way as he loads the last two crates in the back of the truck.

I'm here as a representative of my big brother, who owns Sinful Delights, an establishment that's a restaurant and kink dungeon combined.

Technically, Sinful Delights is owned by the Brennon Consortium, and all four of us brothers have a stake in that venture.

Other than making sure our IT people are doing their jobs and helping my brother Noel out with his kinky resort right when he opened it, I stay out of the daily running of the Consortium.

Though picturing Evan's face as I tell him what wine he's going to put on his menu for the next several months is an amusing thought.

"I'm not a wine guy, and I enjoyed the glass I had when I arrived." I take a step back from Izzy, trying to cement the fact that I need space from her.

"Thanks, Theo. We want this place to work out." Izzy bites her lip, and the hunger she has for reassurance pulls at my memories.

"I keep telling you, it's a dream. It's going to be fine," David grabs his wife and nuzzles her neck, making Izzy giggle.

My stomach drops to the ground.

I'm happy for them, but jealousy slithers through me. It's been a long time since I've had a relationship.

The last woman I shared my dreams with left me and my heart in pieces.

"You've got everything going for you." It really is time for me to go.

"Thank you, Theo," Izzy says quietly.

"Thanks for understanding about not taking your money," David murmurs the words to me as I open the door of the truck.

A stab of remorse hits me in the gut.

I offered David a sum to invest, and he turned me down out of pride.

That's why I'm heading back tonight and not staying for the investor's event.

I get it, and there's a part of me that respects the man for it, but the part of me that longs to be helpful is crushed

"My ego isn't hurt." That's only a slight lie. I clap a hand on his arm. "You're doing a great job here."

"Yeah. I never thought I'd have this place." David takes off his hat and nods, as if he's convincing himself of that.

Three months ago, David's aunt dropped the news that she'd bought this winery and it was her wedding gift to him and Izzy.

Even with the influx of wealth, I know they've been struggling.

There are a lot of costs in an operation of this size, and all the profit is turned right back into it.

But they'll be okay.

I couldn't help but run through the projections, though I stopped myself from asking Evan to give me his read on it.

That'd be stepping too far into Izzy's life, and as much as I wished at one time I was her big brother, the truth is I'm not—because her older sister took that choice away from me.

"Theo, I appreciate all the times you helped Izzy when I wasn't around. But I'm here now."

He doesn't have to say more. I get it.

"You make her happy, David. Merry Christmas."

"Merry Christmas," David says, extending his hand. Izzy gives me one more clingy hug, pressing me against the truck's door.

"Thank you for coming. I guess I have to stop texting you every time I need something, huh?" Her brown eyes fill with tears.

"David is a great guy, Izzy. I will always care for you, and if you needed me and didn't have anyone else, I'd be here, but you calling just reminds me of..." I trail off, unsure how to put it in words.

"The bad times?" Izzy finishes.

"Your New Year is going to be great," I want her to believe it.

"Hey, is it weird if I visit Sinful Bites with David?"

I try to hide my surprise, but I can't. It'd never occur to me that Izzy is kinky, but they say things run in families...just look at mine.

"Not weird at all." I glance across at David.

"Thanks, it's a surprise for David."

"He'll love it," I say, but a hollowness settles in my gut.

"Take care, Izzy." I get in the truck.

They wave goodbye as I drive down the long gravel road. The truck bounces and jerks.

In my mirror, I see Izzy and David kissing, and a rush of jealousy so strong crashes over me I can barely stand it.

Once, I was so sure that I would have a home with someone I loved. And we'd run a business together.

I'm over that. The relationship wasn't good for me, but the what-ifs are so strong.

The truck makes a *chug chug* noise. I chalk it up to it just being an old truck and continue on.

It's not the first time I've driven my dad's truck, but it's completely different from my hybrid car.

And because it's my dad's truck, there are bits of stuff everywhere.

Springs and tweezers, a metal frame and bits of steel, random pieces of wood and material. A box of parts rattles in the backseat.

My dad's an inventor and can't help but bring pieces of his workshop everywhere.

I have his truck because he asked me to drop off old furniture at the donation centre and insisted I should borrow the truck because there was snow heading for the valley.

It's not like hybrid vehicles can't drive through snow, thank-you very much.

But dad pressed the keys in my hand and looped his arm through mom's.

With the way mom's eyes gleamed, I suspect they like my car more than they admit.

I'm driving through farmland and wineries, passing a sign for the small town of Rising Harbour when the truck makes an awful screeching sound, chugs again and I press my foot down on the brake.

The sky is dark now, cloudy and grey.

I should have taken Izzy's offer of a place to stay the night.

Nope, I tell myself sternly. I need distance from her. I can't keep rescuing Izzy. She's not my responsibility.

The truck makes a kind of whirring sound.

I veer left, taking the turn for Rising Harbour, hoping I can find somewhere to stop and call my youngest brother, Hunter, who is way better at car things than I am.

I'm on what looks like the main street when the truck grinds, coughs and slows to a halt.

Doesn't matter what I do, it's not moving.

Leaning back in the seat, I notice I'm right outside a restaurant

At least I can grab a cup of coffee, though the place looks closed.

Glancing at the brick building through the passenger window, the sign reads, **Shel's Diner.**

Scrolled on the window in neon pink is "Shel Diner" again, but the word *diner* on the window is crossed out and replaced by "*cafe*."

The diner is next to a florist and a clothing boutique.

I call Hunter.

My palm is tight on the wheel, like I'm holding on with everything I have.

Suddenly, my chest feels tight.

My ex's face, sneering at me, swims in my mind. The way she curled her lip when she was in a bad mood.

The way she'd put me down for not being a *real man* whenever I insisted on calling someone for help with my car or something around the house, burns through me.

And the feeling of shock I had that this otherwise bright, beautiful woman, who was happy and bubbly around everyone, would say these things to me in moods so changing I couldn't keep track of them. Lynn was everything I thought I wanted: confident, strong, beautiful, and liked to take control in the bedroom.

I was ripe for that experience, foolishly thinking that it was time for me to have a relationship and do the whole marriage and kids' thing.

I didn't realize it'd be a four-year relationship of hell.

One that nobody knew was bad for the longest time, except for my older brother Noel. That's because Noel's first wife, my sweet sister-in-law, Claire, overheard Lynn berating me one day when she came by my apartment to drop off dinner for me.

After Claire and Noel found out, I told Hunter, and I'm glad I did because months later, I needed his help.

I need to pull my head out of the past and focus on the here and now.

But I'm frozen with the gut-wrenching anxiety that always stirs when I think about Lynn.

She wanted me involved in her family, but wanted nothing to do with mine.

We were exclusive—so I thought—but she didn't want to move in together.

I shiver in the cab and realize the temperature has plummeted.

A woman stares at me through the restaurant window. There's something in her demeanor that's so confident and self-assured I feel like I've been rescued from my hall of painful memories.

2

CALLIE

How is it possible my feet hurt *this* much? Oh, right, I've been on them for a gazillion hours. I finish sweeping under the middle tables and empty the dustbin into the trash.

I mentally run through my closing night duties, grateful for the ability to run on autopilot because I am having trouble stringing two thoughts together.

A few short months ago, I would have put in a four-hour day and then spent the rest of the afternoon lounging on the beach and my night partying.

Though it's not the beach, there is nowhere prettier in the whole world than Rising Harbour.

Yep, I'm biased. This place is in my blood and soul.

I always meant to come back, just not so soon.

"Zoom! Zoom!" My seven-year-old nephew drives his Hot Wheels on the freshly swept floor.

"Watch out, buddy." I ruffle his thick mop of curls as I pass by, so much like my sister's an immediate lump rises in my throat.

Done with sweeping, I fill the mop bucket.

"I want more crayons!" Abby, my four-year-old niece, chants behind me.

"You know where they are." I force myself to smile at her because no matter how tired I am, these kids are my world.

I need to make sure they don't feel like any of this is their fault.

"Luke, scramble up onto the bench. You too, Abby!" I call to them, wheeling the mop and bucket back to the middle.

"Why does this take *forever*?" My oldest niece, Madison, flips her long auburn hair over her shoulder but stacks the chairs for me.

I hum in my head, not wanting to start an argument with my tween niece, wishing that I were alone at the diner.

My favourite part of the day? Closing duties. Just me, the lock clicking shut, and scandalous audiobooks.

"She touched me!" Luke screeches. "Did not!" Abby sticks her tongue out at her brother.

"Guys, in a few more minutes, dad will be home." I hope my brother-in-law, Grady, will make an appearance soon.

I need a hot shower, to put my feet up and get back to my audiobook.

I left off where the main character was just about to go down on the heroine, and my lady parts throbbed vicariously.

Considering it's been *forever* since anyone has paid me that kind of attention, I'm eager to return to the fiction world.

The only male power I've had between my legs is my motorcycle Morris.

He's hardy and reliable, but sometimes a woman needs more than mechanics.

Ha. I smile at my cringey joke.

I work the mop under the tables, taking pride in how the peach-speckled quarry floor gleams.

This floor was one of the last renovations my sister did on the place.

When I came back home and stepped into Shel's, I could almost see our grandpa behind the counter, him pointing at the sign of the town in the '50s, telling tourists the story of when he took it over from his father back when there was hardly a road in this town.

This restaurant was one of the first businesses in Rising Harbour, and it's still standing today.

Hopefully, it'll stand another fifty years if I have my way.

There's a tingle in my throat that I'm ignoring. I push away thoughts of the restaurant closing because the town doesn't want a diner.

They want something "trendy and upscale" to bring in new business.

Over the last couple of months, my Uncle Henry and I have fended them off, but I don't know how much longer that's going to last.

Grady and Daphne don't own the building outright, and with the town intent on this revitalization, they can lose the place according to the town's bylaws.

"No! Give me my crayon!" Abby yells, reaching across the table. She snatches the crayon out of Luke's hand.

His little face crumples and breaks into tears.

I know the feeling, kid. Setting the mop down, I make my way to the two kids, noticing Madison is picking up the mop from where I left it.

These three are the best kids in the world.

"Hey guys, there's enough crayons here to share."

"But I want the blue one!"

"I want the blue one too!" Abby says.

"Should we break it in half?" I ask.

Abby's blue eyes widen, her little hand covers her box of crayons protectively.

"No!"

"Hmm," I pretend to think about it. "What else can we do?"

"Take turns!" Luke says with a wide gap-toothed smile.

"Right. Think you can let Abby have a turn with the blue one?"

"Uh-huh. Here, Abby!" Luke gives the crayon back to his sister.

Whew. Disaster averted. I go back to the mop.

"I got it," Madison says.

"Thanks." From the service station, I grab the cart with the silverware, glasses and menus.

I set the tables, so they're all ready for tomorrow's service.

My head cook, Ryan, has the kitchen all set to go with the new specials, and there's nothing for me to do back there.

When I came back to Shel's, one of the first things I did was sit down with Ryan and Brenda—his wife and the person who actually runs Shel's—and changed the menu.

Madison takes the mop bucket back to the kitchen to empty and joins me a moment later.

"I don't understand why I can't visit her at night, after dinner." Madison thumps the rolled-up silverware so hard on the table that the saltshaker spills over.

Placing a smile on my face, I act like it doesn't bother me and set the salt upright.

"Mads, we've been over this. You're a child. A child isn't allowed at night in the rehab clinic."

"I'm not a child." She slumps into a booth, crosses her arms over her chest.

The gesture makes the tween look and sound like an overgrown toddler.

"My cars!" Luke shouts as his Hot Wheels spill.

"Luke! Pick up your cars from under the table!" I call as the Hot Wheels are swiped off the table in what appears to be a crayon battle.

"I wouldn't get in the way. I'd follow the rules." Madison looks away from me, blinking back tears.

"I know you would, Madison, but I'm sure it's a liability thing." I make another mental note to ask our family liaison about it tomorrow night. Even if Madison can say a quick goodnight to her mom, she needs to see her as much as possible.

"You're going tonight with your dad, right?"

"Yeah, after the babies are dropped off at Uncle Henry's. We have just enough time to make it."

The cutoff for kids visiting is 7 p.m.

"She was eager this morning when I saw her, trying to say more words," I say lightly.

"But not all of them. Her speech is still slurred." Madison glances away, but I catch the tears in her eyes.

My heart closes like a fist in pain.

I want to wrap my arms around my niece like I did after the accident first happened, when she sobbed on my shoulder.

"Nope, but it's progress, Mads. Time for us moves faster than it does for your mom. The fact that she's awake and has improved cognitive function is good," I recite the line I say to her about once a day, the mantra I tell myself.

"I miss her, that's all." Madison glances away.

"Me too." Tears threaten to spill from my eyes, but I blink them away. I hate crying.

Daphne is my younger sister, the star of our family, and there isn't a thing I wouldn't do to make her life easier.

She's my little sister, and I've always taken care of her.

Determined to make Shel's a bustling spot in town once again, she and Grady took over the diner when my Aunt Millie was too sick to run it.

Daphne's on the town's tourism committee, organizes charity drives, is the best damn mother I've ever seen, a supportive wife, and my best friend.

She absolutely did not deserve the accident that happened to her in August.

"Auntie Callie, there's a truck outside! Is that man lost?" Luke asks, pointing out the window.

I come over and peer out at a Chevy Silverado that's idling at the curb.

My immediate suspicions rise because I know every vehicle in this town, and I haven't seen this one.

The town doesn't want Shel's to keep standing, and I wonder if it's a messenger from them.

"I don't know, kiddo."

The back door beeps, and Luke immediately charges through the restaurant, Abby following him.

I turn away from the mystery truck, smiling despite how tired I am.

"Hey guys! Who wants nuggets?" Grady calls out.

"Me!" Luke hurls himself at his dad, and Grady swings Luke up into his arms.

"You got it! We're going to get nuggets on our way to see Mommy."

Madison's face falls.

"Mom's had a good day, Madison. I want the babies to say goodnight," Grady says to his oldest. Madison nods, but I can tell she's upset.

"Daddy, can we go now?" Abby asks excitedly.

"You betcha. Go get your backpacks," Grady sets Luke down, and the kids run back to the alcove off the kitchen.

"You okay, Callie? You're looking a little rugged." Grady is a beefy, burly guy, at six feet, with blond hair and a shaggy beard.

"I'm fine. Give Daphne hugs for me."

"Always. Thanks Callie, I couldn't do this without you," he clears his throat.

"Likewise," I tell him. "Madison, I'll take you to visit on your own, I promise."

"Okay, Aunt Callie. See you tomorrow," she runs past me.

Grady rubs his beard. "They were fine?"

"They're always fine," I try to give him a reassuring smile.

This big guy that my sister's loved since high school was a complete wreck a couple months ago, but he's pulled himself together and stepped up for their kids.

"Thanks, Callie. I don't know what we'd do without you."

"I love you guys," I give the kids a wave.

"Let's go, Daddy!" Luke says, running back over to us. He grabs Grady's hand, pulling him along.

"Oh no! I've been captured! I must go!" Grady grins at me as the kids pull playfully on his arms, dragging him away.

"Bye, Aunt Callie!" The kids shout.

"Bye!"

I wait until the back door beeps and I hear Grady's truck pulling out of the back parking lot before I go to see if Mr. Old Blue Chevy is still out the front.

Yep, the truck hasn't moved an inch.

A wave of tiredness rocks me on my feet, but I push it away.

Strolling out the front door, I march right over to the driver's side of Mr. Old Blue Chevy.

Lifting my fist to the window, I rap on it three times.

The guy jumps and then rolls down the window. "Sorry?"

A pair of grey eyes meets mine under the light of the cab. "Why are you parked outside my restaurant?" My defences are up because, over the last year, my sister's dealt with some shady stuff from the people who are trying to get her to close up shop.

"My truck stopped here," the guy says. "Sorry."

He starts to cough, then launches into a full-out coughing fit.

"Sorry," he says again, waving his hand in front of his face.

"What do you mean, stopped?" There isn't much light to see it, and the thought of getting my toolbox and popping the hood makes me feel exhausted, even as my hands itch to do that.

"It made a bunch of noise and then coughed, and no matter what I do, it doesn't go."

The guy glances at me, then quickly away, as if he's afraid I'm going to yell at him.

"Get out of your truck."

"Wh-what?"

"Out, so I can look at it," I stand back to give him room to hop down, bracing myself for him to go into a rant about how he's not going to let *some woman* into his truck.

But he unclips his seatbelt, leaves the keys in the ignition and gets out.

Mr. Tall, Hot-as-Hell Grey Eyes climbs out of the truck.

With his wavy sandy hair falling slightly across his brow, he's kind of adorable. He flashes me a smile of pearly whites.

That smile makes my libido sit up and take notice.

"Theo Brennon." He meets my eyes, then looks away and extends his hand.

"Callie Tremblay," I return his handshake.

His cool fingers clasp over mine, with light even pressure.

Most guys when they shake my hand do it in an aggressive manner, like they're trying to exert their masculinity through that one gesture.

Looking at him, my emotions shift, as if I'm being tugged back in time, to a space where fucking this hot guy in his truck, right here and now, would be something I'd jump on.

"I need to call a mechanic, I guess."

I hop into the truck, turn the key over, and listen to the noises.

"Do you have a flashlight in here?" I ask.

"In the box in the backseat." Theo stands there, with his hands in his pockets, giving me space.

He's not over my shoulder trying to see what I am doing, how refreshing.

I find the flashlight and get out, going around to the back of the truck.

"Do you know the name of a mechanic?" Theo pulls out his phone.

"Henry's is closed." I flash the light under the truck but don't have to do much because the gas leaking is pretty easy to spot.

"I was hoping to get back to the city tonight," Theo runs his hand through it. It's neatly trimmed, a little long on top, and I want to run my hands through it.

"You're going to have to make other plans." Stealing another glance at him, I pass him back the flashlight, noticing how his dress shirt hugs his frame.

"Any other mechanics besides Henry's?" He glances away as he says it.

"Not in Rising Harbour and not open now. You could tow it to Glass Falls, the next town over, and try your luck there."

But I doubt Charlie, the mechanic in Glass Falls, would leave the darts tournament for something he's not going to do tonight.

A wave of dizziness makes me sway on my feet.

Theo's hand finds my arm, steadying me with a gentle touch.

It's been forever since I've been touched by a man, and this casual gesture is making me squirrelly.

I want to both fuck him senseless and run away—that pretty much sums up my MO when it comes to dating.

"I give a good foot massage." He turns scarlet as soon as the words are out of his mouth.

I stifle a laugh. "Oh yeah? I might take you up on that," I say it just to see if he'd blush more. Yep, he did.

"That's the best offer I've had in a long time. Do you *like* feet?" My tone turns sultry, low.

"I..." Theo stares at the ground. "Nothing against them, but I'm not into that kind of worship."

"No? What kind of worship are you into?" The words are out of my mouth before I can stop them.

I take a step closer to him, stopping myself from putting my palm on his chest.

"The whole body kind. Why stop at just the feet?" He meets my gaze, holds it.

The connection between us crackles, my pulse jumps.

No, this can't happen. He's a stranger.

But my adrenaline surges as I drink him in, and I want to follow the impulsive urges that are spiking through my blood.

I take a step back, gesture to his truck.

"I can't do anything tonight, but it might be the seal around the fuel line or the tank itself that needs replacing."

"You're a mechanic?" Theo cocks an eyebrow.

"Yep." I'm stilling myself for when Mr. Sexypants turns out to be Mr. Macho as Theo shakes his head.

"I wouldn't ask you to work off-hours. Thanks for taking a quick look."

He didn't even blink at the fact that I'm a mechanic.

I like him. A lot.

"No problem. I didn't have to go far to look." The innuendo is clear, and now it's my face that's heating furiously.

"If you point me to a hotel, I'll stay the night and then you can work on the truck in the morning?" His cute smile makes my stomach flutter.

I wobble on my feet, my throat suddenly dry. There are two bed and breakfasts in Rising Harbour, but I know the Sleepaway that the Olsen's own is undergoing renovations—they're also trying to stay in business under the new town guidelines.

Looking Theo up and down again, I make an instant decision.

I don't want to send him to the Chansons. Mr. Chanson hates me for that time in tenth grade when he thinks I, ah, borrowed his car.

It was actually Daphne and her friends who did it, but I took the blame for her.

My sister was headed to university, and I didn't want anything to get in her way.

"I have room, you can stay with me."

He tilts his head. A slow, wide smile forms on his perfect lips. "Are you sure?"

"Yep."

We're locked in another heated staring contest; the tension between us is thick.

Snowflakes fall heavily, and the wind whips around us.

"I have an overnight bag?" He says it as a question, as if making sure I'm not going to rescind my offer.

"Grab it." Yep, I'm sure.

He does and locks up the truck.

"This way," I gesture for him to go ahead of me.

The man has a fine ass.

I want to cup my hands around it and squeeze until he whimpers.

I push open the door. "Welcome to Shel's."

"You're a mechanic and have a restaurant?" Theo stands in the middle of the diner, and suddenly the space feels tiny.

I watch him taking it all in, and my stomach flutters with nervousness.

Ridiculous, I scold myself. I don't need some stranger's approval. Daphne has sunk so much time and energy into the renovations.

New benches, new chairs, new lighting.

A half-finished painted mural on the back wall.

"Is the countertop original?" Theo runs his hand along the edge of the stainless steel countertop, trimmed with chrome.

"Yep. The place was my grandparents' for years, my great-grandparents' before that. My sister runs it now."

"It's welcoming and cozy. I like it."

"Thank you. I live upstairs." I walk briskly to the back, passing the kitchen, with Theo following behind me.

What have you done? I chide myself.

I know nothing about this man, yet I invited him to stay over.

Going to blame it on being deliriously tired.

But there's a part of me that wants to see what happens. I crave the chase of new things.

"Up here," I turn up the narrow staircase, my heart in my throat. Upstairs there is a wide hallway, two storage rooms and then my apartment door.

I unlock it. Because I'm actually doing this.

"Callie, thank you so much. Are you sure I'm not putting you out?" Theo asks at the door as I stop the shoe rack from toppling over as we take our shoes off.

If only you were putting out, I swallow the immature giggle that wants to escape.

"No, I have the space. Here's the kitchen," I gesture to the dark space behind me. "And here is the living room."

"Ow! I think I broke something!" Theo grabs his shin.

I flip on the light and I want to disappear, mortified by the state of my living room. I'm a bit of a slob, but not like this.

Little figures are strewn all over the floor, along with beads from a craft kit, foam darts and Lego.

"Sorry, I..."

"Have kids?" Theo picks up a small blaster.

The handle is crushed. "I'll replace this."

"I look after my nieces and nephew." I cross my arms, trying to appear casual and confident. But my throat is dry, and my palms are sweaty.

And between my legs? I'm a river just looking at Mr. Sexypants.

"That must keep you busy." He places the blaster on the living room shelf.

"Yeah, I like to be busy." We stare at each other again, then Theo coughs and looks away.

Get a hold of yourself.

"Bedrooms are back this way," I pass my bedroom, determined not to look back to drink in how hot this stranger that I've just let into my apartment is and what he's looking at as I take him to the spare bedroom at the end of the hall. It's the smallest bedroom, but the kids have been using the other one, and I'm sure it's as messy as my living room.

"This will do, thank you, Callie," Theo steps into the room.

"You're welcome. I can scrounge up some dinner in a few." Theo sets his bag on the end of the bed, takes off his jacket. "You've given me shelter. The least I can do is cook."

It's been forever since someone cooked for me.

For the last few months I have cooked for my uncle and aunt, the kids and Grady, and filled in for my short-order cooks downstairs.

"I have soup in the fridge if you don't mind warming that up." I can't deny that my throat is scratchy.

"Got it," Theo gives me a thumbs-up, then blushes.

He stares at me with those deep grey eyes, as if he wants to say something else and I don't know if it's the relief of my day being over or how comfortable I feel with him I can let my guard down, but that tickle in my throat turns into a full on achiness.

"The kitchen is down the hall," I squeak out. "Obviously. I just showed you that."

"Hey, are you all right?" He takes a half-step like he wants to get closer to me, but he resists.

"Fine." I'm not fine. But I have to be. I've got to drop the kids at school in the morning, visit Daphne and maybe help my uncle with Mr. Sexy Pants' truck.

I try to shake it off, going to the small kitchen.

The old four-seater table is covered with colouring books, leftover homework, every chair has a piece of clothing draped over it.

"This is a nice space," Theo says, looking around the kitchen, then he strides to the doorway and peers into the living room. "Those photos on the wall are gorgeous."

Above the couch, there are framed scenes of Tarragona, Spain, Loket, Czech Republic and Komló, Hungry.

Places I traveled the first year I was a mechanic for the motocross team.

"Thank you. I took them."

"You're a woman of many talents." There's no mistaking how his eyes fill with desire.

I shuffle on my feet, unused to this attention.

"My childhood dream was to be a photographer. I've done a bit of both but nothing to pay the bills with."

I move a pile of clothes and take a seat at the table, not feeling great.

"Callie, you don't look so well."

"You sure know what to say to a woman."

The way his cheeks turn scarlet makes me laugh. He rubs the back of his neck, and I decide to ease his discomfort.

"I think I'm coming down with something." I want to cry as the words leave my mouth and I realize how sore my throat actually is and I can't ignore it.

"Let's see what we can do to make you better." He glances at me, blushes and strides over to the counter. He turns on the electric kettle and opens the cupboards. "What kind of tea?"

"I like mint."

"Okay."

As if he's been in my kitchen forever, he takes down my favourite *Boss Like A Girl* mug and pops the tea bag in it and opens the fridge.

The way he moves, methodical, as if he's not going to rush anything, has my mind spinning, wondering how his muscles feel under his shirt.

"What brings you to Rising Harbour?" I got to cool my thoughts down.

"Driving through on the way back to the city. My ex's little sister just took over a winery, and I wanted to do whatever I could to make sure she's on her feet. I bought several cases of wine from them."

"Your ex's little sister?" We all have exes.

"Yeah," Theo opens the fridge, takes out the container of soup, lifts it up to check that it's microwavable, and pops it in to warm.

"You're still close to the little sister?"

Theo takes down another mug, throws a black tea bag in it.

"At one time I thought she was going to be my little sister forever. Seeing her brings back a lot of memories, so I don't visit her often, but we keep in touch. I've known for a while I had to cut that tie." Theo's tone turns wistful.

"Why? It's obvious you still care for her."

"Just because you care about someone doesn't mean it's healthy—for you or for them. Izzy has a new husband. I don't think he appreciated her calling me when she needed to fix her door or look up the boundary of her property line."

"I get it. Hard to leave, even if it's not good for you." My sister thinks I ran away, but it wasn't my plan.

"Yeah. I was with my ex for four years." Theo pours the kettle and brings the mugs over to the table.

Four years is a decent time for an investment in a relationship. I can't imagine any woman letting this man go easily.

"That's a long time. Who ended it?" I rest my head on my folded arms.

By the stiffening of his shoulders, I think I might have gone too far. "It nearly broke me, but I did. Sometimes loving people isn't healthy."

My own history flashes through my mind.

"I get that. You said crates of wine. Do you like wine that much or...?"

Theo laughs, showing his dimples.

"I hardly drink. My older brother Evan owns a restaurant, and he's always looking to try out new suppliers."

Theo sets down the bowls of soup and the spoons. "Thank you for the dinner."

"It's only leftovers, but you're welcome." I steal glances at him while we eat. He's very tidy, good table manners are definitely a turn-on. I scoff, telling myself to chill.

"What's your brother's restaurant?" The warm soup is making my throat feel better.

Theo's cheeks redden, and he sits back in his chair.

I don't know if I have ever seen a man blush so easily when he wasn't naked, in front of me.

"Sinful Bites in Vancouver."

"The kinky restaurant?" I can't keep the surprise out of my tone.

"Yeah. You've been?" Theo stares straight ahead, his hands curl around his bowl, his shoulders hunched.

I nearly spill my soup because, laughing because just a few short months ago I would have *loved* to go to Sinful Bites with my friend Amy and our group on my way home to Rising Harbour.

"No, I haven't had a chance. But my friend Amy is celebrating her 50th birthday there. A few months ago my sister had an accident..." I have to stop because of the lump in my throat.

"Hey, it's all right," Theo tells me.

I blink back tears. "I can't remember the last time I went out. Heard good things about Sinful Bites."

"Yeah?" He raises his eyebrows, his tone curious.

I have no room for a relationship in my life right now.

No room for kink or much fun. For the last few months, I've been trying to keep everyone together.

But it might be nice just for a moment to toe-dip.

So, I decide to lay it on the table.

"I'm a Dominant and I belong to a FemDom social. We go to dinner and things." I creak out the words in the most un-Domly fashion ever.

"I'd love to hear more about that, Callie. But you're shivering. I think you need to go to bed."

"I think you're right." I set my spoon down, spilling the rest of the soup on the table. "Fuck."

"I got it," Theo rushes up and grabs a cloth.

My body feels heavy, and my throat is on fire. I am past being mortified. Theo picks up the bowls and wipes down the table.

"Thanks," I croak out and suddenly, I'm so tired I slump against the chair.

"Let me help you up." Theo takes my arm, lifts me up from the chair.

I'm too tired to protest. He walks me to my bedroom, and I sigh. The kids had made a fort in here, and all my blankets are pulled off the bed.

"My place is usually not like this," I mutter. Except these days, this is my norm.

"It's fine. I can fix this. Sit here." He leads me to the armchair in the corner.

I yawn and watch as if he does it every day, as if it's no big deal, picks up the toys from the floor, and re-makes the bed without hesitation.

"Thank you."

He ducks his head as he smiles at me. "You're welcome."

I grab a pair of sleeping pants from my dresser and, because I've never been one for modesty, I chuck off my pants and put them on.

Theo doesn't even look at me as I change.

I'm kind of disappointed by his good manners.

"There," Theo says, fluffing my pillows.

"Thank you. I'll look at your truck tomorrow."

"You need to rest, Callie," Theo pats the bed.

The walk from the bed to the dresser isn't far, but I trip over my own feet.

Strong arms wrap around me, catching me before I fall.

"You're bossy," I mutter. He smells good, like the outdoors and fresh laundry.

"In some situations." He guides me over to the bed, and my whole body sighs with relief as soon as I make contact with the mattress.

This is so strange that there is a man here looking after me.

"What situations are those?" My eyelids are so heavy I can't help but close them.

"Work. I tell people—super important rich people, mostly—what to do all day long: how to shore up their security systems and improve their data collection systems. Sometimes with my brothers, though all three of them have bigger personalities than I do. They tell me I'm too serious, though I've saved them from getting in trouble a bunch of times. But when it comes to a relationship? I'd rather *not* be the one in charge. I'm going to get you water." Theo clears his throat, blushing all over again.

"Thanks," I squeak out the words, snuggling into the pillow.

"Anything else?" Theo smiles at me, and my stupid heart flutters.

Just my luck that I meet a gorgeous, subby man when I have absolutely no time in my life for a relationship.

"I have cold medicine in the bathroom."

"You've got it." He turns and walks away, giving me a great view of his ass.

I can feel myself burning up and know that I won't be able to do it all. I hate letting people down.

Theo comes back in with a glass of water and a tablet.

"Here, cold medicine."

"Thanks, would you mind getting me my phone? It's in the pocket of the pants I took off."

He flushes a bit but fishes my phone out of my pants while I take the medicine. Then passes it to me.

"I don't want to get you sick."

"Hey, you can't control that. You offered me shelter, the least I can do is make sure you're okay. Anything else I can get you?"

"No, I just have to get through my pile of stuff, tomorrow." I sigh.

"You'll figure it out," Theo flashes me a grin that's both sexy and confident.

"You've just met me, how do you know?" But his words make me feel bolstered.

"Because you've figured it out this long. Let me know if I can do anything for you."

Is this my real life or am I in some kind of flu dreamlike space where this totally hot, confident, sexy and *submissive* man is in my bedroom?

He didn't jump in and try to rescue me but instead, was totally confident I could sort out my mess.

"I have clean towels in the closet," I whisper. My body is aching with an odd mix of arousal and cold symptoms.

That's exactly my kind of luck.

"I'll be right down the hall. Holler if you need something."

"Okay," Normally I'd brush off offers of help but with how I'm feeling right now, I'm grateful.

Theo gives me a wave and a view of his ass again as he exits the room and I wonder what the hell has just happened to my already chaotic life.

3

THEO

I'm humming as I find the towels and hang them up in the bathroom.

Tucking Callie into bed gives me a satisfied, almost loopy feeling that I haven't felt in a long time.

I feel satisfied that she finally rested.

I didn't want to use my Big Boss, Mr. CEO of Cybersecurity tone on her, but I would have if I thought that'd make the woman lie down and close her eyes.

Callie.

As soon as her bright blue eyes met mine, something pulled deep inside me, like I wanted this moment of meeting her to last forever.

A rush of something beyond attraction stirred within me.

I kept saying things just to keep talking to her, even though I knew I sounded awkward

She's a little shorter than me - maybe "5'10" to my 6 feet-and I want to worship her for hours.

I say her name in my head as I grab an empty fabric basket from the shelf. Then, I pick up the toys scattered on the floor.

Our parents taught us to take care of each other, to do things that need to be done, and it's not like I'm going to sleep.

I *like* taking care of people.

In high school, I got all kinds of flak for this.

I had girls who took advantage of me, who kissed me or fondled me but stopped shy of crossing into "boyfriend material."

My older brothers intercepted more than one situation, and I'm grateful for that.

But nobody could have predicted my relationship with Lynn.

After my long-term relationship ended in disaster, I haven't had the chance to give in to my need for service.

Quick hookups don't tend to last beyond the next morning.

So I can't help but imagine myself between Callie's legs, pleasuring her as her head tips back...

My cock thickens, pressing against my slacks. I ignore it because it's *not* going to happen.

Needing a distraction, I finish picking up the living room. I firmly pull my thoughts to the here and now.

I'm too serious to play the flirting game, and I've been burned so badly.

I don't play games at all, but I appreciate the feminine form, especially the confident, strong, sexy type.

Something crunches under my feet, and I groan, hoping I don't have to replace another toy, but it's only a pretzel.

I finish filling the basket with toys and set it down against the bookshelf.

There's obviously been a renovation in this space. The exposed brick wall gives it a sense of history.

The cork floor beneath my feet is warm through my socks, and the bright blue and gold rugs make the living area feel cozy

I keep glancing at these photographs. The beautiful scenery captured in each frame tells a story.

In the hallway, I open a small cupboard and find a vacuum.

Vacuuming the living room of a woman I just met wasn't how I expected to spend this Friday night, but as I do this kind of mindless task, the tension I've had since seeing Izzy and David finally leaves me.

My brothers always tease me for being too serious, too quiet, and for not taking risks

This for me? Is risky because in Callie, I see a woman who is run down to the point that she's sick, and all I want to do is take care of her.

The way her eyes flashed extra bright when she said she was a Domme.

Not that I'm looking for any kind of relationship.

Nope.

One four-year relationship was enough for me.

And it doesn't look like her life would accommodate a relationship either, but...would she be opposed to casual play?

I finish vacuuming and take a peek inside Callie's fridge.

It's pretty bare, but I find a glass in the cupboard above the sink and pour myself some chocolate milk.

Moving as quietly as I can down the hall, I look in on Callie.

She's sleeping, but tossing and turning.

Back in the living room, I study the place.

It's small with an old teak couch with cushions that have obviously been reupholstered, a large television hangs on the wall and bookcases fill the rest of the wall space.

On the bookshelves are framed photos of three adorable kids, a woman who looks like Callie though her hair is a lighter shade, and a man with a beard who has his arms around the woman and the kids. Other pictures show an elderly couple and a man posing in front of the restaurant—a picture from a long time ago.

I feel intrusive taking in all this history, but I can't stop myself from looking

A picture of Callie, looking up from working over an engine, then several pictures of her in a garage with other female mechanics and a picture of her with a motocross team.

My phone buzzes, and I take it out.

I loved seeing you today. I found this picture of us and had to share it. You guys looked so happy then. - IZZY

The picture of me and my ex, Lynn, standing outside the football stadium and it hits me like a punch to the gut.

It was the season opener, and Lynn had season tickets.

I have my arm around her in the picture; her arm is around my waist. I know her fingertips are painfully digging into me, and I also know that in this photo I'm wearing a cock cage.

Lynn loved keeping me locked as often as possible.

And I wanted it too, thinking I had found my soulmate, someone I could trust.

In the end, it was years of my life wasted.

But having my dick locked is something I dream about, crave way more than I should, even after the hell my ex put me through.

From the guest room, I grab my laptop, settle in, and get caught up on work emails, not looking up until I realize Callie's in the room.

"You're not in bed?" Callie's voice startles me out of my thoughts.

She has a hand against the living room wall as if she has to hold herself up, and her face is pale.

"No. I couldn't sleep. Do you need anything?"

"Water or juice or something. It's clean. You cleaned my house." The half-smile on her face makes me so happy.

"Not the whole place, and it wasn't a big deal. It only took a few minutes." She raises an eyebrow and shakes her head.

"I guess it is easier to do it with the kids not here," she flops onto the couch beside me.

"Thanks."

"You're welcome." I smile, and I want to reach out and give her leg a squeeze, but I stop myself. "I'll get you water. I didn't see any juice in your fridge."

"I have to go grocery shopping," Callie covers her mouth as she yawns.

In the kitchen, I take a glass from the cabinet and fill it with water.

Yes, this is a little strange, but it feels good to look after someone, to see to someone else's needs.

"Here you go," I hand her the glass of water, and her fingertips brush mine.

"Thank you. She's pretty," Callie says, gesturing to my phone, still on the photo of Lynn and me.

"That's my ex," I say, watching her face closely, but she doesn't react, other than to turn her head to the side.

"Oh?"

"Yeah, I haven't really been in a relationship since then—not long term."

"Do you date?" Callie curls her feet up under herself, and I pull a throw blanket off the end of the couch and drape it over her.

"Occasionally, for work events, I have to ask someone to attend with me. A few times, I've gone to a club for pickup play."

When I feel like I'm going crazy from isolation and desperation, and I need someone to beat my ass to feel alive, I go to Club Shivers, a private BDSM club in Vancouver.

"Yeah? What type of play do you like, Theo?" Hearing her say my name like that, with how her voice raised at the end of the question, makes me want to sink to my knees.

"Is this the best time to have this conversation?" I mean, I want to, but I also don't want to start something and get hurt again.

"When my body feels like hell, but the sexiest distraction I've ever seen has just walked through my door? Probably not."

My throat is so dry.

This gorgeous woman called me a *sexy distraction*. I can't help grinning wide enough to show my teeth.

"Technically, I broke down right outside your door," I go to reach for her hand and pause. "Can I hold your hand?"

"Yeah, I'd like that." Callie slides her hand towards me. I wrap my fingers around her slender, thin ones. "Do you need a distraction?"

Callie lightly squeezes my fingertips.

"Yes. No." She shifts her weight, as if trying to get comfortable

"It's been a tough six months."

"You don't have to tell me, but I'm a good listener if you want to talk about it."

I feel her scrutinizing gaze on me and I stay still, letting her analyze me, to come to her own decision.

She squeezes my hand, glances at the ceiling.

"In August, my sister went rollerblading. Five kilometers from here, there is a trail on a hill that leads to a playground by the beach. It's her favourite route. She fell over a piece of driftwood that was left on the path and tumbled against the side of the slope."

"Oh Callie," I place my hand on her thigh, wanting to comfort her.

"It was a beautiful day, lots of people were out. Witnesses to what happened. Someone called for help immediately. She fractured her collarbone and broke her elbow. Suffered a brain injury—yes, she was wearing a helmet. Daphne was in a coma for two weeks," Callie's voice catches.

I rub my thumb over the soft webbing of her hand. "I'm so sorry. You don't have to talk about it."

"That's what everyone says, you know?" Her blue eyes blaze into mine in a moment of raw vulnerability.

I want to drop to my knees and wrap my arms around her.

"It probably makes them uncomfortable. I just don't want you to feel that you have to."

"It's okay. I'm two years older than her, but she's always been so responsible. She has her shit together and always has. Daphne worked her way through college at Shel's diner, married her high school sweetheart, the paramedic, and they bought a house in town and had kids. It's the thing that Daphne always wanted. When our aunt and uncle stepped back from Shel's, she gave up her part-time bookkeeping business, determined to save the diner," Callie pauses, takes a sip of water, shakes her head. "Daphne has always done the *right* thing. She took a break from painting the mural to enjoy the sunny day. I hate that something so normal destroyed her storybook life." Callie glances away. "It sucks."

"How is she now?" I take the water glass from her and set it on the table.

"The experts at the inpatient rehab clinic tell us she's making progress, but it's slow. She can barely walk and her speech is slurred, she forgets a lot of words, and it's hard to tell if she remembers everything we tell her. One day she talks to you and you start to hope that things are going to be normal, and the next she barely recognizes you."

"I have three brothers. It must be so hard seeing your sister like that."

The flash of grief in her eyes makes me want to roar at anything that has ever hurt her.

"Yeah, it is. When we were four and two, she was my whole world. Our mother was an addict. Aunt Millie and Uncle Henry took us in and raised us." She extends her hand, palm up, and I clasp it, gently squeezing her hand.

A sour pit in my stomach bursts open. I've seen what addiction can do to a family, and I shift in my seat, forcing my instincts not to run out the door, even though it's not fair to Callie.

"That's tough." The words don't do enough to convey how unfair that family history is and how inadequate I feel I am to really relate.

My parents struggled in their early days, my dad always chasing his dream and my mom suffering alongside him for it. But they loved us, did everything they could to support us, and eventually their hard work paid off when my dad invented a new cover for solar panels to allow them to absorb more power, and that led to financial success. Financial success that never went to dad's head, and success, he told us, was mostly luck. I can't imagine not having parents who weren't there for you.

"It's the cards we were dealt. My mom got herself clean, but not until we were older." Callie's voice grows wistful. "She's not in contact with us."

"My ex's parents were alcoholics." I swipe the photo away on my phone. "My ex was an alcoholic."

"And her little sister has a winery?" Callie's lips quirk her expression lit with pure amusement, and it makes my dick twitch.

"Yeah," I cough and shift to cover up my growing erection. "Her husband's aunt gave it to them. I know Izzy can handle drinking, but her older sister cannot. That's why we broke up. I tried to help her."

And that resulted in glasses being thrown at me, being told I wasn't a good submissive, that I couldn't please her, that I was a worthless man. I closed my eyes against the onslaught of memories.

"Theo, the odds of winning that battle were impossible." Callie reaches up, and her palm slides against my cheek.

It's warm and comforting, and I can't help but press into it.

"Yeah, I know. I'm an expert in reading data. But still, I had to try." I'm the one who yawns now. "I don't know if I'm ready for a relationship, but I'd like to have that conversation with you."

"Same." Callie shifts position, so she lays her head against my shoulder.

Her soft hair tickles against my stubble, and for the first time in months my head isn't spinning.

"You smell nice."

Callie laughs. "That's impossible, but thank you."

"It's true," I insist. It's something earthy but slightly floral.

"Maybe my shampoo," Callie yawns again, and I copycat her. "I bought it in Barcelona. That's where I was when I got the call to come home."

"What were you doing there?" She's so pretty; the way her eyes crinkle when she smiles makes me melt.

"I'm a mechanic for a professional motocross team." The pride in her voice is clear.

"How long have you been doing that?"

"Three years. I took off because...Daphne and I got into an argument. I had always planned on coming home, but not so soon."

"I'm glad you came home." I loop my fingers through hers, giving a light squeeze.

Her eyes glow with desire as they look up at me. "Me too."

I really want to kiss her and drop to my knees for this woman.

I want to worship her body from head to toe and hold her in my arms, but the timing for that isn't tonight.

"Theo?" Callie tilts her head, giving me a wide smile.

"Yeah?"

"You can kiss me." Her tone is certain, which makes my mouth dry.

"Yes, Ma'am." The *ma'am* slips out as if it were the most natural thing in the world to call her.

Her breath catches, a shadow of longing flickers in her gaze, sending shivers down my spine, firing up every nerve until my toes curl with anticipation.

She takes my chin in her hands, and I gulp. "I like how that sounded from your lips. If you want to call me ***Ma'am,*** beg me for the right."

Her low, sultry tone sends all the blood rushing to my cock, it throbs painfully.

I don't realize that I'm sliding off the couch until my knees hit the thin carpet.

My head drops. I turn my hands palm up, resting them on my knees.

A thrill of adrenaline, of white-hot need, grabs me. In the back of my mind, there's a warning bell that's ringing, asking me if I am sure I want to put myself in this position again.

But I hear the hitch in Callie's breath, her cool fingers squeeze mine.

"Please let me call you Ma'am, Callie. Please, I'll do anything if you let me call you Ma'am, please, please."

She grabs my chin, lifts it to meet hers. "I like you, Theo Brennon. I want you. But tonight, I can't give you more than that."

Her thumb brushes my chin, sending a shiver of pleasure through me, making me acutely aware of the blood rushing to my cock.

"I'm sorry, I shouldn't have overstepped. I shouldn't have used an honorific without a discussion."

"Tonight is all we need to think about right now. You're forgiven for the overstep. And you may call me Ma'am."

"Thank you, Ma'am."

Her blue eyes shine brightly, she presses a palm against my cheek. "Good."

I brush my thumb over her bottom lip, slowly tracing it, feeling the softness of her skin, the warmth of her breath.

She darts out her tongue, licks my thumb, her eyes locked on mine, I let out a desperate, needy groan.

"Come here. Sit." Her tone is all sultry, low and serious.

I scramble up from the floor, my heart pounding. I sink onto the couch beside her.

She places her hand on my shoulder and climbs onto my lap like she belongs there.

The heat between us flares. I swallow hard, captivated by the way her body molds to mine.

Her silky hair brushes against my lips, sending a shiver through me.

She gazes up at me, her eyes gleaming with pleasure, with desire.

"Yes, kiss me."

My stomach is in knots, as if this is the first time I've ever kissed a woman. The fierce need surging through me when my lips meet hers scares me.

But she cups the back of my neck, pulling me closer to her, and I kiss her, slowly at first, exploring her bottom lip. Her pillowy softness makes me want to keep my lips against her.

Giving a little murmur of pleasure as I push against her lips, she parts them, and I explore eagerly with my tongue.

All I want is to keep exploring the softness of her mouth, studying the way she closes her eyes, her long lashes flickering.

Taking control of the kiss, she reaches up to cup the back of my head, moaning into my mouth.

The air crackles with anticipation, and I shift, my cock half-hard against my zipper.

She kisses me, and that connection flares to life between us, pulling me into her.

I'm focused only on her.

My thoughts are becoming heavier as she tugs at my bottom lip, nipping it gently.

I moan into her mouth, eager for more as desperate need slithers through my veins.

"I like how you kiss; don't stop," she whispers against me.

My balls feel like they are going to burst. I want to be inside this strong, fiery woman. I want to know how her pussy feels.

She cocks an eyebrow at me. I feel the command in her tone and know she expects to be obeyed.

"Okay," I say against her lips, as my hands roam over her body.

She slides her hands down my arms, brushing them across my pecs.

When her fingers find my nipples through my shirt, I whimper as she pulls them gently, and then as I push against her, she grabs them, twisting them.

"Good," she breaks off the kiss and leans back, staring at me so intently it's everything I can not to glance away.

"Nice and slow. Can you handle that?" She asks it softly, smiling at me, her eyes glimmering with humour.

"Yes, Ma'am," I drag my lips against her throat, taking my time. "I can."

4

CALLIE

M *a'am.*

Theo giving the honorific catapults me into a mental space I haven't been to in a long time. It sends my blood boiling in a surge of adrenaline, making my heart rate increase.

And the way this man blushed when he knew he didn't have permission to give the honorific? *Oh my.*

I never thought I'd be in a power-exchange relationship again.

Been there, got burned.

Don't want to do it again.

Not to mention? This is the *worst* possible timing.

The circumstances are all *wrong,* but the way his soft lips trail against the column of my neck sends shivers of excitement coursing through my body.

It feels so *right.*

I kiss him; he kisses back, and we're heavily groaning against each other's lips.

This kiss sends me into a buzz of excitement, as if it's the first time I have ever kissed a man.

And it's the first time I have ever kissed Theo, where I am fully acknowledging what he is: a submissive who wants to serve.

He said, *Ma'am*.

There was no way Theo could have known how that honorific sent my system flooding with endorphins I hadn't felt in ages.

No way he could've known it was the right honorific—I'll never use 'Mistress' again.

His hands are tentative, exploring—gentle, yes, but it's as if he's holding back, trying to maintain his control.

And it's seeing him wrangle with it that makes me burn with need, his restraint fueling the fire between us.

I let out a low, gravelly moan from deep within my core as he continues to kiss me.

His kisses are giving me an escape with each stroke of his tongue, stress is being lifted from my shoulders.

Theo tastes faintly of mint. His blue dress shirt has obviously been ironed, just like his pants.

I giggle against his lips, wondering if he'd iron my coveralls.

"What's so funny?" he drags his lips over the hollow of my throat, setting off shivers arrowing right to my pussy.

"Wondering if you'd iron my coveralls." Words are hard to get out because his touch is so electric.

"Were you admiring my crisp creases?" Rich amusement threads his tone.

He caresses my nape, his fingers gentle along my shoulders, moving down to my arm.

"Yes." I sweep my hands down his back, my fingertips exploring his hardened muscles through his shirt.

"I like everything neat and tidy."

"That's my complete opposite."

This boy is setting me on fire, slowly and methodically.

He nibbles behind my ear, and I press against him, wanting more. I want to explore every inch of his body.

I want to see how he comes apart.

Being dominant in my romantic relationships has always given me a sense of confidence when everything else in my life is a complete mess most of the time.

"Opposites are powerful," Theo's voice is thick with lust.

I want to bring this man to orgasm. I want to watch his control being wrenched from him as he gives in to his pleasure.

I want to *command* it.

Reaching up, I hold his face in my hands, and I kiss his mouth, work my tongue around his, and take charge of the kiss.

He lets me explore, staying very still, and a part of me that has been sleeping for a long time is curious, eager to explore this man's patience.

I sense how eager he is to please, how needy he is for my touch.

His eyes burn with heat. He lets out a whispery purr that makes my pussy throb.

I desperately want to feel his cock. I want to know if he's hard for me, I need to know how it looks, how it tastes.

My pulse races as our lips fuse together. I pull at his shirt, wanting it off his body. Tasting him is everything I wanted but told myself I couldn't have.

He follows my lead, controlling himself, even though I know he wants more.

I break off the kiss and, meeting his grey eyes, I slowly unbutton his shirt.

"This is the worst possible timing," I mutter. His pecs are taut. He has a spattering of light sandy hair on his chest. I brush my fingertips through the soft silky strands, and his muscles ripple as he laughs.

"This wasn't on my calendar either. But I'm glad for the unexpected."

"Me too." I mean the words. I slide his belt from his belt buckle.

"I'm on the pill, and I recently had STI testing done. Nothing to worry about."

"Got tested six months ago, all clean. Haven't been with anyone since." His voice is thick with need.

"Six months?" I study his face, but he's not joking.

His laugh rumbles in my ear. "My hand works just fine."

Theo's fingertips lightly trace my jaw, and under his touch, I'm all tightly coiled tension.

The way this man looks at me, with desire and lust, yes, but also hope? I know he's *trouble*.

It scares me.

But right now, I have this beautiful man, in these precious moments where it is just me.

I don't have to play the part of the diner owner or granddaughter who is trying to save the business or mechanic's assistant.

"I think we should move this to the bedroom." I raise an eyebrow, trying to play it all cool, but my heart races, because I want him to accept.

I slide off his lap.

"I like that idea." Theo's low, rumbly voice sends the good kind of chills up my back.

I take a step forward, grab a fistful of his shirt, and pull him. He lets me pull him, lead him, and the endorphins swimming through my head are delicious.

My mouth is dry with anticipation, so many possibilities race through my mind, but I can't do any of them because it's not the right time.

"Tonight, we can give each other what we need, a little of it anyway. You're beautiful, Callie. I'm glad my truck broke down in front of your diner." He has a small, playful smile on his lips, but his tone is so serious, I know he means every word.

"Me too, Theo." I drop his shirt before he can kiss me and climb on my bed, pushing the blankets and sheets out of the way. "Get your sexy naked ass over here. Don't keep me waiting."

He quickly steps out of his slacks, folds them over his arm, and then sets them on the armchair in the corner.

My mouth waters as he peels off his boxers. This man is hung, beautifully.

His cock is long, thicker at the head, and already, a bead of pre-cum gleams.

Theo slides his shirt off, revealing hardened muscles, and I let my gaze roam, studying every part of him.

He's not super built, but he definitely doesn't skip working out. His muscles are well-defined and very pleasing to look at.

After he slings the shirt over the back of the chair, he dives onto the bed.

I laugh, pulling his hair, and tugging him to me.

"That's better."

"Yes, Callie." He slants his lips against mine, kissing me.

My arms are around his back, loving how he moves under my palm.

He kisses me, driving out all of my worries, taking me into this moment, in a flood of desire so strong, I can practically hear it humming in the air between us.

Breaking off the kiss, I push on the centre of his chest, so he lies down.

And before I can talk myself out of it, I've flung my t-shirt over my head, it lands on the floor behind me, and I'm awkwardly getting out of my pants.

"I don't think I've ever ironed a shirt in my life," I tell him, as I ball the pants up, tossing them to the floor.

Theo laughs, a deep, rich sound that echoes in my room. "I won't hold it against you. I've never been under a car in mine."

Catching each other's eye, we laugh, and it feels so damn good, and an arousal shimmers through my body, all my nerve endings poised to flame full blast.

His eyes are lit with warmth, and I drop a quick kiss on his lips.

A spree of hilarity shoots through the headiness, driving me to push him down on the bed.

"Take my bra off, please."

Quicker than I expected, he's undoing the front closure of my bra. "So pretty. May I feel your breasts?"

"I don't know. What will you do if I say yes?" I tease.

His smile slopes, and he moves into my space, our lips almost touching. "Anything you like."

"Anything?" I reach out to him, my hands hovering over his nipples.

"*Please.*"

Oh, the word so softly said grabs at my heart, and I want to lavish this man with praise and give him all the gentle dominance he can handle.

My thumbs brush against his pebbled nipples, then I trace them in a soft circle.

Under my thumb, I feel the shudder ripple through his body.

"Do you like that?" His nipples harden under my teasing touch.

"Yes, Ma'am." He tilts his head back, offering his throat.

My insides clench, adrenaline rapidly taking my breath away.

He's so submissive and vulnerable. It's beautiful.

I press my lips above his Adam's apple as I roll his nipples between my index finger and thumb.

His brows come together as he winces as I apply more pressure.

"Just a bite of pain."

"I expect you to say red if I go too far." I say in my Domme tone.

"I will." His eyes open, and they meet mine, and they're already glassy.

"I want to hear you say, Ma'am." I gently correct him, pulling on his nipple.

"Yes, Ma'am, I will tell you if you go too far." His eyes are filled with heat and desire, and he's so much trouble.

This receptive, beautiful man is in my bed, and it feels good.

I pull on his right nipple, sliding my hand down to cup his cock.

"Yes, oh damn!" he cries out as I grip his smooth steel length, sliding it against my palm, reaching up to his balls.

I give them a squeeze, loving how they feel under my hand, how right here, I have all this control over this man.

He lets out a low whine, and his hips rise.

His cock thrusts against my palm.

"I want to stroke your cock. I want to ride you." I lean down, licking his throat.

His skin tastes like he smells, clean and fresh. He moves against me slowly.

I feel his erection press into me.

"I want you to ride my cock."

I remove my fingers from his chest, sweeping my hands down his pecs. "You may touch my breasts."

His hands are warm as he cups my breasts, gently dimpling his fingertips around my areolas.

"Yes, you can taste them." The little cry that escapes his lips sends a surge of heat firing through my blood.

I feel his smile as he gently licks my nipple, drawing it into his mouth, so his lips firmly close around my hard bead. I can't help the gasp I let out as he leisurely laps it in a slow circle.

Fisting his hair, I tug him even closer to my breast, urging him not to stop.

The sensation of his mouth on my nipple is hot, fiery, and sends my heart fluttering.

It's so good, I forgot pleasure could be this intense.

I pull him off my breast after a moment and bring him to my other one.

It's my turn to cry out as his mouth closes around my other nipple, his tongue pressing on the hardened tip.

My hips arch towards him, wanting more. I moan long and deep.

He lets out his own cry.

I give his cock a long pull; it's hard and thick in my hands, and the way he whimpers is so damn hot, I do it again.

I'm so wet between my legs, my pussy throbs, wanting his cock.

"Do you like it handled roughly? Or softly?" I stop my motion, he shakes his head on my nipple and I am gushing between my legs.

Not breaking eye contact, my lips curve into a pleased smile. I cup his balls, pressing down on the filled sacs.

His whole body bucks, and I do it again, pleased at the whimper he lets out around my nipple, the vibration making my pussy pulse.

"Both. A little of both. Nothing too rough. No crushing, no CBT."

"I'm not that kind of Dominant," I say against his ear.

I let go of his balls, slide my palm along his hips, down his legs, so I can feel his rippling muscles.

"You're so hot, Theo Brennon." I grab a handful of his hair, give him a tug to get him off my breast.

"Feel how wet you made me." I slide down against him, so I'm on my back, my legs spread.

Pulling him by his nipple, I tug him over to me. He yelps but follows, his grey eyes smoulder with heat.

I spread my legs wide, giving him access and love how his tongue darts out, licking his top lip as he stares at my pussy.

He drags a palm up from my foot to my leg, sliding to my inner thigh.

"I can see your pussy is glistening," Theo ducks his head, as if he's shy, and it's so damn cute.

"Yeah? That's what having a hot man in my bed did."

His fingers dip into my pussy, gently around my clit, and I thrust my hips into his touch, wanting more, and he obliges, fingering my clit with the right amount of pressure. He's watching my face intently, waiting for my cues.

"Good. Keep fingering me. I want to come on your hand."

He moves closer, wrapping arm around my body, supporting my lower back.

I turn my head to his shoulder, my lips press against his soft skin. I want to bite him as he slides another finger into my pussy.

Lost in his rhythmic touch, I moan against him, our bodies pressing into each other.

His skin is so warm against mine, sweat trickling between my breasts as his fingers work my sensitive bud.

"That's perfect." He flushes at the praise, but his fingers don't stop, and I thrust again, wanting more friction.

The pressure breaks open from low in my belly, spiraling me upward. I grab his cock, giving it a long pull in my hand.

He hisses through his teeth but doesn't stop fingering me. I take his chin in my fingers, and kiss those lips, with all the desperation this man has sparked to life.

My heart rate is going double time. I slide my palm to the head of his cock and gently finger his slit, all the while feeling his lips on mine, the electricity between us ready to explode.

Taking his drops of pre-cum on my thumb, I drag it down his hard cock, lubricating it so it slides easier in my palm.

"I'm going to come now!" I hoarse whisper against him.

He jerks forward into my palm as I cry out in a shuddering exhale as the orgasm races through my body.

My body tenses, the pleasure shooting me higher and higher. I'm gasping as bliss explodes through my body.

"Fuck," I breathe against him. "I needed that."

He chuckles against me, ducking his head to bring it closer to my breasts.

I drop his length and massage his balls with one hand, slowly, pressing down in a firm circle, it makes him twitch.

"You look so beautiful, Ma'am, all pretty and flushed."

I lay back against the pillows, my hand still on his balls, catching my breath. "I needed that so badly."

Not going to think of how long it was because that's a floodgate of pain and despair I want to keep closed.

"Do you want to come?" I squeeze his balls, loving how he winces.

"Yes please. But I'd love to release inside you," his gaze drifts down as he says the words.

"Yeah?" I tug his hard cock, which makes him cry out, tipping his head back.

"Yes, Ma'am." His muscles are taut and slick with a light sheen of sweat. He's beautiful.

I massage his balls, watching him jerk and twitch, and then with my other hand, I encircle his girth, while pressing down on his taint, working his exterior P-spot.

His hips thrust off the bed. He moans and thrusts, his muscles contract but he holds back, pressing his lips together.

"Your control is so damn sexy. What are you like when you lose it?" I rub his head, wanting to reward him.

His grey eyes meet mine, filled with need and desire that match my own. "Eager to please."

Sliding my hand from his balls, I roam it over his inner thigh, then brush my palm over his light spatter of chest hair.

"Lube, top drawer of the dresser."

He scrambles up, and I take in the sight of his muscled back.

"How bad is that mess driving you crazy?" I can't help but ask as he searches my drawer.

"A little." He turns with the lube. "But it's worth it for this."

Taking the lube from him, squirt some in my hands. "I can't wait to feel your cock inside me."

He cock jumps as I glide the lube over his shaft.

"Thank you."

He's so adorable. He is all trouble, and I don't care. I want this man like I've never wanted any man before.

Kneeling, I kiss his mouth, trailing kisses all the way down his torso, his soft moans urging me on.

I roll on top of him, my legs on either side of his hips. I grab his rigid cock, wrapping my hand around his base.

I slide down his cock.

"I want to tell you when you can release."

"Please." His voice is so growly, so eager.

I kiss him again, our mouths meet, pressing against each other's in need, want, everything that started outside when I first laid eyes on this man, breaking open now.

I ease myself down on his thick length, an inch at a time, loving how he twitches under me.

Taking charge like this ramps up the endorphins, they're surging through my blood with a hot, hungry need that's consuming me for more of this man.

He feels so good deep inside me.

I grind on his cock slowly and his cock hits the right spot high on my pussy walls.

My pussy clenches around him. He lets out a moan that sends shivers down my back. It makes me hot to see his pleasure.

"Your cock feels so good." I grind, rolling my hips, his hands come around my waist and I don't hold back, giving in to the lust that's thumping through my body.

I'm lost in the feel of his cock, the way his eyes are so glassy, his moans, his hiss of pleasure as I take him deeper.

"Please let me come, Ma'am." He writhes back against me. His cry is deliciously hot.

His needy plea pulls at the side of myself I had kept away for all these months.

My body grows hot as I see the pure desperation on his face.

"Do not look away from me," I lean forward, so my breasts are in his face, and I moan as his lips close around my nipples, setting off a new wave of pleasure. His grey eyes bore into mine, and I rock on his cock, feeling so deliciously full. The heat of his attention is focused on me as I roll my hips, and it sears my skin, making me crave more.

"Such a pretty cock."

He keeps his eyes on my face as he sucks my nipple gently, treating it as if it's a delicacy.

I rock against him, thrusting and rolling my hips. He matches me, setting a rhythm that takes away all my thoughts.

"Kiss me." I lean down, meeting his lips against mine, and all of our gentle movements evaporate as with the next downward thrust, his lips crash against mine, as I grind on him.

He fits so good in my pussy, his cock fills me in a way no one has ever filled me before. It's a perfect fit.

"I'm so close," he grits out, his voice breathy and needy.

"Yeah? Me too." I push down on him, and he meets me, thrusting deep, making me cry out with a low moan that echoes around the room.

I flex back, close my eyes and pleasure grabs me, another orgasm starting to break.

Opening my eyes, Theo is still looking right at me.

I push my hands over his and take control of the thrusting.

"Please, I need to come!" His grip tightens on me.

My pussy clenches around his cock.

Pleasure-pain explodes in my clit.

My legs start to shake, and I gab at him, needing to control this moment.

"I'm coming right now! Come with me, Theo!"

He grips my hips, holding me on his cock as my legs tremble, my whole body throbbing with hot need, spiraling me up and up, my body is on fire, Theo's whimpers and rippling muscles, makes me feel like I am going to break. His cock is so damn hard inside me.

His fingers dig into my waist, and I like that. It urges me on to grind harder on him, and he groans, his eyelids start to close. I flick his nipple, and those grey eyes, now totally glassy and shimmering with need, meet mine.

"Eyes on me, *boy*." The searing whimper that rips from his lips sends my blood boiling, the rush of heady Top space filling my head. "Yes, boy."

The primal, mewling sound he lets out makes my body hum with a pleasure so intense all I can feel is his cock driving into me, harder, deeper.

My legs start to shake, my pussy tightens on his length, not wanting to let go.

"Yes, give me your cum!" I order the moment I feel his cock swell, getting even harder, stretching me further.

"Come, boy, now!" Because I can't hold back anymore. The scream I let out is one of pleasure, fiery need, and want.

The break of the crest leaves me gasping for breath.

"Callie!" He shouts my name as he releases in me, a long burst of hot cum.

He thrusts hard, deep into folds, even deeper before his face crumbles. I slant my lips over his, kissing him, swallowing his sweet noises.

"Fuck," I say, breaking off the kiss.

We stare at each other, catching our breath. I don't want to move off of him. I cup his chin in my palm.

"That was so good."

"Yeah," Theo breathes.

"Kiss me."

He gently touches my lips with his tongue and then strokes my tongue, inviting a deeper kiss.

I make a low wail sound into his mouth because it feels so good. I love his little answering moans.

When I pull away, my body is flushed and spasming with the aftershocks.

Taking his hand, I use it to steady myself as I come off of him.

"That was really intense," Theo takes my hand in his and brings it to his lips.

"Yes, it was." I let my head rest against his shoulder, sliding my hand down to his softening cock.

Humming with pleasure, I trace circles on his cock, as we both come back down to earth, but as my body is glowing, that alarm bell is ringing in the far corner of my mind.

I've never experienced a connection this instant, this intense before.

He props himself up, brushes his lips against mine. "I'll be back."

I wrap a sheet around me as I watch him walk out of the bedroom to the bathroom.

My heart rate slowly returns to normal, and the guilt that I had been holding off ever since I kissed this man comes flooding in.

But no, I'm determined not to let those feelings reign.

I'm an adult. One night of hot sex with a very handsome man does not make me irresponsible.

Theo comes back into the room with a glass of water.

"Thank you."

"You're welcome, Callie. Did we cure your flu?"

"Momentary relief," my body all drowsy with the afterglow of sex, is kicking into awareness of how sore my throat is and how tired I feel.

He sits down. I sip my water and then put it on the nightstand.

"We've got to see about your truck tomorrow."

"I'm not in a hurry to leave," he massages my back in a little circle.

"Good," my heart gives a happy leap as I meet his eyes. "Come here," I curl on my side, patting the space next to me.

The grin that flashes on his face is so bright my heart twists.

He slides in front of me, his long body against my smaller one, but I like being the big spoon.

I wrap my arm around his waist, pressing my cheek against his shoulder blade.

"I'm very happy your truck broke down."

He laughs, and I laugh, and it's the best way I've drifted off to sleep in months.

In the middle of the night, I feel his erection against me, and I reach over, throwing a leg over his hip.

We fuck slower this time, still needy.

He waits for me to lead, for my thrust, for my lips on his, and the way he gives up control is so beautiful, I don't know how I can let this man go.

After we're done, I lead him to the shower. He washes my back, and I wash his.

We explore each other's bodies with teeth, lips, and gentle touches.

He dries me off before grabbing a towel of his own.

Yeah, I'm in trouble.

5

THEO

DECEMBER 22ND

"There's a naked man! A naked man is here!" a cute little kid with a thick mop of curly hair shouts after pushing through the door, startling the heck out of me.

Fortunately, I have my pants and undershirt on.

"I'm not naked. I'm putting on my shirt," I say, buttoning up my green dress shirt. "My name is Theo. I'm a friend of your aunt's. You took me by surprise."

The little kid scrunches up his face.

"And you know how to knock," a beefy guy with a beard says, stepping behind him. "Forgive the interruption. A new person is exciting."

"I understand. Theo Brennon." I extend my hand.

"Grady Sullivan and this guy is Luke." He shakes mine.

"Nice to meet you both."

"Come on, let's get your school stuff ready," Grady shuffles Luke out of the room but gives me a *who the hell are you look*.

I don't think explaining I boinked his sister-in-law is a good first impression, so I quietly follow them out, pausing by Callie's door.

"Aunt Callie, you promised you would take me to see mom. I'm going to skip school so I can visit her." A teenager with long hair says, crossing her arms in front of her chest.

"Did your dad say you could miss school?" Callie raises an eyebrow.

"Dad is on days starting like now. Can you get out of bed?"

Callie has a blanket wrapped around her and is sitting on the edge of the bed.

"Good morning," I say. "Are you feeling better?"

"Morning," Callie flashes me a quick smile. "Madison, I wasn't feeling great last night. Can you give me five minutes to get up, please?"

"Fine," Madison turns, flipping her long hair over her shoulder. "Who are you?"

"My name is Theo. I'm a friend."

She scoffs as she leaves the room, in an over-dramatic way.

"Welcome to my chaos." Callie's phone rings, and she grabs it. "Hello? Okay, Pauline. I understand," she tosses her phone on the bed.

"You're very adorable when you look frustrated." I want to put my hands on her, but I wait for her to initiate.

"Then I'm adorable all the time," she gives me a cheeky grin and stands up, wobbling on her feet. "I'm fine. Just need coffee."

"You don't look that fine." She's pale, and she looks sickly.

"I'll take more cold medicine."

"Callie! I gotta leave."

I follow Callie as she sprints into the kitchen. "Got it, Grady. You met Theo?"

"Yeah," Grady nods as he's untangling the kids off of him. "Abby, you need to let go of my leg."

"His truck broke down in front of Shel's," Callie scoops Abby up into her arms and the little girl giggles.

Luke runs into the living room, tosses the cushions on the couch and jumps over them. "I'm so awake today!"

"I wondered whose clunker it was," Grady teases. "Nice to meet you, Theo."

"It's actually reliable." I feel a weird urge to defend my borrowed vehicle.

"I'll be home by eight? I want to see Daphne first."

"That's not fair!" Madison shouts, striding into the small kitchen. "I want to see her, and that's not even on your way home."

"Madison, we talked about this. We'll find lots of time for you to visit."

"Luke, stop jumping on the cushions!" Madison yells. The teenager looks distressed, and I want to do something that will ease her angst, but I just stand there in the middle of a family morning that I don't belong in.

"They're just cushions," Grady says.

"It's fine," Callie waves, patting his arm.

"I'll stop!" Luke barrels into his dad, hugging him around the waist.

"Nobody ever cares what I want!" Madison storms out of the kitchen and slams the door to the room I was staying in.

Grady gives the kids a kiss goodbye. "There's nothing I can say to her right now that'll make it better. Bye guys, have a good day!"

"I want a waffle for breakfast!" the little girl chants.

"One second, Abby," Callie puts her down, and the little girl sits at the table, staring at me.

I make a face. The little girl giggles.

Callie follows Grady out to the hall.

I open the fridge. Yep, as empty as it was last night, and close it again.

"How did the visit go last night?" I overhear Callie say from the hallway.

I pass toy cars to each kid, and they start driving them across the table.

"The staff asked us to leave after twenty minutes, saying Daphne showed signs of distress. I know it's up and down, but this is so damn hard. Madison is pissed. I thought if you had time today you could take her this afternoon. It's right before Christmas break anyway, so it's not like she's going to miss anything. I gotta fly. Love you, Lukey. Bye princess," he waves to the kids. "Be good! Bye Madison!"

"Bye Daddy!" the little kids chorus

Callie comes back into the kitchen. "Okay, guys, it's going to be a good day!"

"Yeah!" Luke echoes.

"Grady is a paramedic," Callie says to me. "The first day back on days is always a little rough, but we make it work. I've got to call Uncle Henry about your truck. But first, breakfast!" She clucks Abby under the chin.

Opening her fridge, she sighs. "Forgot. Need to go grocery shopping. Down to the diner, Miss. Madison, get out here, please!"

Madison enters the kitchen, her expression still tense.

"Hey, Mads. Get Brenda to plate you up something for breakfast, okay? I'll drop the babies off at school. I'll do my best to spring you at lunch. But I've got to cover Pauline's shift."

"Fine," Madison huffs and picks up the backpacks by the door. "Come on, squirts, we're eating downstairs."

"Yay! Waffles," Abby takes her sister's hand, and I see Madison smile for the first time.

Luke hugs Callie, then waves at me. "Bye!"

"Be quick, I don't want to miss the first period!" Madison says. She slams the door behind them.

"Aren't you glad you stayed?"

I step close to her, wanting to take her in my arms because I have never been more glad of anything in my entire life. "Yes. Can I make a suggestion?"

"I don't know," Callie shakes her head. "If you suggest we need more help or to hire someone...I've heard it all."

She blows out a breath, sending the hair that frames her face to the side. I'm not going to give this woman advice. She's clearly been in survival mode for months and is capable of taking care of her family.

But I want to ease her load, even if it's only for as long as it takes to fix my truck.

She brushes by me, opens a cupboard, and takes a cold medicine tablet. "I know this looks ridiculous, but it's how we make it work. Grady wants to spend as much time as he can with the kids, but he works shifts. He gets them up, does their homework, feeds them a snack, and carts them over here so I can drop them off at school. When he's on nights, it's a bit easier."

"It doesn't look ridiculous. It looks like you're doing your best."

She flashes me a smile that doesn't quite reach her eyes.

"You look like you need a nap. Why don't you drop the kids off at school, come home, and get more rest? If you give me a list, I'll go grocery shopping for you, and if you can't find anyone, I'll take that afternoon shift at the diner so you can visit your sister."

She sways against the counter. "I'm a tough cookie who can do anything."

"I know you are a boss babe." Wanting to reassure her, I step in front of her, hovering my hands above her shoulders.

She pulls my hands down to her shoulders, the nearness to her setting off a burst of need that makes my dick twitch.

"I don't need a knight to rescue me." She says it as if she's convincing herself, her tone cold.

"Nope. But a knight only too happy to go do your bidding to win your favour?" I wink, making her smile, which makes me feel like I've won.

"Last night was fun." Her eyes sparkle for a moment, the stress easing from her face. "Even tough boss babe cookies crack under the pressure."

"Yep. I'm stuck here until my truck is fixed or I call for a ride. Let me help. It'll make me happy."

She reaches for my hand and laces her fingers through mine. Her skin is warm and a little clammy. "Service sub?"

I catch sight of the clock. I don't think I've ever had this conversation this early, but here we are. "I like taking care of the people who are important to me. I prefer to say that I'm service-oriented."

"Have you ever been a waiter?" She tilts her head as if she can't envision me serving food.

"In university, yes. At my dad's friend's restaurant." I leave out the detail that I wasn't very good at it because I was a shy kid.

"I still don't know if I can give you anything in terms of a relationship," she drops my hand and crosses her arms over her chest.

"I'm not looking for a commitment, Callie. I'm looking to be a friend."

She bites her lip, then her eyes meet mine, stirring the heat between us.

"Last night," she takes one of my hands and places it on her waist. She leans forward and brushes her lips against mine. I let out a whimper because I want to kiss her, but she pulls away, teasing me. "Was so *good*, Theo. I don't want to say goodbye. I just don't know how this can fit into my life right now."

"I don't want to say goodbye either. Can we say we're starting something? Slowly?"

She runs that cool gaze over me, and I stay still, wanting to show her I can take what she gives me.

"Okay. I graciously accept your offer of free labour."

"Service," I whisper.

"Service," she brushes my lips with her index finger and stands on her toes, and leans in, like she's about to kiss me and as if my mouth remembers how she tasted, I salivate with pure need to taste her.

A knock rings out, making her dash to the door. "I'm coming, Mads! There's still lots of time."

She squeezes my ass as she walks by, giving me a sly smile over her shoulder.

"Madison, we have time—oh, hi Mrs. Stewart."

"Hello dear. I wanted to come by and say that I didn't see your name on the Rising Harbour Christmas party list. You know that is tonight. As a business owner, it is an event you should attend, especially if you want councilors to read your application to stay."

The whiny voice makes my skin crawl, and I'm curious who it belongs to, so I step into the hallway and see an older woman wearing a fuchsia dress with lipstick to match.

The woman raises her eyebrows to her hairline after glancing at me.

Callie glances at me, then back at Mrs. Stewart. She grins slyly. "I've been busy."

"Callista, I know Daphne has gone through a great ordeal, but for the moment, you are the business owner on the application of proposed revitalization."

"I'll try to get there, Mrs. Stewart. Shel's is a staple to Rising Harbour, and you know we intend to stay."

"I knew your grandparents, Callista. If you want to stay, you have to convince the town that you're a good fit. Being part of the town's celebrations will help with that. I hope you change your mind. Good day."

Callie closes the door, leans against it.

"Hello, Callista." I take a step closer to her, grinning.

"You make my name sound sexy," she drags her hand down my chest, making me shiver. I swallow hard, my breath catching as her fingers trace lower.

"It is *sexy*."

"Not when the elders like Mrs. Stewart say it," she steps toward me. My mouth goes dry. I want this woman so much an electric hum rolls through my body.

"Say my name again."

The cool, dominant tone in her voice has me wanting to whisper her name over and over as she shudders against me from climaxing. But right now, I'm on a mission to make her morning better.

"Callista," I caress her name with reverence and lift her hand to my lips, kissing the back of her hand.

"When it's just you and me, I want to hear either Ma'am or Callista. Acceptable?" Her eyes are glued to my face, studying me intently.

I swallow but don't look away.

"Yes, Ma'am. Are we doing this?" The burst of hope at the thought has my pulse leaping.

"We need to have a conversation about the rules of engagement. But I'd like to... not say goodbye."

"Me too," I whisper. "I want you to kiss me, Callista. Please."

"Yes, boy." She cups my face in her hands as if she's committing my every pore to memory. Her breasts brush my chest as she stands on her tiptoes and kisses me, tasting my lips slowly, flooding me with need. I stumble back as she breaks off the kiss and traces my lips with her thumb. "You made my morning."

That makes me happy. The invite to tonight's dinner seemed force?"

"Welcome to small towns. There's this Christmas fundraiser shindig that all the other business owners are supposed to go to, but it's like a thousand dollars a plate and I didn't know if Grady was going working. I had nobody to go with."

"I look good in a tux," I say, wrapping my arms around her waist. "And a thousand dollars is pocket change."

"You shouldn't tell that to a mechanic," she says, patting my face. Her eyes are warm, and her complexion looks better.

"Go ahead and overcharge me. Can I kiss you again?"

"You may," she flashes me that pretty smile. "But I'm going to get you sick."

"I don't care."

Her breath hitches as she leans against me, parting her lips to let me taste her. I take my time, kissing her slowly, wishing we could stay here all day and tangle each other's tongues.

"If it would help your case with the town, I'd love to take you out tonight."

Callie's eyes go wide; she bites her lips. "Theo, I can't bring you into my mess."

"I'm offering." Attending a crowded dinner isn't my favourite thing to do, but if it helps her, then I want to get into that tux.

"I don't usually let people in," she looks beyond my shoulder, her expression closed.

"Hey, I get it."

Her vulnerability feels like a precious gift that I want to hold and guard.

"Come on, I'll introduce you to Brenda—the diner's head server. She's the one who really runs the place. I've got to get the kids to school." She slips her hand into mine, tugging me out the door. In the hallway we meet each other's eyes and smile.

I had spent the last month gridlocked with a client who refused any and all suggestions I made and kept sending me back the proposals.

Meeting Callie has let me step out of my work mind that I desperately crave a break from, of where I have to be *on* all the time and not flinch.

With her, I can pour all my nurturing and giving into whatever she needs, and it feels damn good.

Are you sure, Theo, that she's not going to hurt you?

The voice in my head sounds like my younger brother's, and I exhale.

Whatever this is between Callie and me, it's just starting, but the attraction between us is demanding to be explored.

My palms are suddenly sweaty on the smooth wooden banister as I follow her downstairs, admiring her toned legs, letting my gaze drag across her body in appreciation.

At the bottom of the stairs, the noise from the diner filters in.

Callie turns to me, placing her palm on my chest.

Chill, Brennon, you can do this. I don't want to screw this up and it's been decades since I've asked people if they want a refill on their coffee.

"Ready?" Callie raises an eyebrow.

"Yes, Ma'am."

She brushes a finger along my jaw.

"Yes. I can do this."

"This is nuts. I usually don't let people into my life."

"Hey, I got you. It's just one shift."

"Okay. You might hear things about me. Please ignore them."

"Callista, there is nothing anyone can say that would alter my opinion of you."

I rub small circles on her back, and she straightens her shoulders.

"Okay, we are going to go with it."

"Yep."

I recognize that this situation has us both like fish out of water, but she swings open the door and I take a step back. I don't know what I was expecting—maybe a half-empty place, because the town is trying to shut this business down—but every seat in the diner is full. Three waitresses wearing yellow shirts are racing about.

As we pass the kitchen, I spot two line cooks and a cook calling out tickets.

A woman with a perm that'd be at home in the '80s smiles broadly at Callie. "Good morning, sunshine! Those kids get more adorable by the day."

"Good morning, Brenda. This is my friend, Theo. He's going to take Pauline's afternoon shift."

"Hello there, handsome," Brenda winks at me.

"What does it take to get some coffee around here?" an old man with a baseball cap calls out.

"Saying *please,* Norm, usually does it." Callie grabs a coffee pot from the service station and marches over to the table by the corner.

Brenda is still staring at me, making a 'tsking' sound.

"Hi."

"You don't look like you work in a restaurant."

"I don't, but I did in college. I can take one shift."

Brenda clucks her tongue at me as if she doesn't believe me, and honestly, I don't blame her.

"Might as well jump right in. Grab an apron from the back, and you can shadow me for a few minutes."

"Sure," I can't help the silly grin on my face as I find my way into the hallway and grab a yellow apron. I tie it around my waist, then come back to Brenda.

The place is busy, and the breakfast smells are making my stomach grumble, but I follow Brenda as she takes orders, watching Callie out of the corner of my eye.

Every table she stops at, the customers smile at her, but I notice a couple of tense shoulders and hear clipped tones from some.

"I see you're already at work," Callie says as she brushes by me.

"Yep. Brenda is a great teacher."

Brenda snorts and wags her pen at me. "You're a charmer, I can tell."

I meet Callie's eye, and she flashes me a grin. "Got to take the kids to school. Here," Callie presses a key ring into my hand. "For when Brenda lets you take a break, use my car out back. You drive a stick?"

My face turns scarlet, but someone calls Brenda away, and Luke runs over to Callie, grabbing her hand.

"I can. My dad's old car was a stick."

"Good. Don't grind the thing, okay? Light touch. Grocery store is up the hill. I'm going to take Daphne's truck to drop the kids off."

"Got it. See you later."

"Aunt Callie, we have to leave now!" Madison stomps her foot on the floor.

"Coming, Mads."

"Not until that's table bussed, Miss," Brenda says.

Madison rolls her eyes but clears the counter of dishes, with her little sister and brother helping her.

"See you later, Brenda, Theo." Callie gives us a wave, scooping her little niece in her arms.

"Come on!" Madison shouts through the restaurant.

I wave at them and turn my attention back to the diner, because as soon as Callie is out of sight, it feels like everyone has something to say.

"That Madison is just like Callie, eh?" An old man at the end of the counter says. "So much attitude."

"You stop with that talk, Phil. Madison is a good girl. Daphne's done right by her."

"Callie looks worn out. I don't think she can handle the place." A small woman with red hair says.

"I think that girl can handle a lot," a tall man with a full head of gray hair says. "I taught her in high school," he says to me. "Callie always gets dumped on, and it's not fair."

"If she acted less like her mother, it would be fair." Another woman pipes up.

"Hush, all of you, and finish your breakfast. You know she's doing her best trying to keep this place afloat. I'm grateful to her for coming back home," Brenda says.

"Yeah, with her tail between her legs after breaking a whole family part," the man with the ball cap says.

"I told you to stop. Now, do you want a butter tart for the road?"

Phil raises his coffee cup. "Yes, please."

After that,, the customers return to their plates, chatting among themselves. Brenda shows me the ropes, and my days of being a waiter come rushing back to me.

It feels good to do something I wouldn't usually do, and if it helps Callie, I'm happy to do it.

"Daphne worked her butt off to get this place up and running," the man who had defended Callie from earlier says to me as I'm refilling his coffee. "Too bad the town wants to take anything good out of this place."

"I heard something about that." I reach in and clear his plate.

"Who hasn't?" The man crosses her arms over her chest. "Daphne had done everything the town asked, and you should have seen the place before she took it over. But now the town wants to make sure the business owners aren't going to abandon shops, so they have to buy the building, and Mr. Hops won't let the girls have it. Even though it belongs to them."

"That's not how I remember it, Gus. Shel lost the building to old man Hops, fair and square." Phil says, standing up.

"And who has paid the property taxes on it ever since?" Gus glares at Phil.

"I thought the town wanted a tourist destination?" I say.

"They do," Gus huffs.

"The town doesn't know what it wants. They're making every business owner go before the council and state their case." Brenda says.

"Making good, hardworking people buy in. Did you know that Mellie at the bookstore had to buy tickets to the Christmas dinner?" Gus says.

"Hey, that dinner is to help the children!" Phil shouts.

"It's a waste of money," Gus says again.

I smile and turn with my hands full into the kitchen, and Brenda meets me at the pass.

"Hey, ignore them. They don't know what's happening, and only Callie can tell you the history of this building. But the town does want a business commitment; that part is true. Callie has a history of leaving when things get tough," Brenda shakes her head. "I think the world of her though, and Daphne too. The future is uncertain with Daphne still recovering."

"I think the world of Callie too," I reply.

Brenda smiles, swatting my shoulder. "I knew I liked you! Now get out of here before your run off your feet and don't get back to cover Pauline's shift."

She doesn't have to tell me twice. I hang up my apron and step out, drinking in the chilly air.

I find Callie's car and adjust the seat, hoping I don't screw up her vehicle. Is it even possible for a town to tell businesses they have to own their buildings? I don't know.

But my brother Noel would.

At least, I think he would. He's a corporate lawyer—or was before opening his adults-only resort, Vixen's Paradise.

As the oldest brother, Noel loves to pretend to know everything, and the annoying thing about him is, he usually does. But Christmas isn't an easy time for him since his wife died, so I hesitate on calling him and pull up the directions to the nearest grocery store instead, just as my phone chimes in with a list from Callie.

My cheeks heat as I read her text after the grocery list.

And one hot, willing submissive man in my bed.

You have that, Ma'am

I exhale, telling my cock to stop twitching. I don't know where this thing between Callie and me is going, but I'm happy to find out.

6

CALLIE

I drop the kids off at school and, without even realizing it, find myself driving the same stretch of highway Theo took into Rising Harbour.

Theo could have taken Daphne's truck, but there's something intimate about being in her space.

She surprised Grady by asking for a truck for her twenty-eighth birthday.

Her fruit-shaped air freshener dangles from the mirror.

In the backseat is a novel she was reading.

Her sunglasses and her favourite shade of pink lipstick are in the cup holder.

Maybe it's silly, but driving her ride gives me a sense of relief—like I can pretend she's at Shel's, and she'll be pissed at me when she discovers I took her truck.

Driving into Glass Falls, I think of stopping by my best friend Amy's place, but I don't think I'm ready to tell her about Theo yet.

Not that I want him to be a secret.

I know what it's like to be someone's secret, and I'd never put someone else in that position.

It's more like I don't want to break the bubble that this new hot-as-hell attraction has me in.

Before doing something totally nuts—like driving all the way to the Okanagan Valley to check out the winery Theo's almost-sister-in-law owns—I hit a drive-thru for a hot chocolate and pull over at the start of the trail to my favourite lookout in Glass Falls. The hike up that path gives you a great view of the waterfall, the mountains, and the hill of Rising Harbour.

It's too wet and snowy right now, but just thinking of bringing Theo here makes me all gooey.

A light dusting of snow is falling, so I turn the windshield wipers on, happy that I found a moment last week to change them.

It's not rest, just me parked on the side of the road, but it's the first time I've felt like I could breathe in a while. Something in me loosens, the tension finally giving way.

Daphne always told me I couldn't keep running from my problems, but running away is exactly how I became a mechanic—I'd always run to Uncle Henry's shop.

If I had a fight with a classmate, or if my sister's friends were mean, or if Daphne and I argued, I'd head straight to Uncle Henry's.

The smell of grease and oil always made me feel better. His soothing voice and calm demeanor made me feel safe. I liked fixing things, taking them apart and putting them back together, and that's how I ended up a mechanic, by accident.

Photography was my dream, but nobody thought it was something I could make a living from.

Helping my uncle out, I discovered that problem-solving on my feet kept my thoughts from spinning.

Sipping my hot chocolate, I want to call Daphne. I want to tell her that I met a guy, but she's always had feelings about who I date.

She can't help but be judgemental.

Daphne's always the person who does the *right* thing, and having kinky sex doesn't fall within that perimeter. When I first told her I was interested in being a Domme, she scrunched up her face and suggested I go to therapy.

So, of course, I found my way to my first kink party and, luckily, fell into a group of other female Dominants who were more experienced than I was and showed me the ropes.

But for a few years there, I took risks I might not have otherwise because of my sister's disapproving stare, her occasional asking me about it, making assumptions like I step on men's balls for money. Every criticism my sister uttered drove me to the next one-night stand or the next kink party until I found the man who made me fall hard and fast.

With John, I started to ease off the casual hookup train. He took me on trips, brought me gifts and encouraged me to think of something outside of Rising Harbour, and because of John's encouragement, I picked up my camera again.

That's one good thing that came out of that heartbreaking experience.

But if it hadn't been for Daphne interfering, I wouldn't have left Rising Harbour. This place has its own weather system, its own sense of time, and I belong here.

I had been seeing John for almost two years, and the rush of dominance he allowed me was amazing. It wasn't like some of the encounters I had at clubs, where men only wanted a transactional relationship.

It started to look like what Amy had with her husband, Clive.

John brought me my favourite hot chocolate, would give me back rubs, and was happy to sit under my feet while I binge-watched the car show I was hooked on. But he wasn't happy to introduce me to his friends or family.

I wipe away tears I didn't even realize were falling down my face, wanting not to be mad at my sister.

It wasn't her fault that the guy turned out to be engaged and that she was the messenger to give me that news.

I yelled at her and told her it wasn't true. Then she begged me to look at the social media posts she'd found. I blamed it on her being postpartum and having baby brain.

Terrible of me, I know.

When I found out who the guy I was in love with actually was, I crumbled.

I did what I always did: I ran away by accepting Gianna's offer to be the mechanic for the motocross team and spent three years on the circuit in Europe.

It was the best time of my life.

Until the phone call brought me home.

I finish the last sip of my drink, pull out of the parking lot, and head back to Shel's, wondering why I'm being so stubborn.

Because I'm the *Domme*.

I laugh, my hands tensing on the steering wheel, but that's part of it.

Theo told me to have a nap, to rest.

I bristled at that, even with how kind his grey eyes were, how sweet his expression when he made the suggestion.

He didn't give it as a command, but as a caring suggestion, so why couldn't I take it?

As someone who thrives on control, it's hard for me to accept help.

Delegation is not my strong suit.

And that's what Theo's given me.

A fresh swathe of caring interference.

I'm not ready for a relationship. I don't know if I could give a submissive everything they need: an emotional safe place and physical intimacy.

How can I when my head isn't straight?

But Theo is different from any other guy I've been with before.

The instant attraction is more than a one-night stand. It feels like a connection that's full of heat, and I don't want to walk away from it.

I come in the back way and right upstairs, unlock the door. "Theo, I'm home."

The little apartment gleams. Every surface shines freshly cleaned. A vase of flowers sits on the kitchen table. I hang up my jacket, take off my shoes and open my fridge.

Fully stacked, everything neatly arranged.

A girl could get used to this.

The door to the guest room is closed, and I pause, hearing his rich timbre.

"As we discussed at our last meeting, the legacy needed to be deleted. I can see the breach, and I have a team member on their way to you. I can be there tomorrow, but my assistant is more than capable, and you are fortunate that we caught it in time. We'll touch base in the morning."

I knock softly against the door because I don't want to feel like I'm eavesdropping, but the door opens, and Theo grins at me, reaching for my hand.

"Hey."

"Hi Callista." His tone is almost shy, not the commanding rich voice I overheard.

"You cleaned."

"I can't help myself," Theo's mouth quirks.

"You bought me flowers."

"Yes." Two dots of scarlet appear on his cheeks.

"Thank you," I plant a kiss on his mouth, the scent of his aftershave wafting in my nostrils. I reach behind his neck and slide my hand into his hair, rubbing little circles on his scalp. He practically purrs.

"It's more than just sex for you, submission?" Theo's hair is silky beneath my fingers as I keep twirling it, watching his expression closely.

A flash of hurt crosses his face, and the zillion ways I could fuck up his ex's car flash through my mind.

"Yes. I resort to the occasional pickup play, but prefer a relationship. I don't want something transactional."

"Me neither." I cup his face, and he gives a soft whimper. "I've had a few bouts of guys treating me like I'm an on-demand kink dispenser, and I'm not interested in that bullshit." I kiss him again, deeply, feeling his restraint weaken as I tug on his bottom lip.

My hands find their way around his ass, and I knead, squeeze, enjoying the firmness beneath my fingers, the way little shudders roll through his shoulders.

"This is a fine little town you have."

"Yeah? I couldn't wait to get away from it." That wasn't entirely true. I love it here and long to be part of it, but the town hasn't always returned the same love.

"Uncle Henry is going to finish your truck by tonight."

"Good," Theo glances down.

I grab his chin, lifting his gaze back to me. "What is it?"

"I have to leave on Saturday. Morning."

There's a hitch in my breathing, my stomach knots with disappointment. We knew this was coming to an end.

"Work?" I brush my lips across his.

"Yeah. I have to present the findings of my team at a company board meeting. Have I mentioned that I hate public speaking?" His lips purse as if in distaste, and I tickle him under his chin, lightly.

"No, you didn't."

"Yes, it's a huge part of my job. I have the perfect person on my team to delegate it to, and I don't."

"Because you're the boss," I tease.

"Yes," he strokes my hair softly, with extreme gentleness. I want to arch my back under his touch.

"After giving a presentation or the occasional press conference, I have to decompress in a dark room, no noise."

"How long does it take you to bounce back?" I grip him around the waist. I understand what it's like to wear a mask.

"Depends. I wish I could stay longer." He drops his head, then lifts it to peer deeply into my eyes.

"But we're going to keep going." I need to say the words.

"Yes, Callista, if you want me."

He stands with his hands at his sides, glancing up at me with those soulful grey eyes.

"I do want you." I drag my palm down his chest, squeezing his balls through his slacks. He hisses through his teeth. I rise onto my tiptoes, press my lips over his, and twine my fingers through his hair, pulling him closer. He groans softly into my mouth.

"I can't remember the last time someone bought me flowers. Thank you. I remember how your cock throbbed inside me." I undo his button, his fly, shove his pants off of him.

Slipping my hand under his boxers, find his half-hard cock.

"Your pussy gripped my cock perfectly." His breathing hitches as I press on his cock, the smooth length of him thickening in my hand. *I deserve this*, even if this is the wrong time and I'm not in the headspace to be a full-time Domme.

But the way he waits on my every touch, so willing, it's impossible to resist. We're diving in again without words, and when he throws his head back and groans, I can't stop myself.

"Give me your limits." I lift my hand off his cock and cup the back of his head. His Adam's apple moves as he swallows.

"No blood play, or scat. I'm not into CBT, trampling, or sissification—those are hard limits. I don't enjoy being spat on, and humiliation is also a hard limit for me. I don't love electric play."

"Noted," I scrape my fingernails along his arm. The fine material of his dress shirt probably costs more than every single garment I have in my closet.

"Anything else?" I cup his face against my palm.

He kisses my fingers as I run them across his lips. "I don't like being grabbed from behind."

I wrap my arms around his waist, hugging him against me. I noticed this morning how he flinched when people were moving behind him in the diner, and I can guess this stems from his ex.

"What about yours?" Theo's voice is silky soft.

"I don't like being tickled. Don't call me 'mommy', no verbal abuse. If you go too far into the scene to stop communicating with me, I end it. Got it?"

"Got it."

This was a flyby negotiation, not the deep conversation we'd eventually need to have, but it'll do for this moment.

"I *do* like a little pain," Theo admits, blushing slightly.

I drag my fingernails across the nape of his neck. "Yeah?"

"Yes, please, Callista?"

I laugh softly, my fingers curling around his lips, tugging until he winces.

"I love giving pleasure. It's what drives me."

"And giving up control of yours?" I press my palm against his cock.

"Yes, Ma'am."

"Beautiful." I grab his shirt and kiss him, sweeping my tongue deep into his mouth. He groans, and the sound sends my pulse into overdrive.

"I didn't take that nap."

"I noticed," Theo trails his lips against my neck. The rumble of his laugh sends a vibration rolling through me, making me want him. I'm so hot for this man, it's not going to take much for me to combust.

"I wonder what would help me sleep?" I pull him even closer to me, undoing the buttons on his shirt.

"Tell me how I can worship you?"

He's so eager, so raw, I look away, pushing down a wave of fear that this is too much.

He gently cups my face. "It's okay to be vulnerable, Callista."

And because I'm me—and probably need therapy—I've always challenged and growled my way through life.

There's a part of me that wants to test him, to see if my words will make him run.

So, I throw out the wildest thing I can think of on the spot.

"Eat my ass." My tone is sharp.

"I would love to eat your ass, Ma'am."

And this beautiful, strong man sinks to his knees, wraps his hands around my waist, and presses his mouth against my thigh, through my pants.

I am so fucking gone.

My pussy is dripping wet. "Get my pants off me, boy."

The weight of his hand on my waist intensifies as he pulls down my jeans. I grip his shoulder for balance, stepping out of them, then trace his cheek with my fingertips before turning and folding myself over the bed.

"Can you be a good boy and save your come for later?" I say over my shoulder. His cheeks heat and he bows his head.

"Yes, Ma'am," his finger skims along my ass. The cool air sends shivers over my flesh as he pulls down my plain panties.

He squeezes my ass cheeks, the pressure both gentle and firm, a wave of pleasure rippling through my pussy.

His cool hands knead my ass, then his lips press on my cheeks, and he licks, long strokes of his tongue, working his way across to my centre. My legs start to tremble as he kisses the other cheek with a slow, deliberate focus.

"Oh god!" He licks each curve, sending anticipation soaring through me and I shiver, as his tongue slides over my sensitive part, the warm flicks of his strokes, sends heat through every nerve, igniting a fire that steals my breath, makes me whimper and raise my hips.

His mouth lifts up, he blows a hot breath over my ass crack, making me cry out before that sweet tongue of his licks me between my ass crack again.

"Ooh, that's a good boy." I reach back, placing a hand on the top of his head. He whimpers under my touch.

He grabs my ass as if he's holding a precious object

Oh fuck me, this boy is damn good with his tongue, methodical and precise, taking his time to explore with his lips while his tongue keeps working.

My nipples tighten, and the breath leaves my body. His tongue keeps rolling along my skin, setting off nerve endings I had forgotten about.

I push back into his face. He yelps but drives right in, licking my crack, in and out, his soft breath blowing in my most sensitive places.

It has me standing on my toes, grabbing the bedsheets.

Fuck, I'm going to come just from this sensation.

I pull his hair, and the strangled cry wrenched from his lips is full of desperation, vibrating against my skin, making me feel all hot and powerful.

"Such a good ass licker, boy."

He spreads my cheeks, his hot mouth pressing against the curve of my ass, lips caressing the inner flesh. The sensation is so fucking divine—he's devouring me, and my pussy pulses, wanting attention.

"Very good boy." My breath hitches on the words, my eyes roll back in my head as pleasure swamps me, drags me down.

In response, he moans. The vibration ripples through me, making me even wetter.

His tongue is in my anus; it probes, then circles, probes and circles.

The motion makes me want to scream.

I'm panting, shivers rippling across my skin, and I can't help but wonder—who's in control now, when I'm the one struggling not to come?

I don't know if I can let go like this, but then his fingers sweep around to my clit, pressing his thumb against it. It's my high plea of pleasure that echoes around the room.

"Did I say you could touch my clit?" I bounce back against his face.

His fingers drop.

He whines, and I smirk, savouring his frustration

"Put them back where they were, but I'm going to spank you for this." I keep my tone light, despite how close to exploding I am.

Theo bounces against me, his eagerness clear, and I laugh as he fingers my clit hard, in time with the rhythm of his tongue—flicking, teasing, and driving me even closer.

I grind back against him so hard I must be cutting off his air, but his tongue continues relentlessly.

Circling.

Lapping.

My calves shake as I press into the floor, and like a sparkler igniting, I'm flaming into a burst of pleasure as the orgasm builds and then crashes through every sensitive nerve ending.

I roar out, grabbing his hair, and push back harder against him as the most intense wave of pleasure slams into me, leaving me shuddering.

"Fuck."

For a moment, the room spins, and I struggle to catch my breath, reaching for Theo's arm. He catches me, guiding me down to sit next to him on the floor.

I drape an arm around his shoulders and kiss his forehead. "That was so good, boy. Thank you."

"You're welcome, Ma'am." His voice is syrup, dripping with satisfaction.

He glances up at me, a pleased smile on his face.

"Being on my knees for you, Ma'am, made me feel like being on top of the world."

"Theo. You pleased me very much."

It's an effort to keep my voice steady.

I run my fingers through his hair, enjoying how he dips his head against my hand and slides my fingers down to feel his cock.

It's wide, thick, hard.

"What about denial and control?" I whisper in his ear, dragging my hand up and down his cock.

His lids droop, and I squeeze his balls. He lifts his head, his eyes open and lock onto mine with such intensity my pussy clenches.

"Love being teased. I love wearing a cock cage." His eyes are so glassy and wide that my heart thumps in my chest.

"I will always reward you, but I think I'm going to enjoy making you wait. What do you say to that?"

"Yes, Ma'am," Theo heaves a sigh as I drop my hand from his cock then cup his balls, pressing on his filled sacks.

"I need to tell you something?" His grey eyes meet mine, his blush climbs up his neck.

"What's that?" My mouth hovers near his, and there's a drop of sweat forming on the top of his lips.

"I bought tickets to the fundraiser this evening." His sly smile makes my pulse jump.

"Did you?" My heart flutters so fast, it's going to burst out of my chest. The gentleness in his eyes melts away all my worries, all my doubts.

"Mrs. Stewart came back as I came in with groceries." Theo looks damn pleased with himself.

"Why did you do that?" I press my thumb at the base of his cock.

"It seemed like the right thing to do." Theo lets out a hiss between his teeth. I drag my lips down his neck, licking the column of his throat while squeezing his balls in a gentle rhythm.

"If you can be a good boy and save that come for me, I'll reward you by allowing you to take me to this fundraiser tonight." I kiss his cheek.

He shudders deliciously. "I can wait. I'm a very patient boy."

"Good," I trace the shell of his ear, my limbs heavy with exhaustion. I stand and peel off the rest of my clothes.

Glancing at the clock. I have an hour and a half to take a nap before I pick up my niece.

"Is there anything I should know about tonight, Ma'am?" Theo asks from where he is, kneeling on the floor.

I reach down and hold his chin in my palm, feeling my throat dry.

We might run into my ex.

"Nothing."

I slide under the covers, noticing that the sheets have been changed and my Kindle is charged.

"Thank you for looking after me."

"It's my pleasure, Callista," Theo rises, strides over to the window, and closes the curtains. I extend my hand to him and pull him to me. "See you later, sweet boy."

He exhales a breath, drops his head down, and gives me the biggest, shiniest smile ever.

"Later, Ma'am."

He walks out of my bedroom. I hear him in the washroom, and then finally, my eyelids close as I feel safe for the first time in a long time.

7

THEO

A four-piece orchestra plays 'Jingle Bells' in the hotel lobby, and gold garlands are strung over every surface

The mingled, sickly scents of colognes and perfume clog my nostrils, and the murmur of the crowd makes my head woozy.

But there's nowhere else I'd rather be.

Gold vases with poinsettias sit on high-top tables.

A dozen or so Christmas trees, all uniquely decorated, stand by the windows.

I want to check them out.

People are buying raffle tickets to win the trees, several people have stopped to talk to Callie, and already, I'm feeling drained but trying not to let it show.

The doors to the banquet hall are open, and there is a crowd mingling, waiters with appetizers are circling the room.

I'm starving and would love to get in there, but Callie squeezes my hand, and she pulls me off to the side towards the window.

"Have I said how stunning you look tonight, Ma'am?" I keep my voice pitched low, for her ears only.

Her blue eyes widen under a swathe of shimmery makeup, and the red lipstick she chose is the exact same shade as the deep red in the dress she is wearing.

It hugs her body, and wearing stiletto heels, she's at eye level with me.

"Theo, you might hear people say things about me tonight."

I want to brush away her worries, but she looks so upset, I rub her arms, feeling such a powerful sense of gratitude that she shared her anxieties with me.

"Let's see, today I heard about the time you were caught smoking weed behind the bleachers."

"Do you know what it's like to live in a small town? I needed an escape. It was only once," Callie raises her chin as if I'm going to challenge her.

"Some old lady told me about the time your sister broke your favourite Barbie, so you wrecked her bike."

"Look, I wanted that Barbie for two Christmases before I got it. She knew it. I didn't wreck her bike—I borrowed it and crashed into the neighbour's fence," her lips quirk.

"I heard that you were a horrible student-"

"We can't all be computer geeks like you."

"Right? That's what I said, and then they said If it weren't for your sister, you wouldn't have passed high school. You know what I told them?"

"What?" She tilts her head, her expression curious.

"That's exactly how it was for my younger brother."

"Yeah?" Her face relaxes into a grin.

"Yep. He's the athlete of the family. A smart guy, but he hates reading and doing anything bookish."

There's no way I'm going to repeat to Callie the comment about her ruining a family I heard from that old guy this morning.

"I bet you're a good older brother."

"You'd have to ask Hunter that. I can't wait to tell them about you." I place my hands on her shoulders, dropping them to her waist.

She takes my hands in hers, her grip cool.

"You're going to tell them about me?" The pleasure in her voice makes me want to lift her on my shoulders and spin her around.

"Yes, how I met a cute barista outside a diner that's having an identity crisis."

She tilts her head back and laughs, the high, lilting sound drawing glances our way.

"I would have given you and Brenda a warning if I had known that Flo was dropping off her art stuff. What else did you learn about me?" She slides down her hands to cup my ass.

I can see the crowd in front of us, but there's nobody behind us. I'm backed against the closed curtain.

"Mr. Ellison told me about the time you took your uncle's car for a joyride-"

"Small town rumour, it never happened," she gives me an exaggerated wink.

"And how you spent all your time in your uncle's garage, not having to prove yourself."

"That's not true! I had to fight my uncle to get him to give me a job. He didn't want to, but Aunt Millie's health had taken a turn, and he wanted to keep me home, so he finally gave in! I got my mechanic's license without his help." Her lips set in a thin line.

"You are so *cute* when you are indignant, Ma'am."

Her fingernails dig into the skin above my cuffs in reply, and I chuckle.

"I also learned how you made out with your first boyfriend in church, that you fixed your highschool geometry teacher's mother's car for free, how your uncle missed you and moped around town when you left and how you are the first to pitch in. Ma'am, if you didn't want me to hear gossip, taking that shift at Shel's today was a horrible plan."

Callie closes her eyes briefly. "I am very grateful that you spent only a few hours in that place today." She drags her hand along my chest, and I grab it, raising it to my lips and kissing it.

"And I'm happy to be here with you. It doesn't matter what I hear, I'm *not* running away."

I can see how my words have struck a nerve, and it seems to give her some strength because she draws herself up, puts her shoulders back and pulls my hand. "Let's go."

"Yes Ma'am. I can't wait to dance with you, but I also can't wait to get my reward."

"Yeah?" The way her eyes darken a shade has my cock. throbbing and impatient.

"Yes."

"You've been a very good boy. I've been thinking about your dick all day."

My throat goes dry at the thought.

But Callie puts on a dazzling smile and turns to greet an old man at the door with a full beard. "Hi Roger, how are you doing?"

"Hey Callie, I'm glad you came out. You have to stop letting the council bully you. How's Daphne?"

"She had a great day." Her smile is real, and I wonder who this man is.

When Callie got home this afternoon, she was practically giddy.

Daphne had a good day, able to hold a conversation.

She called her aunt, who met them with the little kids and then came home to me, throwing her arms around me, laughing.

"Glad to hear it. Have fun tonight," he gives her a wave.

"Who is that?"

She grabs my hand, positions it around her waist, and I pull her closer to me

"Roger was a friend of my grandfather. He gave me my first job at the grocery store, outside of Shel's. He's always stood up for me."

"Then he's one of my favourite people I've met here."

She flashes me a grin, steps into the banquet hall, and I follow. She leads us over to the appetizer trays, thank god and I shove something that's wrapped in pastry in my mouth.

"Hungry?" Callie brushes a crumb off my dress shirt.

"Starving," I say, raising my eyebrows and nuzzling into her shoulder. "Some gorgeous Domme has made me *very* hungry. Are there going to be speeches?"

"Yes. Do you want to stay?" She says it teasingly, but there's a challenge in her eyes.

"I am curious as to what the town will say and see if I can be of any help to you."

"Theo, you can't help me with Shel's."

"Am I crossing a line?" I soften my voice.

"I don't know. The last two days have been an exception. I usually don't let anyone in, and I feel like it's my mess to clean up."

"Callista, so nice to see you!" Mrs. Stewart, now dressed in a sparkling black dress, slings an arm around Callie. "Let me take you to your table. You're with Mickey from the Sleepaway, Derek from Rosette's Bakery and the Flints." Mrs. Stewart leads us to a table near the front, but off to the side in a corner, where the view of the stage is blocked.

"Thanks Mrs. Stewart. These are *perfect* seats." Her tone oozes with sarcasm.

Mrs. Stewart doesn't pick up on her tone and squeezes Callie's shoulder. "We're so happy to have you here!" And the woman flutters to the next table.

I pull out Callie's chair for her, and she sits down, then I take the seat next to her. "What do the Flints do?"

Callie busies herself with some water. "They run a little hobby farm. That was Daphne's first job outside of Shel's. She loved working with horses."

"And it's not unique enough for the town?" I lean toward her, my knee touching hers.

"The council identified businesses that they determined had too much overlap. Their names were on the list. I don't know who they pissed off." She hooks her ankle over mine, and I sit back in my seat, drinking in the sight of her.

"The problem with Shel's is they don't think it's unique enough to draw tourists."

"But the diner has been there since the town's inception."

"Literally," Callie leans into me, and below the table, she squeezes my thigh.

"Thank you for buying tickets. My aunt and uncle are happy I'm putting in an appearance."

"Not a problem. I like to be helpful."

I was going to ask to kiss her saucy lips, but the other guests joined us at the table.

Then the speeches started.

The mayor comes on first and starts talking about how Rising Harbour is the last of its kind.

I tried to listen so I could help Callie out later, but I only focused on the feel of her hand on mine, how her thigh rubbed against mine under the table.

Not that I needed this dinner to confirm it, but by the time we got out on the dance floor, I realize how completely in lust I am with her.

"What are you thinking, Theo?" Callie says against my lips as we slow dance on the floor, her arms over my shoulders.

"Honestly?" I lean down to her ear, brushing the outer shell with my lips.

"Yes, please."

"How this is the wrong time for this, for whatever is between us, and I'm thinking I also don't care."

"I knew you were trouble the moment I saw you." I hear the smile in her voice. She leans closer to me, pressing her hot body against mine.

"Me trouble? I heard about you." I let out a low growl, holding her closer.

"What else?" Callie blinks her eyelids dramatically.

"The owner of the Sleepaway told that tale about how you put sugar in her gas tank." My tone is light and friendly, but Callie stills in my arms.

"Have you ever covered for one of your brothers?" She cocks an eyebrow.

"Hell yes." As soon as she asked the question, the times I covered for all three of them flashes through my mind. I was the shy one, the one who didn't speak much.

Nobody expected me to get in trouble.

"Sometimes it's like that with sisters," Callie winks at me.

My mouth goes dry as she slides her hands along my ass, pulling me closer. "I've made nice with every one of the council members. I think we can go now. If this is our last night, I want to make sure it leaves you plenty satisfied."

"Last night for *now*," I murmur.

She grabs my hand as the music ends and says her goodbyes.

I make a beeline for the coat check to grab our jackets when I catch Callie's expression—like she's seen a ghost.

"Thank you," I say to the attendant, grabbing our coats, throwing down a ten-dollar bill. I stand in her view of the window, holding out her coat.

"Your jacket, Ma'am."

She doesn't say anything, just slips her arms into the jacket stiffly.

Without putting mine on, I walk in the opposite direction, heading for the back exit.

Callie's not looking at me, so I tug her over, just inside the doors. "Everything okay?"

She closes her eyes and nods against me. "I'm sorry. I'm the one who should be driving, whatever this is between us, and we're rushing."

"I don't feel that we are rushing. We know what we want." I wrap my arms around her and press a gentle kiss to her mouth.

"Your being here has...paused my stress. But you're the submissive, in the vulnerable position."

"Come on, give me some credit. I know what I want. I'm a grown-up. Submissives are just as responsible for keeping themselves safe as the Domme is."

Callie shakes her head, a smile playing about her lips. "Tell me something horrible about you, please."

I laugh. "I hate pineapple on pizza?"

"You're completely terrible." She leans her head against my chest. "I'm not a catch."

"Don't say that. You were upfront with everything that's been going on with your life."

The hurt in her tone, the wobble of confidence, makes me want to drop to my knees and give her reassurance.

"Mostly everything," Callie murmurs. She shivers, and I tighten my grip on her. "Can you promise me one thing?"

"Anything, Ma'am."

Her eyes are filled with tears, and I lean down and kiss the corner of her eye, and a shudder rolls through her under my lips, I keep kissing a trail to her jaw, before she pulls me back to meet her eyes, that are now so serious my mouth goes dry.

"If this gets hot and heavy, if you fall *in* love with me, if you want more than what we agree to... you tell me."

I know what she's asking. She wants me to be honest, yes, but she also wants the space to decide if a serious relationship is something she can handle.

That's fair, but I don't want to agree to this... because I'm halfway in love with her already.

"I promise." As soon as the word is out of my mouth, her expression relaxes.

"Thank you, boy. I will be honest with you too." She rubs her thumb across my jawline. "When the town came out with that list deciding they needed to boost their tourism, business owners who owned the building were given an exception...I know," she says at my expression. "Small towns."

Her face loses colour again, and I offer her my arm. "Let's get some air."

I shrug on my jacket, hold the door open for Callie, and step through after her into the steady rain.

"Believe it or not, we had six cupcake bakeries here at one time. Grady and Daphne's plan was to buy the building, but there were back property taxes owed. Their goal was to purchase it outright, but they can't do that until the taxes are cleared."

"Who owns the building?" I keep my voice soft, gentle because with the way she is shifting, her eyes darting everywhere makes me think she's going to bolt.

"My great-grandfather helped everyone he could. But he needed the down payment for Shel's, so he went to his friend, Paul Hops. My great-grandfather paid it back within the year but, as a gesture of friendship and because Paul was expanding his business, Shel split the building with him, fifty-fifty. The Hops still own fifty percent of the building. My aunt and uncle thought the property taxes had been paid by the Hops, and they were until my grandfather passed."

That's enough to make my head spin, and I want to call Noel because he has the skill set to untangle this.

"Okay. Are they involved in the business?"

"No, not at all. Nobody heard from them for years, they were too busy with their construction company." Callie bites her lip and looks down at her hands.

"Ma'am? Have I told you how gorgeous I think you are?"

The pleased smile spreading across her lips makes me feel giddy.

"Whatever this is between you and me, the timing..." Callie reaches for my hand.

"I know. I don't care. Why can't Daphne and Grady buy the building from the Hops?"

She squeezes my hand hard, and I stay still, letting her take her time. "Because they don't want to sell it. Jana Hops will never sell it. That's the granddaughter."

"Why not?" Rising Harbour is a cute little town, but the Hops Construction company is massive.

"Because for years, I had a relationship with her fiancé... I didn't know he was someone's fiancé," she swallows.

"I hate the motherfucker," I spat out with as much force as I could.

She shakes her head. "No, Theo, it was entirely my fault."

"Callista, it's not your fault," I boldly take her chin in my hands, wanting her eyes on mine.

"No, I ruined her mother's plan. Broke up a marriage."

"You didn't break up a marriage, Ma'am. He was not married but promised to another."

Her lips press together in a thin line, and I want to find the man who hurt her and make him pay, the protective urge thumps in my chest.

"Why do you believe me? You're a stranger."

"Callista, because you're so obvious about the truth. So bold with it."

"There's people who have known me all my life and think it's my fault. But I swear, I had never met him before. I met him in Glass Falls, where I was living with my friend Amy."

"It's not your fault."

"No, it's my fault. I'm kind of impulsive, I rush in. It felt so good to have someone new, someone who didn't know me. He took me on trips. I thought there was a future with us..." She shakes her head, her long hair falling against her cheeks. "I was stupid."

"This guy led you on while stepping out on his fiancée. This isn't on you, Callista."

I can't get my head around the business in and outs, but some guy who was almost married to another woman decided to have an affair with Callie? That guy's an asshole.

She gives me the tiniest smile. "I tell myself that. It doesn't help. Getting the building back isn't the only problem. The town has to approve your business, and so far, they haven't given Daphne the green light. They want to see a commitment to the town. I think they would have given it to Daphne, but with me here..."

She shrugs a shoulder. "I have a habit of running away sometimes."

"You haven't run away from me."

"And I don't want to."

She grabs a fistful of my shirt and slams her lips into mine, backing me against the wall.

I kiss her with all the pent-up frustration I have. I kiss her like her lips are the only thing keeping me breathing.

Her mouth is soft, insistent against mine, and all I can do is moan.

She kisses me like she's trying to drive out the thoughts in her head, and I'm more than happy to be her sexy distraction.

My hands roam over her coat, into her hair, where I thread my fingers through her silky strands.

She breaks the kiss, cupping my cheek.

"One more thing. Daphne is the one who told me about my ex... that he was engaged. I didn't believe her at first. She's never approved of my lifestyle. I accused her of not being okay with my being happy."

"Hey, siblings argue." I wrap my arms around her, wanting to take away her worries.

"That was a big one. Next thing I know, I'm signing with the motocross team and partying in Europe, living my best life—until the call about her accident brought me home."

She wipes her arm across her face. "I love when she's having a good day and recognizes us and her eyes light up. But there's a part of me that dreads it. A part of me thinks she's going to scream at me to leave—because in our last conversation... I wasn't nice."

"Callista." I lower my voice, keeping it soft. "You spent years with a man your sister suddenly claimed was taken. I don't think many people would have reacted calmly."

"How do you never say the wrong thing?" She asks, slipping her hand into mine.

"I say the wrong thing all the time. There's a whole YouTube video of me fumbling through a presentation at the firefighters' association—trying to explain how our tech could secure their data. It was right after my breakup. Go watch it. It's horrible."

She laughs. "You make me feel..."

She pauses, then shakes her head.

"Like what?" Hope leaps in my chest. I want this woman to want me as much as I want her.

"Like I want to take you home and spank your ass before you leave tomorrow."

My cock twitches. Yeah, I like that idea.

"Please, Ma'am."

"Get in the car."

I do as she says.

In the car, her hand finds my thigh, then sweeps up to my crotch and rests there. She presses down. I groan, annoyed and impatient.

Yeah, we might be rushing in but who cares?

We're adults.

I can't deny the attraction, or how I feel around her.

And I love feeling like I can make her world better.

We pull up to Shel's. Before I can open her door, she runs around to mine.

I get out.

She kisses me, pushing me against the car. I'm so desperate for her, she could order me naked in this parking lot and I'd happily obey.

"My ex wasn't there tonight, but his father and uncle were."

"Okay. You got through it."

"Yeah, thanks to you. Are you still good and ready for me, Theo?"

She slides her hand between my legs.

"Yes, Ma'am."

"Good. I want your cock hard and aching by the time we reach my apartment door."

8

CALLIE

Pure, hot need courses through me. Tonight, I want whatever this man is willing to give me.

Yeah, he's trouble, but damn it, I more than want him, I *need* him.

The door is barely closed before I push him against it, grabbing his cock through his pants. I hold his chin and press a scorching kiss on his soft mouth.

His moan is low and needy.

He kisses me back, our lips and tongues meeting, our moans echoing each other's.

The high this submissive boy gives me is like stepping into an alternative world, a fresh change of pace that I desperately needed.

When his head drops and he pulls back, guilt crashes over me.

"Thank you for tonight. I know crowds aren't your thing. If you want to watch a movie and take it slow, cuddle, I get that." I pat his cheek gently. He turns into my touch, nuzzling against my hand.

His outpouring of affection is what my soul has craved for so long.

"There are times when that's exactly what I need. But I heard there might be a spanking?" His lopsided grin makes mine spread into a goofy smile.

"What if I grabbed a paddle from my toy chest?" I dance my fingers along his chest, loving the way his eyes light up with pleasure.

"Hell yes."

"I have plans for you, boy." He blushes just as I hoped.

Laughing, I grab him by his fine tux, pulling him into the bedroom. At the end of the bed, I cup his face and bring his head down to mine, slanting my lips against his.

He shivers deliciously as I work my tongue into his mouth.

His taste is intoxicating.

I'm quickly becoming addicted to everything about Theo Brennon. That's bad news for me because not a single relationship I've ever had has worked out.

I brush my palms along his abs, pull at his waistband, getting his pants off. Stroking his cock through his boxers, I feel his hardness. "You are so damn hot."

He swallows as my hand presses through his boxers. I squeeze his sac, and he groans.

"Ma'am, you're making me so needy."

"Good."

"Wait for me. Naked. On your knees."

"Yes, Ma'am." The way his voice becomes so gravelly makes me purr.

I walk away all casual, though it's not as easy as I'm making it look. I can't wait to run my hands over his ass, to see how he takes a spanking, and finally reward him for his good behavior.

Then why am I freaking out?

Because, from the moment my sister burst my bubble, I convinced myself that I didn't deserve a relationship. I sought out casual play faster than I could change my panties and lived it up while I was in Europe.

Whatever this is between Theo and me, it feels different. It has weight. For the first time in weeks, my mental clarity has returned, and my mood has lifted... all thanks to this stranger who's affected not only my libido but my emotional equilibrium.

He didn't barrel his way into my life. He showed up and said, *"I'm here. Use me"* with no expectation of anything in return.

The enormity of it hits me, and I reach out to steady myself on the wall. Needing to pull it together, I square my shoulders and do a quick refresh in the bathroom.

There's so much I haven't explained to Theo... stuff he needs to know... but I don't want to trauma dump on him right now.

Right now, I want to be the Domme I strive to be. I want to be giving, loving, and in control.

I'm eager to reward my sub for his good behavior, and the thought alone has my panties soaking wet.

Done in the bathroom, I grab a storage box from the closet and search through my kinky toys. I pick out a light acrylic paddle—one with lots of flex—and put the rest back.

My heart races faster than a metal drummer's beat as I stride down the hall and open the bedroom door.

The sight of his muscled back, his palms pressed to his knees, is so beautiful that I pause to drink it in. His breathing is even and steady. He doesn't glance back as I close the door.

Mine.

"This is a very pretty sight." I place my hand on his shoulder, caressing his back. "You're a very patient boy."

My heel grazes his leg as I thread my fingers through his hair.

He flinches, a tremble rocks through his body.

I rub circles on his head, but he isn't relaxed. His breathing is quick, his hands clenched into fists.

"Theo, look at me." I kneel beside him, running the back of my knuckles against his scruffy face. "Are you okay?"

He glances at me, then away, swallowing hard. "Yes. I want this." He reaches for my hand, but I stop him.

"When I walked in, you were all serene. When I touched you, you reacted. Any reason?" I keep my voice soft and light.

His grey eyes cloud as they meet mine. "I didn't know. When your heeled foot touched my skin, my ex trampled me with heels. And when your heel brushed my skin..."

I take off my heels, tossing them across the room. "You got triggered."

"When she first started, it was fine. I liked kneeling. I liked being under her bare feet. But later, when I tried to help her, the more she'd increase the intensity of her control." His voice is barely above a whisper.

I set the paddle aside and rub his back until he relaxes.

He grabs my arms, drops his head, and I hold him as he exhales shakily.

I'm so mad I want to punch something, but with effort, I lock that emotion away to process later.

After a moment, his breathing returns to normal. I turn his face toward me and kiss him sweetly.

This man might be a stranger to me, but I know he's a good boy. His ex didn't deserve him.

Theo groans softly, the tension finally leaving his body.

"Do you want to continue?" I drop a kiss on his cheek.

"Yes. Green all the way, Callista." His heated gaze is filled with lust, and my pussy tightens.

"Good." I lightly kiss his lips, then rise to grab a water bottle from the nightstand.

Uncapping it, I hand it to him. He sits back on his heels.

"I'm sorry."

"Don't apologize for hitting a trigger you didn't know about. I've got my own stuff, too." I glide my hand to his and squeeze it as his fingers grasp mine.

"That's the reason I wasn't looking for a relationship."

"Same," I giggle, and then I can't help but take his face in my hands. "But I think one happened to us."

"I think you're right, Ma'am." His eyes meet mine, his lips turning upward in a small smile. "Continue, please."

I pick up the paddle, slide my hand up his naked back, and goosebumps rise on his smooth skin.

Cupping his nape, I hold the paddle to his lips. "Kiss it."

He does, and I feel the wave of anticipation run through him as his lips brush the paddle, his breath hitching.

"Lean over the end of the bed and hold on. I'm not going to go easy on you, boy."

"Yes, Ma'am!" He gets into the position.

I run a hand down his spine to his ass, reaching around him to play with his balls, sliding down to his half-hard cock.

While I'm playing with his dick, I slide the paddle along his ass, around, in a slow circle.

He murmurs, arches up to the touch, clearly asking for more.

Dropping his cock, I take a step back, release a breath of my own and swing the paddle through the air.

It makes contact with his ass with a light thwack, and I bring it down again.

He's braced, waiting, accepting, taking what I give him, and I feel the slide of my mind into Top space, and I give in to its depths. I want to make this boy's ass red.

So I swing the paddle through the air, and down on him, hard.

Even harder.

"Thank you, Ma'am!" He stays still, doesn't flinch.

And that's a green light for me. I strike again.

He takes it, not flinching, accepting every hit to his skin.

I keep swinging the paddle down, the rhythm builds as the flush of pink spreads across his skin.

As the paddle lands hard on the bottom of his ass he falls out of position.

I stop, stride over, and fist his hair. "Back where I told you to stay, boy."

"Yes, Ma'am."

"Give me a colour."

"Green." He meets my gaze, holds it. His tone is sure and confident.

I'm going to take him at his word.

Letting go of his hair, I bring the thin paddle down again.

The sound of the acrylic hitting his flesh, so satisfying, it's making me so wet.

His breathing is heavier now, intense, as I don't let up.

The pink flush on his ass turns to a deep red.

He's going to be sore tomorrow.

While driving home.

Away from me.

I swing the paddle through the air, bringing it down harder, loving how he jumps.

Along the bruise of his ass, I give him another two slaps with the paddle.

It flexes against his ass, but doesn't break.

I press the paddle into his ass, then bring it away. I run my palm along the red splotches.

He lets out a little whine. "Thank you, Ma'am."

"You're welcome. Get on the bed on your back."

He scrambles, diving on the bed, and he spreads his legs wide.

"Come here." I climb in between his legs and brush my lips against his.

A slow, soft kiss at first, but then I wrap my arms around him and kiss him like I mean it.

Like I never want to stop kissing him and I deepen the kiss even more, my pussy clenching.

His body tenses, and the low, sultry growl he lets out bounces around the room, making my pulse race.

"That's a cute Wolfie," I break the kiss, look into his eyes, searching to see if he's okay.

"Yeah?" A small smirk tugs at the corner of his lips. "I like the name.

"Good. How can I make you growl like that again?" My palm slides down his leg, then over to his half-hard cock.

I take it in my hand and stroke it.

"Just like that," his lips hover over mine.

I form a ring with my thumb and index finger and slide it down his shaft, moving slowly up and down.

He twitches, groans, I flick his slit with my thumb, he growls and I don't let up, gliding my thumb down along his underside.

The ripple of power that shoots through my bloodstream, watching him thrust on my fingers, has me soaking wet between my thighs.

"Kiss me b-"

He cuts off my words by slamming his mouth against mine. His strong arms come around my back, holding me against him.

His kisses are desperate and hungry, each one lingering on my lips and sealing the connection between us.

My nipples tighten. I stroke his shaft, cupping his balls as his lips lock against mine.

"Oh...please, Ma'am." That low, growly vibration sends fresh shivers down my spine. It's completely adorable how needy and open he is with me.

"How do you want to come?"

"In your pussy, please, Callista."

His cock twitches in my grip. Pre-cum leaks onto my fingers.

I bring my hand to his mouth, slide my fingers past his lips, and he slurps them clean.

"Good boy. Up!"

He shuffles back, so quick and eager to obey. I lay down, shoving all the pillows behind my head and spreading my legs.

This boy needs little direction.

His hands glide up and down my legs before his face moves between them, kissing either side of my labia. The feel of his lips on my sensitive skin makes my hips jerk off the bed, and I press my hands against his shoulders. "Give it to me, Wolfie."

His laughter shoots vibrations through me as his lips seal over my clit and his tongue strokes it, in a quick, plunging rhythm that's ripping the breath from my body.

Tingles explode throughout my core, his hot mouth against my pussy lips, amazing.

"That's a good boy." I grasp a fistful of his hair and push his face exactly where I want it. "Higher with that tongue, yes, there."

Oh my god.

His flicks of tongue are enough to stop my thoughts, making me let out a soft moan of my own.

My nipples are strung tight.

I could so easily come right now, but I need to reward this gentle submissive that showed up and tossed up my world.

"Get your reward now, boy, before your tongue makes me scream. I want to drain your balls."

His body shudders, and he lifts his face out from between my legs. His lips are shiny with my juices, and he tackles me in the softest way, his face right to my collarbone.

The electricity between us sparks, the air is thick with need.

I knead his red ass. He flinches, shudders.

"Does it hurt?" I dig my fingers in his burning flesh, just because I want to.

"Yes, in the best way, Ma'am."

He presses his body into mine with such abandon it steals my breath. His lips on my skin are perfect, waking every sensation, making my pussy tingle with need, and I grab his head as he presses his lips above my nipple.

"Taste them, boy."

His tongue lavishes my nipple, sucks on the hardened tip, until I groan, my pussy throbbing, ready and so damn wet for him. I yank his head off my breast so I don't come from him sucking on my tits.

"Now, Wolfie. Show me how you use this beautiful cock."

"Yes, Ma'am," his eyes laser-focused on mine.

He takes his thick cock in his hand and strokes it, up and down the shaft, looking so strong, so beautiful, I want to memorize every feature of his, forever.

Gently he lowers himself to me, bracing on either side of me on his arms, his cock pressing against my opening. I cup the back of his neck, and he moves with me as I lean over to nibble on his ear.

"Nice and slow. Put your big cock in my pussy. Give me all of your cum." I clutch him against me, licking, nibbling, my hands sliding up and down his biceps.

"Yes! Your pussy is gripping me so hard, Ma'am. It feels...so...good."

"I said slow, boy!"

"Yes, Ma'am."

And inch by hard inch he pushes into my pussy. I brush his nipples as he starts to move, rocking his hips, oh... so slowly.

He doesn't take the lead, instead, he responds to how I move.

I lift my hips, he meets me, I pull on his nipple, he leans down, and our panting and moans fill the room. I'm lost in the rhythm of slow thrusting, of watching his muscles ripple as he controls himself.

He doesn't pound into me but slowly glides his cock in and out while holding my hips. I let go of his nipples and press down on his biceps. He closes his eyes, his brows furrow.

"Harder, Theo!" My voice breaks as I ask for what I want, but he obeys, giving me more, longer, deeper thrusts.

He pumps faster, the heat between us escalating, making me cry out, and I can feel every inch of him as he thrusts into me, and I cling to him, wanting to feel him as he finally breaks control.

He thrusts. Harder. Deeper as if he wants to possess me, and I meet each thrust, not letting him override me, reminding him I'm still in charge, I squeeze his ass, my pussy gripping his cock, craving more.

"Come for me now!" I wrap my legs around his back.

He stills. His body tenses, and then his face scrunches in a way that is powerful and raw.

A strangled groan escapes his lips as he lets out his hot release, making me hot for more of him.

He comes and comes until he's shuddering.

"Thank you, Ma'am," he murmurs, rocking his hips, driving me closer. My toes curl, my breath coming in quick, shallow pants.

"Welcome," I gasp, "I'm going to come, boy."

And I do on his next thrust, electricity shooting through my veins, my orgasm exploding from my centre, my head swaying, overwhelmed with the sensations, the pleasure.

He doesn't throw himself on top of me, but balances on his arms, keeping his weight off of me, even though his eyes are closed and he's shuddering with aftershocks, matching my own.

"Fuck." I touch my lips to his bottom lip and tug on it.

He bucks my hand, gives me that Wolfie noise that lights me up.

"Good boy. I love how your cock feels in my pussy."

He makes a sound that's half whimper and half growl. I shift under him, and he slowly detangles from me.

"Clean me up."

"Yes, Ma'am," he exhales, moving down between my legs.

My heart rate finally slows, my entire body is soft and languid with the aftermath.

The long stroke of his tongue to my clit makes me jump, and he licks me as if he's starving, each touch of his tongue sending jolts of pleasure through my core.

"That's a good boy," I gently rub my foot along his back.

He stiffens for a second, and I remove my foot, then I repeat, as softly as I can. "Is this okay?"

In response, he taps my leg, and I bring my foot back, dragging it along his ribcage, down to his ass again.

I won't ever trample him, but I want to give him a better memory of having feet on him.

I drape my leg across his back.

This man could give lessons in how to lick a pussy.

My clit hardens again under his strokes.

"That's it! Don't stop!" He sucks my clit as if his life depends on it. I clutch his head as tension coils and then breaks, ecstasy crashes into me, intense and overwhelming.

He growls between my thighs, it shoots me over the crest, and I'm flying, ecstatic tingles tightening in my core, shooting through my veins, and then the orgasm explodes, dragging me down.

"Fuck, baby!" I scream, pulling his head away from between my legs. I close my eyes, the room spinning around me.

Theo shifts and lies beside me. I wrap my arm around him, moving so his head is on my breast.

"You good?" I open my eyes, ruffling his hair.

"Very good, Ma'am." He's all hard muscles but soft with release beside me as he glances up at me from under his dark lashes.

"That was... yeah." I run my fingers through his hair, soaking in this peace that's settled over my mind.

But before we crash, I want more.

"Let's get cleaned up." I tug him out of bed. In the bathroom, I turn on the taps. "Get in."

Theo steps in, his long cock slack, but I want to lick it. I push him gently under the spray. "Turn around."

I soap his back, his ass, in between his legs. He jerks as I run the sponge over his balls and along his cock.

I quickly soap myself off, rinse and then, with Theo standing in front of me, I kneel, play with his cock, my hands kneading his balls.

His cock springs to life, and I take it in my mouth.

The taste of him coats my tongue, and I lick slowly, loving how his control is slipping.

He jerks against me.

I swallow his length, his cock velvety hard against my tongue. I taste my own juices along with the taste of his skin and keep swallowing, taking him even deeper.

"Ooh! Callista!"

His pure cry of happiness has me changing rhythm. I stop swallowing, switch to teasing his cock's head, twirling my tongue over his length.

"Fuck! Ma'am!" His hips jerk, his muscles taught under my hands.

Laughing around his length, I reach up, play with his balls, pressing them in my hand.

"Can I please come?" He presses on my shoulders lightly.

In reply, I dig my nails into his ass, moving him closer to my mouth.

I swallow deep, it hits the back of my throat.

Glancing up, his face is upturned to the ceiling, his muscles rippling with each shallow gasp, his jaw clenched in concentration.

"Now! I'm coming!" His cum shoots down my throat in long, ropey spurts. I greedily swallow it, every hot drop.

"Oh God, Callista!"

I stay like that on my knees, running my hands up his legs. "You're a good boy, Wolfie."

Standing, I take his face in mine and kiss him long and slow. He moans against me, his lips making my skin buzz with pleasure, a soft growl of approval rumbling from his chest. I'm so pleased with this boy, so consumed by him.

I turn off the shower and step out. Theo is already reaching for a towel, holding it open for me, anticipating my need.

That makes my throat go dry and my pussy flutter.

I step against him, and he dries me gently, as if I'm something precious, his touch tender.

"Thank you, boy."

He grins, drying himself off, and I can't help but run my hands over his ass, then reach around his front to grab his softening cock.

"Callista!"

"I can't help it. I love teasing you. You gave me so much pleasure tonight."

He blushes as I lead him out of the bathroom to bed.

He climbs in, and I pull the blankets up to his chin before getting in on the other side.

I wrap my arms around him, spooning his back. "We will talk

tomorrow."

"Yeah," he snuggles against me, yawns, and is asleep in seconds.

I lay in the dark, trying to calm my beating heart, anxious about going forward, but as my eyes close, I know with certainty I want Theo in my life.

My phone rings from somewhere far away, stirring me awake.

The spot next to me is empty. I pull the sheet off the bed and walk into the hall. Theo is already up, and he's handing my clutch to me.

I dig out my phone, taking a seat at the kitchen table.

"Hi, Aunt Millie."

"Callie, I wanted to let you know that Uncle Henry parked Theo's truck right out front, and the keys are in the mailbox.

"We are all going to see Daphne tomorrow for lunch, if you want to come along. The staff seem positive."

My aunt's voice breaks, and my heart squeezes. Aunt Millie and Uncle Henry are good people. These last few months have taken a toll on them, and it hasn't been fair.

I don't want to think about tomorrow because tomorrow is going to take my boy away from me, but being with my family will keep my mind off of it.

"I'll be there."

"Good. Thank you for going to the fundraiser last night, Callie. I've already heard about how delighted people were to see you. I love you."

"Love you too, Aunt Millie," I say to her before hanging up.

"Good morning."

"Morning, Ma'am. I made coffee."

How can I ever not live like this? Theo pours me a coffee, adds the cream and sugar, and hands me a mug.

"You look so awake."

"I had to check in with my staff this morning."

"You okay, Wolfie?"

Theo sips his coffee, glancing away from me.

When he looks back, I swear his eyes are shiny with tears.

"You know, I didn't want to take my dad's truck. But I think my mom loves my hybrid car, and they were going to do something Christmassy, and I did want to come see Izzy. My brothers tease that I'm a pushover, but I don't know. Is giving in to people you care for so bad?"

"I don't think so...even the toughest of us do it. But if those people are toxic–"

"Yeah. I'm really glad I took his truck," Theo grins, waggles his eyebrows. His expression is so adorable, my heart does that skipping a beat thing.

"Thanks for the fundraiser last night. I'm so... you came in like a whirlwind and fixed me." I hate crying. I furiously blink back tears.

"It was my pleasure, Ma'am." His sultry voice warms my soul. "But you don't need to be fixed."

He places his hand on mine, and I don't know how we're going to make this work, but I know I don't want him to leave.

9

THEO

My stomach has been in knots since my alarm crashed into my sleep this morning.

I have to leave today to go back to the city, and I don't want to.

My phone buzzes with a message from Jayden, my second-in-command, asking if I could fit in another presentation. I'm going to have to delegate this one.

I can give it to Jayden, who is the type of person who's happy to sell ice to polar bears. I put away my phone to find Callie assessing me.

"Sorry."

"No, it's fine. You know, last night at the fundraiser was the first night off I have had in months. Aunt Millie has an autoimmune disease, and sometimes she's not up to taking the kids. Grady's parents have flown in several times, but honestly, as tiring as it has been, I haven't minded having my nieces and nephew."

"They adore you."

"My point is, the day before the fundraiser, this guy shows up who doesn't blink at spending money for tickets, who happens to have a tux in the truck-"

"Izzy wanted me to come to an investor's event, but I ended up saying no."

"Right. And do you know how lucky it was that Uncle Henry found that tank?"

"I like it when things work out."

"We haven't had much of that lately around here. But you," she reaches for my hand. "I'm upset that you're leaving."

She turns her head away from me.

This is a woman who doesn't like to cry.

I stop myself from smiling as huge as my cheeks are aching too.

"I'm a wreck about leaving. I didn't think I'd want another relationship after my ex, but this feels right."

"I know," she trails her fingers along my arm, and I squirm on the seat, wanting more of her touch, knowing we have to focus.

"How do we move forward?" I turn my palm over, and she puts her hand in mine.

"Slowly. Good morning and good night texts."

"Yes." Her hand in mine feels right, and I don't ever want to let go.

"We can try to have dinner together through video call."

"Good with me. But I have a secure app I prefer. Let me send it to you?" I make sure she hears the question in my voice.

"That's fine. I'll try your app. How do you feel about wearing a cock cage?" Her fingers wrapped around mine, and that's the only reason why I didn't bolt, but my jaw clenches.

I close my eyes as the question triggers the remembered feeling of being locked, coursing through my system.

Being in chastity is powerful.

Nothing has ever made me feel more submissive.

It's something I'd love to experience again, just for that feeling.

"Theo?" Callie rubs circles on my wrists.

"I want to. I dream about it all the time. I crave it. I don't know if I can get there. My ex left me in a cock cage and didn't allow me access to the key. I don't know, Callista. That's a jump for me, from where I am right now." Something in me rises to the surface, a wave of hurt, but as Callie squeezes my hand, the intensity of that open wound eases.

"Because it's a deeper form of submission?" Her voice is gentle.

"Yeah. And because... if I were to have a key holder, it'd mean they earned my trust." The need in my voice makes me shift, but Callie presses firmly on my wrists, keeping me still.

"She didn't deserve you." Her tone is all controlled, but the anger sparks off of her.

I pull away from her touch, needing to move.

"I know I wasn't perfect either, though I tried. I had to call my younger brother to help me. He got a key."

"I'm glad that he was there for you." But her tone is crisp, annoyed.

"I'm sorry your ex didn't appreciate what she had."

"You don't have to be sorry," I say it with more bite than I want to.

Callie's eyebrows rise as she changes the subject.

"You can get keys from the manufacturer. Did your brother know you were a submissive before that?"

I bite the inside of my lip, and because I need something to do, I stand and fix the calendar that's hanging askew on the wall.

"Hunter and I are close. He was in his own dynamic at the time," I say, swallowing hard, shoving away the memory of the voicemail I got before leaving the office on Friday because I don't know what to do about it yet. "Yes, he knew I was a submissive. Tried to tell me that Lynn wasn't good for me."

"How did you meet her?" Callie twirls a piece of hair around her finger, leaning toward me.

It's an innocent question, but it brings back a flood of memories.

"Is that relevant?"

"I'll tell you about mine if you tell me about yours. It's best to start knowing the baggage, don't you think?" She stands and takes the mugs to the sink and leans against the counter.

"Yes, Ma'am," I shove my hands into my pockets. "After university, I met Lynn during my first job at a large security firm. I had impressed the higher-ups, and they were giving me more responsibility. It was a perfect fit. All my fears about being too serious or too shy vanished as people only cared about the work I was doing."

"I like your serious and your shy." She moves to stand in front of me and cups her palm under my chin, and the warmth of her touch eases my anxiety.

"It would have been perfect until the senior partner accused me of stealing money because I was one of the newest people to have access to those accounts. My world crumbled around me because I'm not the greatest at handling conflict, and I didn't know what to do. The firm sent in a forensic accountant."

I turn my cheek so it's in her palm, close my eyes as she brushes my cheekbone with her thumb.

Her gentle dominance is centering me, making me feel safe to continue. "And it was her." Callie keeps touching me, slides her thumb across my cheekbone, and I exhale, trying to keep myself right here in this moment.

"Yep." The first time I saw Lynn, flashes through my mind. She had on a leather skirt, high heels, and a black blouse.

Her blonde hair was perfectly styled, and she wore a diamond-encased brooch.

"After weeks of worrying about it and making myself physically ill thinking everything that I had worked so hard for was going to be taken away from me, in no time at all, Lynn proved that it wasn't me who appropriated the funds but the daughter of the firm's president. I was so relieved and super glad I hadn't told my parents or my older brothers about the investigation. It would have caused my parents stress, and my dad doesn't do stress well, and my mom has enough with my dad to deal with."

"That sounds like an awful time." Her touch is feather light on my face, and I whine softly against her fingers as they linger over my lips.

"Yes. My older brothers had a lot going on at the time. Evan wasn't in the country. I'm forever thankful that I told Hunter because I also told him when I started dating Lynn. I was twenty-four when I met her and twenty-eight when our relationship ended."

"That's a lot, Theo. But you came out of it. Maybe not unscathed, but you're here now." She removes her hand from my face, presses it on my chest.

"With you." I exhale and run my thumb along the back of her hand.

"That time wasn't all wasted, despite the kerfuffle with the firm, they gave me glowing recommendations. I worked with another firm for a year, then went back to school for an accelerated degree program that earned me further qualifications. During the whole time I was with Lynn, and despite all her faults, I don't know if I would have achieved the professional status I have without her encouragement. If it weren't for Lynn, I wouldn't have looked at the possibility of having my own business. But she pointed out how I am good at organizing data and relaying it to people, and parceling it out in layman's terms. Feeling gratitude towards her is a huge step in the healing process, I guess."

"I'm proud of you for leaving that relationship." Callie takes my hand and leads me to the living room.

She pushes me down on the couch, straddling my lap, and kisses me.

I groan as soon as her tongue swipes mine, my head buzzing with the high of tasting her, but I pull away from the kiss.

"We're supposed to be having a conversation, Callista." The ends of her hair brush my lips.

"I know people pay you a lot of money to keep them on track, but I'm annoyed at the moment."

I laugh, and she climbs off my lap, slumps beside me.

"The garage in Glass Lake hired me. A friend of mine, who is kind of like a mentor to me, lives out there, and I leaped at the chance. That's where I met John. His alternator stopped working. I took a look at his car, and its bearings were worn down. He had a nice smile. I was feeling horny. He invited me to dinner, and I accepted," she threads her hand through mine. "I know now that he had a weird fascination with a female mechanic. Anyway, we dated. He got me out of my pick-up play phase." Her voice is quiet, like she's spinning over regrets in her mind.

"We don't expect people to lie to us."

"I know. I was happy being with him. Finally, I found a guy who got me and who allowed me to be my true self, you know? He didn't want a pro dominatrix, but he wanted to give up control. He was comfortable in letting me take the lead. He took me on trips."

I don't know what to say, but the pain in her voice is tearing apart my heart.

She glances at a spot on the floor, her hair falling to cover her face.

"I honestly thought he was who he said he was. I was so excited that I had to get Daphne to meet him. To be honest, I was being spiteful."

"By introducing your boyfriend?" I rub my thumb in the webbing of her right hand, and she exhales.

"I wanted to be the one for once to have something good. For weeks, I had asked John to come to Rising Harbour with me, and he refused.

That should have been a red flag... I missed many of them. Finally, he agreed, and I took John around town, showed him where I grew up, but didn't let him meet Daphne. When she heard my new boyfriend was in town, she begged me to let her have dinner with us. As soon as she saw John, I knew something John did or said didn't meet her approval, so I confronted her in the women's washroom at the restaurant."

"That must have been upsetting."

"Yeah, not my best moment. She told me she recognized him as Jana Hops' fiancé. I called her a liar. She brought up Jana's social media feed. I threw up."

"That seems like a perfectly acceptable response." I lean my head against her shoulder.

"I marched out to confront him. He denied it, even after I showed him proof. Then my sister left, and that's the last time I saw her when she wasn't brain-damaged." Callie leans forward. "I'm selfish and horrible."

"No, you're not. You are human and gorgeous and have dealt with being second place to your sister your whole life."

The need to whisper reassurances to her and to ease her discomfort is so strong, it vibrates through my body.

Her hand runs along my leg, and we quietly hold each other, lost in our thoughts.

A few minutes later, she turns her head up to me with that gorgeous smile.

"What about orgasm teasing and denial, long distance? You ask me for permission before you masturbate?"

The suggestion sends me into panic mode and makes my dick stand up at the same time.

"I think...yes, I'd like to try that. What else do you need from me?" I ask, snuggling against her.

"I need communication. For you not to disappear. If this doesn't work out-" "It will. This will work out." I try to keep my voice even, but I am so sure Callie and I will be together because I am going to do everything I can to make sure this does work out, whatever it takes.

"But if it doesn't, I need you to be honest with me, okay?"

"I'm a grown-up. I can do that."

"Anything you need from me that we haven't covered?" She brushes her fingers through my hair, and I can't help but let out a soft whimper.

"The same. Communication and honesty. I do have a request, though?" I slide off the couch, kneeling beside her.

I put my hand on her calf, gliding it up her leg.

"Theo, we're supposed to be negotiating." Callie shakes her head back and forth, but doesn't order me up.

"I can negotiate on my knees. For you."

She throws her head back, giving me a fleeting glimpse of that enticing column of her neck, and laughs, the sound low and teasing.

"What is it, Wolfie?"

"That you do one nice thing for yourself a day." She scrunches up her nose, making a face.

"I knew you'd react that way." I gently rub the tops of her thighs.

"Is this because of your ex's addiction?"

"Partly, or maybe it's knowing you have a lot going on right now. I thrive when the people in my life are happy." The voicemail from Friday pops up in my brain in mock protest.

"Fine, I'll do one nice thing for myself a day. Like riding Morris."

A smirk plays on her lips, scares me a little.

"Morris?"

"My motorcycle. Uncle Henry rides his with mine when he has the time."

I shake my head, even as I'm smiling, because, of course, she rides a motorcycle.

"Does your uncle's bike have a name?"

"Church," Callie laughs.

"Have you ever ridden a motorcycle?"

"Nope. I passed when Hunter tried to make me." "No objections?"

She plays with my hair, making a growl escape from my lips.

"I figure you know what you're doing."

"Good," she leans down and kisses me sweetly, her hair falling in her face, brushing my eyes with her silky strands.

"As long as riding Morris counts, I can do this self-care thing."

"It wasn't your fault that you dated an engaged guy. That's on him."

"Oh, Wolfie," she kisses me again, slowly, seductively. My dick twitches.

"Are you sure you have to leave?"

"Ask me to stay and I will."

She leans forward and taps me on the nose. "Nope. I'm not going to be your reason to get out of the work thing you hate, and there's Christmas."

"Fine. It was worth a try."

"Guess you have to go now."

"Yeah. I really should." I have to meet with my team tonight to finalize the talking points that I am going to deliver to the organization tomorrow.

"As soon as I can get back here, I will." I stand, a lump in my throat. Giving a little cry, she slants her lips against mine, kissing me so hard they hurt.

She breaks off the kiss, pats my cheek.

"Wait here." I do, and she strides down the hall, stopping at the closet.

"Take this." She thrusts a package at me.

"A present? What is it?" Delight bubbles up in me at the simple gesture. "It's an eye mask. The kind you put in the freezer. Maybe it will help you when you decompress from public speaking." She glances away from me.

"Thank you, Ma'am." I wrap my arms around her and kiss her, committing how she tastes to my memory, how she feels in my arms, and the scent of her shampoo.

I'm not taking a single second of our time together for granted.

"Be a good boy. Text me when you get home."

"Yes, Ma'am."

She comes with me to the door.

I pick up my bag and see the sheen of tears in her eyes.

"Take care of yourself, Callista. We'll text tonight."

"Can't wait," Callie says, opening the door for me.

My pulse is racing so fast I don't want to leave her, but I have to.

"Bye."

"Bye, Wolfie." She gives me a small wave, then steps behind the door. I wait until I hear the door click closed, and then I take the stairs two at a time and, in the cool air, I grab the keys and dash to the truck. Without looking back, I drive out of Rising Harbour with my heart ripped out of my chest and left behind.

10

CALLIE

> Home, Ma'am. Wishing I wasn't so far away from you.

I grab the phone like it's a lifeline—tight, like I can't let go.

From the moment Theo left, I threw myself into keeping busy. In the diner, I spilled every coffee I poured until Brenda told me gently to go, that we had enough staff to close.

With nothing else to do, I paced the floor of the apartment and hated myself for doing so.

I was apparently recovered from my flu symptoms.

This is silly. I shouldn't be lusting after some guy.

I didn't want to be in this position again. I probably mean nothing to him.

I was just a good lay, a distraction while his truck broke down.

But the thoughts were hollow. I knew I was lying to myself.

His text made my spinning thoughts subside.

The phone chimed again with a picture.

It's a photo of a living room, with leather furniture, bookcases, a fireplace and a view out the window of the mountains.

If I had to guess what Theo Brennon lived in, it would be this; a professor's study, calm and classic and masculine.

> Nice pad.

I flop down on the couch, grab a pillow, and hug it to my chest, convincing myself I can smell Theo's aftershave.

> It'd be my pleasure to show you, Ma'am.

My cheeks are blazing, this text exchange making me feel all flirty and out of my mind.

> I'd love to see it, boy. How was your drive?

I stretch my legs out on the couch.

> The roads were fine. But I hated moving further from you every second.

My pussy clenches.

The boy knows what words to say to me to make me swoon.

My hand strayed between my legs, hovering over my mound.

> How much time do you have until your meeting, Wolfie?

> I'm leaving to meet my team in twenty-three minutes, Ma'am.

I snort a laugh.

The precise countdown is exactly like Theo, I read the text in his calm tone.

Still using the app, I switch it to video call.

The screen greys out, and a moment later, Theo's handsome face appears.

He smiles, those gorgeous dimples on display. "Hi there, Mr. Sexy Pants."

"Hi Callista. I couldn't stop thinking about you the entire way home. I still have the taste of you in my mouth."

My heart races. "That's sweet. I can't stop thinking about your thick cock. Show it to me, boy."

His face turns deep red, and I stifle a laugh.

Theo moves across the room and must have put the phone on a tripod because the next thing I see is him dropping his pants and palming his half-hard dick.

My nipples tighten, not just at the sight of his dick but at the fact that he obeyed my command, without question or hesitation.

He's not even in the same room as me.

Not in the same town.

The heady surge of adrenaline shoots through me, sending me right into Top space.

"Stroke your cock for me, while I finger myself. Tell me what you'd do to me to get me to come, and if I can reach orgasm before your time is up, you can come too. Would that help you get through your meeting?"

"Yes Ma'am, it would," his voice purrs.

"Let me see you stroke it, slower, Wolfie."

Theo slows down his strokes, and I can see his cock throb in his hand.

My mouth waters, remembering the silky feel of his cock in my hand, how he cried out under my touch. "That's good, just like that. Now tell me what you'd do to me."

"I don't know what to say, Callista. I've never done this before." His nervousness is like a splash of cool water.

What kind of idiot am I that I ordered this boy to give me pleasure moments before he has to go into a meeting that he's told me is going to cause him stress after?

"I'm sorry. I went too fast here. When I heard your voice, it lit me all up, in all the right places. As soon as you left, I convinced myself that this wasn't real, that I was just an overnight lay for you. And I jumped right into sexting or video sexing."

His hand slows and drops to the side. He strides over to the camera, and I can't say anything because I think he's going to turn it off and end the call.

"If I were there, Callista, I would drop to my knees, wrap my arms around you and then I would slowly take down your pants..."

Oh. I giggle with the rush of the fact that this submissive is showing up for me again.

I exhale and get comfortable, spreading my legs.

"Then, starting from your feet, I would massage all the sore spots away in your body. I would stroke your strong calves, part open your legs and put my face in your beautiful cunt."

I suck in a sharp breath. I toss my pants off, flinging them across the room.

Slowly, I slide my hand under the waistband of my panties, fingers pressing into my wet pussy.

The thrill of doing this with him through a screen makes my heart thud.

"You're so good to me, boy. Show me your cock again."

On screen, Theo stands back and strokes his cock.

"Faster."

His head tips upwards, showing me the column of his neck, those strong shoulders that look like they could carry a lot.

I moan softly, the memory of his skillful tongue between my legs flooding me.

"I'd take my time and worship you, sliding my tongue up one side of your slit, then the other. Slowly, my tongue would make a circle, and I remember the taste of your wetness right now, Callista. You taste fucking gorgeous."

My nipples ache, pressed tightly against the fabric of my shirt, ready to split the seams.

"You're saying all the right things, boy. I'm so close."

My pussy clenches. I keep fingering roughly, wanting to hear his next words.

"I feel you tremble underneath my hands, and I love that you have given me the privilege of tasting your clit. My mouth is on it right now, sucking it, flicking it with my tongue."

The pressure explodes, sending me soaring, panting for a breath as I tumble into a powerful orgasm that feels as if it's pulling me from my body.

"Theo!"

On screen, his hand is moving faster, stroking his cock, and I see pre-cum leak from his head.

"Come now, Wolfie!" Somehow, I get the words out, even as pleasure still ripples through me.

I sit up, clutching a pillow, and watch as his eyes flutter shut, his face drawn tight with release—until he moans loudly, and his hand is slick with his own seed.

"Damn, that was intense."

"Yes, yes, it was, Ma'am." He disappears out of view for a moment and then comes back with a washcloth. Holds it up to the camera.

"Oh yes, clean that up, boy. Wouldn't want you to have a wet spot in your pants during your meeting. Why don't you forget the boxers?" He laughs deeply, cleans his cock, then picks up his boxers, shows them to me and tosses them behind him.

"If I told you to leave those on the floor, how much would it bother you?" His eyes go wide. He slaps his palms against his cheeks.

"That'd be a very cruel punishment."

"I'll have to save it for later then, Wolfie." But I'm teasing, and by his matching grin, he knows it.

"I'm sorry I pulled this on you right before your meeting." He brings his fingers to his lips, then presses them to the screen.

My heart melts, this man is turning me into a puddle of goo, and I don't know if I can cope.

"I'm glad you told me what you were feeling, Callista. I know both of us are entering this relationship with past scars, and maybe they're not fully healed yet, but I'm willing to be in it with you anyway."

A lump forms in my throat. I can barely swallow. Does he mean it? I want to believe his words with my whole heart.

I want to be in this relationship with him as much as he says he wants it, but my romantic history makes me wary.

"Me too," I squeeze the words out. "Remember to put the eye mask in the freezer."

"I'll try it, thank you, Ma'am."

"Go kick ass, Wolfie. Good night."

"Good night, Ma'am."

The screen goes blank.

The pleasure that's rippling through my body is pushing away my fears.

We can make this long-distance Dom/sub relationship work.

I can be open and vulnerable with Theo. My phone rings in my hand and my heart leaps, thinking maybe it's Theo, but it's a number I don't recognize.

"Hello?" "Yes, hello. It's Wanda Graveston, I am downstairs at the front of Shel's, but the diner is closed. I was supposed to take measurements tonight."

"Measurements for what?" I stand, shove my feet into my shoes, and glance at the calendar that I had copied from Daphne's notes.

"For our Christmas party tomorrow? Daphne said it wouldn't be a problem. I took measurements months ago, but our drummer got a new kit. It'd make me feel better if I could just check my measurements. You know Shel used to play the saxophone."

"Really?" I can't recall my grandfather playing the saxophone, but it's something that sounds like him.

"Yes indeed. Many of our members remember Shel's throughout the years; that's why we wanted to have our Christmas dinner celebrating our 30th Anniversary there."

"What's your organization called again?" I'm taking the stairs two at a time.

"The Musicians Guild of Rising Harbour."

I didn't know we had an official guild. I knew that there was a choir that gathers around the Christmas tree outside of the town hall every year and musicians that play at different festivals in the summer, but a guild brings to mind something grander that Rising Harbour has.

I open the door to see a thin woman wearing cowboy boots and a fancy hat in a wool coat.

"Come on in, Wanda. I'm happy to help you take measurements. I'm Daphne's sister Callie."

"Nice to meet you. You must be the famous mechanic who works on that girl's team."

Nerves swirl low in my belly as Wanda brushes by me and I close the door.

Having Theo here took me to a different place, where I had a break from the guilt that's been my constant companion since I've come back home.

"I don't know about famous, but I do know my way around an engine."

"That's what Daphne said. Now here we are. "I think we can set up the drums here if we move these front tables."

"I can't believe Daphne mentioned me."

"She is very proud of you! Now I'll just stand on this chair to take a measurement of the window. There. I emailed Daphne the latest menu update, but I haven't heard from her . Is she here?"

Wanda peers at me from her perch, the chair wobbles.

"I'm handling the diner right now. Daphne is unavailable." It sounds lame, but I don't want to tell this stranger that my sister had an accident and is in a rehab facility.

"Okay, I'll just send it over to you. It's standard Christmas dinner stuff plus those butter tarts Daphne promised me from Aunt Millie."

"What time are you coming in?"

"As soon as you close tomorrow. Daphne thought it was perfect timing because she and her family are—or were going to leave for Spain on the same night, but I guess that's not going to happen because you came home? Oh! Did you surprise them for Christmas?" Wanda beams at me.

My insides twist with anxiety, and i swallow past a bundle of nerves.

Other than making sure the kids are covered, Christmas is not something I wanted to give a lot of attention to.

Daphne's the one who went all in for Christmas, she and Aunt Millie.

We all agreed that we were going to scale it back this year and keep it simple.

"Okay, got all I need," Wanda says as she steps down from the chair. My mind is whirling. Daphne had a Christmas vacation planned to Europe, and they were going to surprise me?

"Here's my number and email. If you could send me over your menu, I'll get it to my cook." I hope Ryan knows about this event.

"I'll do that as soon as I'm home! It was nice meeting you, Callie!"

"You too, Wanda!" I'm just locking the door, about to call Ryan, when I realize I still have gifts to wrap. Fortunately, the medical team has cleared Daphne for a visit home, but I know Christmas is going to be hard.

***

DECEMBER 25TH

"I don't want to open gifts in front of Mom. It feels like we're playing pretend," Madison's lower lip trembles.

"Madison, I know it feels awkward for me too." I wipe away a tear on my niece's face.

We're in Grady and Daphne's house, opening presents under the Christmas tree.

Grady is working tonight, so we skipped dinner and had a huge breakfast. Luke and Abby are laughing hysterically at Uncle Henry's puppet show.

Daphne is sitting next to Grady, taking it all in. She seems relaxed when the kids are near her. I drape my arms around Madison and guide her back into the living room.

Daphne has Luke on her lap. Aunt Millie is bringing in a tray of hot chocolate from the kitchen, raising her eyebrows.

I give her a nod to say I have this one. Uncle Henry tosses the puppets aside and is now putting batteries in a light-up unicorn that Abby opened.

"Mads, your mom is the kind of person who's organized. She plans."

"I know that. Before she became brain damaged."

"Madison!" I hiss, taking her arm.

Her eyes go wide in shock, then she shrugs.

"What? It's true."

I take a deep breath, count to five and exhale slowly.

"Yes, it's true. I know how hard the last few months have been on you, honey. Your mom is here now, and we're going to enjoy the rest of this day, okay?"

Madison nods. I give her a hug, bringing her close to me.

"Your mom had your presents wrapped in her closet. My guess is she finished off her whole list by June. So all the Santa presents you opened were picked by her. Now don't spoil it for the babies."

"I won't!" Madison grins at me. She skips into the living room, grabs a present under the tree and hands it to Luke.

"Look from Satna!"

"For me?" Luke asks.

"Yep!" Grady says, ruffling his hair. "Look, Mommy!" Luke gives the parcel to Daphne.

Her hands shake as she tries to hold it, and Grady steadies it for her. "Pppresent for you?" my sister says with a smile, but her mouth is lopsided—and it pulls at my heart.

She's the kind of woman who buys Christmas presents for her family in advance. And I had to be mad at her for bursting my bubble? I swallow past the lump in my throat.

"Yes!" Luke tears the wrapping paper open. "What about me?" Abby cries. Madison dives under the tree and pulls one out for Abby.

"Callie, there's one for you!" Aunt Millie pats the seat next to her, and I sit down beside her.

She squeezes my hand. "Thanks for helping her through that." I nod, my throat tight.

"Least I could do." Grady gives me a look I can't read, but then turns to his kids and shows Daphne everything they opened.

Uncle Henry stretches out his hands behind his head. "Guess I didn't need to get you munchkins presents, eh?"

"We love presents, Uncle Henry! Mommy, what's your favourite present?" Madison asked.

Daphne's face scrunches up, like she's going to cry.

Grady pulls her close to him. "We're just happy to have you home for a bit, Daph."

"I-I-I want to go home. Now."

"You're home, Daphne. We love you," Aunt Millie pats her knee.

"No, no. Back home. Take me back home."

"Why don't you want to stay with us?" Madison stands, kicking wrapping paper everywhere.

I hurry over, taking a small parcel from the tree.

"Daphne, you didn't open mine!" I thrust the present in my sister's hands.

She nearly drops it.

Grady helps her open it.

Daphne looks at me, then at everyone in the room and bursts into tears.

The window chime I bought for her crashes to the floor, but fortunately Uncle Henry catches it.

"They told us it might be a lot on her," Uncle Henry says.

Aunt Millie wipes away tears from her eyes. "I know."

The kids aren't saying a word, standing around looking at their mom in shock.

"Kids, take a toy to the basement! I'm going to make a fresh batch of popcorn, and we'll start the Christmas movie before we go skating!"

"Come on, guys, first one down there gets to pick the movie!" Madison says.

"Mommy come?" Luke asks, his hopeful look tugs at my heartstrings.

"Mommy will come in a minute," Grady says. "Go ahead, Lukey." My nephew follows his sisters and I tiptoe to Daphne.

"It's okay if you don't like it." I pick up the star. I thought it would be pretty on Daphne's window in the facility.

"Daphne, if you want to go back to your room, we'll take you," Aunt Millie says. "We just want you to be happy."

"I don't. It's so loud here," Daphne presses her hand against her ear. "Stay."

"Good," Uncle Henry clasps her on the back.

I gather cups and plates to take them to the kitchen, Grady coming in behind me.

"We shouldn't have pushed it, Callie."

"I didn't make the decision to bring her home." I stack the dishes in the sink.

"You said it'd be good for the kids."

I rinse off dishes, taking a breath. Grady's a good guy, but the way he's standing in the kitchen right now, staring me down? I could do without it. I'm the peacemaker, and usually, I'd let this slide—but my empathy feels a little raw around the edges.

So, I turn from the sink and lean against the counter.

"You got a problem, Grady?"

"Yeah, my wife is a recovering vegetable and you couldn't care less because you're still mad at her." The words sting like little paper cuts.

I freeze, and it's like all the noise in the whole house freezes, too.

I hear the drip of the water, the buzzing of someone's phone.

Aunt Millie is talking softly to my sister. Uncle Henry waltzes into the kitchen, his hands in his pockets. "Shit," Grady says.

"It wouldn't be Christmas without airing the trauma, eh? We've all done our best. We all love Daphne. Sisters argue."

"Yeah, but some sisters forgive," Grady says.

"You think if I forgave her it would make her heal faster? You gotta be kidding me." I turn my back to him and start scrubbing down the counter.

"You barely talk to her, Callie."

"What am I supposed to say, Grady? 'I'm exhausted from looking after your kids and your business? I gave up a job that I loved to come home, but I guess that's not enough either." I furiously scrub at the already clean counter.

No matter what I have tried to do for Daphne, it's never enough.

I took extra jobs while she was in university so I could help pay her tuition.

She took the money but made digs about how I wasn't going to do anything with my life because I wasn't going to university.

"Callie, we appreciate that you came home. You know Aunt Millie and I do. The kids love you. Grady, I know you're running on too little sleep and your phone is going to buzz off the table. The facility said we could bring Daphne back if it got too much, but I'd like to try to keep her for the night. We have a nurse coming in."

"I can take care of my wife," Grady spits out.

"We know. But you have three kids to take care of too. Millie and I thought it would be just in case, in case you get called out to work. My shop is closed for another few days. Shel's is closed for two days. Let's enjoy the time together."

"We have to make it good for the kids." Grady rubs a hand over his face.

"We will." Uncle Henry looks at me, his blue eyes smiling.

"We always have, right, Callie?"

"Yes.That's right." They are my family, and I'll do anything for them.

Uncle Henry grins, swipes a cookie from a tray, and hums on his way out of the kitchen.

Grady sighs and rubs a hand over his face.

"Sorry, Callie."

"It's no biggie. I know I'm the one who isn't responsible."

Grady shakes his head. "No, you're the one who is easy to blame, and I joined in. Do you know I keep blaming myself? If I hadn't been at baseball practice, Daphne wouldn't have gone rollerblading."

"Grady..." I give the big guy a hug.

He hugs me back.

"Thanks for being here for us. We love you."

"I love you guys too." I pat him on the back and hear the buzzing of his phone again.

"They want you to come in."

"I know, but I'm going to ignore it for a little longer," he grins, looking so much like his youngest, I laugh.

"Perfect," I smile at him, feeling the tension roll off us.

Our home is cozy and warm, and the people I love the most are here.

Back in the living room, I sit beside my sister and pick up a memory game.

You have to press a button that makes a sound and make a pattern, then the other person has to try to remember the pattern.

To my surprise, Daphne seems to get it, and the kids find us laughing when they come upstairs.

"You forgot the popcorn!" Abby says, hurling into me. "Sorry, Abby. Do you want to play with your mommy?"

"Yes!" She grabs the memory game and they settle in to play. Aunt Millie comes beside me, squeezes my shoulder.

"I love you, Callie."

"I love you too, Aunt Millie."

The kids all pile on the couch, taking turns with the memory game, and my sister's laughter feels normal and real, and I don't want to be anywhere else at this moment.

But in the back of my mind, I'm looking forward to talking to Theo later.

I'm feeling drained and exhausted, and I can't wait to get back to the apartment to tell Theo about this Christmas.

It's never going to be a good time for a new relationship, not with how my life is and I'm glad Theo has rolled with that. Taking my phone out of my pocket, I quickly send him a text.

Hey Mr. Sexypants. Your Christmas merry?

It's merry. I wish it was naughty :-)

> Wait until later when I give you your present...

A meme of a panting wolf crosses my and I laugh out loud.
My mood lifts, making the rest of this Christmas a little easier to get through.

11

THEO

DECEMBER 30TH

"Hey, Mr. Sexypants. How was your flight?"

A rush of heat rolls through me. The way she says it all sexy teasing but with a deep possessiveness in her voice, like she's claiming me makes me so hot.

I shiver into my jacket, brushing past people on the sidewalk.

Large snowflakes are landing on my jacket.

"I caught up on work."

"Distracted yourself, you mean."

I can hear the smile in Callie's voice.

The clinking of dishes rattles in my ear.

I picture her in her cozy apartment, putting away dishes. The kids must have just left.

"You may be correct."

"I know my Wolfie."

There was no denying it.

My cheeks warmed against the cool air at the sultry tone in her voice. Maybe this relationship was only eighteen days old, but it was already the most intimate I'd ever had.

Even long-distance, with our daily texts and video calls, we were growing even closer.

"Do you think I'm doing the right thing?" I sidestep out of the way of a couple holding hands and a mother rushing by with two toddlers.

"I can't say whether you are doing the right thing."

Her tone lost all the teasing lightness, shifting to thoughtful and open to listening.

"I'm glad you didn't sugarcoat it and lie to me."

"I'll never lie to you, boy." Her tone sent a shiver down my spine.

I called Callie after I gave the presentation, as this part of my job always does it sucked the life out of me.

I stumbled into my dark condo, stripped my clothes off, threw on the eye mask Callie gave me, and then flopped down on my bed in my dark bedroom.

Remembering I told Ma'am I'd call her when I got back, I sent her a quick goodnight text.

When I woke up the next morning over breakfast, I asked Callie if she had time, and she did, so I opened up the video in the app.

"Is everything okay? You look so serious."

"I want to tell you something."

"I'm listening."

She tucked a stray piece of hair back behind her ear.

I blew a breath out, trying to figure out where to start. I'm uncomfortable because it isn't my story to tell.

"My brother Hunter... had a nasty breakup with the love of his life."

"Okay." Whatever Callie thought I was going to say, that wasn't it, because she leaned forward, her expression relaxing.

"He was with this guy for two years. They were hot and heavy. They broke up. Hunter crashed at my place during this time."

"That sounds heavy." She didn't even blink that my brother was gay. I exhaled.

"Yeah, but this was right when my break-up happened. My ex wrecked me. I didn't know how to cope with the shit in my head. I thought I was broken."

"Theo, no. I hate her so much."

A part of me bristles that I didn't want Callie to hate Lynn, but another part likes that she has my back.

"When it finally ended and Hunter saw how wrecked I was, he called his ex. They got me a key to the cage and then..." I swallow, glancing away from her on the screen, shame colouring my cheeks.

"Tell me, boy." Her cool tone snapped me to attention. I wanted to please her, so the words loosened in my throat.

"I needed to know that I was a good submissive and that it wasn't my fault. I couldn't sleep. I couldn't function. I couldn't let myself have an orgasm. Hunter got in touch with his ex. Cy came. He set up a session with a Domme he knew and stayed with me."

"Dude is a stand-up kind of guy."

Cy is also an asshole, but he has a code of honour. The way my ex left me brushed up against his Dom ethics.

"When I was done with that Domme, Cy was the one who gave me aftercare." I stood needing to move.

I paced my kitchen, remembering how Cy held me and rocked me.

He swept the hair out of my eyes and told me: "You're a good submissive. The problem isn't you. You gave her everything. She let you down. You'll find someone."

I don't know if he was saying it to himself or to me.

Cyrus took me home, and Hunter wasn't there, telling me it hurt too *much to be in the same room with him, but he knew I would be taken care of.*

Cy made me drink a glass of water and get into bed, and then he told me to take care of my brother.

"Before I left to drive down to see Izzy, I got a voicemail from Cy requesting my professional help. Something is going on with his sister. He wants me to look into it. I have to tell Hunter."

"You could not take the job," Callie leaned into the frame, a small smile on her lips.

"You know I can't do that."

"Because you feel that you owe him."

"Yes."

"I'm glad your brother and his ex were there for you. I see how you're in an impossible situation."

"Day before New Year's Eve, I'm flying to Toronto anyway, to meet with a client and check on my team there. I'll tell him then."

"Sounds like you have a plan."

"Always."

"Do you want some relief, boy?"

My cock twitched as she said it.

"Yes, please."

"Go into your bedroom. Let me see you stroke that cock that belongs to me."

The way I hurried into the bedroom, my balls tight with her call of ownership.

"Here I am, Ma'am," *I said after placing my phone in a holder.*

I turned so Callie could watch me peel off my boxers.

I stroked my cock, up and down, groaning.

"I miss my cock so much. Play with your balls."

My hand slides up to my balls. With my fingertips, I gently squeeze them.

"Oh, I like that. Pull them, squeeze them towards your thigh."

I do, applying firm pressure. My nipples zing kind of painfully, they want attention, and my cock is still hard.

It's hard to wait like this, but I keep playing with my balls.

"Good. Take those boxers you left crumpled on the floor. Stuff your face with them."

The command freezes me for half a second, but my fingers have already moved to crumple them up and stuff them in my mouth. I moan around the wad of fabric, making hungry groaning noises.

"Oh, that's such a pretty boy following directions."

I whimpered, hot shame rippling through every nerve end, making my balls tighten.

"Stroke that cock again, but don't you dare touch the head."

"Yes, Ma'am," I gritted the words out, the cloth in my mouth hard to keep there. I'm drooling a little, but I stroke my hard length up and down.

"Faster."

I followed the direction, gliding my cock against my palm.

"Edge, boy. Let me know when you're close."

I squeezed my penis harder, then let go, feeling it soften a little. "Edge."

"Show me how you make yourself come, but don't. Tell me when you're close again."

I released my grip and stroked from my base to my tip, closing my eyes as I bit down on the cloth. "Edge!"

"Good boy. You may come now, and at the exact moment you do, I want you to spit out your boxers. Next time, it's going to be my panties in your mouth."

The threat of that makes me so fucking hard, my nuts are going to *burst open.*

My cock is rippling with need, so hot, so ready, spurts of pre-cum leak all over my hand.

I spit out the boxers, gulping air. I throw my head back, and an electric charge shoots up my back, grabs my balls, and I shoot hot cum over my hand.

"Good boy. I'm so pleased with how you followed instructions."

"Thank you, Callista, for letting me come."

"You're welcome. Wipe your hand off with that dirty underwear."

Oh God, with the release, it felt hard to follow her direction. It took extra focus, as if a caveman part of me wanted to hurl a "fuck you" at her.

But I did it because I am driven to please, I want to cede control to her, and the release she just gave me warrants obedience.

"Very good boy. I'm so pleased."

***

"I'm standing outside his apartment now." My stomach is in knots.

"I can't tell you if you're doing the right thing because I know you're worried about hurting Hunter's feelings. In my opinion, the benefit of having a secret never lasts as long as it should."

"I know. Thanks, Callista."

"I got you, my sweet boy. Now I'm going to curl up on the couch and watch a monster jam, getting my self-care in for the day."

"Good. You need a break." Christmas and the days after had been rough on Callie.

"Someone is teaching me to look after myself."

"It makes me happy to hear it."

"Go knock on the door or ring the doorbell or whatever."

"Yes, Ma'am. Talk later."

"Later, boy."

Still smiling from the conversation, I take the stairs two at a time. A woman with a little dog is coming out and holds the door for me.

"Thanks."

This converted warehouse has a long marble entryway. I go down the long hallway to loft number 8.

I knock twice.

I don't hear movement, so I hold my thumb up to the lockbox above the door handle.

This apartment is one of the Brennon Consortium properties, and as long as Hunter didn't change the code, I can let myself in.

The door flashes green and allows me to push the handle open.

I close the door behind me and take off my shoes.

I set my bag down by the shoe rack and strode inside.

"Hello?" I call out.

The kitchen is on my left, the marble counters cluttered with take-out containers and dirty dishes. In the living room, other than the pristine leather couches, the floor seems to be covered with every piece of clothing my brother owns.

The small kitchen table facing the patio doors is covered with welding parts and tools.

Going over to the windows, I pull back the curtains and let the deceptive sunlight in; it looks warm out there, but it isn't.

I go up the open-plank stairs, stopping at the bedroom.

Hunter is sleeping on his stomach.

He's always had this thing where when he's intensely focused on something, nothing else matters, and he turns into a slob.

He drove my mother nuts days before a tournament game, but in that way, he's like our dad.

I wonder what's going on with him, but I know not to push him.

When I was twelve, I begged our parents for a room of my own so I didn't have to share with him because I couldn't take it anymore.

They gave in, and I took over the shoebox-sized room that mom had started using as an office. Evan and Noel grumbled about us younger brothers getting spaces of our own, but it was good-natured.

They didn't want to share a space with Hunter's mess.

Plus, they saw the sense in Hunter having his own space when he was the only one of us to get up early for hockey practice.

Clothes are thrown over the armchair in the corner. A bunch of tools are on a side table, uncapped blue nail polish is on a nightstand.

"Good morning!" I pick up the clothes that are on the floor by the bed.

My brother stirs, turns over, and opens his eyes.

"You're not my mother," he grumbles at me.

"Nope. But I'm thinking I should send her a photo of this pigsty." I take out my phone and snap a pic of the space.

"You wouldn't." He throws off the blankets. Yawning, he scrambles up and rubs his face.

"I might," I grin, dumping the clothes in the hamper.

"What do you want?" He runs a hand through his messy, wavy hair. It's long enough that it brushes his shoulders.

"I was in the area. Had to come by. It's almost noon."

"So? I was on a job last night. Stop touching my stuff."

I put down the mug I'm about to take to the kitchen. "Go shower."

Hunter growls. "Only because you ask so nicely," he pats my cheek, then pulls me in for a bear hug.

My younger brother is a big guy, the tallest of us.

I feel swallowed by his big shoulders and thick arms.

"I'll be out in ten."

Relief shimmers through me that he hasn't told me to fuck off yet.

In the kitchen, I tidy up the mess.

After I've cleaned the counters, I pop a pod into the machine. I'm cracking eggs into a bowl for an omelette when Hunter emerges, dressed in a blue Henley and a black pair of shorts.

"Breakfast and maid service? It must be good," Hunter opens the freezer, takes a carton of something out. "Veg. Toss it in the omelette, okay? There's cheese in there, too."

"You're so bossy." I roll my eyes.

"Only to my big brother."

I exchange a knowing smile with him. Hunter and I don't have a lot in common, but the fact that we are both submissive men has deepened our bond.

He drinks his coffee, watching me cook. I flip an omelette onto a plate, then another, and he takes both plates to the table. Before I join him, I go to my bag and take out a tin.

"For you. From your mama."

"I'm her favourite." He grins as he lifts the lid and takes out a piece of fudge.

"That's not a secret." I tease.

Hunter rolls his eyes but still grins at me. He pulls his phone from his pocket, fires off a text—no doubt to mom—then leans in beside me. "Smile."

I comply, and then he sends the selfie.

"The parents missed you at Christmas."

"My flight's booked for tomorrow. I'll be there on New Year's."

"Good." I shift in my chair.

"I thought you were trying to save a cafe or something."

"Still working on that. I came to see a client."

"Couldn't you delegate it to someone?" Hunter cocks an eyebrow.

"Then I wouldn't get to see your ugly face."

Hunter snorts, continuing to eat his food. His nails are painted metallic blue, and I wonder why, and if he's seeing someone, and what he's doing for work.

He takes a bite, not breaking his steely stare. I ignore his stare, used to his silent observing.

"Thanks for making breakfast," Hunter says, taking the dishes to the sink.

"You getting to the gym?"

"Yep."

"Playing hockey?" I sort unopened mail into a tidy pile.

"Some. Got a hitting partner for tennis."

"Glad to hear it." After his breakup, Hunter stopped doing all the things that he loved.

The back of my neck grows hot as I think of Cyrus. My feelings about the man are complicated. I'm grateful that he got me out of the mental lockhold my former Domme had on me. I hate him for breaking my brother's heart.

Hunter takes the coffee cups, stirs sugar into mine, sugar and cream into his, and brings them to the table. "Spill it, Theo."

I sip, considering how much to tell him.

"Meeting Callie was unexpected. But things are getting pretty serious between us."

"How serious?" He sips his coffee, raising an eyebrow over the rim of his cup. "Does she have your dick locked up?"

I bite the inside of my cheek, staring down my brother, but he stares back at me coolly.

Nothing much can ruffle his feathers.

He got through high school because I did most of his schoolwork, along with Noel and Evan.

Our parents did everything to help him, and as far as I know, his scholarships were never once in jeopardy because of poor grades. But as much bluster as my younger brother has, I know a lot of it stems from his feeling inadequate because of his dyslexia.

Hunter's a gifted athlete.

Didn't matter what sport. Give him a stick or throw him a ball, and the big guy is poetry in motion. He hated playing hockey in college, but that's what got him there on a scholarship.

Our parents would do anything for us. They worked their asses off so we could have a good life, and they insisted on education being a priority.

Hunter did the first two years of university, got injured, took time off and then he switched schools to a small college in Wisconsin to finish his degree.

"Not yet." I blink, looking away.

"Get a fucking backup key this time, keep it somewhere. Make it hard for yourself to get to or whatever, but do it. I don't know how you'd ever trust a keyholder again."

"I know," I push my hand through my hair, knowing my cheeks are warm. "She's different. I like her."

"Thrilled for you. But you haven't told me why you're here."

"I did. I have business for my business. You know, I think we should buy mom an electric vehicle."

"You can mention that in our next video call or on New Year's at Evan's."

"Yeah," I stand, needing to move. I pace along the kitchen, with my coffee cup in my hand. I stop and look at Hunter.

Our parents really don't have favourites. They've never played us against each other or anything like that, but Hunter is a lot like our mom, and his blue eyes are steely as he glares at me.

"I got a call for a job. A celebrity is being harassed. They've had several serious data breaches." The words tumble out, and the knot in my stomach tightens.

"Right, that's what you do. What does this have to do with me?" Hunter's gaze is sharp, his shoulders hunched.

"Cyrus is the one who called me."

As if I had turned off a light, his face darkens.

"Yeah? Which relative is it of his?" His tone is like thunder rumbling.

"His sister."

"I'm sure you'll do a great job. Is that it?" He spits out the words.

"Yep, that's it."

"You can accept money from whomever you want, and he can hire whoever he wants. It has nothing to do with me."

"I wanted to tell you. Didn't want to keep it a secret."

"Your conscience clear now? Thanks for the visit. I've got shit to do."

Hunter turns away from me, staring out the window.

"Do you want to get dinner?"

"No, Theo, I don't. I'll see you in the new year if you're around. If not, I'm sure we'll be dragged to Evan's birthday," Hunter's voice cracks.

"You seem upset. I didn't want to make you upset. I don't want to leave you like this."

"I'm fine. I know how to take care of myself. But I think it's best if you get on with your business. You can see I have this mess to clean up."

"Call me later if you change your mind about dinner."

"Yeah." Hunter turns, walks briskly past me to the door. "I know you thought you were doing the right thing, but I can't help but feel manipulated. Did he ask you to tell me?"

"No. This is my choice." I squeeze his arm.

Hunter touches his chin to his chest.

"Bye Theo," He hugs me, keeping a distance, not like the crushing hug he greeted me with, but I'm grateful he's seeing me out.

My emotions are all over the place.

I know that telling him was the right thing to do, but it leaves me unsettled.

But did I expect him to throw me a party?

Five blocks from Hunter's, I find a cafe, grab a drink. I take a chance and call my client to see if he can fit me into his schedule earlier, and to my surprise, he does. That done, I call Noel to tell him I want to look into buying Callie's restaurant.

He asks me if I'm bringing her to New Year's Eve.

If I hadn't just had that conversation with Hunter, I might have answered Noel differently. But because my mind is tripping over itself with ghosts from the past, I downplay what Callie means to me and brush it off.

After hanging up with Noel, I'm on the phone with the airline, trying to see if I can change my flights when Callie rings through.

"Hello, Ma'am."

"Theo, I know I'm interrupting you. Is this a bad time?" Her voice hitches.

"What's wrong?"

"Daphne's had a setback." I hear the pain in her voice and spin my coffee mug around on the table.

"Callista, I'm so sorry."

"The staff said at first it might be just the stress of the visit home for Christmas, but now it appears she's had some seizure activity."

If anything happened to one of my brother's I would lose my mind.

"I'm going to switch my flight to fly into Kelowna, and then I'm going to rent a car and get to you. We can spend New Year's Eve together."

"Theo, I can't ask that of you." Her voice is husky, like she's holding back tears.

"You're not. Callista, I'm offering. You can accept."

There's a long pause, and I hold my breath. If she tells me to stay, I will obey her, but all I want to do is be there for her and hold her in my arms.

"I'll probably have the kids." But her tone is back to being level.

"I don't mind. I just want to be with you."

There's a pause. It's not uncomfortable, but it's heavy, as if we're both contemplating what this means. "This isn't a big deal for me to do. Let me do it, Ma'am."

"Okay, boy. Let me know when your flight is getting in. I'll pick you up."

"Sounds good. Talk to you later."

"Thanks, Wolfie." She clicks off, and I finish my coffee, then order another one while I'm stuck on the phone with the airline.

Knowing I'm going to do everything I can to get to her eases some of the tension I had since leaving Hunter's apartment, and I can't wait to show her how eager I am to not only please her but to give her whatever she needs.

12

CALLIE

DECEMBER 30TH

During the entire drive to the airport, I bite the inside of my cheek, pushing down my anxiety.

I feel guilty about leaving Shel's, even though I know Brenda has the place in hand, and guilt about leaving Aunt Millie with the kids, but she shooed me out of the house.

"It's been another stressful week, Callie. Go get your friend from the airport. I'm holding down the fort just fine, right, Mads?"

"Yeah. We're making stuffed red velvet cookies."

But as I get closer, excitement ripples through my body. I can't wait to see Theo.

My sister is being looked after by the best team on this side of the country, and the latest update is that she's steady.

They're keeping a close watch on her, but it's not as severe as they first thought it was.

Guilt gnaws at me as I tap the steering wheel.

I can handle my own shit—I don't need a white knight riding in to save me.

I bite my lip so hard it almost bleeds, regret swirling through my body.

I want to crawl away from myself.

But you can't get away from yourself.

And maybe... it's nice to have someone to lean on for once.

Even if I am the Domme and I'm supposed to be taking care of him.

Maybe, like Theo has said, we can take care of each other. That feels very grown-up and *not at all* like my past relationships.

I force myself to take a deep breath.

Everyone's healthy and safe.

Aunt Millie unexpectedly raised my sister and me and did a good job. If she says this was one of her good days, then I have to take her at her word. I respect and love her too much to insist that she can't mind the kids when she's telling me she can.

Uncle Henry is at the shop.

He has a brake line to fix, and I know that was his way of dealing with the stress.

The shipment of produce has been delayed, but there wasn't a single thing I could do about that. The staff is pushing the pies, and who needs a vegetable?

I allow myself to exhale.

It's so weird how since Theo came into my life, I've been letting go of the stress and the tension I've clung to since Daphne's accident.

The self-care I agreed to hasn't hurt either.

My Wolfie is a sly one when he wants to be.

Knowing all the people in my life are as fine as they can be at the moment, sets me free to indulge in how eager I am to see my submissive.

My submissive.

So what if he flew across the country to see me? That should make me feel like a fucking queen.

After I have my way with him—if Daphne continues to be stable—we can talk about the building.

The more time I spend in Rising Harbour, the more it feels like I never left.

I want Shel's Diner to last another fifty years. I don't know how I'm going to buy the building, but there has to be a way.

Finally at the airport, I pull into short-term parking.

Inside the airport, it is busier than usual, and I patiently make my way through the crowd.

There.

I catch sight of his sandy hair, his tall frame, and I know I'm blushing. My beautiful boy strides toward me, his eyes brighten when he sees me, and he quickens his pace until he's standing in front of me.

The air between us is charged with heat and anticipation; it pulsates between us. I cup his face in my hands, rising on my tiptoes to kiss him.

He groans softly, sending vibrations through my mouth, shooting tingles right down to my pussy.

It's so good to touch him. I savour his lips, rolling my tongue against his, and both of us let out loud pleasure-filled moans.

Taking his hands, I squeeze them in mine.

"Thank you for coming, boy."

"There's nowhere else I'd rather be, Ma'am." He opens his arms, and I step into his embrace, pressing my head against his muscled chest.

I feel the thump of his heart and am energized by his offer of strength.

"Let's go." I take his hands in mine, squeezing his fingertips.

"Can I grab snacks first?" He gives me a cute little wink.

I didn't think of it, eager to pull him toward the parking lot because I wanted him in my apartment, naked.

"That way we won't have to stop." There's nothing much open between here and Rising Harbour.

Theo walks over to the vending machine. "Anything you like?"

"I'm partial to the gummy bears."

He smiles, makes his selections, and taps his card to the machine. "Drinks too."

He selects my favourite coconut-flavoured drink before I can ask for it, takes the blue one for himself, and slides them into his laptop bag. "Ready now?"

"Yes, Ma'am." There's nobody around who heard him say Ma'am, but the fact that he said it out in public makes me tingle with pride.

He opens my door for me, tosses his duffel and laptop bag in the back seat, then buckles himself in.

I concentrate on getting out of the parking lot—there's a tour bus in front of me.

Theo places his palm open on my thigh.

I brush my fingers against his until we're on the highway.

Then I push his hand back and squeeze his thigh.

He yawns, covering his mouth.

"Sorry, Callista."

"You must be exhausted. Thank you for coming." I say it again to assuage the guilt that's eating me.

I'm used to doing things on my own.

"With brain injuries, things can change rapidly. It's been weeks of ups and downs. Daphne is doing better now, it's not as urgent as we thought, and you came..." I stare straight ahead, not wanting to chance seeing pity on his face, but I can feel his eyes roam over me.

"There isn't anything I wouldn't do to make your life easier. That's good that Daphne is stable." Theo places his hand on my thigh, and I let him leave it there, liking the comfort. "I talked to my brother, Noel, about how the building is for sale."

My throat closes up, but I have to focus on the dark highway. I want to give this boy so much pleasure while he's here.

My pulse races, thinking of what I have planned for him.

I go to open my drink, but Theo twists the cap off for me.

"But it isn't." I turn to look at him, and he has a sly smile on his face.

"I know. But sometimes people sell things if they get an offer. Noel said he'd look into it for me."

"Thank you, Theo." Keeping Shel's and dealing with the other owners is a constant source of stress. If I could find a way to save Shel's, then it'd make all the sacrifices Daphne gave worth it.

"Hey, I'm happy you gave me the go-ahead to talk to my older brothers." The smile he gives me makes my pulse quicken.

"How's your younger brother?"

I sense Theo shifting in the seat and pat his thigh.

"Hunter is complicated. He's kind of a lone wolf. His breakup changed him."

"A breakup can mess you up."

"We both know that. There's a part of me that is mad that Cyrus could fix me, help me, but left Hunter. That he didn't look after him. But I don't know the details."

"It's not your fault that someone was there for you, Theo. You deserved that."

"Yeah." He pats my leg.

The next time I look over at him, he's asleep, his head against the window.

DECEMBER 31st

My alarm buzzes in the dark early morning, yanking me to consciousness.

I shift Theo's head off my shoulder to grab my phone so I can silence the intrusion.

"Good morning, beautiful Ma'am." His sleepy voice wraps around my soul, and he snuggles next to me. The weight of his arm around my waist feels so good.

"Good morning, boy." I cup his stubbly cheek in my hand and tip his face to mine, kissing him deeply, his tongue stroking mine.

He releases a low moan, which sends pinpricks rolling down my spine. I tease his tongue, sucking on it, and he shifts, so he's wrapping me in his arms.

His strong arms are a great place to be first thing in the morning. He presses his chest to mine, his hand sliding down to my ass.

I jerk into his touch, my body all awake with hot want that slithers through me.

"Desperate this morning, Wolfie?" I lick the shell of his ear, tracing the line down to his jawline, then to his neck. His pulse jumps under my tongue.

He smells like sleep but in a good way, clean and fresh, and I don't think this man has ever intentionally put a foot wrong, he drops kisses along the column of my neck in reply, then brushes soft sweet kisses on my breasts.

I fist my hand in his hair, pulling his head up so I can see those grey sorrowful eyes.

"I didn't hear you." My tone is sharp, all in control Domme.

"Yes Ma'am. Feeling so desperate." He props himself up on his elbow, with my hand still on his head.

I slide my free hand down to cup his balls. They are full against my palm.

"How many days has it been since I let you come?" I give another squeeze, delighting in how he winces and tries not to.

"Three," his voice is so needy. I can see the ask in his glazed eyes.

"Is that all?" I drag his head up to me and I kiss him, a long slow kiss.

"Yes." He kisses my bottom lip playfully.

I slide my hand out of his hair, cup his face and tug gently on his bottom lip, mirroring him.

"I like waking up with you in my bed." I take his hard cock in my hand and slide it against my palm, careful not to touch the head.

He's already leaking pre-cum, and it's tacky under my thumb.

"Please, oh please." His whine is cute and pulls at my heartstrings.

Three days is the longest I've held him off from having an orgasm since we started this relationship.

The thrill of that is heady, it makes my pussy throb.

I stroke his cock as it pulses in my palm, then I scoop a drop of white liquid, putting it on his lips.

He shudders.

Licks his lips, stares right at me and it sends a blazing trail of fire from my pussy to my nipples, to my throat, the blaze so hot it steals my voice as all I can do is stare at this boy be pleased at the perfect obedience he gave me.

"Earn that orgasm, boy." My tone is harsher because I had to fight to get the words out, and I lay back against the cool sheets, spreading my legs wide.

He's on me in a nanosecond with a half growl. I laugh, my fingers twirling in his soft, wavy hair.

"This is a reward," he breathes, as he pushes my legs further apart.

The image of his sculpted back as he puts his face between my legs is beautiful.

Such a strong man, handing over control of his pleasure to me.

It makes me feel powerful and very fucking needy all at once.

Theo licks my inner thighs, sending shivers racing down my skin.

His mouth seals against my labia, and his tongue is stroking with little flicks.

That's setting off electric heat that's making me lose my mind.

"Faster, Wolfie," I pull his head right into my pussy, lifting my hips off the bed.

Pushing down, I grind my pussy against his face. It feels so damn good. The first lick of his tongue on my clit sends an arrow of electric heat firing through my veins. I push his head down, further, like I'm suffocating his face in my pussy.

The low, desperate moan he makes in response echoes through the room.

He works me with his tongue, his lips sealing around my clit, sucking me as if he needs me to come, as if driving my pleasure is his only goal. I drape my feet over his shoulders, stroking his ass with my foot, gently brushing it along his ass cheek.

"Yes boy, just like that," I pant, grabbing his strong forearms.

My body is getting ready to explode.

Pleasure is coming to a point, like a gathering cloud, his tongue circles my hood. His warm, wet mouth is on my clit. His tongue massages it, sending it pulsing. I'm gasping, whimpering low moans at the sensations, all hot and too much.

I can't hold it back.

A bursting hot electric current sends me soaring, up further and further from this man who is worshiping my pussy with his mouth, until I can't go any further.

My legs fall from his back, trembling as another wave of intense sensation breaks through, sending me tumbling over to an orgasm that hits me so fast it steals my breath. I grab his biceps as I come, feeling them ripple under my fingertips.

"Fuck! You're so good with that tongue," I croak, my mouth dry.

Aftershocks of hot pleasure roll through me—this boy knows exactly how to make me feel alive.

Theo lets out a startled cry, his back arching off the mattress. Wet liquid heat spreads against my thigh.

I pull his head up, sliding out from under him. "Did you come?"

Oh, yeah. He definitely did.

There's a large white puddle of his cum on my red sheets.

He gazes at me, his grey eyes wide. "Yes."

My lips twitch, trying not to laugh because he is staring at the mess on the bed, like he doesn't know how it got there.

"That's what you do to me, Ma'am. Make me lose all control." He runs a hand through his hair.

"Did I give you permission, boy?" I stand, walk around the bed and reach for him, running my knuckles against his face gently.

"No, Ma'am," his tone is all surprise.

"Who does your cum belong to?" I drag a nail across his nipple.

He shudders, his throat working hard as his cheeks are bright red.

"You." He whispers the word like it's an apology, his eyes flick down then up to my face.

He's studying me as if he's wondering what I am going to do.

I smile, ruffling his hair. I snake my hand along his spine to the base of neck and push his face right into the mess he made.

"You can clean that up, boy. You will control yourself. You will only come when I tell you to. That's what we agreed to. Hands behind your back."

He lets out a muffled laugh. "Yes, Ma'am!"

"Good." I grab a fistful of hair and move his face in the wet puddle, from side to side.

He whimpers. His tongue shoots out between his lips, and he licks up his mess.

The sight of him willingly accepting my discipline is turning me right on. This big man could easily overpower me.

And without the adrenaline of arousal, he is accepting his predicament.

The power of this literally rushes to my head, making me a little lightheaded.

What did I do to deserve this submissive? Nothing.

I loosen the grip on his hair, trailing my fingertips down his back.

"Yes, that's it. Clean it all up, you bad boy," I say it playfully, dancing my fingertips along his back.

He moans, loud and low, but keeps his head down, set to the task. I slide my hand down and cup his ass in my hands, then I let go, draw back my hand and spank him, the sound of my palm hitting his flesh echoing in the room.

He jumps as my palm meets his flesh, but his tongue is still busy cleaning up.

"At least you're cleaning up your mess. I think you need a spanking. What do you think?" His back arches towards me, his muscles rippling deliciously. He lets out an adorable growly whine.

"Why does this turn you on?" I pull a fistful of his hair, turning his head so he looks at me. His eyes are glassy.

"I want to make you happy. You're putting me in my place. And..." his wide smile makes me giddy. "You're keeping it fun, still."

"It's supposed to be fun," I trace his lips with my index finger, his pulse jumps.

"Yes Ma'am. This is turning me on."

"Ask me to punish you," I scratch his head, and he leans against me, practically purring.

"Please punish me, Ma'am. I want you to make my ass red."

My throat goes dry, my nipples hardening into tight peaks.

"Stand up. Lean over the end of the bed, hands behind your back. I'll be right back."

Still keeping his eyes down, he scrambles to the end of the bed.

The sight of this gorgeous man leaning over, baring his ass to me, with his hands on the small of his back, completely steals my breath.

From the closet, I take out my favourite crop. I swing it through the air, making it whoosh, then tap it against my hand as I come back into the room.

"You can be an obedient boy." I brush my fingertips along his ass cheeks, loving how he holds himself still.

"Yes, Callista."

I run the flapper of the crop across his shoulders. He flinches but stays in place.

"You're beautiful, Wolfie. Do you know how treasured you made me feel? You knew I was in distress, and you dropped everything to see me. You are my *very* good boy."

He lets out a growly cry that I love so much. I run my knuckles against his cheek.

"Your face is so sticky from cleaning up your own cum. I think you wanted to be punished. You wanted to see what would happen when you disobeyed me."

I bring the crop down above his tailbone. He doesn't flinch.

"Answer me, Wolfie." I grab his ass and squeeze, digging my fingers in the sensitive underside of his skin.

His muscles ripple, he shakes his head. "Yes. No. Maybe."

"Which is it?" I bring the crop down once, twice, three times, on the same spot on the centre of his ass. He flinches but stays in place.

"I don't want to disappoint you. You make me so needy and desperate that I lose control. But it wasn't on purpose."

"But you like this?" I bring the crop down hard on the unmarked ass cheek. His hiss echoes around the room. I trace the bright line left by my crop.

"Yes! Oh yes! Thank you, Ma'am."

His cry propels me to bring the crop down, again and again, the stinging noise it makes sending arousal climbing through me, so hot and fast I feel like I'm the one who is going to lose control.

Theo's breathing becomes ragged and short as I cover his ass, bringing the crop squarely across the middle.

He takes it, staying in position, his knuckles turning white as a stripe appears across the top of his thighs, cutting into the delicate flesh of his ass.

His ass is covered with white lines of the crop, and is all red.

With a flick of my wrist, I bring down the flapper high on the left side of his ass, right above the last white line. He jumps, but still stays right where I told him to.

Taking two steps, I lay my palm against his ass. "Your butt is red and is giving off its own heat."

"Thank you, Ma'am."

"You're welcome, boy," I drop the crop to the floor. I sit on the edge of the bed and pat my lap. "Come here, Wolfie."

He lifts his head off the bed and lays it on my lap, letting out a deep sigh of pleasure.

"You're such a good boy," I massage his shoulders, enjoying how his muscles flex and ripple under my touch.

"Do you know, I had planned to shower with you and give you a blow job to start our day?" I circle his ass, getting close to his opening, just a tease, not quite there.

He whimpers, dropping his head. "You did?"

"Yes, but this was a good way to start our day, too. But I'm going to shower, and when I get out, I expect the bed to be stripped, made and the coffee on."

"Yes, Ma'am."

"I need to pick up the kids from Aunt Millie's. I said I'd take them skating. Do you skate?"

"Yeah. Hunter is the superstar, but all of us played hockey."

"You're pretty super yourself."

He blushes almost as red as his ass. I slide my hands through his wavy hair.

"Thank you, Callista."

I cup his face, pat his cheek. Without looking at him, I stride towards the shower.

I can't wait to see this man on ice skates while *wearing a cock cage* a thrill races through my viens, thinking about how gorgeous cock would look locked.

I push the thought down and away. If he's ready, I'm ready.

That feels like the next stage of commitment, and the part of me that always runs, panics.

But I'm all in to take this further between us...at least that's what the post-session flood of endorphins is telling me.

13

THEO

I'm ending my call with Jayden when Callie comes out of the shower.

The scent of her shampoo engulfs me as she reaches a hand out for mine, then wraps her arms around my waist.

I love being held by her, and I let out a happy growl.

"Bed made. Coffee just finished brewing."

"Thank you, boy. Your turn to shower. I left something for you to use on the counter." She licks the shell of my ear. I shudder, and she laughs.

My cock twitches. "I can't wait to see it."

She drags her nails lightly down my back, to my ass. She spanks me once with enough force that I bend forward, clutching the counter.

I'm still upset about losing control this morning. I'm a trained submissive who should know better.

"Theo?" She lays a hand against my cheek.

I turn my head and meet her calculating gaze.

"Yes, Ma'am?"

"I like I make you so hot and bothered you lose control. There's no punishment here, so stop beating yourself up over it." The way she reads my mind is so hot.

I work my tongue against my lip. "I will. And I know." I shake my butt. "Funishments."

"Oh yes, *funishments*. I'm going to run downstairs and scrounge us up some breakfast. I expect you to be finished by the time I get back." Callie opens her closet, steps into a gorgeous pair of deep burgundy boots.

"Thank you, Ma'am."

She blows me a kiss, I return it before stepping into the bathroom.

I spot the anal douche kit on the sink. An icy wave of anxiety crashes over me.

Taking a deep breath, I push away the edges of the memories that want to crowd in, determined to keep myself in the present and not in the past of a relationship where I was mistreated.

Instead of Callie turning mean, humiliating, or punishing me with extreme force, she made it into a cute *oopsie*.

When I have my mind unfrozen from the past, I use the douche kit.

That done, I step in the shower, letting the warm water work away the tension in my body.

I have to fly out the day after tomorrow, and I'm determined to give Callie everything I can during the time we have together.

This relationship between us is hot and heavy and intense, but feels familiar in a way no other relationship has. I feel comfortable with her in a way I never have before. It's not like any power exchange relationship I've had, and that's electrifying.

With us, there is a deep level of respect. It isn't just a one-time session where we are getting our sexual needs met. I know she cares about meeting my emotional needs, and I hope I'm supporting her in the ways she needs me to.

"Mr. Sexypants! Get over here!" I quickly dry off, step out of the washroom to find Callie leaning against the kitchen table.

"Ooh, I love the sight of you in the morning. Turn, Wolfie."

I slowly turn so my back is to her. Her footsteps thud on the floor behind me. She comes up behind me, rests her palms on my back and sweeps them down, cupping my ass cheeks.

"Did you use my body wash again? I love that you smell like me." The sultry tone sends heat to my face. Makes my cock rise.

"I did, Ma'am. I love those boots on you."

She turns me to face her, and the approving smile that makes her eyes gleam with something like mischief deepens the aching need rising in my cock.

"Come here, Wolfie." With the gentlest tug on my elbow, she leads me to the counter, passing the table that's been set for two. The aroma of the diner food is making my mouth water. She pushes me forward.

"I'm keeping the boots on. You call yellow or red or stop, and we stop. Hands on the counter."

I whimper. Placing my palms flat on the counter grounds me.

On the counter, in my sightline, is a bottle of lube next to a glove.

She presses her hands over my nipples, nudges her booted foot between my legs. "Spread for me."

I spread my feet shoulder length apart. My mouth is dry, my cock twitching.

"Lean forward on your forearms...." Callie gently pushes me into position, and I duck my head, staring at the backsplash.

"Stay exactly like this. Don't move."

"Yes, Ma'am." My belly knots, I lick my lips.

In my periphery, I catch the movement of Callie picking up the glove.

The snap of the glove makes me jump.

The squeeze of the lube bottle sends a shudder from the base of my spine to hot tingles up my back.

My mind is half gone in a buzz of anticipation so sharp it makes my skin feel like it's being cut. With her bare hand, she grabs my ass, pinches it hard. Kneads it.

And grabs, pinches, kneads harder.

The sequence fires up my nerves, makes me fight for control to stay standing. Not enough to be pleasurable, but enough to be *irritating* with an edge.

A slap on my ass makes me jump, the pattern changes.

Slap, squeeze, knead. Slap, squeeze, knead.

Each time her strong grip lands on my ass, it drives my thoughts further from my mind, sparking a relentless want rippling through me.

I want to move, to turn and kiss her or to drop to my knees.

But I stay exactly where she has placed me, dialed into the energy in the kitchen.

Something is going to happen here, and it's going to bring me more into being *hers*. I can feel it, as if it's waiting for me to step into and accept.

She drags her gloved hand over my butt, then with her fingers, spreads my ass cheeks. I feel the brush of cool air.

A shudder rockets through me as her finger circles my anus. I have no time to think about it, I gasp as she slips a finger in my ass.

Oh, god.

The room spins, but as I relax around her finger, getting used to the pressure, it starts to feel good.

"Good boy. You're taking my finger very well," she circles it in my ass, then draws it out. Before I can exhale, she slips it in again. And out.

I thrust back on her as she slips it in again.

Her palm comes down hard across my ass. "None of that now, Wolfie. You stay still while I explore what's mine. You're going to take another finger, aren't you?"

She says it as she's stroking her finger past her knuckle. "Yes…" I croak the word out, my mind buzzing with pleasure.

"Yes *who*?" She wraps her ungloved hand around my shoulder, pulling me back against her.

"Ma'am," the honorific squeaks past my lips.

She laughs softly, pressing herself against my back. "You're such a cute Wolfie. Ah, just relax for me. That's it." Her second finger slides in.

My chest tightens as she curls her fingers downward. Shivery heat erupts as she brushes my prostate.

"Ma'am! Oh, Ma'am!" The sudden pressure in my balls takes away my breath.

Her fingers caress in a slow, agonizing motion that sets my mind buzzing with a pleasure so intense it doesn't quite touch me, it's just out of reach.

"Does that feel good, boy?" Her voice comes out in a low, predatory purr.

"Yes, Callista. So good," I heave out the words.

She pushes her fingers deeper, in and out, and my mind slides down into subspace. All I can feel is her hot, erotic touch, dragging my flesh, demanding that I open even wider, that I take what she's giving me.

She stretches me, a delicious burning ripple through my body, one that makes me want more and fearful that I can't take another second of this sweet torture.

The keening, wailing sounds are from me, and they cocoon us in a deep state of intimacy I don't want to leave.

When her digit strokes my prostate, I yelp, my knees buckle.

It feels so explicit, so blissful.

And I don't know how much more of it I can take. I start to pant, sucking in long, deep breaths.

It's been a very long time since this part of me was played with.

"I want all of you, boy," she taps her booted foot against my leg, giving me something to focus on that isn't the building furnace in my balls.

She runs her foot against the back of my calf, up and down.

The cool leather adds to the sensations, splitting apart my resolve.

I want to stay exactly where she's put me, but her every touch is making that a challenge.

I feel like I'm going to lose.

Her fingers thrust deep, deeper. Oh fuck.

Before I realize it, my hips are rocking back against her.

"I said stay, Wolfie." She grabs my ass and pulls.

I cry out as she massages my prostate. Electric heat and pleasure zing through me. It's like I have to come right *now,* but I can't. More than fucking anything, I want to empty my balls, but I can't because there is too much pressure.

But not enough.

Not where I need it.

My cock throbs painfully pressed against the counter.

"Please, Ma'am, I need to come."

Tears are leaking down my face. I need this elusive promise.

Pinpricks of pleasure flood my system, hammering desperation into me so hard, I'm going to fall apart.

"Please, please, Ma'am, let me come."

"Oh, I *love* hearing you beg, sweet boy."

I want to thrust against her fingers so badly, but I stay exactly where she told me to.

She drags one finger out, then the other.

I grind my molars, fighting to hold on.

"I know you are a good boy. You'll wait for me to give you permission to come." Callie sweeps her bare hand across my shoulder, along my neck, and then she's ruffling my hair.

"Yes, Ma'am." I squeeze my eyes shut against the burning pressure, the desperation that makes me suck in deep breaths.

"Good boy. But one more thing." The glove comes off. I hear the squirt of more lube. Then, a moment later, I gasp as a plug slides in my ass.

"Fuck!" So stretched I burn. I desperately cast about for something to fill my mind with. A replay of a hockey game, the dirty slushy snow in Toronto.

"I need to have fun with my boy while he's here. You keep that in until I remove it."

"Yes, Callista." I'm a whimpering, crying mess.

"Yep, not yet. You're *not* going to come yet."

The command is said low and whispered, but it's still a command. Disappointment slaps into me, like it's a physical thing.

She removes her fingers from my body, taps the plug between my cheeks.

I'm catching my breath, my eyes are shut.

The heat of her body comes beside me.

She washes her hands and snakes a hand up my back, grabs my hair and pulls me up, freeing me from leaning on the counter. Standing on her toes, her lips brush mine in a punishing kiss that leaves my lips tingling.

"Good boy." She reaches into the cupboard for a glass, sets it under the tap. Holds it to my lips.

"Drink this."

I do, and the water cools me off slightly, but I am hyper-aware of the butt plug in my ass. My nerve endings are supercharged.

My mind is still half in that altered state. Her eyes drink me in, studying me.

"Yeah, that's a good boy."

Safe.

I'm safe with this woman, to show her my vulnerability.

"Come eat." She grabs my arm and pulls me over to the table. "Sit." Her eyes are brimming with heat, the little curved smile on her face sends shivers up my back. My cock is half hard as I slid into the seat. I'm naked. She's not.

That's enough to keep my cheeks flaming.

Ah, fuck, the sitting is hard with the plug.

"How do you feel?" Callie gives me that sultry smile, that beautiful Domme glance.

As aware as I am of the plug, I'm even more aware of her. How slender her fingers are around the fork, how a piece of hair drops over her shoulder as she leans forward.

"Horny as fuck." She lets out a peal of laughter that echoes around the room, making her eyes extra bright.

"Good boy. After we eat, we're going skating. The kids want to watch the ball drop at the town hall, and then we can come back here."

"That's...forever from now."

"Yes," Callie smiles, batting those pretty eyelashes. "Anything wrong?"

"Not a thing."

She picks up a fork, reaches across my plate, fills it with food and holds it to my lips. I open my mouth.

"Good boy."

I wiggle in my chair, my cock aching. "It's going to be the best New Year's Eve ever."

"Yeah?" That smile is sexy and gorgeous.

"Yes, Callista. There's no other place I'd rather be."

I swallow though, thinking of how we were all supposed to be at Evan's for New Year's Eve and other than Hunter, that plan has fizzled out.

But it's true. I don't want to be there. As loyal as I am to my brothers, this woman has given me back a part of myself that I thought was lost. In giving my submission to her, I feel stronger. Healed.

"What are you thinking?" Callie leans forward, her eyes bright.

"That I'm happy being with you."

"Good," her fingertips dance along my arms. "You're my whole resolution for the new year."

She gives me a wink, and that makes me laugh, and she's letting out that adorable high pitch laugh again, and then she's gasping for breath. I get up and get her a glass of water.

"Thanks, boy," she wraps an arm around my neck, bringing me down to kiss her.

I groan as her tongue slides against mine.

She sucks on my lips, deepening the kiss so hard it's making my cock throb even more. And I am so certain that I want this woman in my life. I want to surrender to her as fully as she'll take me.

I take her hand, give it a squeeze and kiss her back, loving how her lips feel against mine.

"Get dressed. We have twenty minutes." Her cheeks are flush, her eyes are bright. She deserves the world, and I'm going to treat her like the queen she is... like my queen.

"I'll be ready in five."

"Good boy," Callie gives me a slap on the ass as I clear our plates. I shimmy because I thought it might make her laugh, and it does.

"Are you sure we don't have time for a quickie?" I raise my eyebrows.

"And you asked so nicely too, but no," Callista stands, wraps her arms around my waist, pressing her breasts against my chest. "But if you're very good, you'll like the reward I have in mind."

"I can't wait."

My poor swollen aching balls can't wait either.

14

CALLIE

Satisfaction swims through my veins, knowing I teased my boy and left him needy—and that's exactly what he craves. I throw on my jacket.

"All set?" Theo holds the door open.

My bag with my skates is on his shoulder.

"Yes," I kiss him and chuckle at his instant moan. I cup his face, tilting his head back to deepen the kiss, sliding my palm against his balls.

His hips buck under me. I break off the kiss, ruffling his hair.

He sighs against me. I dig my fingers into the crease of his ass and tap the plug.

"You're making me feel desperate."

"Good. That's exactly how I want you." I slap his ass, hitting the plug.

He closes his eyes, his long lashes fluttering. "Ma'am."

The trust Theo has given me has started to heal the wound I've been carrying around for so many months.

I was convinced it was a permanent part of myself.

I give two more sharp slaps right on the base of the plug before nuzzling his neck, the heat from his body seeping into mine, his breathy sounds zing right to my pussy. I'm so wet for him.

"As soon as it's the New Year, I'm going to let you come inside me. After I peg your ass."

His mouth falls open, his breathing catches.

"I can't wait," he brushes his lips against mine. I fist my fingers in his hair and pull his face to mine, teasing him with a kiss that I don't give. I pat his cheek.

"Later. Now it's time to go skating."

"Fine," Theo runs a hand through his hair. "Lead the way, Callista."

My phone rings halfway downstairs.

"Hey Grady, I'm on my way to take the kids now. Everything okay?"

"She called me, Callie."

I grab the handrail. The emotion in his voice makes me stop.

Theo offers an arm for support, but I shake it off and sit on the stair.

Grady isn't a guy prone to emotion, but he's not afraid to show his feelings.

He cried rivers when Madison was born.

"All by herself?" Hope flares through me.

"Yes. Her words are still slow in coming, but I'm on my way to pick her up. She asked to come home for New Year's Eve. I can't tell her no."

All the information I have read on brain injuries in the past months spins through my mind like a carousel of too many facts.

But I recall reading something about how sentimentality can be a pull.

"I know we still have a long road, and a setback might be around the corner, but it's New Year's."

Grady proposed to my sister on New Year's Eve fifteen years ago.

"Thanks for telling me. I'm so happy." My tone is low as I say the words because I'm feeling a ton of emotions right now, and most of them I thought I had stored away.

"Our neighbour is with the kids. If you still want to take them skating, that'd give me time to get dinner."

I glance at Theo. He's reading something on his phone, with a frown of concentration on his face.

I think of how much I want to tease this boy until he loses it, of how much I want his hands and lips on me, and of how much I want him under me.

But then the guilt crashes over me. I am not my sister; I don't plan every second of my life, so I'm not sure where I would be if I wasn't here, but it probably would have been somewhere in Europe with Gianna and the team—while my sister juggled saving our family's legacy because of my fuck-up.

"Let's not change plans, Grady."

"What do you mean?"

I reach over and squeeze Theo's thigh.

There's a part of me that's already regretting what I'm about to do, but this is a chance for me to be the good sister.

"You haven't had a lot of alone time with your wife. If she's having a good day, then you should enjoy every second. I'll take the kids skating. You can even pick them up tomorrow, or you can see how it goes. Daphne is usually better in the mornings, right?"

"Callie..." His voice breaks. "I have always liked you."

I snort a laugh. "That's not true, but I know you love my sister. Does Mads know you're picking up Mom?"

"No, I needed to see her for myself before I told the kids."

"Perfect. Then go take your beautiful wife out or bring her home and dote on her. I got the kids."

"Thanks, Callie."

"You're welcome." I slide my phone back into my pocket.

"Theo..."

He gives me a steady, cool glance, squeezes my thigh.

"The plan was skating with the kids, right?"

"Yeah." I press the heels of my palms into my eyes.

I don't think being a good sister or being a good friend means sacrificing your happiness for someone else's time and time again—but I need to give Grady this night.

Maybe it'll ease the guilt inside my chest that always flares up when Daphne's having a good day.

Maybe it's because I'm bracing myself for her anger, for her to tell me that it was my fault because I left when she told me the guy I was in love with was engaged.

Theo's arm comes around my shoulders, lightly as if he's just placing it there. I need the touch, and he knows it.

I lace his fingers through mine and lean back in his arms.

"I don't know why her having a good day makes me an emotional mess."

"Because you hope that it's going to last. You fear that it won't." Theo brushes his lips against my forehead, as if he can soften the impact of his words.

But what he said is true, and I know it.

"Are you very good on skates?" I drop his hand and stand.

"I can hold my own," Theo flashes me a grin.

"Yes, you can."

I take the stairs two at a time. The sound of the diner fills with laughter and talk, and I can't wait to take the kids to the New Year's feast at Shel's because they were looking forward to it. Theo opens the car door for me, and I slip in.

Never once has this man complained about me driving, and I like that a whole lot.

He gets in, buckles up, and glances at me.

"I can't think of a better way to start a new year."

"Me neither." I drag my hand down his arm to the waistband of his slacks.

I let my hand drop to press against his junk.

He squirms on the seat. I laugh.

"I know you're going to be a very good boy and wait for me. Who does your cum belong to?" I love how he blushes when I say it.

"You, Ma'am." Theo takes my hand, lifts it to his mouth, and presses a kiss to it.

The desire in his eyes tells me that he wants everything I am willing to give him, and knowledge settles deep into my chest.

***

Growing up, Daphne always talked about wanting to get married and having babies. I'd scoff at her and roll my eyes.

"Why do you want to have kids? What if you turn out like our parents?"

"I'm not going to. I'm going to turn out like Uncle Henry and Aunt Millie."

For her, it worked out.

She got everything she wanted, and I know that a happy home doesn't just happen, it's a credit to her and Grady that her kids are so great.

I never wanted kids.

I didn't want to risk abandoning them or passing on trauma I hadn't dealt with.

But watching how Theo so effortlessly skates with my nephew and nieces? I get the hope my sister had.

"I'm cold!" Luke says, grabbing my hand.

"Yeah, I think we're almost done here, buddy." I ruffle his hair, glancing across the ice.

Madison is doing some kind of turn on one foot, and Theo is cheering her on.

Abby is trying to spin like her big sister and falls down. Theo offers her a hand and, still holding her hand, skates over to us.

"This guy is getting cold."

"I think the girls are done too," Theo says.

"I am not!" Abby skates away, gliding gracefully.

Luke takes two steps on the ice before reaching for my hand. His little fingers curl around mine, and I want to soak all this in so I can tell Daphne later.

"I'm getting hungry, and I know the special at Shel's tonight," I tease.

"Is it pigs in a blanket?" Luke asks, pulling on my arm.

"What? No! Why would you wrap a pig in a blanket?" Theo asks dramatically, clutching the side of his face. Abby laughs, and Luke giggles, and my silly heart leaps.

"What?" Madison skates up to me so fast she sprays me with ice.

"We're discussing dinner," I reply.

"Oh, same boring food at Shel's," Madison sticks her tongue out at me.

I see Theo out of the corner of my eye, hiding a smile.

"Yep, same boring food. Let's go!" I take off on my skates expecting her to take off after me, but she stands still, her hands in her pockets.

Abby is spinning around making a figure eight, and Luke is clutching Theo's hands.

"What is it, Mads?" I skate back to her.

"Same boring food, but without Mom making a hot fudge sundae."

I touch her arm gently. "I know it's not the same. We're almost through the holidays, and you don't know what's going to happen in the new year."

"I want Mommy to come home."

Her whine tugs at my heart, and I chew the inside of my lip, regretting my earlier decision. But if Daphne is having a good day, Grady deserves to have time with her before adding the kids.

"I want her home too."

"So you can go back to Europe?" She sniffs, looking down at her skates.

"Hey Mads, I don't know what's going to happen with your mom. But I'm in no hurry to pack my bags. Race me to the gate?"

"Fine!" She takes off on her skates, her long hair reminding me so much of my sister, I blink away tears. I follow her, slowing down my stride.

"You got me!" I tell her. "I'm starving. Let's go eat some boring food."

"The fries are the best in Rising Harbour."

"Yep, they are!" I find Theo untying Abby's skates. "Thanks, I can take over."

"Sure," he brushes his finger against mine as he unlaces the rented pair of skates he borrowed and returns them to the counter.

I get everyone's skates off and packed, and Madison is talking to her siblings about the biggest sundae, and my heart is lighter. I have dodged the preteen moodiness until we are in the car.

I buckle up the little kids, Theo holds my door open for me and then slides into the passenger seat.

Abby and Luke are using their gloves as hand puppets, and this happy bubble lasts until I turn onto the main street.

"Theo, are you going to disappear just like the other guy?" Madison's snark instantly causes my shoulders to tense.

"What other guy?" I fall for the trap as soon as the words come out of my mouth.

"Like that rich guy with blond hair. Where did he go? He just disappeared."

My belly twists in a knot. I can't recall when Madison saw me with John, but it makes my head spin.

"Mommy says that guy is sufferable!" Luke chants from the back.

Thinking of John's annoying habit of constantly clearing his throat, and how he never gave you a straight answer, I can see why Daphne would think that.

"I think you mean insufferable," I tell Luke. "And everyone has their opinion."

I keep my eyes straight ahead through the windshield, checking the cars behind me.

"Madison, I don't know what the new year will bring, but I am not going to disappear," Theo says. His voice is even and confident.

My cheeks flame, my pulse races. How can he make that promise? I don't like telling the kids things I don't know for sure.

"Good," Madison says. "I like you!"

"I like you too!" Luke says.

"Me too!" Abby shrieks.

Soon the kids are laughing and listing off things they like.

But an irrational wave of anger fires through my veins.

"Have a crystal ball?" The words come out with more bite than I intend, and I keep my voice pitched low enough not to be overheard by the backseat passengers.

I feel his gaze shift over to me.

"Don't need one. I don't break promises, Ma'am." The words are spoken as quietly as mine were, and they cause me to choke up with tears.

"I don't want you to disappear either."

I see his smile out of the corner of my eye, and my heart skips a beat.

"Why is Dad here?" Madison asks as I pull into the parking lot behind Shel's.

"I don't know," I say. As soon as I'm parked, Madison jumps out and runs over to Grady.

He hugs her, twirling around in his arms. I get the little kids out.

"Happy New Year," Grady says to me. He gives Theo a nod.

"Happy New Year. We didn't expect you until later."

"Home daddy! Let's go home!" Abby says.

"Yes, princess, that's what we're going to do." He meets my eyes as he swings Abby up into his arms. "Thanks, Callie, but I need the kids at home with us. Uncle Henry is at the house. Brenda packed our order."

"Everything is good?"

"Yes, come over tomorrow, please." He glances at Theo. "You too."

"I'm flying out tomorrow morning," Theo says.

Grady raises an eyebrow and then looks at me. "Join us when you can. All right, munchkins, say goodbye to Aunt Callie and her friend."

"Bye!" Madison huffs, dragging herself to the car.

Luke and Abby throw themselves at me. "Bye Theo! Bye, Auntie Callie!"

I wave them goodbye and turn to Theo, suddenly feeling bereft.

"Ma'am?" Theo cocked an eyebrow.

I push aside the feeling of feeling left out and all the tangled, knotted feelings I have about my sister.

Standing four feet away from me is a sexy submissive who is waiting on my word.

The rush of power that gives me turns the Domme part of myself all the way on.

"Get upstairs. I want you nak—."

The back door of Shel's opens, and Brenda steps out. "Callie! Good, I thought you were coming in with the kids. Natasha called in sick again. I'm getting slammed."

"I'll be right there, Brenda, and I'll call in reinforcements."

"Good!" She closes the door.

"Are you hiding me?" Theo tilts his head to the side, his eyes lit with amusement.

"I didn't want you to get pulled into work. Are we hiding this?"

"I didn't think so. I thought that's why you let me around your nieces and nephew."

"Yeah," I drag my hand across his. "Being hidden is a red flag. I should have...." My voice trails off. John's refusal to let me meet his sister spits up from my memory banks. "I don't know if you caught everything. I'm sorry I didn't tell you what the phone call was about on our way to get the kids."

"You didn't have to, Callista." Theo brushes a hand along my arm. His touch is comforting, and I exhale.

"My sister is having a good day. Such a good day that she called Grady all by herself. That's why he came and got the kids."

"That's great! Isn't it?"

"Yeah. But..."

"You can tell me," Theo says softly against my ear.

I blow a breath out between my lips. I feel ridiculous. "They need family time. It's stupid to feel left out."

"Your feeling left out is valid. It's the not knowing how your sister is going to be that's probably amplifying that."

"Yep. Half of me wants to run over there and crash their party."

"And the other half?"

"Wants to take you upstairs and have my way with you." I raise my eyebrows, smiling.

"Good," Theo grins so huge I can see his molars.

Laughing, I pull him down to me. I trace his lips with mine before I kiss him, a desperate, needy kiss.

"I need to go in and be a diner owner. But I have a task for you."

I take his face in my gloved hands, staring into his grey eyes. All I see there is anticipation, acceptance.

"What can I do for you, Ma'am?" Theo asks in that sultry way of his that sends a new wave of hot neediness right to my pussy.

"Go upstairs. Get naked. I want you to stroke that gorgeous cock of yours, get all hard and then when you're close, edge for two minutes. Do this every fifteen minutes until I come up. Make sure you get yourself water and get up as you need to. I'll call you if I am delayed more than an hour. Do you want boring food for dinner or something else?"

"I want your pussy for dinner," he says so deadpan, it takes me a moment to register what he says.

It startles a laugh out of me, and I kiss his nose.

He scrunches his face. Adorable.

"I'll take care of dinner."

"Sounds good, Callista. I can't wait until you get up there."

I press my keys into his hand. "Be a good boy." His lips are soft against mine as I cup his ass, my fingers finding the plug through his slacks.

"Yes, Ma'am." He gives me a little wave as he takes the stairs up to my apartment.

As I step into Shel's, I call my friend Amy.

"Thought you lost your phone." Her sarcasm makes me grin.

"I know I owe you a visit. I've got a hot submissive boy upstairs, and I'm short-staffed. Any chance your kid wants to pick up a shift?"

"He's going out with friends so I can have my way with the hot subby boy I married. How long do you need him for?"

"We close at nine."

"Hold on."

I wave to Brenda, throw on an apron and get into the fray. Kids are climbing off their parents' laps, tired looking moms are trying to get their kids to eat something before their sitter shows up.

It's pretty much the chaos you'd expect. I bus two tables before Amy gets back to me.

"He's on his way. You could have called him yourself."

"Then I wouldn't get to hear your voice."

"That bad, eh?"

"Yes," I move out of the way for Brenda as she comes by with our newest server, who is still learning to balance plates.

"Enjoy your night and give me the details soon."

"You're the best, bye!" I hang up with Amy and find Brenda. "Hugh is coming in."

"Good! Where's the council when this place is packed, eh, Callie? I hope Hugh still remembers how to take orders."

I laugh. "He will."

Amy's son worked here during high school and until he left for college last summer. He's a good kid.

While I'm bussing tables, I make an order for my favourite food besides Shel's in Rising Harbour.

"You got it, Callie!" Allison Qin says after I ordered the New Year's special. The warmth in Allie's voice surprises me. "I called Brenda earlier for our order! I'm sure you guys are just as swamped as we are!"

Allie and I grew up together, but her parents homeschooled her, so I only really know her from council meetings as an adult.

"If only the council could see us now!" I mutter.

"I don't think it matters, Callie. I don't think anything will budge them from their weird idea of how to preserve Rising Harbour's industry. But we need places like Shel's, that's what brings people here. Good food always has. Qin's Charm has won top restaurant, ten years running." The imitation of an announcer makes me laugh. "Hey, this might be the year Shel's takes first place! We've tied twice."

I laugh. "True, Allie! Good luck tonight."

The next hour passes in a blur, but seeing how happy everyone is in Shel's takes me back to the good parts of my childhood.

Hugh comes in and joins us, lightening our load. I stay through the dinner rush until it's back to a trickle.

"Thanks for taking a shift," I squeeze Hugh's arm.

"I could always use the cash," Hugh says, grinning.

"I figured you could."

I'm going to spend New Year's with the man I know is a good one. I don't want to let him go. The unknown scares the crap out of me, but

that boy is worth risking my heart for because I know he won't break
it.

15

THEO

The hardwood floor bites into my knees through the thin carpet in the living room.

But I shift slightly, using the discomfort as a way to focus myself, even as my cock pulsates with need, the head swollen and flushed purple as I keep stroking.

The only thing I want at this moment is to come and give in to the pressure that is mounting in my balls.

But I want to please my Domme more, so I hold back, rocking on the uncomfortable floor, keeping that release in with everything I have.

Beep beep, the timer rings out.

I wipe the sweat from my brow. Get a glass of water.

As I put the glass to my lips, a wave of guilt swirls low in my stomach.

No, I'm not going there. My Domme told me to take care of my own needs. She didn't tell me to stay kneeling long past my point of discomfort.

I'm here in the present, not back where my mind wants to take me.

I wish my past didn't drag itself into my now. It's like I have to fight the remnants of the toxic relationship I left, even though what I have now is good and healthy.

Callie cares about me as a man, not just someone who serves her sexual needs.

I take a quick moment to read through my messages, confirming there's nothing that can't wait.

Kneeling again, I take my half-hard cock in my hand and stroke it, the skin so sensitive the touch fires a rocket of need that makes my hips tilt. All I want to do is spill my seed. But I grip my cock, grit my teeth. I am so close, I'm gasping.

I reach out, my fingers trembling with exertion, I restart the timer.

I don't know how I'm going to hold off for two minutes.

But I jerk off, writing code in my head, focusing on a half-finished protocol.

It cools me down a fraction.

I tighten all my muscles and feel the insistent press of the plug up my ass.

The timer goes off, and I gasp for air, trying to bring myself back to focus.

I rest against the couch before I pull myself up, my legs wobbly from the exertion.

In the bathroom, I grab a cloth and give the counter a quick wipe down, for something mindless to do.

Force myself to sip more water before I settle back into my spot, grabbing my cock.

It's so sensitive, I almost spurt as I hold it.

I start stroking, playing with my balls lightly, and close my eyes.

Callie's smile from across the rink flashes through my mind. She's so beautiful the way her hair shone in the sunlight took my breath away.

I'm leaking pre-cum, so I stare at a spot on the wall, forcing myself to run through the security codes of my building.

The code to our server room.

The code to my father's safe, which after years of grumbling he finally agreed to get, though it's empty and I have all his important documents in mine.

My balls are boiling. I don't know if I can hold off anymore—the timer goes off sparing me. I drop my dick like the live wire it is, exhaling a shuddering breath.

I stretch my arms above my head.

This is slow, sweet torture that I have willingly accepted.

But this tease and denial? How many nights have I lain awake *wanting* this? Craving this.

At one point, I would have done anything to get it and paid any amount of money to receive it.

My cock is still hard when I grip it.

I imagine what it would feel like to be caged again, the press of the steel against my cock, how tight my balls would feel... knowing that Callie held the key.

My mouth waters.

Heat shimmers up my spine.

My vision hazes over as I reach out for my phone and set the timer.

I squeeze my eyes closed, sweat breaks out across my back. I hear myself pant as I fight for control.

I think of the mess in Hunter's apartment, of the coldness of his stance as he turned away from me.

Even with the wash of sadness and guilt, my stroking hand is getting me so damn close.

I'm leaking.

I pinch the head of my cock because I will hold back, no matter what it takes, and I bite my bottom lip so hard I taste blood.

The door clicks.

I exhale. Relief swims through me.

I hear the groan of the wood as the door closes, Callie's soft footsteps.

My shoulders tense, waiting, wanting her to know that I followed her orders.

I rock on my heels, increasing the speed I'm stroking my dick.

"What a sight this is to come home to." Her fingertips graze my shoulders, then she digs them in with enough pressure to send me backward.

The coolness of her boot against my back is comforting.

"Open your eyes, baby." Her low, seductive tone pulls at my heartstrings, she knows the power she has over me.

It feels like everything before this moment was leading up to *now*, that this power exchange between us has just gone up a notch.

My whole body vibrates with need, but I want to bask in her tenderness.

I do as commanded, meeting her startling blue eyes, gazing up at her from my spot on the floor.

"I can see what a good boy you've been for me, waiting, edging but not allowing yourself to come." The pleased smile that spreads across her face makes my pulse jump.

Another moan escapes my lips as she cradles my chin in her hand. I want to stay here forever, resting in her awareness of me.

My timer beeps.

Her arm brushes my jaw as she reaches across me as she picks up my phone, sending a shudder up my spine.

The glow of approval in her eyes makes me want to roar.

I will do everything I can to care for this woman, to support her, to serve her.

"I once heard that you should spend New Year's Eve doing what you want to do for the rest of the year. I want to be with you, Wolfie."

I drop my chin to my chest. The purr of her words carries an emotional weight that feels heavy

It's what I want.

Our desires match, and it makes my cheeks blaze with heat. I stare right at her.

"Me too, Ma'am," I can barely get the words out. She rubs my head in a slow, seductive circle, then moves behind me.

She didn't tell me not to look, and that's good because I can't take my eyes off her.

Her legs are so shapely in those boots, the jeans hug her ass like they were made for her. She sits down, her arms resting on the armrests.

"Come here."

The words have barely left her mouth and I'm in front of her.

"Turn around." I do, turning so my back is to her.

She runs her nails down my spine softly, then taps at the butt plug.

"I think it's time for this to come out. Do you feel you're properly prepared to take *my* cock?"

Red-hot need flares through me at the question.

Ready?

Yes, a thousand percent.

I am so damn ready for anything this woman wants to do to me.

"Yes, Callista." My body spasms under her palm.

"Nice and slow."

I whimper as she tugs at the plug.

She grabs the base of the plug, the heel of her palm pushes on my ass cheeks, as I gasp, shudders rack my body at the thought of Callie pegging me, my hips jut forward with the scream of need that runs through me.

"Here it goes." She parts my ass, turns the plug.

My toes dig into the floor, fighting to stay upright.

Sweat breaks out at the base of my spine.

She pulls the butt plug out.

My ass gapes for it, wanting it back, desperate to be filled again.

My heart beats so loudly I am sure Callie can hear it.

I hear metal teeth ripping through fabric and the soft give of the chair.

"My beautiful boy." Her palm splays against my lower back, trails down to my ass, comes around, and cups my balls with the slightest of pressure.

Fuck, they are boiling, ready to burst. I roll on my heels.

"Are you still so close?" Her mouth is on my ass cheek.

"It's what you do to me." My voice is broken with need, desire flaring across every nerve of my body, all of it needing somewhere to go.

I shift my weight, trampling down impatience, my mind racing, wondering what she is going to do next.

I want to lick her pussy until she shudders and cries out my name.

She gives me a little push, stands, and grabs my ass. "Come, Wolfie."

In the bedroom, she pushes me face down on the bed. "I'm going to ride your ass, boy. How do you feel about that?"

My throat goes dry with anticipation. But her focus is on my face, she's studying my reaction.

"Yes, Ma'am. *Please* ride my ass."

Her laugh vibrates through the room, low and pleased as she comes towards me, then the bed shifts under her weight.

A sharp tug at my hair jerks my head back, forcing my gaze up to her smile.

Her lips hover close, brushing mine with a soft, taunting sweep that leaves my whole body straining toward her.

I'm going to burst with how much I want this woman.

Her tongue probes against mine, commanding me to give her more access to my mouth, and she kisses me with the force of a windstorm that spins us out of reality and into this intimacy where is just her and me.

We're lost in moans, tongues twirling, the heat of our bodies pulling each of us in, keeping us where we are.

She breaks off the kiss, sweeps her hands over my nipples, then touches her forehead to my chest. "I'm going to be gentle and slow."

"I know, Callista."

"Want to see me put it on?"

"Yes!" Hell, that's going to be sexy. My mouth salivates in anticipation.

"Sit. Stay here."

I do and watch her stride to the closet. She takes off her boots, then the jeans, tossing them to the side.

"Does that bother you?" She turns her head over her shoulder.

"Nothing bothers me at this moment. I like seeing you naked, Ma'am."

I drink in her slender curves, watching as she opens the closet, then takes out what she needs.

She shows me the harness.

Her body is toned, fit, and gorgeous, and I let my eyes roam over her body as she puts on the harness.

I want to help, but I sit as I am commanded.

Oh dear heavens.

"You look so hot." The harness is leather and black and so damn sexy. I feel like I'm going to spurt all over the bed...again.

The dildo is curved. Big.

"The very first time I tried this, I felt silly." She puts her hands on her hips, and her uncertainty is endearing.

But she looks so damn hot.

"You look *gorgeous,* Callista."

"Thank you, Wolfie. Now, I feel pretty damn powerful wearing this. One sec." She steps into the washroom, then comes out, and seeing what she has in her hand makes me swallow.

"I said I'd take care of you."

"You did, Ma'am."

With her holding a lubricant syringe, she looks like a sexy nurse from my hottest fantasies, but no fantasy could ever come close to how she struts over to me with a roll of her hips and she takes, takes my chin in her hand.

"You're going to take everything I give you, Wolfie."

"Yes, Ma'am."

"Get this nicely lubed up for me before I lube your ass." She strokes the dildo she's wearing, right from the base to the head, and a shot of rapid-fire jealousy runs through me. I wish her hand was on *my* cock. But I part my lips, and take the fake-cock deep into my throat.

She threads her fingers through my hair, closing her eyes.

"Oh, I can feel every lick, every motion, right on my clit as the harness presses against me."

That incites me to lap and lick the dildo more. I swear I can smell her sweet, tangy arousal.

She strokes my jaw as I suck, making me moan around the dildo. It feels like we're standing on the edge of a cliff.

The more I suck, the more she touches me, and I keep it up, watching as her eyes roll back in her head.

"Good boy. Time to get on your hands and knees."

"Yes, Ma'am." I get into position, arousal pumping through me, my cock standing up straight.

The bed shifts as Callie settles behind me.

"I love your body." She slaps my ass, and all it does is make me more desperate.

"Thank you, Ma'am." Warmth spreads through me as she kneads my ass cheeks. I'm not a jock like Hunter, but I work hard to stay fit, and it's nice to have that noticed.

"I'm wearing a double-headed strap-on. Every time you move, I will feel it right against my clit. Hold those ass cheeks for me, so I can lube you up." Her commanding tone has me instantly moving.

I reach back and do as I'm told. Shivers, making sweat break on my brow.

The cool press of the applicator invades deep, making me clench and squirm as the liquid plunges.

"There," Callie shifts her weight on my hips feels good. I like having her this close.

"Relax, Wolfie. Your shoulders are tense."

I didn't realize I had tensed up until she kneaded them.

"Sorry, Ma'am."

"That's better. I'm going to slide in this ass now, here I go."

There's the tiniest of tension, then my arms shudder, the pure fission of sensation swallowing my every nerve ending.

"Fuck!" I cry out as the press of the dildo presses even further.

Callie rocks her hips, discharging heat and need, and want through me.

The pleasure is so intense my mouth is bone dry.

She stays like that, her hands sliding around my waist, her fingers curling around my hard cock.

"You're nice and hard for me, Wolfie. I love that."

She stays right where she is for a moment, allowing my body to adjust to the size and feel of the dildo.

"Oh! Ma'am!"

"Tell me how this feels, Wolfie."

"Like you belong here. Like you *own* me," I cry out as her fingers come off my cock and around my hips.

"I'm going to own your ass with my cock, boy."

"Yes, please," I grit the words out, as she thrust harder, sliding back to me. Her fingers dig into my hips.

She thrusts hard, deep.

Her breathy noises as she rocks her hips are sending pure liquid heat up my spine, making me hard as steel.

"Oh fuck! Yes!" Callie's low, guttural tones swirl around the bedroom, taking me deeper into pleasure.

Hot white fire shoots up from my spine; my balls are going to burst.

She thrusts.

Rides me deeper. Takes what she wants.

Nonsensical babble pours out of me as I'm shot up higher into a different atmosphere.

"Yes, more!" I ask for it, closing my eyes against the tide.

She pounds me and rocks and in this moment she owns every damn thing I have.

From my ass, to the dusting of fine hair on my back, to my bank account.

As she takes and takes, my cells merge with hers, wanting her to take even more.

My cock is leaking pre-cum.

I cry out, a stream of babble, lost in the hot waves of pleasure, the gaping abyss of need. I press back on her. She slaps my ass, once, twice, over and over. The sound rings out in the room.

And it's all just sounds against a tide of heat that's so hot, I know I'm going to shatter.

My growly grunts, her high cries.

My cry, her low throaty approval makes me feel like I am going to orgasm any second, as if I'm already there, even though I'm not.

Her roll of the hips feels so good, shivering pleasure consumes my breath as I shudder, wanting more.

"How are you feeling?" She tilts her pelvis forward. The cock rocks low in me, touches the right spot and I can't help it, I'm humping the bed as if my life depends on it, crying out for release.

"Good! This is so fucking good! I love you taking my ass."

"You're being a very good boy!" She grabs my hips, digging into my flesh with her nails. It drives me wild, I can't help but buck back against her.

She shifts, going even deeper.

Blazing heat, an explosion of sensations that's making me so horny, as filled with need as I've ever been, ramps through my every particle. I need her to grant me permission to release.

"Please, Ma'am, please!" Her hands are on my cock, gripping me, jerking me off against her soft palm.

She thrusts with her hips, fucking my ass hard, splintering.

All I want is to explode, all I need is this woman and the promise she's offering.

My breath is short and hollow.

"Please, Callista, please let me come!"

She glides her hand up and down my cock.

"Not long now, boy." She grabs my cock's head, gives it a pinch, a pull, rubs the slit.

A thousand sparking lights enter my brain, my vision grows fuzzy.

All that's there is her scent, the press of her skin against mine.

Her next thrust has me screaming, it's so hard.

"Now! Come now, boy."

Thank fuck. I'm gasping for air as my body ripples with tension, as the furnace consumes me, heating up my every cell.

I spurt long shots of come all over the bed, until I collapse, panting and spent.

She laughs, the best sound, and her teeth graze my shoulder. "You took my cock so well, Wolfie."

"You are... thank you, Ma'am," I lift myself up, but she keeps me there, wrapping her arms around me. She rests her head against my back. I'm drifting on the high.

In the far corner of my mind, I realize that she has gotten off me, my skin cool where her body was, and I hear her in the bathroom.

But I am floating on a thrill of sensation that's so pure that my body feels incredibly heavy but weightless at the same time.

A warm washcloth is pressed against my ass, then she's moving me off the bed, straddling my hips.

She reaches between my legs, cleaning my cock.

"Good boy." Her lips are like heaven on mine as she kisses me, slow and sensual. How pleased she is with me is on her face, her eyes light with admiration and pleasure.

"Let's get you in the shower."

Fortunately, her arm is under mine, helping me up because I'm wobbly on my feet.

Callie guides me into the shower, turns on the taps and soaps my body with her body wash.

"Need clean sheets again," I say against her lips.

"Totally worth it," she kisses me, long and deep, until I mewl under her tongue. "I'm going to do that again."

"Yes!" The bleakness of reality enters my mind, and I shake my head. "I'm sorry I have to leave tomorrow-"

She presses a finger against my lips. "We're not talking about it. It's New Year's Eve, Wolfie. We're spending it together. That's all that matters right now."

With brisk effectiveness, she washes me off, wraps me in a towel.

"Stay here."

I reach for her ass.

She swats my hands away with a smirk. "Later."

I slump against the counter, staring at myself in the mirror.

It's the same face I woke up with today, but *everything* feels different.

In the centre of my soul, I feel peace.

Owned.

"Here," she hands me one of my folded t-shirts and a pair of boxers.

"Thanks." I get them on, still feeling light headed.

I brush my lips against hers, but she breaks off the kiss, grabbing my hand. She brings me to the living room and gently pushes me on the couch.

"You need this," she wraps one of her fuzzy throw blankets over my shoulders.

"No, I don't-"

"Take what you are given, Wolfie."

She twirls her fingers in my hair, makes those calming, soothing circles, then she skips away, to the kitchen.

I hear her rummaging in the fridge, but my eyes are feeling heavy. I grab a pillow from the armchair and snuggle down.

The blanket smells like her, and I snuggle into it.

Callista can still my thoughts, like nothing I have ever experienced before.

She's brought me a peace I have never known, and I'm so hungry for this connection we have to continue.

16 CALLIE

My vagina still tingles from the orgasms I had while pegging Wolfie.

I'm blown away by how he dove in, fully accepting this was happening, and offered me his unfiltered trust.

But that's this gentle, kind man.

He doesn't play games.

His actions have shown me he means what he says... so why do I feel this fractured?

I don't want to hurt him, and my track record with past relationships would say that there is no way this ends without heartbreak.

He's curled up on his side, looking all adorable and sleepy, and after the performance he just gave me back there, he definitely deserves his rest.

I reach for my phone, scrolling through messages I missed. Aunt Millie sent me pics of Daphne at dinner with the kids.

My heart twists, happy for my sister.

For all these months, Daphne getting healthy and things going back to normal is all I wanted.

Then why do I feel like I'm losing my mind, now that it's happening?

Needing to do something, I grab the cleaning supplies under the sink and march into the bathroom.

From the hall closet, I grab a toy cleaner from my stock.

My hand shakes as I detach the dildo from the harness, remembering how Theo felt beneath me.

His sexy back, flexing, as shivers rippled through his muscles, the clench of his ass, the movements pressing against my clit... I shake off the memory and concentrate on cleaning the toys.

That task finished, I gather all the debris in the bathroom, including the kids' toys, and throw it all in a basket.

Then I spray down the shower and tub, spray down the sink and the mirror.

Under the bathroom sink, I find toilet bowl cleaner and then spray it furiously until the toilet is covered with foam.

I grab a clean sponge and start scrubbing.

It's ridiculous, but hot tears are stinging my eyes.

There is no reason why I should be crying right now. I had the *best* sex of my life, like I do every time with Theo.

The fumes make my nostrils hurt.

"Callista?" Theo leans against the doorway, his arms crossed in front of his chest, his cock half hard.

"Hey." I glance up from my scrubbing.

"I think you have covered every surface with some type of cleaner." His lips are upturned in a wry smile.

"Wanted to be thorough." I cough and can't stop coughing.

Theo steps into the bathroom, holds out his hand. "I'll finish here."

"You don't have to." But I put my hand in his. He grabs it, helps me to my feet and walks me out of the room, his hand presses on my back, he guides me to the kitchen and gets me a glass of water.

I drink until the scent of the cleansers is dislodged. "Thanks."

"Is there a reason why you're scrubbing the heck out of the bathroom on New Year's Eve?" His grey eyes glint with amusement.

It makes me want to kiss him.

So I step into his space, put my hand on his bare chest and kiss him and nibble his lower lip, making him groan.

"Something to do." I mumble.

"Sorry I fell asleep on you."

"You needed rest. That was quite a workout." I run my fingers over the bite mark on his shoulder, watching him flinch, yet he leans into me, his breath hitching.

I press harder, feeling the tense ripples of his muscles under my touch.

"Yes, it was." His strong hands slide down to my waist, pulling me against his chest. I let him embrace me, melting against him.

He so good, and I press my face into his warm skin, he breathes a soft groan.

"What is bothering you?" He rubs little circles on my back, easing more of my tension. I could brush him off and tell him nothing.

That'd be the easy way out.

But this boy has given me so much vulnerability and shown me so much strength, that I can't help but give him the same in return.

Even if I don't like the thoughts in my head.

"Guess I'm feeling on the cusp. I don't know what's going to happen. I want Daphne to come back and be healthy and resume her life again, but now that we're close to that... I'm happy, really, but it feels..."

"It's that unknown feeling?"

I glance up at his face and see no judgement, just calm acceptance. "Yes. I don't like that feeling."

"Because that means you're not in control." He brushes a thumb along my jaw with such tenderness, I want to weep.

"I'm not that great at cleaning."

His mouth twitches. "I know that about you. I think I should go clean it up before the chemicals decide to react or something."

"I think that's a very good idea," I brush my hand along his pecs, just because I want to touch him.

"Did you think this is how we'd spend New Year's, with me cleaning your bathroom?" He grins and gives me a little butt shimmy.

"I'm a lucky woman," I press a kiss to his lips. He kisses me back, with one of those growly noises, and then I can't help it. I pull his head closer, slam my lips against his, deepening the kiss, tasting every inch of his mouth. His cock rises between us.

"Later," I give him a quick little pat as he heads toward the bathroom.

"Yes, Ma'am, I can't wait."

I laugh, and the sadness I was feeling lifts away.

That's one of my favourite things about Theo: the boy makes me laugh.

I change into a comfy pair of leggings and a sweater and pause by the bathroom to admire Theo's strong arms flexing as he wipes down all the surfaces. "There, that's done."

"Thank you, boy. It looks great."

A knock sounds on my door. I had almost forgotten about the food I had ordered.

"How's it going out there?" I ask, taking the bags from Allie's brother.

"The rain is starting to change to freezing, but the tips have been good tonight. I'm not complaining!"

I pay for the food, close the door with my foot, and take the bags to the table.

"That smells amazing."

"Wait until you try it."

We unpack the food, exchanging smiles with each other as we plate.

"You would be with your brothers if you weren't here?"

"Yeah, but I talked to them all earlier. Noel isn't at Evan's. I'm not the only brother missing."

"Try this." I lift chopsticks to his mouth, feeding him a bite of the spicy shrimp.

His eyes water, but the sound of pleasure he makes has me reaching out to squeeze his ass.

"That's good."

"We're full of hidden gems in this small town." We bring the food into the living room and sit down together on the floor.

I feed him again, my arm brushes against his, and a rush of desire coils deep inside me, fueled by the heat of his gaze on me.

"Do you feel like you should be there with them?" I shift slightly, ignoring the building ache between my thighs. Later.

"No. When Noel had just lost his wife, we all stayed close, but he seems to be in a better place now. Last time I spoke with Noel, I brushed off his accusation that there was anything between us. Not because I want to hide you..."

"You told Hunter about me."

"Yes, I'm closest to Hunter. I guess I wanted Noel's focus on helping with the legal stuff for Shel's not on our relationship. Maybe I just wanted to keep it to myself. But I did tell my parents."

The sly smile he gives pulls at my heart.

"Yeah?"

"Yes. They're happy that I found a relationship. I told Jayden and Alex, they're the senior members of my team."

"I don't have to worry about a work wife?" I tease, brushing my fingertips along his arm.

He blushes, shaking his head. "No. Jayden is very happy with her wife. She thinks it's about time I had a relationship instead of—"

"What?"

Theo shrugs. "Casual dates that don't last," he leans his head on my shoulder, and I slide my palm on his leg.

"I think we can both leave that behind going into the New Year."

"Oh yes, Ma'am."

I kiss him, tasting chili on his lips. My hand taps his half-hard cock. "It's going to be a very good year."

We seal the words with a long, sweet kiss.

My pussy is throbbing, wanting more.

I kiss him until my lips are swollen. I pull him to his feet, leave him standing there, and then I stride over to the armchair. I toss my clothes off, sit and spread my legs.

The heat of his eyes on me makes my clit throb. I pop a leg on each armchair and drag my finger through my clit.

"This is what you do to me. Show me how much you want to be inside of me, Wolfie."

"Yes, Ma'am!" He basically jumps across the room, kneels between my legs, his hands resting on top of my shins. He parts my labia with a cool, gentle touch.

"Hands behind your back."

His grey eyes are smoky with desire as he meets mine. He laces his hands behind his back.

The way he obeys makes me so pleased. So turned on by his submission.

"Anything for you, Ma'am." His voice is deep, husky, and I lift my hips off the chair in response.

He presses his nose to my seam. I can't help but moan at the first stroke of his tongue. It's methodical, so gentle I want to climb out of my skin.

I grab his hair. "Pick up the pace, Wolfie."

His laughter sends vibrations hitting my clit. But he gets on with it, sucking, lapping, licking, driving me wild with every tease, every pull of his tongue.

"Boy!" My muscles tense like a bow, waiting to be set free, the pleasure hums through my body. He takes my clit in his mouth, sucks hard.

I'm damn close. I want this orgasm so much, but I press my legs against his face and with my fingers still entwined in his hair, I pull up.

The boy takes direction well, because he lets go of my clit but keeps lapping.

"More! I'm almost there!"

My legs are shaking against his face.

Oh my God, I'm so close to coming, the vibrations build up even more, tingles flare across my skin as my need grows and as he works his tongue, it feels like liquid lightning up my core.

"Theo, Theo, Theo!" I gasp out his name as the orgasm pulls me under, sizzling pleasure swimming through my veins. I'm floating in space, nothing matters except this wave that I'm riding. I lean my head back in the chair.

His hot mouth is still on my pussy, licking me with short strokes that make me tremble.

"Come here, boy." My tone is gravelly. I guide Theo's hard cock, loving his whimper as I put his dick exactly where I want it, right in my pussy. The chair shifts below us.

"I think it'll hold us."

"I don't know." Theo brushes his warm lips against my cheek.

"Do you doubt me?" His eyes widen at my change of tone, but I have a relentless desire for what's between us to be real. I want all the evidence I can soak in to squash the doubts in my head once and for all.

"I would never doubt you, Callista." He rubs his lips against my cheek.

I believe him with my whole heart.

I want this man so much that it hurts. I want to take care of him and treasure him and eat food with him on my living room floor every day.

"Good."

"The structural integrity of this chair from the seventies, however," Theo snuggles against my neck, setting off a new wave of heat that arrows to my pussy.

I laugh. "It's probably from the fifties, actually."

"I think we're good though."

"Oh *boy*, we are very good," I purr against his ear. I slide my hands down his waist, drawing him tight against me, feeling the heat of him as I line him up.

When he's hit the right spot, I rise, slowly at first, and lower myself with deliberate control on his iron cock.

His groan is all guttural, making me want more.

"You stay right there and let me do the work. I'm taking what I want."

And I do, pushing myself up and down, claiming control.

"Yes, Ma'am," he grits out through clenched teeth.

The ache is delicious as I rise on his cock again, the sensation almost unbearable.

The stretch burns as I slam down again and fuck, I don't want this to end.

I love teasing him. I love rubbing my pussy against his cock. I love how tense he is, as if he's holding his breath, not wanting to disappoint me.

His brows furrow, his muscles strain with the effort it is taking for him not to move, and that's pleasing me, coating my veins with approval.

I grind myself on his throbbing cock, and this is exactly how I want it.

"Your cock feels amazing. I love watching how the tip of your cock disappears into my pussy."

He lets out a low moan. His eyes are hazy, and I laugh and kiss him.

As my lips meet his, he responds instantly, all that pent-up passion erupting as his lips crash into mine, fierce and unrelenting. I rock forward, digging into his shoulders, and slam myself down on his cock/

"Oh, fuck, Ma'am!" He closes his eyes, and I thrust my hips forward.

"Take me, Theo. Show me how much you want me."

His eyes open, and they gaze at me with such love and need and want, I lose my breath. His cock moves in me, slow at first as he thrusts deep, then he lifts me up, shifts me forward, and he's pumping into me, so powerfully I feel stretched to my limit.

It's exactly what I want. I snake my hand to his neck, feeling the pulse of his heartbeat beneath my fingers as I give it a firm squeeze.

He might be fucking me, but every inch of him inside me is at my command, every movement controlled by my touch.

Our moans collide, hot and breathy, filling the air as we rock together. The chair creaks under us. Every thrust of his cock makes me burn for him, sending my pleasure soaring.

"Deeper, Wolfie! Harder!"

He grunts, thrusting deeper, sweat slick on his chest.

I'm going to explode. "Now Theo! Come in me right now!"

He pants against my ear, thrusts once more, so hard the chair vibrates under us. "Callista! You're beautiful!"

His eyes close tightly, his body tensing as he lets out his release. I clench around his softening cock, feeling him jerk beneath me, a whimper escaping his lips.

"Good boy, Wolfie." I kiss chin, his ear, under his eyes, his jawline. He drops his head to my chest, sighing like a contented wolf.

The chair squeaks at that moment.

Theo untangles himself, lifts me up just in time, because the back leg of the chair breaks off.

"It almost held," Theo grins.

"It was so worth it," I laugh, and catching sight of the time, I sling an arm around him. "We're just in time for the countdown."

Theo grabs his phone from the corner of the coffee table and finds the ball drop feed.

"Here we go." He nuzzles against me, placing his chin in the crook of my clavicle.

"Five." My voice breaks on the word.

"Four." He holds my hand.

"Three." We say together.

"Two," Theo whispers.

"One!" I lift his chin to mine, kiss him.

He drops his phone, wraps his arms around me and we sway together, our lips fused.

My cheek is wet with tears when I break off the kiss, but I wipe them away with the back of my hand. Theo glances away, pretending he doesn't notice.

I start to gather the plates, and Theo chips in and silently we clean the space. After the dishes are in the sink, I press the palm of my hand to his ass and push him towards the bedroom.

"Let's start the New Year how I intend to spend it... with you in my bed."

Theo shimmies his hips, making me laugh, and we tumble onto the bed.

"Happy New Year, Callista," Theo says.

"Happy New Year, boy."

I don't know what this year is going to bring, but I know I don't want it to be without him.

17

THEO

"Did I mention I just shaved my legs?" Callie says teasingly.

I close the file I had been reviewing, settle back in my desk chair, giving her my full attention.

"Anything you do makes me horny."

Callie laughs. "I like hearing that, Mr. Sexypants. Does that mean you're hard for me right now?"

The Domme knows how to push my buttons. I'm scrambling out of my chair, walking to the door to make sure it's locked.

I lean against the door, my mouth dry as she shows me a picture of her bare legs, stopping just above the hem of her skirt.

"I'm always hard for you, Callista."

"Get that beautiful dick out and start stroking it."

All the blood rushes to my cock. I unzip my pants, shove them down. My hand grabs my cock.

"Thank you, Ma'am, for letting me touch my cock."

"You're such a good boy. I know you haven't had a release in a couple of days."

"Four. But who's counting?" The reminder has me grinding my molars.

"You better believe I am." My head tips back against the wall, my cock throbs, growing harder in my hand as I stroke it up and down.

In my mind, I am seeing her with her legs spread in the armchair; her legs spread wide, her nipples rosy.

"I miss having you in my bed. I love having your back to my front." Her tone changes from breezy and light to lower, sensual.

I groan as my cock starts leaking.

"I love being in your bed. I miss kissing you."

My jaw clenches. I want to hold off as long as possible, but my cock is twitching, it's not going to take long.

"I miss kissing you."

"What else do you miss?" I can hear that slow, sly smile in her voice.

"I miss feeling your ass in my hands. I miss tasting your skin."

"I'm going to take your cock into my mouth and suck it so good next time we are together. What else would you like me to do, Wolfie?"

"I want..."

"Yes? I hope your hand is still on your cock and you haven't come yet."

"I haven't, Ma'am."

"I know," Callie laughs. "Tell me what you want me to do next time we see each other."

My mouth goes dry. I close my eyes, needing to take myself mentally out of my office.

"I want you to tie me up. I want you to tease me and have your way with me."

I'm blushing like crazy, even though she can't see me. I curl my fingers into a fist, my shoulders hunch with the tension that slithers through my body.

"Boy, I can't wait to tie you up and put my mouth on your nipples, run my hands down your chest, till I get to your cock. And then I get to play with it. That makes me so hot, I'm almost ready to come. What about you, Wolfie? Think you can come for me right now?"

My hips thrust up off the wall. I'm pumping into my hand with such force, I'm biting on my lip to keep from shouting.

"Yes, Ma'am!"

"Good boy, Wolfie. Ten..."

"I don't know if I can make it!" My muscles tense, trying to hold back.

"Yes, you can, Wolfie. You're a good boy. You will not lose control. Nine..."

I'm leaking pre-cum all over my hand; my legs are shaking with the effort of staying up right. I visualize Callie's fingers playing with her clit.

My mouth waters, like I can taste the salty sweetness of her clit on my tongue.

"Eight. Send me a picture." Her command makes me whimper, but I grit my teeth, stopping myself from spilling with an iron will, and I snap a pic, send it to her, and wrap my hand around my cock again.

"Oh, it's such a nice cock. It looks so big. What a pretty cock. Seven." Her voice is liquid honey, warm and smooth, making me want to please her.

"Ma'am! I'm so close." But I want to please her.

"I know you are, baby. Play with those balls. I'm sure they need some attention. Give them a nice pull for me."

Oh, geez, the entire world is shrinking to my hand on my cock, my panting breath. I do as I'm ordered, cupping my balls, I give them a good yank, letting out a groan this is so maddening and I want to please her, to hold off but as my balls tighten, I don't know if I can.

"I love hearing those sounds, Wolfie. Give me more of them. Let me hear how much you want this release."

"Please Ma'am! I need this! I'm close," I let out another loud groan. It echoes around the room as my cock pulsates in my hand, pre-cum spewing even more.

"Six. Five. Four... slap the head of your cock, Wolfie. Now."

"Ma'am!" I cry out, but I bring my hand down until the head of my cock turns red, shouting as the self-inflicted spank hurts.

"You're a good boy, Wolfie. You're going to come for me. Three."

"Please, please, Ma'am, I need to come."

"Two... now Wolfie, one!"

An inferno swallows me whole as I give in to the release. Stars dance behind my eyes. I tug my cock furiously, panting as the orgasm breaks open over me in a white feverish need.

Hot cum spills all over my hand.

My legs feel like they're going to give out, and I slide down to the floor

A soft chuckle rings out in my ear. "It's so fun to play with my boy in the middle of the day. "You good?"

"So much better now, Ma'am. Thank you for the release." I get up and stride across the office to my small private bathroom.

"You're very welcome. What's next for your day?"

It amazes me how Callie goes from getting me all riled up to talking about mundane things.

I wash my hands, taking a moment to gather myself before answering her.

"Have a meeting with a client over dinner and then I'm going to FaceTime with Hunter and Noel. We are planning Evan's birthday party."

"You guys have been working on that party for a while."

Holding the phone against my shoulder with my ear, I wash my hands and splash my face clean.

"It's the first time all four of us are going to see each other in a while. Callista, do you want to come with me to Evan's party?" I hold my breath, even as I utter the invitation.

I believe Callie when she says she wants this relationship between us, and there is no denying how much she cares for me. But she's wrestling with her own conflicts, and I don't know exactly why, but I think the thought of being seen with me in public is making her nervous.

"You know, being a four-hour drive away from each other is pissing me off. Uncle Henry's birthday is also that weekend. We're having a small party at home."

"What if you came to me after your uncle's party?"

"Daphne is still doing well at home with the care they have coming to the house, but I feel like I have to stay close. Aunt Millie might need me, and I don't want my staff at Shel's to be overworked."

I swallow the disappointment, pressing my tongue to the roof of my mouth.

We agreed to take our time, to take this relationship as slow as we both need.

"Hey, no problem. It was just an idea." I fail to keep the disappointment out of my tone.

"Theo, it's not that I don't want to be seen with you."

"I know, Callista. I know how you feel about me."

"Thanks for understanding, Wolfie. Sometimes the distance between us is annoying." Her voice sounds so small. I wish I were there to comfort her, to hold her in my arms and dot her face with kisses.

"When you're ready, I can't wait to show you off." As I move back into my office, there's a knock at my door.

"That's a kind thing to say, boy."

"You're amazing. Got to go, someone's at my door."

"Call me before you go to sleep."

"Yes, Ma'am."

I end the call, open my door to find Jayden, running her hand through her short spiky hair.

"Everything okay?"

"There's a man here who insists on seeing you. He says that he needs an update immediately."

On purpose, my office isn't flashy, and there's no sign advertising that we are here. Most of the experts who work for me, work remotely. We go to clients.

I follow Jayden out to the front office, which consists of her desk, a desk for my employee Alex, whose home is being renovated.

"He's right there," Jayden says, going back to her desk.

He doesn't turn around. He doesn't have to.

It's how all the energy in the room tunnels toward him, because he's in it.

Cyrus Sebastian Rawlings, in the flesh.

His black hair, his wool jacket, the way he's standing bring back a wave of memories that I push away.

"You could have called." I turn on my heel before he turns around. He follows me back to my office.

"I needed to see you." Hearing his voice in my office makes the mask I wear at work wobble for a moment.

But this man hurt my brother.

I won't forgive him for that.

"I just read through Morgana's case. It looks like all measures are in place and reports have been filed with the cybercrime unit. Is there anything else we can do for her?" I shove my hands into my pockets to keep him from seeing them tremble.

Cyrus crosses his arms as I lean against the small window.

His deep brown eyes bore into me with an intensity that makes most people squirm.

He cocks an eyebrow. "How is he?"

"Fine."

As grateful as I am for this man's help, the hurt he caused my brother is too much to ignore.

"Theo..." Cyrus strides over to my small seating area and sits on the couch.

After a moment, I take the seat across from him.

"How is he?" His eyes are filled with pain as he asks me, his voice breaking.

"Last time I saw him, his apartment was a mess, but he was fine. Until I told him you had called me."

"What did he say?" His tone is gruff, like he's holding back emotion.

"That I could work for anyone I wanted, but he wondered if you had told me to tell him."

Cyrus shakes his head. "I guess he knows me pretty well."

"I guess so."

"Where is he staying?"

I shift in my seat. I know Hunter loved Cyrus and thought he was going to be with him forever.

But after five years... I don't know what this man wants.

"I want to make it up to him, Theo. I need to see him."

If I tell Hunter that Cyrus wants to see him, that puts the ball in Hunter's court, but it also puts the emotional burden on Hunter.

I don't want to add that kind of emotional stress to my brother.

"Cy, I don't know if I can help you."

"Please." He blinks at me with those serious eyes.

Something in me balks at the sight of this man—asking, begging me for what he wants.

"We've worked hard on Evan's birthday party. Can you wait until after that to see him?"

Cyrus's mouth sets in a hard line. "Yeah. I can do that. You'll tell me where he is then?"

"You know, Hunter. He doesn't like to stay in one place for too long." I don't want to promise him anything.

"Yeah." Cyrus stands, holds out his hand.

I clasp it. "You were good for him. For a while."

Cyrus nods, glancing away. "Thanks for looking after Morgana."

"Of course."

I watch him go, his stance lighter, and I wonder if I am going to do the right thing.

I haven't given him anything yet, but I know I will—and I hope my brother doesn't hate me for it.

18

CALLIE

FEBRUARY 3RD

"I can drop the kids off, I don't mind." My tone comes out like I'm an eager puppy, and wince.

The Domme side of me that is usually dormant while I'm with my family, cringes.

"It's on our way. This gives you time to spend with Daphne," Aunt Millie says, patting my arm.

"Callie, you've got to talk to her at some point," Uncle Henry says. He gives Aunt Millie's cheek a kiss. "I can't believe you got a lead on the Cobra roadster."

"Yes, I did! Perfect timing," Aunt Millie gushes.

Uncle Henry grins, his eyes sparkling behind his thick glasses. "Even if my bank account says no, I still want to look."

"I'm looking forward to a night at the hot springs!" Aunt Millie says. "Come on, kids!"

"They're saying goodbye to Daphne." I tell her.

Aunt Millie frowns, the joy leaving her face. "I know it's hard on Daphne not being able to look after them herself overnight. The nurse is coming at ten, Callie."

"I know." I say and smile through the knot in my stomach.

"Grady's parents really want to take them to the waterpark, and this was the only weekend they could do it." My aunt squeezes my shoulder.

The kids' grandparents came for Uncle Henry's birthday dinner as a surprise for the kids.

"I'm happy for them," Daphne says, coming into the kitchen with Luke holding her hand.

"Oh! We didn't know you were up. Are you okay?" Aunt Millie rushes over to Daphne.

"Fine with this little guy," Daphne says and runs her hand through Luke's hair and grinning, he ducks under her touch.

"Mommy!"

The happiness on Daphne's face is like looking at her old self even as she wobbles on her feet and grabs the counter and then she points at me.

"Me and you. Girls' night."

"Yeah, it's girls' night." I grit out.

My sister's progress has sped up, though she still misses words, but she's so much better. The physical therapy sessions are helping.

But yeah, my uncle is right; at some point I have to talk to her.

I've tried to avoid her.

Guilt is a cruel mistress.

"Mads! Abby! Time to go!" Uncle Henry calls.

Daphne hugs Luke, coos softly to him, so I can't make out the words, but the lump in my throat makes it hard to swallow.

"Do I have to go?" Madison says, coming into the kitchen with the kids' bags.

"Yes. You do," Daphne says.

Her words come out so clear, with no stutter that it makes everyone in the kitchen go still and Madison smiles, and hugs her mom.

"Okay, I'll go."

"Be good," Daphne brushes a piece of hair off of Madison's face.

Uncle Henry blinks back tears, and I look away because I know we are all thinking the same thing.

For months we wondered if Daphne would be okay. If she'd be able to come back to us and be the mother she's always wanted to be.

Seeing these little everyday interactions between her and her kids is making us cry like babies.

"This girl is always good," Auntie Millie says, giving Madison's shoulder a squeeze. The kids give me hugs, hug their mom one last time.

Moments later, Uncle Henry and Aunt Millie leave for their overnight trip, and I'm left with my sister alone in her house.

"You can go," Daphne says, sitting on a stool at the counter. "Don't need a babysitter."

Her speech might be slow. Her movements might be a little awkward. But that haughty, superior tone is my sister.

"Where would I go? I've spent barely any time with you since you've been home."

"Noticed."

"I've been busy."

Daphne turns her head and raises her eyebrows. "With what?"

"I don't know, running Shel's. Looking after some amazing gorgeous kids."

She grabs my hand. At first, I think it's for balance, because she leans over the chair, then I realize she's crying.

"Dammit. Daph, I didn't want you to cry." I pull a kitchen towel off the stove handle and dab at her eyes with it.

She swats it away, but her hand tightens on mine. I drape my arm over her shoulders. "I'm sorry, Daphne, so sorry the accident happened."

"Not your fault." She shakes her head.

"I should have been here."

She scrunches her face up. "You came back. I'm happy you came back."

A choked sob garbles her words, but I understand the meaning.

"Let's go into the living room. Your couch is so comfy," I guide her up from her seat, and she holds onto my arm for support.

She flops onto the couch, closing her eyes.

"You're tired? We don't have to do anything. I thought we could watch a movie and have snacks, but I can help you to bed."

"No. No movie. Hurts my eyes. Snacks, yes. Candy," Daphne grins at me, and she looks so young, so much like my sister, I lean down and hug her, brushing my lips across her forehead.

"I missed you."

"Me too. No candy at the therapy place. Unless Grady brought it."

I didn't think of bringing my sister candy.

"Sorry Daphne, I should have brought you some."

She shrugs. "You couldn't have known. You cleaned up my room, moving... like a...," she brings her hands together.

"Like a butterfly?"

"Yes. Always Callie on the go."

"I didn't like seeing you there."

"I didn't like being there." Daphne reaches for a tissue on the side table and blows her nose.

"I'll be back with snacks. And nail polish," I say as inspiration hits.

"In my bathroom upstairs."

"Okay!" I squeeze her shoulder, then go up the carpeted stairs, down the narrow hallway to my sister and Grady's bedroom, grab the nail supplies.

I'm racing downstairs when my phone chirps from the coffee table.

"Here we go. Silver or purple?"

Daphne points to silver. I sit next to her and start in on her nails.

"Thanks. You were always better at this."

"There's not much I'm better at."

"You're better at leaving."

I bite the inside of my cheek, not wanting to say something that I'll regret.

Daphne is still in a fragile state, and I already upset her once this evening, but her comment stings.

I blink back tears as my phone rings again.

"Who's calling?" Daphne nods towards my phone.

"Theo," his name is out of my lips before I can hold it back. Maybe I wanted to say it because thinking of my boy brings me comfort.

Maybe I wanted to see the look on Daphne's face.

But regret washes over me.

I concentrate on finishing her nails, then cap the bottle of polish.

"There, you need to dry."

"Tell me about Theo."

But I don't want to. Daphne's never approved of my relationships.

She and Grady have been together forever, and I think that makes it hard for her to understand casual dating.

I've been judged by her in the past, even before the whole John thing, and her criticisms land in a way that nobody else's would.

"Nobody tells me anything. Everyone treats me as if I am going to break."

"You are fragile right now," I curl into the corner of the couch, taking my phone out of my pocket. I scroll to a selfie of Theo and me and flip the phone screen to show her.

"He's so handsome. You met online?"

"No. His truck broke down right outside of Shel's."

Daphne's eyes go wide, then she laughs so hard her face turns red and her eyes water.

"It's not that funny." I get up to get her a glass of water.

She sips the water, looks at me, giggles. "It is funny. Did you ever think you'd meet anyone at Shel's? You go all over the place looking for men. One lands in your lap right outside your front door."

I bite the inside of my cheek. "I don't go, 'all over the place looking for men'." Yeah, she's annoying.

"You've driven eight hours just for a date before, Callie."

"That was once." I glare at my sister, heat climbing up my neck. I wish her opinion didn't bother me, but it does.

That was years ago, right when I was exploring being a Domme for the first time.

It was at a private party in Tofino, and I met a lot of new friends.

The guy and I enjoyed a weekend together, and then I came home.

"I would never do that." Her speech might be slurred, but the judgmental tone comes through, clear as crystal.

"We can't all marry our high school sweethearts." I sit back down. "Where does Theo live?"

"In Vancouver, but we're making it work."

"That's only four hours. Not far. When you break up with him, you won't run into him around town."

You can't throttle your sister. She's recovering from a brain injury.

I get up from the couch and start cleaning things.

I wish Theo were waiting for me back at my apartment or that he had come to this dinner with me.

Or that I had gone with him to his brother's birthday party.

In so many ways, Daphne has had it easy.

Before the brain injury.

Oh God, I know I am a terrible person. I finish emptying the dishwasher.

Daphne yawns, stretches her arms above her head. "Next girls' night, can we go out?"

"You want to?"

"I'm tired of being inside. Want to see Shel's. Grady said we'd go on Sunday."

"It's the same as usual. Nothing changes."

"At least you can count on that." My sister rubs her eyes, and for a moment, she looks so small and broken that my anger—her words having landed in wounds I still carry—eases.

I sit next to her, pulling her beside me in a hug.

"I'm really glad to have you home."

"You too. Me too. I'm happy you're here."

"Thanks."

"Can you call the kids for me? I am going to go to bed."

"Sure. Do you want help upstairs first?"

"Yeah." She stands, wobbles and then reaches for my arm. "Sorry."

"It's okay." I wish she were apologizing for the hurt she caused me and not for needing my help, but that's a selfish need of mine.

We make it over to the stairs; her face drains of colour from the effort.

"Everyone treats me like I'm broken. I know I am." She slides to the bottom step, and I sit next to her.

"You're going to get through this, Daphne. We're here for you."

"I know. I didn't expect Shel's to still be open."

"It's a family legacy, right?" I offer her my arm again. "Ready to try?"

"Yeah. The first few nights I was home, I slept on the couch, but I want to get back to normal." Her body tenses with the effort it takes her to climb each stair, but we make it to her bedroom.

I help her change into pajamas and then I tuck her in, giving her my phone to talk to the kids.

While she's talking to them, I tidy up the hallway and lower the lights. She's hanging up when my phone buzzes.

"From Theo." Daphne giggles as she hands me the phone. "It must be nice to have fun."

I have nothing to be embarrassed about, but my face is hot.

> *Have a good night, Ma'am. I wonder if I'll dream about how your pussy tastes or how your cock felt in my ass?*

"Yep. I like having fun with Theo." Did I say it just to make her uncomfortable? Yeah.

"Is he a good guy?"

"The best," I mumble. "Daphne, what happened to your phone? Grady couldn't find it after the accident."

Her eyes glaze over, and I curse myself for asking.

"I don't know. Getting me a new one has been on the list."

I don't want to leave her alone at night, but everything in me wants to bail.

This night has brought up a lot of emotions, and I don't know what to do with them

Other than get in my car, drive four hours, and jerk my boy off over and over again until he's dry

Or edge him until he begs me, in that hopeful, needy way that makes me want to give in and hold off while staring into those smoky eyes of his.

"Callie, the doorbell. The nurse is probably here. You can go."

I know Grady will be home in a couple of hours and that my sister is safe, but I feel so guilty as I kiss her cheek and say goodnight.

Forcing myself to take the stairs slowly, I let the nurse in, throw my jacket on, and grab my car keys.

Daphne is home, and everything is returning to normal.

But I don't know what I want my normal to be.

19

THEO

FEBRUARY 14TH

It's just a dumb Hallmark holiday.

But telling myself that doesn't make the awareness of this day any less, nor does it dull how much I want to see Callie today.

It does nothing to cool down my half-erection as I think about how much I want to kiss those soft lips of hers, run my hands over her cleavage, feel her hot mouth on my cock.

Eight days since she's allowed me to release.

It's wearing on my nerves.

There comes a point in orgasm denial where the feelings of arousal and the subspace I get from being denied turn to frustration that borders on the edge of resentment.

This is the first time I've experienced that with Callie. I know it's natural, but I don't like having a negative thought directed at her.

I do my best to push the feelings down and climb my way through the backlog of emails.

My phone buzzes with a text.

> How is my Wolfie doing? I'll see you soon, boy.

I open the attachment.

Seeing her cleavage sends all the blood right to my cock. I can't help myself. I'm out of my chair, marching into my bathroom.

> Not soon enough…

The weekend is three days away, and that's the next time I'm driving down to Rising Harbour. My phone buzzes with another photo.

A cleavage shot, but without the lacey black bra, with Callie's nipple pinched between her thumb and index finger.

My hand is working my fly down, even as I know I'm going to regret it. But I can't focus on work; I'm crawling out of my skin.

I *need* to come.

Closing my eyes, I think of her in those purple boots that hug her calves, of her striking her crop on my ass.

I long for her touch with such force that I'm panting with need. I take my cock in my hand and stroke it long and slow.

It's so sensitive, it tingles in my hand. I'm already leaking pre-cum.

I wish Callie were here to stop me—or to ruin my orgasm.

Or to plunge her fake cock into my ass, commanding me to come for her.

My body shudders as my balls tighten, and I can't stop myself from pumping my cock in my fist, thinking of my gorgeous Ma'am.

"Fuck!" I tilt my head back, feeling her hands roam over my body, as my liquid fire strikes the base of my cock.

I'm coming so fast and hard my legs tremble. I bite back a groan as I come all over my hand.

"Fuck," I say it again, as I wash my hands, and stare at myself in the mirror, my cheeks flushed.

I agreed to give my orgasms to Callie.

I just broke that agreement, and a hollow, empty feeling comes over me, and so does the memory of my ex's words.

But they're chased by the memory of Callie cupping my face, telling me I was a good boy.

I hang on to that as I finish tidying up, then return to my desk.

> Ma'am... I'm sorry. I needed a release so badly. I couldn't wait.

The jerking off made me feel physically better, so I put my head down, turn to the pile of work I have, including a conference call with two of my employees, and I don't even notice the time, until Jayden knocks on my door

"Hey boss."

I glance at the clock. "What are you still doing here? Go get your wife. Have a good night."

"Thanks, Theo. " Jayden gives me a wave, and I go back to my screens. Half an hour later, I'm interrupted by the buzz from the door.

I check the security camera, then shut down my systems and grab my bag, smiling as I open the door.

"What brings you here?" I say after letting Hunter inside.

"Figured we could grab a beer." Hunter flashes me a smile.

At Evan's birthday party, he seemed better than the time I saw him in his apartment. I had no idea he was still in town.

"Sounds good," I say, locking the door and following my brother down the steps. "I didn't know you were still here."

"I've got some work to do. Here for a few more days."

"Where are you staying?"

"Parents."

I take that as a further good sign because if Hunter was still in his funk, he wouldn't want to stay with them.

We take my car and find a sports bar and a booth in the back.

We order burgers and fries, cold beer.

"I was thinking of hitting Club Shivers tonight." Hunter glances away from me, spins his beer around on the coaster.

"Yeah? I haven't been there in ages."

Hunter and I are both members of the upscale private BDSM club. I hate crowds, but sometimes I need what the club provides. And my ex loved the place.

"I thought that, and then it felt empty, you know? Like I was seeking sex just because of some dumb day."

"A Hallmark holiday." We clink our beers together.

"I blame the parents for this, you know? All those lovey-dovey things dad does for mom. Notes every morning." Hunter rolls his eyes.

"He sends her a dozen red roses."

"And don't forget the chocolate that she pretends she doesn't want."

"And then he takes her out for dinner."

"They're going to a murder mystery dinner tonight. Can you believe that?"

I think of how much I want to take Callie out. "Lucky fuckers."

Hunter tips his glass towards me. "Exactly. It's amazing how we all ended up in screwed up relationships."

"That's not their fault."

"I don't know. We were shown a standard that is hard to meet."

"I think we were shown be," I take a sip of my beer, and Hunter runs his hand through his hair.

"I miss them."

Asking about Cyrus was on the tip of my tongue but I stop myself, cluing into the fact that Hunter said, "them."

"Want to come back to my place? Shoot some pool."

"Sounds good."

I settle the tab and we ride over to my apartment, Hunter is silently staring out the window.

I want to ask him who it was he was talking about missing but I also don't want to fish for something he doesn't want to tell me yet.

"Can't wait to beat you."

"When have you ever beaten me at pool?" Hunter asks as he racks the balls.

"It's happened."

"In your dreams."

We play and Hunter is laser-focused on making his pocket shot with the same concentration he used to have for scoring goals. "Why aren't you with Callie tonight?"

"She's at her niece's school volunteering for the kids' Valentine's Day party."

One of the things I love about Callie is how she is always there for her people. Even if I want to be with her tonight, I respect her obligations.

"Noel said something about turning her diner into a kinky bed-and-breakfast?" Hunter waggles his eyebrows.

"I was joking. The diner's really cool though. It looks like something out of a movie set."

"Maybe I'll visit one day." Hunter lands his shot in the corner pocket. I stand, taking my shot, miss. But I nail it the second time.

"I'm thinking of where to live next." Hunter glances at me, searching my face.

"Yeah?"

"Mom thinks I should move back here, but I don't think there's much work for me out here."

"We have stuff for you to do with the Consortium."

"I don't mind helping Noel around his properties but that's not a day to day job," Hunter lands another pocket, because everything my younger brother does is a success.

"Theo..." His tone changes to being serious and I take notice.

I lean my pool cue against the wall. "What is it, Hunter?"

"I've been offered a coaching job. In Latvia."

"A coaching job?" Hunter has said that he never wanted anything to do with hockey again.

My doorbell chimes. I'm so rattled by his words that I brush past him and go right to the door without checking my security feed.

"Callista." My heart leaps and I want to sweep her into my arms.

She's here, on my step. Her hair swept up in a messy bun, a swish of purple eyeshadow bringing out those deep blues of her eyes.

Standing right in front of me, wearing a leather jacket that hits her waist, jeans that hug her ass, and a low lacey blouse.

"Hi Mr. Sexypants." She pushes me playfully inside the apartment, closes my door, and then grabs a handful of my shirt, with the most gorgeous smile on her face.

I go with her movement, letting her spin me so my back against her door, she cups my face in my hands and kisses me.

Damn. What was my name again? She kisses me like she wants to ravish every part of me.

Her scent fills my nostrils, goes right into my bloodstream.

My cock presses against my zipper.

She puts her hand on my hard cock through my pants.

I moan against her lips, break off the kiss.

"You're here."

"Surprise," she twirls her fingers through my hair, then pulls my hair lightly. This close, I can see the sparkles in her lip gloss and I need another taste of her.

I lean forward. She laughs against my lips, brushing her nose against mine

A long, passionate kiss that steals my breath.

Her tongue strokes mine as we moan against each other, vibrations that go right to my cock

She cups her palm against my cheek, breaking off the kiss. "Good Wolfie, down now boy."

Swallowing, I sink to my knees in front of her on the floor.

She pulls my face against her crotch.

This is... Callie's presence, her aura, is the peace I've been searching for ever since I last left her.

This is what I need—to please this woman right here.

Nothing else in the world matters. I rub my fingers against her jeans, inching them up to her ass, my eyes fluttering closed as she strokes my hair.

"What if I told you I came all this way so I could have my way with you?" Her eyes glimmer with amusement, her tone sultry.

"Thank you Ma'am!"

Her laugh makes me grin up at her, basking in her gaze. "But I saw your text. I thought you were saving all your cum for me." She makes a tsking noise and gives my hair a hard enough tug that makes me wince.

"I'm sorry Ma'am, I really wanted to. I like that you have that control over me but thinking about you makes me so wild, I couldn't hold it back."

"I know you're a very good boy, Wolfie, shh," Her palm presses against my face, and her foot nudges between my knees.

I gulp back a sob, the relief of knowing she isn't going to hurt me or reject me, enveloping me whole. The trance is broken by soft footsteps.

Hunter.

"I'm interrupting. I'll get going."

I shift on my knees, starting to stand, embarrassment heating my cheeks, but Callie's firm touch keeps me in place.

"Callie Tremblay. You must be Hunter."

"I am. Nice to meet you."

Callie slides her hand off my shoulder and extends it to me, inviting me to rise. My face is as hot as hell as I turn to my brother.

But his eyes are amused, there's a smirk on his face.

"Theo didn't know I was coming. I surprised him. I'm the one who interrupted you two."

"We were just shooting pool." Hunter shrugs but I see the disappointment flash in his eyes.

"I'm good at pool. Stay, Hunter. We can get to know each other a little."

"I don't want to be a third wheel on your Valentine's Day." His tone turns bitter.

"You're not! Theo hasn't had a chance to introduce me to any of his family or friends yet. Besides, I'm way too tired from my drive. Theo foiled my plans," Callie gives me a wink that makes my cheeks burn hot.

"Hunter, stay and hang out with us. Can you be on my team? I don't want Callie to know how bad I am at pool."

My brother chuckles his blue eyes filled with an ease I haven't seen in so long. "Callie, we're going to crush him, aren't we?"

"Definitely. I like busting his balls ever so often," She slaps my ass and walks over to Hunter, sliding her arm through his. "Show me to the pool table."

Knowing my balls aren't going to get any attention tonight, makes me grind my molars but I trample down the frustration that's kind of delicious and get in line behind them.

20

CALLIE

FEBRUARY 15TH

Theo presses his bum against my front, sleepily stretching beside me.

He's so adorable, with half-closed eyes and a curved smile on his face. I love being in bed with him first thing in the morning. He stops my thoughts from going on to my to-do list.

"Good morning, Callista."

I love the way he says my name, like every syllable has meaning.

"Good morning, Wolfie. Ready to wake up?" My hands dance over his pecs, brush down his chest, cupping his balls gently.

"Do we have to leave this bed?" He turns in my arms, brushes his lips against mine.

I laugh. "I guess you could lick my pussy before breakfast." I turn, so I'm on my back, my hand cradling his cheek.

"Yes, Ma'am." He moves down my body, peppering me with little kisses, but I tug him back up, wanting to kiss him. I fist his hair, tilting his face up.

"You're so eager, but we're going to go at *my* pace this morning." I trace his top lip gently with my tongue before cupping his nape.

He lets out a sweet groan, and I kiss him, a hungry kiss, driven by need.

I don't have much going for me. Technically, I have no job.

If you want to get really technical, I don't even have a home of my own.

But somehow, I have this gorgeous, submissive man in bed with me.

My nipples draw tight, so I shove his head down. "Carry on, Wolfie."

"Yes, Ma'am."

His lips around my nipple wake up a deep, aching need in my pussy.

I push his head down, wanting more pressure, lightly scratching his back. "I like that, boy."

He keeps it up, sensations ping-pong through my body as he suckles my nipple, setting off a throb between my legs.

The moan I release hums through me, wanting to come apart under his hot mouth right now.

My hips arch off the bed. To slow it down, and to remind Theo I'm still in charge, I pull his head up, lean towards him and kiss him, slowly, before I push his head right into my other nipple. I stretch out on the bed, my hands tracing the path between his broad shoulders, while enjoying the sight of my sub pleasuring me.

He whimpers around my nipple, the pleasure surging to my veins, but I want more.

I want his mouth between my legs.

Letting out a half-scream, I swing my leg over his back, press my heel on his ass.

His head lifts off, his grey eyes shining.

"Lower, boy."

He kisses my stomach, sweeping his hand between my legs. I spread my legs wide, pressing on his shoulders with my heels.

The first swipe of his tongue has me whimpering like an animal in heat.

Gasping, I feel his tongue on my clit, fluttering in a one-two rhythm, and I can't help but moan, yearning for more.

His tongue. So fucking good.

I clasp my legs around his face, press his head down, keeping him there.

His mouth claims my pussy lips with fierce urgency, like he needs to taste every piece of me.

I yank his head up and scoot down so I can kiss him hard and fast. I taste myself on his mouth.

"You're making me feel so needy, boy. Finish me." I push his head back between my legs, keeping my fingers twirled in his hair.

He inhales my clit, sucking hard on it like it's his favourite treat.

My toes point, I feel his cheekbones against my legs, and he looks so hot right now.

"Good boy. Keep it up, I'm so close!" The word tears from my lips as he moves his head up and down, swirling his tongue over my plumped-up nerves.

My hips arch off the bed in time with his long, quick sucks.

Pulses roll through my body, setting me aflame with all-consuming ecstasy.

I pull on his hair, silky strands caught between my fingertips, as my neck strains back.

The pleasure rolls through me in a wave I can't control. It crashes through me, tingling hot sensations through every particle.

"Fuck, boy! I'm coming!"

I'm gasping for breath as the orgasm explodes, sending me into a mind-blowing climax that leaves my legs shaking.

If I could wake up in bed every morning with Theo Brennon between my legs, I'd be a happy woman.

Then why don't you?

If I told him I wanted that, I know he'd walk through fire to make it happen. He'd give up everything in his life to accommodate me. And I can't ask him to do that.

"Stop, boy." I let go of his hair but keep my hand on his neck.

"Come here," I open my arms.

He slides against me, and I snuggle against him, back to the position we were in when we woke up this morning.

"Thanks for giving me a great start to my day. You take the first shower, I'll make breakfast." I brush the head of his cock with my fingertips, circling it lightly. "You can be a good boy and wait until I take your cum, right?"

"Yes, Ma'am. Soon please?" He gives me a cheeky grin that makes me laugh. I ruffle his hair, and he leans into my palm, making that adorable purring noise.

"Someone should have thought of that before they jerked off in their office yesterday." I gently slap his ass as I get up, grabbing my robe from where Theo hung it up for me last night after his brother left. Theo gets up, comes behind me, doing up my belt of the robe. "I love waking up beside you."

"Ditto. Now get showering."

Everything has its place in Theo's kitchen.

It's all sleek, deep-tone backsplash, wooden cabinets that look like they came out of a glossy magazine and stainless steel appliances.

I feel out of place, like I'm playing house somewhere unfamiliar, and I guess that's true, but as I open the fridge and rummage for breakfast ingredients, I relax.

I make the coffee and check my phone, making sure Daphne and the kids are all right.

I'm replying to Grady when a text from Amy appears.

> Hey! We're in the city. Want to bring your boy toy to Club Shivers tonight?

My mind floats off in a rush of possibilities. I haven't been to Club Shivers in forever. The last time I was there, I went with Amy and the FemDom social group I belong to.

> He's more than a boy toy, I'll have you know.

I throw together eggs and bacon while sipping Theo's really good coffee, thinking the possibility over.

He said he wants to take me out, but I don't know if a club environment is what he had in mind.

And if we go to the club and he meets my friends, does this make it more real? More permanent?

A ball of anxiety forms deep in my belly, but then I think of how hanging out with Hunter last night came so naturally.

I told Theo to tell me if he fell in love with me.

But he doesn't have to say it for me to know how he feels.

He has to say it because if he wants more with me, then my boy has to ask for it.

"Thanks for making breakfast, Callista." I step over to Theo, run my hand through his freshly washed hair, brush it out of his eyes.

"You're welcome. Plate up for us." I take a seat at the island.

He hums a little as he plates up, naked and clean, and passes me a plate.

He pours himself a coffee, fixes his own plate, and joins me.

"Thank you for including Hunter last night. When I opened the door and saw you there, I wanted to throw him out."

I take a sip of my coffee and slide my palm against his thigh. "I know. But we had fun, didn't we?"

Last night, we played two rounds of pool, where Hunter and I kind of ganged up on Theo, then we talked and laughed with each other until midnight.

"Yeah. I can't remember the last time I hung out with Hunter like that. He was in a sociable mood."

"I like him, Theo. He has a good sense of humour." There's something so cool and confident about Hunter that if Theo hadn't told me he was a submissive, I would have definitely assumed he was a Dom.

"Yeah, when he's in the mood, he does. And I guess kicking him out on Valentine's Day would have made me an ass."

"Glad I saved you from being an ass to your brother."

"Sometimes he deserves it," he grins at me playfully.

"Speaking of Valentine's Day, Amy and her husband Clive are here in the city for a romantic getaway. She wants to know how I'd feel about going to Club Shivers tonight?" I climb off my chair onto his lap. He grabs my waist, and I place both hands on either side of his face. He licks his lips.

"I want to go out with you, Callista. Let's do it."

Something in my chest relaxes as he says yes, and I brush my nose against his before kissing him deeply.

I feel his erection stir beneath me, and I grind slowly up and down on his cock.

"Tell me what your limits are when it comes to the club."

"I don't like public play. I'm open to doing a scene with you in one of the private playrooms."

"Can my friends watch?" I ask because I'm curious.

His cheeks pinken. "Can I give you a maybe on that?"

"Of course you can." I run my thumb across his lip. "I want you to enjoy tonight."

"I don't want to walk naked through the club." Theo closes his eyes as I trace his jaw with my lips.

"Okay, but can I dress you up?"

"I have stuff in my closet." His eyes open, and he grins.

"I can't wait! Anything else?" I pull back, take his chin between my fingers.

His eyes flick away from me, and a painful expression crosses his face briefly.

"Baby, tell me." I brush the hair off his forehead.

"My ex...I don't want to have sex in the club, not tonight."

I place my hand over his heart and feel it leap rapidly. "Why?"

"At the end... that was the only way she'd give me relief, if she had an audience. That's the only way she'd satisfy me."

I have never wanted to cut someone's brakes so badly. The more I know about this woman, the more grateful and proud I am that Theo got out of her clutches.

"Maybe next time we can have sex there and we can make a good memory. I want it to be fun for you tonight. I understand your reservations, and I hear your boundaries."

"Being out anywhere with you is going to be fun, Callista." His lips are almost touching mine.

"Kiss me."

He does slowly at first. Then he pokes his tongue into my mouth, making me open.

The kiss turns needy, and he whimpers against me.

I break off the kiss but twirl my fingers in his hair, wanting to keep touching him.

"If we aren't having sex at the club, are you against pleasuring me while we're playing?"

"No, Ma'am, that's fine."

"Good. But if we aren't going to have sex, that means you're going to wait even longer for relief. How do you feel about that?"

I ease back so I can reach down and grip his cock.

"Pure torment, but I know it'll be worth it."

"How would you feel if I locked your cock tonight?" His eyes widen and heat climbs up his neck.

He glances down, blushing. "I don't know. Yes, I want you to. But that means something to me."

"It means that you trust me. That's all for right now, Wolfie. It means I have control...literal control of your orgasms. It doesn't mean a long-term commitment. Just a night of play, of locking you up to make you feel every second of denial that much more."

The air between us is heavy, sparking with heat and anticipation. I hold my breath, wanting to give this to Theo, wanting him to accept.

"Yes, Callista. I can't wait for tonight."

I kiss him while keeping my hand on his cock. It twitches and hardens. "Me neither."

21

THEO

"We have time to relax before leaving for Club Shivers. Come here, boy." Callie pats the couch. "I expect you to be on your best behaviour tonight."

"Is that any fun?" I reach to touch her hair, but she dips out of the way.

"Don't mess up my hair, boy. Be good and I'll reward you." Her makeup is done. She's just out of the shower.

I shake my hips at her, causing her to laugh. "Can't wait."

She grabs my ass and squeezes. "Sit, Wolfie."

"Yes, Ma'am." She studies me as I take her in because she looks amazing tonight. Her hair is in soft waves, framing her face, and deep brown eyeshadow has brought out her crystal blue eyes, and they glow with warmth as she trails her fingers around my nipples, down to my stomach, to my knees.

"Stay like that."

She stands in front of me with that smile that makes her eyes sparkle.

Licking her lips, she slowly unties the belt of her robe and lets the fabric fall open

My breath stutters.

I ache to reach for her, to palm the weight of her breasts, to taste. But I don't. I stay exactly where she put me.

Her eyes flicker with approval. She steps closer and places a hand on my shoulder, her grip firm and grounding.

She slides one leg over and settles onto my lap, the heat of her centre pressing through the thin fabric of my pants.

Every part of me strains toward her, but I'm still holding back—because she hasn't said go yet.

My cock stirs as she presses her palm over my nipples, rubs them in a circle.

"Callista, you're teasing me." My hips thrust forward.

"Yes, I am, Wolfie. Don't move." She presses a finger on my lips, and I want to suck it into my mouth, but I bite the inside of my cheek, keeping myself still, obeying her command.

I try to control my twitching cock, knowing I can't.

It's impossible for me to stem the tide of simmering fire of want that runs through my veins for her.

She grinds on my lap, rising up and down against my cock so slowly it makes me grit my teeth. Desperation starts to build and simmer through my body.

My eyes roll back in my head as her pussy brushes against my erection. "I want to tie your ankles with the sash of my robe. That good with you?" I swallow hard.

"I'd love to be restrained for you, Ma'am."

"Restrained and locked-up. Didn't we pick out the prettiest cage?" Her smile glows as she teases my lips, sending shivers rippling through my skin.

I can't answer her, but a cry of need escapes my lips.

Tonight, I want to surrender control... complete control to her.

She slides off my lap, kneels in front of me, and I swallow as her eyes darken with intensity and everything in me tenses in anticipation. Her hair falls, hiding her face as she wraps the silky sash around my ankle, tying it to the leg of the chair.

It's not tied tightly, and if I wanted, I could easily break free from it.

She finishes the other tie.

Then her hand slides in between my legs, and she takes my hard cock in her hand and pulls hard enough to make me rock forward.

"Yeah, we did, Ma'am." My breath hitches as she gives a tug on the sash, just enough so I can feel it against my leg.

She smiles like a cat lapping cream, and it takes all my willpower not to squirm on the chair.

We spent the morning shopping, browsing through boutiques. I bought Callie a pair of delicate amethyst studs. They catch the light now, sparkling against her ears.

After lunch, we visited the sex shop to pick out the cage. My prior experience made that part easy.

The sales clerk gave me a little smirk and told us to have fun.

"It's going to look so pretty on my cock."

She trails her fingers up and down my shaft, her palm sliding against me, thumb flicking the head of my cock with agonizing slowness.

It drives me wild, and I hiss through clenched teeth.

She turns so that her back is against the chair, reaches for the remote and flips on the TV.

"Thought we could watch a show." Still holding my half-hard penis, she finds a reality show and seems to turn all her attention to it, ignoring me.

My hips buck off the chair. This sweet denial is what I agreed to, but fuck. The timing.

She slaps my thigh playfully. "Stay still, Wolfie. We need to relax before we leave for Club Shivers."

"Yes, Ma'am," I grit through my teeth.

The show plays, and I try to distract myself.

But she smells so good, and her warm hand on my cock, giving it the occasional rub, the slightest pull, makes me crawl out of my mind with need.

Halfway through the show, I start to squirm, my control breaking.

"I said sit, Wolfie. I can't lock you up until you're nice and soft, sit back and relax."

She leans down, brings her mouth to my penis, and gives me another steamy kiss, making me ache with desperate need that I can almost taste.

"Yes, Ma'am."

I breathe through my nose, concentrating on how silky her hair feels against my leg.

She pushes her head against my penis, and I catch the sly grin on her face.

It's so frustrating; it's like pinpricks of fire are lacing through my veins, and I can't do a thing about it.

Her touch is just there, but it's not giving me enough sensation to stay hard, and I want more.

"Would you ever compete on a reality show?" I need to distract myself further. She turns to face me, gives my cock a good tug, before removing her hand.

"Daphne actually thought I should go on that show where you try to get to a remote place before the other team. I thought she was joking." Her tone is wistful, and I want to hug her.

"Did you play sports?" I throw out the question, wanting to distract her further.

"We both did. She was great at soccer. I guess if it's something she wants me to do, it's fine if I go do it."

"Callista, I didn't mean that question to bring up anything." I'm definitely soft now, concerned about what's going through her mind.

"She's made comments to me over the last couple of weeks about how I always run off. I should be used to it, but it still bothers me."

"I'm sorry she said something to upset you. I think you're amazing."

"Yes?" She tilts her head back to me, her gorgeous eyes all sultry.

"Yeah. I think she's jealous." It's something I have thought about for a while, but I haven't dared to say it.

Callie's mouth opens, but she shakes her head, startling into a laugh. "Daphne's never been jealous of me, Wolfie. She's the golden girl. I'm the one with oil under my nails."

This woman is the one who can command a room with her presence, who people look up to and respect. It's not like Callie abandoned her family.

She ran to an opportunity.

Finally, she turns off the television, sits on her heels and stares at my penis.

"Good, look how soft it got for me. I guess we might as well lock it up." She reaches under the chair and takes out a bottle of lube. "Here you go, boy, get it nice and covered."

I squirt lube into my hand, taking my time to coat my balls and work it all over my dick.

"I think you need even more," Callie takes the bottle of lube from me, squirts some into her hands and slathers it over my balls, pinching slightly.

Her grip makes me jump.

My mouth waters, I want this so much.

"Now here it is, just for you." Her eyes gleam with dark desire. I let out a little whimper.

Reaching under the chair again, she brings out the gold cage she'd picked out.

She places it in my hands. "Go ahead, lock it up for me."

Her tone is as smooth as honey.

My blood rushes to my cock. I squirm in the chair, my legs open. I'm exposed in a way that makes me feel vulnerable.

I swallow. I can't believe I'm willing to do this, but I trust her.

And I want to do this for her.

To prove my devotion, to offer her this level of submission, is what I long for.

I slip it on, holding the cage close to my body. I get the ring part over my balls and let out a hiss.

Callista's hands come over mine, and she puts my dick in the metal. My breath is heavy, and I'm a little shaky. But the way she glances at me, as if he's making sure I'm okay, is reassuring me. I'm going through with this.

She holds the cage closed but doesn't lock it.

"Hmm, I think that lock will hold. Oh, the key." She dangles the key that's on a chain in front of me. "Can't forget this."

A mixture of cold fear and excitement washes over me. "No, Ma'am."

"Keep holding that lock for me, yeah, I just want to see-" Callista slips her finger under through the bars, poking my penis. "I love how squishy and snug it looks."

My cheeks are blushing furiously, but I sit here, hardly able to breathe, taking every ounce of her attention, soaking it in like a wilted plant.

I'm awkwardly holding the cage together as she's inspecting it, running her fingers over the smooth lock, to the point and then back again.

Her smile of glee is the only thing that is keeping me here.

That and my raging desire to do this.

"Yep, it's going to do. I'm going to lock it." She takes the lock off of the cage, snapping it closed in her hand. "Perfect."

My whole body is tense; my heart is beating so fast. She slides the key into the lock and slides the lock onto the chastity cage.

"Time to shut it."

I exhale, breathing through the nervousness.

Callista squeezes my thigh. "You're such a good boy for me, Wolfie. You're pleasing me so much. Put your hands on your thighs, palms up."

I do, feeling calmer as she holds my gaze. I know what she and I have is rooted in care for each other.

"I'm going to wear this key around my neck. The extra key we're going to put in your wallet."

"Ma'am, you don't have to-" She presses a finger against my lips.

"Wolfie, I need you to know that you have the means to unlock if you must. I want to be sure that me and your past are separate. Even if it is for one night. Do you have a safe here?"

"Yes. All my important files are in the safe."

She unties my legs, tossing the belt aside. "Show me."

I get up, feeling the cage against my cock like firm pressure. It's like a hand holding me in place.

"You look so sexy with my cock all locked up." The approval in her tone sends shivers down my spine. I can't help the grin on my face.

"Yeah?" I stop in the doorway of my guest bedroom.

"Yeah, boy," she squeezes my ass, snakes her hand on the back of my nape, pressing my mouth to hers.

She kisses me, a wet, hungry kiss that has my cock jumping.

"Show me the safe." My lips are tingling as I step into the guest room and open the closet doors.

"Here's my safe." I gesture at the black box.

"Open it for me, boy."

I tap in the code on the electronic lock, and it beeps open.

The only things in my safe are paperwork, most of it my dad's patents because mom had asked me to store them—documents from the Consortium, and documents for my business.

"Put the extra key in your safe if you don't want to keep it in your wallet. I care about you, and I will never let you suffer."

"Thank you, Ma'am." The gesture has me choking back a sob as I slide the spare key on top of my work documents.

Something in me is healed with this gesture, and I feel my defenses coming down even further.

I believe Callie will look after me, that she'll give the space I need to service her in a sexually submissive way, that's connected and vulnerable, the kind of submission I crave to give.

"Come here." I walk into her open arms, and she holds me, then rubs her pussy against my cage.

"It looks so cute and small in there, I like it," she brushes her lips against mine.

A wave of desperation, of neediness, sweeps over me. My thoughts are heavier, and I know I am not far from sinking into subspace.

"Can I do anything for you, Ma'am?" The need in my voice is so raw, I want to please her so much. I want her to order me to do something, anything to ease this open need.

"Is my boy feeling all needy? All wanting to please?" Callista wraps an arm around my torso, pulls me close to her, licks behind my ear, slowly draws her tongue against the shell.

Needy. Yes.

"Yes, Ma'am! I want to do something for you, please." Oh yes, I'm begging. It's the only way I can express how much I need her to accept my offer of service.

"I think I want to watch you mop your floors," Callista says. Her tone is low, the amusement laced through it makes me smile. "I need to do my nails before we leave."

"You got it!"

She slaps my ass as I pass by her. "We're going to have the best night."

***

"I'm happy to call a car, Ma'am."

Callie takes my bottom lip between her thumb and index finger. "No, I'm driving us. Your job tonight is to be mine, okay? I want you to concentrate on what I tell you to do. I want you to relax and let go."

I whimper, exhaling a shuddering breath as my heart drums rapidly.

"Yes, Ma'am."

"Good boy."

Callie slips on her coat, and I take her bag. "Amy is already there. Last time they came, it was at capacity, and they didn't want to miss out."

She's saying normal words, but my gaze is focused on the deep red lipstick she's wearing as she caps the clear lip gloss she just applied.

I feel the cock cage every time I shift, and it's like it's an invisible leash, connecting me to her. I touch the leather band on my neck.

"You look so handsome in that collar, Wolfie."

"Thank you, Ma'am."

It's just a play collar, but my mind is leaping into situations that we haven't talked about.

Maybe it's a half-fantasy combined with the cock cage that is making me feel like it's real.

Like I already belong to her. Permanently.

I think of how I want to wake up with her in my arms every morning.

And at night, I want to rub her feet and listen to her talk about her day.

I want to serve this woman so completely that all her self-doubts are forever banished from her mind.

And I know...I need to tell her how I feel. But that thought makes my throat close up because I don't want to lose her.

"Wolfie, let's go." She gives a tug on the leash, and I follow her out the door, down the hall.

My eyes watch how her legs take every stride, how she presses the elevator button with her index finger that is painted a deep purple.

I'm fully zeroed in on her.

Callie guides me to her car. I get in, and the short ride is a blur.

I'm acutely aware of how my cock pulses in the cage, the pressure like an unyielding grip on my penis with every movement.

Just like my cock, it feels like every part of me is bound, waiting for her next command.

22

CALLIE

What are you doing?

My inner voice screams loudly as I park behind the converted warehouse.

I wonder if instead of engaging in all that foreplay, we should have just changed at Club Shivers.

Putting that cock cage on Theo... all that trust and vulnerability, laid open for me and the enormity of that I don't take lightly.

My boy is so driven to please.

Making him hold the cage in his hands while I "inspected" it? So *much* fun.

Was that too much?

Stop it, I tell myself. I'm not going to spin tonight.

Tonight is about taking care of my boy.

I want to show him how much I appreciate him and to have a fantastic time.

"Are we here?" His voice is low, groggy, and I know he's still out of it.

"Yes, boy. Let's go." I get out of the car and hurry around to open his door.

Ever the gentleman, he usually opens mine—but my boy is halfway to subspace and I want to make sure he's steady enough to walk to the front door.

I should call this off right now. I went too fast. I'm playing with his emotions.

All the self-doubt ping-pongs around in my mind as I reach for the leash under Theo's cashmere coat and walk us up the steps of Club Shivers.

A man in a dark suit opens the door for me as we approach. "Have a good evening."

Inside, a short, curvy woman with spiky hair checks us in against a list on the system.

I lead us to the coat check and lockers down the hallway, right before the change rooms.

Theo helps me put my bag in the locker.

I slowly unbutton his coat. "You look so handsome in this shirt."

The way he dips his head gives me a surge of desire so hot, I want to slam him against the row of lockers and make him beg me for release right here.

"I can't believe I get to be with you tonight, Callista. You are a beautiful goddess, and I'm just a guy in suit pieces."

I laugh, pressing my palm against his cheek.

I kiss his strong chin. Electricity crackles between us.

My nipples harden as I trace his jaw, then take my time licking his throat around his Adam's apple.

"Very fine suit pieces."

When I went into Theo's closet, I found that he had a whole assortment of fetish pieces, but I discarded them.

I didn't want him to wear something that he had worn with another woman.

This shirt is so luxurious, it feels like strands of silken gold between my fingers.

"Hands behind your back, Wolfie, feet shoulder-width apart."

I sense other people bustling by us, the thud of music coming from the door to the main floor of the club as other patrons open it.

All of Theo's focus is on me, and I suppress a shiver from the blazing heat in his eyes.

Tonight, it's about him.

About what he is willing to take and what he can give.

Tonight is about how I can give him the experience his submissive soul craves.

"Good boy," I coo, my tone light. "You are mine to play with and mine to control. Your only concern tonight is my pleasure."

"Yes, Ma'am." His voice is shaky.

I circle him, taking in his bowed head, his strong shoulders, his toned muscles, and exhale.

I'm so proud that this boy is mine.

There's a bead of sweat on his upper lip.

He's swallowing as I take my time, leaving him to be on display for me, in this quiet corner of the club.

He whimpers as I glide my hands around the curve of his ass, his pants smooth under my palms.

The fake leathers were in the back of his closet from a Halloween party.

I knead his ass, Theo lets out a soft whine as I press my hand against the cock cage.

"Let's go, boy."

I give a slight tug on the leash.

My shoulders back, head up, I project the confidence I only ever feel when my boy is with me.

"Have a good time," says a slender man wearing a leather vest as he opens the door for us.

"Thank you." I feel regal in my platform boots, my leathers fit snugly and my corset top is pushing up my breasts.

The main floor of the club is definitely the voyeur zone.

There are three stages throughout the space, with different demos going on.

The bar and seating area are at the back, and throughout the space, there are play areas with lots of seating, inviting people to watch.

I pull up short, by a stage, watching a rope demo.

"I would love to tie you up, just like that." I run my hand through Theo's silky hair, my eyes peeled on the Dom/sub pair on stage, watching as the Dom finishes tying a chest harness.

I feel Theo's gaze watching me, watching it, taking in my expressions.

He reaches for my hand, his expression all serious. "Yes, Ma'am."

I throw my arm around his waist, hugging him. His trust is the most precious thing I have ever been given, and I need to honour it.

"You will use yellow if you are unsure about anything tonight."

He tips his head back, his eyes so filled with need, it wraps around my soul.

"If you say red, all play stops. I will take care of you, boy, do you understand?"

"Yes, Ma'am, yellow and red." His lips upturn in an adorable smile.

"And if I say green?"

"Then we're having the best time, Wolfie." I pinch his ass, he yelps.

A tug of the leash has him following, moving on through the crowd of people to the seating area.

Anticipation slithers through me. I can't wait to play with Theo.

"Callie!" I turn and see Amy sitting at a corner table and wave back. "

"Hey." I lean down to give her a hug.

She flips her long purple hair off her shoulder.

"It's so good to see you!" And as I'm hugging her, inhaling her preferred scent of some expensive perfume, I realize it's true.

Since my sister's accident, I have isolated myself. Not on purpose, but because that's what I needed to do.

Seeing Amy brings my regular life back to me, and it makes me feel off balance.

Like the flashbacks of when I was happy and carefree, don't belong to me but to someone else.

Amy is the kind of Domme who never lets doubts go through her head.

Or if she does, she crushes them as soon as they appear. "And who's the not-boy-toy?" Amy's eyebrows raise.

"This is Theo. Theo, say hello to Amy."

"Nice to meet you, Amy," Theo says, glancing up.

"You too. Clive is serving as my footstool under the table, but I'm going to send him for drinks."

"Wolfie, go with Clive. Get me a strawberry virgin daiquiri and water for yourself."

I unhook his leash from the collar and place my hand on his cheek. I pull his face down to me, crushing my lips to his. "On your way back, check out the demos. Tell me if there is anything you want to try."

"Yes, Ma'am."

"Hi Callie, good to see you," Clive gives me a nod hello.

"You too," I grin, seeing the tall man with the shaved head wearing a leather harness and a leather kilt.

"Go on, boys, leave us to our girl talk," Amy says.

"You're so cute when you're in command mode," I tell my friend as we sit in the booth.

"I am always cute," she flips her hair again, peers at me with a dark gaze. "So, does having a boy toy help?"

"Help with what? And I told you, he's *not* a boy toy."

She puts her hands up in a placating gesture. "Okay. Does he help give you the release you need from taking care of everyone else?"

"I don't take care of everyone," I cross my heel over my leg, trampling down the annoyance I feel. "I came back home to help, and that's what I've been doing. But Grady takes care of his kids, and my uncle and aunt help too."

"And you stepped in to take care of the diner, put in a brake belt, and look after your aunt when she's having a bad day."

"So? I'm capable of doing that. And you mean brake line. Uncle Henry doesn't have me in the shop often."

"Why so touchy?" Amy's eyes gleam. I feel like I've been played.

"Because looking after people you love is what you do. And Theo is not a boy toy." I say it again.

"Oh? Tell me more."

I turn to look out at the crowd, spotting Theo and Clive near the middle stage. "He's fun. He makes me laugh. The sex is good."

"And those are all good reasons that fill a short-term need."

I wish my friend would put away the therapist's hat.

"I don't see your point." But I can hazard a guess.

Out on the floor, people are dancing, engaged in play, laughing and having a good time.

Over here, it feels like a black hole of doom.

"You say he's not a boy toy. But you always prefer short term relationships, and the reasons you gave me are checkboxes on a pickup."

"He's mine, okay?" I glare at her, heat rising up my neck. "I want to take care of him. I want to commit to him."

"Wow, that is big. Does that mean you're going to stay in Rising Harbour? If the team calls you tomorrow to come back, what are you going to do? Daphne is better."

With one breath, Amy tosses my fears on the table, right in front of me. She's that kind of friend.

"Look, if I need a psychology appointment, I'd call your office. Tonight, I'm going to take Theo upstairs and play with him. What are you and Clive going to do?"

"Oh, that boy is getting roughed up down here for everyone to see. Want to watch?"

I catch sight of Theo striding towards me, carrying my drink and two bottles of water. He meets my gaze and shimmies his hips.

"He is very easy on the eyes," Amy whispers to me. "Thanks, boys."

"Here you are, Ma'am," Theo hands me my fruity drink. I take a sip of the concoction, and sugary sweetness coats my tongue. "Perfect, thank you."

"Callie said she wants to take you upstairs to one of the private dungeons. Are you sure you don't want to stay down here?"

"I'll go wherever Callista wants me to," Theo says.

"You two are so cute together," Clive says.

"They really are. Why are you standing?" Amy points to the floor. Immediately Clive sinks to his knees. She opens her legs, spreading them around the chair, and Clive buries his face in her crotch.

"Let's go." I reattach the leash to Theo's collar. He exhales slowly, eyes fluttering shut for a brief moment as if grounding himself in the gesture.

When his grey eyes open again, they're glassy with devotion.

"Thank you, Ma'am," he whispers, voice tight with need. His fingers twitch at his sides, his whole body humming with restrained energy, like he's waiting—eager—for the next command.

I cup the back of his nape, rubbing a small circle on his neck. He drops his head, his arm brushing mine.

"We'll catch up with you two later."

"Have fun," Amy gives us a wave.

"You doing okay, Wolfie?" I ask, keeping a hand on his ass as we get through the crowd.

"Yes Ma'am. The people in here are making me feel a little overwhelmed."

I place my hand on his shoulder, cursing myself for forgetting how draining Theo finds crowds.

"We could leave if you want. I'm sorry I forgot how crowd-averse you are."

"I want to be here, Callista. I'm not speaking tonight. I'm fine."

"You'll tell me if you aren't?"

"Yes, Ma'am."

"Good." I give the leash a strong tug on the leash, pulling him down to me until his lips are a breath away from mine.

I trace my tongue over his lips, my body heating up with the contact. My pussy is tingling. I want this boy to fuck me long into the night.

"Let's go upstairs."

With every step I take, I feel Theo's eyes on me, like a heated blanket of laser-focused awareness.

I pause to watch a man in a cowboy hat, using two floggers on his sub. Theo's pupils grow large. I wrap the leash around my hand and start to pull in time with the rhythmic thuds that land on the submissive's back.

"Lovely," Theo says.

"Yes," I pull on the leash, shortening my grip so he'll feel more pressure. shortening my grip.

Theo sags against me, and I reach around the front of his slacks, pressing my palm against his cage.

"I know you don't like pain."

"A little pain. Double flogging is a heavy sensation that I could get into."

His comment sends flutters of anticipation through my body as I think of the new toy in my bag that I want to try out tonight. "Come." I steer him to the desk near the elevators. "Go get my bag, please."

"Yes, Ma'am."

While he does that, I make a request to the attendant.

"I'm giving you dungeon number five." She hands me a key fob, then passes on my request into her mic.

"Thank you." I take a seat in a round plush chair to wait, but a moment later, Theo appears.

"Thank you, boy." We go to the elevator, and a Dom with two subs sporting kitten ears gets on beside us, then another Domme I don't know with her male submissive, he's in a chest harness with nipple clamps.

I brush my palm along Theo's chest, pinching his nipple through the fabric of his shirt.

He lets out a soft whimper and I smile, amused by the good natured chuckles of the people in the car with us and I place a smile on my face, throw my shoulders back and walk out of the elevator, my sub right at my heels.

My emotions are a jumble of excitement, anticipation and fear that I'm going to let Theo down.

Needing a moment, I steer him to the railing, and we look at the view from this vantage.

"I like the thump of this place, the energy. It makes me feel like there's always something new."

"You crave new things," Theo slides a glance at me.

"Yes, I don't want to be bored." I tug his leash, bringing him closer to me.

He takes my hand in his, lifts it to his lips and presses a kiss on it. "I will do my best to give you all the stimulation you need, Callista."

"I know, Wolfie."

But a shiver of dread rolls through my body—because that's always been my problem.

The insatiable need to seek out more stimulation.

"Time to play," I cup his nape, bringing his face to mine.

Kissing him deeply, passionately, until the heat from our tongues mingling blazes across my skin.

"I can't wait," Theo says as I pull away from his lips.

My pulse jumps as I open the door. "You're mine, boy."

23

THEO

My cock swells against the cage—not uncomfortably, almost like a backward hard-on—and I know in time I won't be as hyperaware of it as I am now.

Being in chastity is driving me deep into submission and making me so horny, I would do anything for release.

"I almost forgot that your cock is all locked up," Callie sings teasingly as she closes the door.

The dungeon has a high ceiling and soft light. It's quiet in here.

The walls are exposed brick, and everything in the space, from the furnishings to the fixtures, has a polished look.

There's a sink in the back with cabinets, and a rolling cart beside the bondage table.

Bondage table. I swallow hard, taking it in.

Callie gives me that sexy, in-control smile and pushes me back so the back of my thighs hit the table.

"Ma'am," I say against her lips as she slips her tongue over mine, kissing me so hard I whimper.

The way she's kissing me right now is my entire reason for living.

I could stand here and kiss her until the end of time, waiting for her next command.

She puts her hands on either side of my neck, breaking contact.

I exhale a shuddering breath and touch my forehead to hers.

I don't know what's going to happen this evening, but I'd bet my entire portfolio that whatever happens here in this private dungeon is going to change the way things are between us.

I try to stamp down the smidgen of fear that is making my palms sweaty.

I want Callista.

She knows I want her.

"Time to ditch the clothes." She starts at the bottom of my shirt, unbuttoning me slowly, until she reaches my belly button.

A button falls off and hits the floor.

It's partly nerves that make me laugh.

"What's so funny?" she traces my lips with her finger.

"That you made my buttons pop off." For three hundred bucks, I'd expect the damn shirt to hold up better.

Nerves pulled me out of the altered headspace.

"Yeah? I want to push all your buttons tonight, baby." She kisses me as she works my pants off, shoving them down my legs, gliding her warm hand back up and around to squeeze my ass. "There's my boy. Get those shoes and socks off."

I unlace my shoes, kick them off and then get my socks off.

The golden floor is cool under my feet.

I drop my forehead to her chest, and she rubs the back of my head.

Her touch is so heated, so dominant. Little mewling sounds escape my lips as I melt further.

"That's a good boy," she grips my chin between her forefinger and thumb, slanting her lips against mine.

"You're mine, boy. You're going to please me tonight," she says against my lips, then gives me a sloppy kiss that leaves me wanting more.

"Yes, Ma'am." I mumble against her soft lips as she kisses me so hard my head is spinning.

She breaks the kiss, but skims her lips against my collarbone, setting off a new trail of shivers.

I'm nervous. But just because I'm nervous, it doesn't mean I don't want this.

"Let's get started. Lie down on the table, on your back."

She takes a step back from me, creating physical distance between us, her expression expectant

It's a subtle way to transition into the scene.

We aren't mere friends in this moment; we're submissive and Domme, and my Domme just gave me an order.

With dread and need coursing through my veins, I get on the table.

The table is padded, black leather, and easily holds me.

Thick leather straps with buckles are at the top of the table all the way down.

My throat goes dry.

The silence in the room is almost as loud as my drumming heart.

I want to do this and, despite my nerves, a thrill of excitement races down my spine.

I glance at her one more time, clad in that corset that hugs her breasts, the perfect purple leather mini skirt, those platform boots.

She's so gorgeous, and I'm so lucky she's standing in this room with me.

Callie comes beside me and starts buckling my ankles, then straps above my knees, and above my waist.

"Good boy." She presses a soft, feathery kiss to my lips. "Give me a colour, Wolfie. Are you enjoying this or feeling panicky?"

She slides her hands under my calves, rubs them in slow but vigorous circles.

And I realize that I am okay.

I'm here because I want to be. Because I trust this woman, my Domme, not to hurt me, to look out for me.

Relief shimmers through me, yawns open my submission to her even further. Callie said she wanted to push me tonight, and this is me, stepping into that space.

"Green, Ma'am. I'm not panicky, and I feel good."

"That pleases me so much." Callie plants her lips across mine, kissing me so hard my lips feel swollen.

The key she wears around her neck swings against my chin, sending a shiver that ripples through my entire body.

In this moment, I belong to her, completely and utterly hers.

"Let's keep securing you." She buckles the straps across my shoulders.

My arms are next, and I force myself to breathe deeply.

"Now just your head. Tell me how you're doing." She buckles the strap across my neck.

I take a deep breath, forcing myself to relax.

She drags her hair over my face, a slow, sultry motion, my cock twitches in the cage.

"Fine. I'm good, Ma'am."

"Perfect. This is about me teasing what's mine regarding you giving up control and letting go."

Her platform boots thud on the floor as she moves away from me, towards the sink. "You please me so much, Wolfie, and I know you're going to do fine tonight."

Something wet and cold presses into my right palm.

I clutch the ice cubes in my fingers.

"Good boy. You're going to hold these ice cubes for me, just like that. Don't drop them."

She traces my hip with an ice cube, runs it down to my thigh, then back up again, repeating the process several times.

"Ouch, fuck!"

An ice cube presses against my testicle through the cage. It doesn't hurt, but the cold shocks me.

But then her warm lips are on my sac.

She's making me so hot and bothered, I'm going to burn.

I pant. My head is spinning, trying to anticipate the sensations, as she keeps dragging the ice cube across my balls, then her hot lips ease the path of cold.

It's driving me wild.

"Callista, this is making me crazy."

"Good." She taps the cage with her index finger, and a slow smile curves across her lips.

Vibrations dance across my sensitive skin, making me wince and squeeze my eyes closed tight.

Callie's on my left side now, dragging another ice cube down my arm to my hand. "Hold this one and don't drop it."

Never did I think holding a fistful of ice cubes would be a challenge, but it's taking everything I can to squeeze my hand around the slippery cubes.

She turns her back to me and goes across the room to her bag.

I hear her rummage through her bag, then her footsteps beside me, and then the roll of the cart.

"Here, Wolfie, now hold this in your left hand. If you squeeze it, it'll squeak and I'll stop the scene and check in on you." She pushes something round into my palm.

"A little brush of pain," she says as she slaps something cool against my thigh, making me jump.

Slap. Slap.

The coldness of it makes my muscles tight.

She continues, bringing it down across my hip, then across my chest.

"Fuck!" I cry out as it slaps against my nipple, then the other.

Callie laughs softly as she flicks her wrist and the red silicone strands of a pastry brush meet my other nipple.

The little bite of pain sends all the blood rushing to my cock, making me so damn aroused, I want to burst out of this table and fuck her.

But that's not what's going to happen.

I close my eyes, calm myself, as she flicks the brush all over my shoulders.

"I love how red this is making your skin." She brings the brush down over my pecs, drags it across my arm, and my fingers almost slip on the ice, but I hold it.

I'm determined not to fail her.

She brings the pastry brush down on my nipples, a quick snap, snap, that makes me moan in protest.

"You can take this, Wolfie," she coos to me as she snaps the brush over my other nipple, again and again.

It's an innocent-looking thing, but it's packing a punch.

It stings and leaves rug-burn sensations in its wake.

As my mind is being enveloped in the pain, my fingers turn colder.

I almost drop the ice cubes, but Callie presses her lips against mine, anchoring me to her, and I close my fists, determined not to drop them.

"How does this feel?" She flicks the brush on the top of my shoulder.

"It stings a little, but not in a bad way." My voice is so thick, every syllable syrupy, I feel like I have something stuffed in my mouth.

"You're taking it very well, and you're still holding those ice cubes," she says as she brings the brush down on my wrist once, twice, but I clutch the ice cubes.

They will not hit the floor.

She reaches across the table, swinging it at my other wrist.

"I think I want an orgasm. But you're all tied up. I wonder how you can pleasure me?"

"Any way you want. You could let me out of the cage."

"Hmm, I could, but what fun would that be, Wolfie? I was hoping to go twenty-four hours."

A rushing mix of desperation and arousal rolls through me, wrenching a wail from my lips.

"Oh, I think you could take it. And I think I know a way you can pleasure me without unlocking you."

"You're very creative," my words come out in a whine.

"Thank you, Wolfie. That's sweet of you to say. I hope you feel that way after I've used your face to come."

My mouth instantly waters, remembering how she tastes. "You can use my mouth."

"I can, can't I? I'm so glad you've offered."

My racing pulse jumps as I hear her footsteps move away from me.

The anticipation fuels the ember of need even more, sending me spiraling higher.

My dick twitches and constricts in its cage.

Despite holding ice cubes, I feel a trickle of sweat break out across my lower back.

"Open for me. This is the only way you're giving me dick tonight. Nice and wide."

Oh god. Her tone is so cool, commanding, and I only obey.

Something smooth and leathery is pressed against my lips; she pushes it to my mouth.

Callie reaches behind my head to tighten the straps, and I lift as much as the restraint of the table allows me to, automatically.

A flat piece of leather is fitted against my lips.

My gag reflex kicks in as I feel the ball press on my tongue, and I cough.

"Relax, Wolfie. I got you. You're doing such a good job for me. You look lovely swallowing this penis mouth gag. I can't wait to ride your face."

She's going to ride my mouth, but I'm not going to be able to taste her.

The torment of it all shoots burning arousal down to my cock, which is constricting against the cage in protest.

Fuck. I'm going to explode.

I let out a moan as she pinches my nipple, a wail escaping as she presses her hot mouth to it.

Her warm breath sends shivers down my spine.

Water drips along the bottom of my palm. Between the wetness and the increasing numbness from the cold, it's harder to maintain my grip.

I squeeze my eyes tight, determined not to drop the ice cube.

"Look at you, accepting what I give you, loving every minute of it. It turns me on, Wolfie, I'm so hot for you."

I let out another little sound behind the gag, turning my head to her, my eyes wide.

I want to feel her hand on my cock so badly, I'm pulsating with that fiery need.

"Almost forgot this," she slides a piece of silk against my cheek.

Fuck. She's going to blindfold me, then I won't be able to see what's going on.

I'm at her mercy.

It's a place I never thought I would ever be again, a submissive offering I didn't think I'd risk to anyone ever again, but Callie...Callie makes me feel safe.

She slips the blindfold over my eyes, and her hair tickles my chin as she leans forward to secure it behind my head.

My hips try to rise against the strap I'm restrained with, because I want more of her touch and I need her to know it.

I want her to give in to me.

But I don't.

I want her to know that I'm doing this for her, because it pleases her, because she's commanded of me...but I need acknowledgement.

Maybe that makes me a bad submissive. I don't know, or just a needy one.

The blindfold is a good one, I can't see through it, just shadows.

Without sight, without the ability to speak, to move, my mind is thrown somewhere else, half panic, half arousal, until I feel her hair on my chest.

Her hand over my cold ones, making me moan for more of her touch.

"You did so well, there's hardly anything left of this ice cube."

She takes the remainder of the ice from my hand, then something soft is rubbed over my palm... it feels like a towel.

"I have to tell you that I was going to spank you if you dropped the ice on the floor. A pity."

Mewling pours out of me, behind the gag, in protest, horrified that I've lost out on a spanking.

She dries off my hand, leans down and presses a kiss above my wrist. "Don't worry, I don't need a reason to spank that adorable ass of yours. How is my cock doing all locked up? It looks so good." She touches it through the cage, poking at it, and the heat from her touch is making me roar inside.

Heat climbs up my neck. My cheeks are on fire.

Wounded animal noises slip from behind the gag, raw with need for her touch.

I'm so needy, so eager, I will do anything she asks of me.

Callie presses hot, lingering kisses along the tops of my thighs, trailing them up the length of my body until she pauses at my chin. Her mouth is soft, searing heat against my skin, each touch branding me with her touch.

"Time to ride, my boy."

I've never been so aroused in my entire life, and there isn't a damn thing I can do about it, other than give this gorgeous woman everything she takes.

24

CALLIE

Theo's cute little sounds, muffled by the gag that is in his mouth, ring around the room.

He's moving the dildo side to side, up and down, and it's so hot, my pussy is throbbing.

I am so proud of my boy that my heart is close to melting into a pile of goo.

Everything I have asked of him, he has given, and I can't wait to reward him.

His submission fuels my need to Dom in a way I have never experienced before.

I want to be better for him.

And I want to take his submission further because he's so needy.

Raw need flares and hums through my body as I remove my corset.

I glance at my boy, drinking in his body laid out for me on the table.

He's so strong, so capable, and yet he's lying in the bondage I placed him in.

To do what I want to him.

His trust takes my breath away, makes my head swim.

I drape my corset over the cart, then I shimmy out of my mini skirt but leave my platform boots on.

The table moves a little as I climb on top, positioning my legs on either side of his head.

I grab the dildo.

It's nice and slick from being lubed up.

I slide forward, my pussy just above the tip of the dildo.

"I'm checking to see how wet I am, baby." I coo to him, slipping my fingers into my pussy.

I'm already soaked.

I take my fingers out and hold them under Theo's nostrils.

The moan he lets out is so primal it raises goosebumps along my flesh.

"I know you love tasting me, but right now, you're going to pleasure me with the only dick I have access to."

His cheeks flame with a red blush.

The table moves a little as I climb on, kneeling on the padded arms on either side of Theo's head.

Rocking my hips, I test the weight—perfect, the table doesn't even creak.

My hand glides along the smooth dildo, slapping it against my palm.

"You're going to fuck me like you mean it. I want to feel this dick work."

I cup his cheeks, wanting to give him reassurance with my touch.

Sweeping my thumbs along his cheekbone, I make soft cooing noises.

"I'm going to ride your face so hard, Wolfie."

I slowly lower myself onto the dildo one inch at a time, easing it into my soaking wet pussy.

"Perfect!" I rock my hips, testing it out. "Yeah, that feels good, boy."

With the way my nipples are tightening, it's not going to take me long to get to climax.

I lean back slightly and let out a primal growl of my own.

"This is so good, Wolfie." I fist his hair in one hand as I grind against his face, letting the dildo take most of my weight.

I close my eyes as the surge of control flares through me.

Yes, this is exactly what I needed.

Rocking my hips, I let out guttural moans.

The dildo moves in me, hitting me even deeper, making me burn, in the most delectable way.

I stop moving, let go of his hair. "Show me how much you want to please me, boy."

His chin lifts up, sending the dildo up into me deep, I roll my hips. "Give me more!"

Biting back a scream, I rock.

His head moves up and down. He's so intent on my pleasure, I can feel it in the strength he's using to move the dildo in me.

"Give me more, boy, I'm almost there!" I can't believe how close I am, but pleasure is coiled tightly in my lower belly, and I can feel the orgasm hovering, waiting to claim me.

He tilts his chin up a little more, and the tip of the dildo sinks deeper in me, hitting me high on my inner walls.

"Yes!" I bear down with all my weight, rocking my hips forward.

I grab either side of his head and hold on, his cheeks covered with a sheen of sweat.

My pleasure surges, flooding my veins with heat, boiling over the surface.

"I'm cumming!" My nerve endings are exploding like fireworks. I shudder as the ecstasy consumes me, making me blank out as I'm floating above the room, in particles of bliss, screaming Theo's name.

I lean back, reaching for his waist, grabbing at him.

Needing to feel him.

"Good. That was good."

Leaning forward, I slide off his face with a slow, deliberate shift of my hips.

My hands glide up his legs, fingertips digging into the tender heat of his inner thighs.

He squirms, restless beneath my touch.

"Good boy."

I climb off of him, stride to his head, lean down. "Lift your head, Wolfie. I'm removing the gag."

He does as I ask. I unbuckle it, then I wipe the saliva that's on his chin off with my palm.

"How are you, boy? Give me a colour."

This scene tonight reached an intensity I wasn't expecting...one I had hoped for maybe, but it exceeded all expectations.

"Green, still." Theo croaks out.

"Good," I turn the dildo side towards his mouth and he's opening for me before I even ask him to.

"Yes, boy, clean up my toy."

He makes a keening noise that makes me want to reach in, grab his heart, and keep it safe with all my might.

This gentle man has found me and has given me the gift of his submission, and I am going to guard it like the precious gem it is.

I reach across his shoulders, dragging the key along his cheek as I unbuckle his head strap.

"Work your mouth, that's it," I fist his hair, move his head up and down.

He sucks it so hard he's slurping, desperate for every drop.

"That's it, good boy. Lick it all up—clean every bit of my mess like the needy little thing you are."

Every sloppy, urgent suck only proves how completely he's under me, and the shields I keep around my heart shatter a little more.

"You're so cute, Wolfie." I pull the dildo away from him and set it to the side.

I stride over to the bucket of ice, and, taking a glove, I fill the glove with ice cubes, then from my bag, I grab another toy.

"I think I need to cool you down."

"I am burning for you, Ma'am."

"Yeah?" I tie the base of the glove and hold it in my hand, then run it over his feet.

His toes jerk.

It's so adorable, I can't help but laugh, slapping his thigh lightly as I do.

"I thought you'd appreciate being cooled off." I run the glove over his other foot, then between his legs.

I lean down and kiss him, blowing my hot breath across his skin.

"Callista!" His aching cry makes me chuckle as I glide the ice over his slender knees, then plant gentle kisses.

His skin is soft and clean.

I love how much this man takes care of himself.

He wasn't waiting around for a woman to do his laundry or to order him to wash his feet.

I bite the fleshy skin on his thigh, sinking my teeth deep.

Theo yelps, his fists clench. It's so damn hot.

I swipe the bite mark with my tongue, soothing it. "Here, I'll cool that off for you." I press the gloved ice to the spot, holding it there.

His legs shake, and he lets out breathy moaning sounds that are driving me wild. His eyes are closed, and I think my boy likes these sensations. At his caged cock, I lean down and kiss his balls that are constricted by the cage.

"Aww, I'm almost sorry this isn't getting out to play today. But I can still play with it." I take the bullet vibe I had grabbed from my bag and press it against the cock cage.

"Ma'am!" Theo cries out, his feet point toward the ceiling

"You please me so much, boy, with how needy you are for every touch. And I'm so pleased with how you are taking everything I am giving you, even this." I drag the ice glove over his balls, pressing it to his sensitive skin.

I slap his thigh and then press the vibe on his other testicle. I repeat this because I can.

The power of being in charge rumbles through my veins, shudders rack his body, he squirms, pulls at his restraints, eases himself back on the table.

"Please, Ma'am!" he moans, his deep rumble echoing around the room.

I love how his face scrunches up when I press the cool glove to his balls. And how he relaxes when the bullet vibe gives him a surge.

The moment his hand forms a fist, I turn off the vibe and ice those balls.

"You're torturing me!" It's the whiniest tone he's ever given me. I give his testicles a good slap, and he yelps.

"No, that'd be torture, my sweet Wolfie. This..." I slap the glove ice against his sack, above his cage. "It's play, and you're pleasing me. Now be quiet or I'll put the gag back on you." I flick the bullet vibe to the highest setting and press it against his cage.

Glancing at his face, I see a drip of sweat forming on his brow.

Reaching up with my icy glove, I swipe at it. "Can't have that, boy." I take the vibe off the outer ring of the cage, I then I press it against his balls.

"Ma'am! I'm going to come!"

"Not in my cage you're not!" I swipe the bullet away, then slam the icy glove against it.

Theo shakes his head, his fist clenched.

I exchange the ice for the bullet, keeping it there for a count of twenty.

"You will not come tonight, boy."

"I want to please you, Callista." His tone is hollow, like he's sliding back into subspace.

"Oh, you are." I slide the glove in between his thighs, dragging it over his sensitive flesh. I hold it there, squeezing him until he cries out.

"That's a good boy." I move my hand to his smooth chest, my fingers playing with the fine down of brown hair he has there.

I hold the vibe over his nipple and the other icy bag over his other nipple.

"Ahh!"

"Do you like this?" My tone is sugary sweet.

"Yes. No."

"Why no?" I switch, setting the vibe to the lowest setting before placing it over his other nipple.

"Because I'm all frustrated. I don't know what you're going to do next. Maybe I was thinking you'd let me out of my cage to orgasm."

"I'm taking the blindfold off now." I want to see his eyes.

I reach behind his head and undo my knot.

Leaning down, I brush a kiss on his closed eyelids.

I kiss his closed eyelids. "There. Open for me."

He blinks in the light, and I see how glassy his eyes are.

"I just locked you. I don't want to let you out so soon. I'm thinking tomorrow after breakfast? Would you sleep in it for me?" I trail my hand back down to his nipple, flipping the vibe on.

"Yes, Callista." His tone is so filled with willingness, it takes my breath away.

I don't know what I expected him to say when I asked if he'd sleep in the cock cage.

There was only one answer he was going to give me.

But knowing how Theo feels about cock cages, the level of submission that represents to him, this has moved from casual play to a serious commitment.

No longer abstract.

The awareness tightens my throat and knocks me off balance.

That loss of control? Unacceptable.

I need to be in control right now.

Mentally, I do my best to shove all these emotions to the side for later.

I dig my nails into his hip bone as I lean over him.

I tug at his bottom lip, then slant my lips over his.

I moan into his kiss as his lips work against mine.

My heart is beating so fast, I kiss in time to the beat, the heat of our skin blazing.

This is so real. The connection between my boy and it can't be ignored.

I break off the kiss and, not being able to speak for fear I'd cry, I unbuckle him.

He stays still until I undo the last buckle, then he stretches his arms above his head.

"Over." The word comes out far harsher than I mean it to, but my heart is still racing.

He obeys without question, giving me his beautiful strong back.

I adjust the table. The padded section near his torso rises, giving his cage a little more room to breathe.

My hands glide over his ass, pinching and squeezing the soft flesh before bringing my palm down with a sharp slap, the sound echoing through the room.

He grunts beneath me, moaning.

I want to bite his ass and see my handprints on his skin. So I spank him as hard as I can, he lets out a grunt, as I land another slap on his lower thighs.

His shoulders tense. I bring my palm down on his flesh again, loving how he tightens under my hand.

I'm lost in spanking his ass, the red welts on his puckered skin sending me soaring.

I draw back my hand, bring it down hard again, then I dig in with my fingertips over his hot flesh.

I lean down and press my lips to his ass, sinking my teeth into his skin. He lets out a half-scream. A tremor ripples through his body as I lick and lap the bite mark, needing to soothe it.

Standing, I bring my palm down again, as hard as I can, on his ass, so hard the table bounces.

"Yellow." His sharp tone freezes me.

"What can I do? Are you okay?" I want to touch him, to reassure him, but I force myself to wait until he speaks.

He props himself up on his arms, giving me a cool look.

"Physically, I'm okay. But I feel like you're mad at me. You haven't said anything to me other than 'over' in a while." His eyes are wide, and he frowns.

I run the back of my hand over his cheek. "You *are* pleasing me so much. I should have told you I wanted silence. I'm sorry, Wolfie. When you said that you would sleep in the cock cage, it made me so wet, I wanted to mark you."

Theo presses a kiss on the back of my hand. "I'm sorry. I need more verbal affirmation. We can work on it."

"Wolfie, I don't mind giving you reassurance, and I'm so proud of you for slowing the scene down. Do you want to end the night here?"

"What was your next plan?" He shakes his head even as he asks the question.

"I was going to bring out my deerskin flogger to warm you up and cool you down. Make this gorgeous ass heat up more."

"I'm okay to continue. Can you please speak more to me, tell me what you're doing? I just feel very vulnerable, and I like the feeling, but I need to know your silence doesn't mean you are mad at me."

His request makes me want to burn down anything in his way. I will look after my boy.

I kiss his forehead. "Yes. I should have realized how challenging taking that gag was for you. I'm so proud of you."

"I liked it, Ma'am."

"You're a good boy, Wolfie. Give me your arm. I'm going to buckle your arms and legs and then throw my flogger."

He wiggles his butt on the table, and I laugh. "Yes, Ma'am, please."

He extends his arm, and I secure it. "And now this one."

I pull the strap tight, lean down, and drag my tongue along his arm. His skin is clean and salty.

At his feet, I buckle his left ankle, run my hand between his legs. I stick my fingers through the cage. "How is my cock doing?"

I move to buckle his right ankle.

"Fine. It wishes it could be let out."

"It'll have to wait a little longer," I hum on purpose as I stride over to my bag. I want Theo to hear me. I want him back to being relaxed.

My hand clasps the handle of my deerskin flogger, and I can't help the thrill of anticipation.

I lay the tails against my hand, loving the softness of this flogger.

"This should feel like a massage. Or at least that's what I've been told."

I press the handle to his lips, and he kisses it.

Because he's a good boy.

My throat is tight as I stand at the side of the table and throw the flogger.

It lands with a thud, and I brush the tails down his back.

I throw it again, right left, right left, working it across his wide shoulders, then down on his ass.

"The way your skin is red and shiny and so pretty, boy." I lightly skim my fingertips over his ass, he lets out a huff.

Thud, thud. I draw back, throw the flogger, loving how the tension leaves his shoulders.

He makes little mewling sounds as I work his shoulders, all the way down his back and over his ass again.

"How does that feel?"

"So good, Ma'am."

"You deserve it, boy," I throw the flogger again, watching as his skin turns a deeper shade of red.

I watch as the tails cover his ass. I get lost in the rhythm of throwing. The flogging calms my mind, makes me feel like I'm back in control.

I work the flogger in a figure-eight pattern, dragging it across his body, over his shoulders, down on his ass.

"Yes!" Theo cries.

"Your ass is now pink and looks so delicious." I throw the tails, loving how they cover his ass, the swell of his back.

I slow down my throw to drag it over his legs.

His gravelling whimpers make me clench between my legs.

"You were a very good boy tonight."

I lift the flogger and set it across his shoulder blades.

"A very good," I bring my palm down on his ass, the smacking sound loud in the room. "Boy," I spank his other cheek.

He turns his head to look at me over his shoulder and gives me that dimpled smile that I love.

I drag my palm over his ass. His skin is warm, and give it a gentle squeeze. "Time to unbuckle you."

I start at his hands, kissing his wrist where the buckle was, then his feet. He waits until I come to the end of the table.

"You may sit up now."

"Thank you, Ma'am." Theo pushes himself up off the table, sits up. He reaches for my hand.

"I loved every part of tonight."

"Me too." I'm pushing down emotions that are threatening to overwhelm me, and I'm feeling guilty that I haven't shared how I am feeling with Theo.

But he's so happy, the smile on his face is so adorable and dopey, I don't want to say anything that will take him out of this state.

Besides, this is my guilt to deal with.

From my bag, I pull out a pair of sweatpants and a black t-shirt, and pass them to Theo.

"Thank you." He says it with so much appreciation, tears leak out of my eyes.

"I said I'd take care of you."

"Yes, Ma'am, you did. You are." The dimpled smile combined with the glassy eyes that follow me, makes want to lock the door of this dungeon and stay here forever.

But I have to keep moving.

I gather up the clothes he started the night with, throwing them in my bag. I'm picking up my skirt when Theo reaches out a hand to me.

"Callista, come here? Please."

I can't deny him. I stand in front of him. He pulls me to his chest, hugging me close, and in his arms, I feel safe.

"I just needed to hold you for a moment," he snuggles into my collarbone.

I close my eyes, letting his strength comfort me, easing away the churning self-disgust that's starting to rise up in my head.

"Let me finish cleaning the room while you get dressed?" He ducks his chin as he asks.

What more can I do to show him I'm not going to reject his offer of service? I grind my molars, knowing that I'm not going to hurt him because I won't be able to accept everything he has to offer.

"Thank you, boy."

I throw on the clothes I came in with, pack up my bag as Theo wipes down the bondage table and empties the ice from the bucket into the sink.

I watch as he cleans, noticing he's a little heavy in his movements.

My plan for aftercare was to take him downstairs to the quiet lounge, but I realize I don't want him out there, not yet.

"Wolfie." I sit on the small couch in the corner, drawing my legs up to my chest.

"Can I do something else for you, Ma'am?"

"Yes, come here," I pat the seat beside me. He sits, leans against me, but I pull him towards my chest, so his head is on my breast.

I take the blanket that's on the back of the couch and drape it over him.

"I'm proud of you for calling yellow." My voice is thick. It dawns on me how far Theo has come.

From tip-toeing around me to telling me what he needs is huge. "I always want you to tell me what you need."

He rubs his head against my breast, and I cup his cheek.

"This. I need this." His eyes meet mine and our gazes lock, and I exhale in relief that this man is okay, that he's still here with me.

I hold him, letting our combined warmth and strength settle my own wounds.

I wanted to put distance between us because I didn't want to be vulnerable.

But I needed this too.

His eyes close. I trace his strong jaw with my index finger, twirl my fingers through his hair.

As Theo's body grows heavier on me, I notice he has drifted off to sleep. I remind myself that this man is unattached.

He's not going to hurt me like my last relationship.

All he has done from the moment I met him is make my life easier.

But what can I give him in return?

Aside from getting his sexual needs met, Theo's life is stable.

The feeling that I am not playing a role or that I'm holding him back churns through my veins.

There are reasons why I'm not good at commitment.

Theo stirs against me. "Hey."

"Hey my boy. You ready?"

"Yeah." He sits up, leans toward me, his lips asking for a kiss.

I grant it, taking my time feasting on his state, slow and gentle.

"Let's go."

Theo stands, takes my bag, and holds the door for me.

Outside, the air is less heavy, like the feeling of an empty space, though there is still music pumping through the speakers.

"Looks so empty."

"It's late." I check my watch, realizing that our scene went on longer than I thought.

"We played," he waggles his eyebrows, grinning.

"Yes, we did." I grab his hand before turning towards the elevators.

As soon as the elevator door opens, Amy runs towards us. "Clive is just in the shower."

"Were you waiting for us?" I ask.

She grins at me, gives Theo a wink. "I was hoping you'd come to breakfast with us."

"Theo?"

"I'll go anywhere with you, Ma'am." Tears choke me up.

"Oh, I think this one's a keeper, Callie," Amy gives me a wink and grins.

I smile back, but my heart is galloping on the inside. Because I know he is a keeper.

This man said yes to sleeping in a cock cage, and I should have ended the scene right there.

I don't want to hurt him.

And I knew, before locking him up, because he told me, because he is open, honest and good, that he sees the cock cage as a sign of commitment.

I'm commitment-phobic. I don't know if I can handle this, and the guilt that's eating up my insides over it is tearing me apart.

But I'd rather be torn apart than hurt my sweet boy.

Even though it's going to kill me to leave him, I know I have to.

25

THEO

FEBRUARY 16TH

"You look like you had the best night of your life!" Clive claps me on the back outside Club Shivers.

He has a dopey grin on his face that matches my own.

"I did." My throat is tight, I still feel like I am floating high on the post-scene endorphins.

Callie pauses her conversation with Amy and reaches over and ruffles my hair.

"Breakfast," Amy says. "Or you could open Shel's for us?"

"It just might be worth the drive back and watch these boys cook naked for us," Callie says, fisting my hair, tilting my head down. "But Ryan would blow a gasket if I let them into his kitchen. The place on Maineland has good grub." Callie's eyes glimmer as she slants her lips across mine in a sweet kiss.

"Yep," Amy loops her arm through Clive's. "See you there."

In the car, Callie has her hand on my thigh the whole time, checking me over to make sure I'm okay.

"I'm fine, Ma'am. I loved it. Thank you for tonight."

"You're welcome, Theo," she flashes me her real smile, the one that shows her dimples and makes me glow inside.

When we're settled in a big booth by the window, Amy teases Callie about Shel's not being closer when you need a good breakfast, but it's obvious Amy cares about her and Callie doesn't mind the good-natured teasing.

Callie keeps her hand on my leg the whole time, which is exactly where I want it.

The post-scene feeling has hot need dancing along my skin, and I want to touch her.

I lean against her shoulder, listening to Amy and Callie talk.

The conversation is light and teasing.

They are obviously old friends, and I'm so touched to be included in Callie's circle.

When we say goodbye, Amy whispers in Callie's ear, and Clive shakes my hand. "Hope to see you again, Theo."

The look he gave me made my stomach flip-flop. As if he didn't think he'd see me again, at least not with Callie.

"I'm sure I'll see your face again," I tell him, but glancing at Callie, who stares straight ahead, not meeting my eyes, forms a knot in the pit of my stomach.

She did tell me this wasn't good timing.

That she wasn't available for a relationship.

Stop it. I don't want to take myself down that path. Callie holds my hand the whole way home, and it makes the fears subside.

"Bed boy, now." She grabs a fistful of my shirt, pulling me in for a long kiss that leaves me gasping.

"Yes, Ma'am." My lips are tingling from her kiss. I shuck the shirt and throw it to the floor, noticing how Callie has corrupted me.

I'm taking my slacks off when she grabs my ass.

"You're so damn sexy." Her bare leg slides against mine.

Between the kitchen and my bedroom, she'd stripped naked.

My pulse gallops the way it always does when she gives me praise.

She hugs me from behind and pushes me onto the bed, her breasts swaying.

No other woman has ever turned me on like she does.

With that sly, sexy grin, she flops down beside me, spreads her legs wide, and gives me her best mock "come hither" gesture.

"Give it to me." Her voice is all hot command, and I don't need to be ordered twice.

I bury my nose in her pussy, inhaling her scent, like I'm a football player running for a touchdown.

She grabs my head with her hands, pushing me against her sweet, tender flesh.

Her pussy is swollen, already slick, and I lap up the fresh juice, savouring how she tastes, wanting to drown in it.

"Good boy!" Her praise keeps me going, eager to get her to orgasm.

I know how she likes it by now, and I suck her clit until I feel her legs start to tremble.

She pants above me, little breathy sounds that send shivers down my spine.

My nipples zing as she brushes her thumbs over them.

"I'm coming!" She lets out a high-pitched wail as I keep my face buried in her sweetness.

I feel her body heave, her legs come close around my mouth.

I'm content to stay here. Knowing that I gave her pleasure makes me feel satisfied and want to give her more.

Even as my balls constrict.

I feel her nub getting swollen, her breathy pants above me, demanding me to give her more, until I feel her tighten underneath my tongue.

Her legs clamp against me. I suck hard on her sweet clit, wanting to hear her explode.

"Theo! Theo!" She pants my name, and it goes right to my caged cock, constricting against the metal bars, pushing back into me.

She arches her back under me, raising her pussy to my lips.

I don't let go, sucking her clit even though her nails are digging into my shoulders.

A high-pitched cry rips from her mouth. "Fuck!"

Her body relaxes under mine as the orgasm recedes.

She lifts my head from between her legs.

Her beautiful face is all drunk with pleasure.

"You're my sweet boy," Callie says as I move myself up her body.

She pulls me down and brings my head to the crook of her shoulder, brushing her lips against my forehead.

Callie snuggles against me, wrapping her leg over mine, right next to the cock cage.

"Thank you, Ma'am, for tonight. I had the best time." I nuzzle her neck.

She gives me the glowiest smile, cupping my cheek, and there is nowhere else I want to be or stay, forever.

"Go to sleep."

I don't think I can drift off. The amount of pent-up frustration coursing through me is so high, I can't calm down.

Callie nestles my head against her warm, soft chest.

"I said sleep," she says, amusement evident in her tone.

"Yes, Ma'am," I whisper, and with her arm around me, I drift off.

But a nighttime erection wakes me up, not much later.

Callie has tossed all the blankets in her sleep, leaving us chilled in the cool night air.

She cries out, a breathless moan that reverberates between us, reaching for something that she doesn't find, and tugs the blankets off me as she rolls onto her side.

I wrap her in my arms, wondering if I should wake her up or let her sleep in this restless state.

Glancing at my phone, it shows 4:00 am.

My balls feel like they're going to be ripped off.

The nighttime erection woke me up because I'm not used to sleeping with the cage around my dick.

Callie turns towards me, and I can't help but wrap a finger around a silky, cool strand of her hair.

The night we had at Club Shivers healed something in my soul, soothing my past wounds.

Every second thrilled me.

The sting of the flogger ignited a craving that only grew stronger.

Her touch demanded more—more control, more fire.

My mouth ached to be claimed by her, desperate for her to take my submission even further.

Whatever way she wanted me, I wanted her to demand it of me, so that I could satisfy her.

So I could please her. But most of all, I wanted to ease the worry and doubt that I saw flicker across her expression.

One of the things I love most about Callie is how vulnerable she allows herself to be.

My ex treated kink like a porn fantasy to be acted out.

Kink with Callie is fun, mutual pleasure, satisfaction, and the more we are together, the more I see it as being part of our relationship and not just the reason for the relationship.

The sweet, musky taste of her pussy still lingers on my tongue.

"Hey Mr. Sexypants. Did I wake you?" she asks with a yawn.

"No, I've been up for a while."

"Why?" Callie yawns again, stretching then sits up. "I don't think I slept well."

"You were tossing and turning," I wince as the burning tugs at my balls.

"Wolfie, what is it?" The panic in her voice pierces me like a dart to the heart.

I don't want to make her upset.

"The cage... I'm not used to-"

Callie sits up, reaching for the chain around her neck.

"Nighttime. It's burning and pulling."

"Why didn't you tell me you needed me?" she slides the chain over her neck.

Her tone is harsh, and I hate myself for it, but I flinch.

She grabs my shoulder, pushing me towards the mattress.

"You're a good boy, Theo, but it's my job to take care of this cock, and if you were uncomfortable and needed me, then it was your job to tell me. I'll never be mad at you for telling me what you need."

She unlocks the cage with a soft click, then slides it off me, releasing the tight grip.

"Yes, Ma'am." I get the words out as I rush to the washroom.

After I pee, I splash cold water on my face, and come back to her.

"I'm sorry."

"It's okay, boy. Come here." Her tone is soft, reassuring as she pats the bed beside her, and I slide back into it.

She throws her legs over mine, runs her hand down my chest to my balls, cupping them in her hands.

"How are they doing?" She asks softly, concern flickering in her eyes.

"Fine. A little tender maybe, but fine." And I'm so horny, her touch makes me hiss through my teeth.

"I need to see," she lifts the blanket off of me, moving between my legs.

She strokes my dick, then her beautiful lips close around the head of my cock, dropping teasing kisses all over my shaft.

I can't help it; my hands find their way into her silky hair, and I growl in pleasure.

The feel of her mouth is molten silk, and I could drown in the feel of her tongue.

My hips buck off the bed. My cock is super sensitive, and the slightest touch makes it jump.

"You're a good boy," she runs her hands up my legs.

Her praise, combined with her touch, makes me want to roll on my tummy.

But there is something in her tone that makes me pause, that sends a mini bolt of fear dashing the hope I had felt.

"Ma'am, is everything alright?"

"You're perfect, Wolfie," she presses her breasts against my chest, the heat of her body soaking into me.

Her silky strands tickle my nose.

"My boy." Something in her tone has me shifting, but she touches her lips to mine, and a part of me veers off from this moment.

Her gentle stroking, teasing my bottom lip, is undoing yet another wound from the past.

But it's also making alarm bells go off in my head.

Because trauma is fun that way.

"Callista?" Her name comes out like a panicked note.

"I got you, Wolfie." She slants her mouth against mine, parting my lips effortlessly.

Our tongues meet, a dance that I'm being lured to take part in, but I don't need to be convinced.

I kiss her back with such intensity my lips bruise.

She reaches between us, her hand circles my cock.

"I want you inside me," she spreads her legs open. "Now."

"Yes, Ma'am." She presses my shoulders down, till my mouth is hovering near her breasts.

I get the hint.

My mouth comes around her nipple, and I suck on it, moaning deep and low from my belly as the taste of her skin fills my bloodstream.

My cock throbs as I suck until she grabs my hair and pulls me off to her other breast.

I circle her nipple with my tongue, tasting the saltiness of her delicate skin, then suck on the tip.

Her hips rise above me, like she's trying to mesh us together, and she grabs my ass.

I drop little kisses along her skin, up to her face, where I kiss her, twirling my tongue against her.

"Oh."

That little sound makes my blood surge with heat.

I rise up on my elbows, staring into her gorgeous eyes.

"My Callista," I whisper.

She shakes her head, cups my face, holding me there. "Get that hard cock in me, boy."

I kiss her again as I line up, then she's pulling me into her, and my cock sinks inch by inch into her wet heat.

"You're so big, boy."

I'm so fucking sated my eyes roll back in my head as I move, my blood heating with desire.

Never has another woman done it for me like this, and I want to stay here forever, buried in her pussy in my bed, forgetting that everything else exists.

All that matters is this strong, beautiful Dominant woman who controls my every move.

She rolls her hips, wraps her arms around my waist and moves with me, rising to meet my every stroke.

We start slow, staring into each other's eyes, and in hers I see acceptance, love, a home I didn't know I could ever have.

She cries out as I drive her to the next peak.

"Harder. Faster!"

"Yes, Ma'am," I say as I dive deeper, sinking so far into her depths, my thoughts cease to exist.

Every thrust I gave her, she met me. I thrust harder, longer, she rocks beneath me, never missing a beat.

She lets out a cry that bounces around the room, a sweet song to our lovemaking that makes my breath hitch in my throat.

Her nails dig into my flesh, scoring me against my back. Her touch burns, electric and demanding.

I growl with need. The want for this woman to make me hers forever is in the air between us.

She rolls her hips, digging her nails into me more. The bite of pain sends adrenaline through my body. My cock is so damn hard I don't know how much longer I can last.

"Yes boy! I'm coming! Come with me, come now!"

A wave of pleasure so forceful it grabs me until all I can do is pant her name.

Her pussy clamps on my cock, gripping me so tight, keeping me buried in her.

Her brows furrow as her orgasm drives her over the edge and she screams—that's what makes me come undone.

The bed shakes with the force of my release, arms trembling as a low growl slips from my lips.

Stars blur my vision while spilling into her sweet heat, her legs wrapping around me as panting steals my breath.

Lying against her, careful to keep my weight off, she draws her legs over mine, pressing my cheek against her breasts.

She kisses my nose, my jaw, then finds my lips, kisses me slowly and long.

"That was good."

"Perfect way to start my day."

She cups the back of my neck, runs her hand through my hair. "I have to go home."

"I know. I'll come see you this weekend." I nuzzle against her shoulder.

"What if I ordered you to come with me?" Her tone is wistful.

"I have a presentation tomorrow."

"If I ordered you to, would you?" Her hand snakes into my hair, grabbing a fistful and tugging my head up and she stares at me with an intensity that sends chills down my back.

"Callista, what's going on?"

She gives my hair another tug, hard enough to bring tears to my eyes. "Answer me, boy."

"If you ordered me to come home with you?" I can't believe I'm even considering this. "We agreed that this couldn't interfere with our work."

Fear chokes me as I say the words.

"Yes, we did. And that this wouldn't be a long-term thing." Her hand drops from my hair, she cups my cheek with her palm.

"Callie? Tell me what's going on." My mind is in overdrive, thinking of all the possibilities, and I don't like that is where my thoughts are running to, but she told me from the beginning she has a habit of bolting.

"Nothing," she shakes her head. "I know you have your business, and

I wouldn't do anything to jeopardize that. It was a silly question. Can you please go make us breakfast?"

"Are you sure we're okay?" I take her hand in mine and lay a kiss on the back of it.

"We're fine, Wolfie. I think I need more recovery from last night."

"I want to go to Club Shivers with you again." I watch her face as I say it.

She smiles slyly, then sits up against the pillows.

"That would be fun. Shower before you cook."

"Yes, Ma'am," but my nerves are jumpy. I'm wondering if things are okay between Callie and me or if I have done something to make her rethink this.

After my shower, I'm making us breakfast when she comes out of her shower, smelling like that familiar body wash.

"Hey Mr. Sexypants. I'm going to have to eat and run." She doesn't quite look at me.

"Everything okay?" The words are hollow. I want to drop to my knees and beg her not to leave me, but I want to trust that this isn't the end for us, that she meant all the words she said to me at Club Shivers.

"They got another packet of documents from the town. Grady wants to go over them with me."

In all the time that I've known Callie, Grady has never shown an interest in the diner.

She won't quite meet my eyes.

"Callie, I really want you to accept help with this. Let my brother look at it and see if you can make the Hops an offer to buy them out."

She draws herself up, smooths down her top. "Even if they did, we'd still have to convince the town to let us stay, but I think it'd be easier. Maybe they're worried about bad blood spilling to the next generation."

"I'm going to come next weekend." I say as I pass her a plate.

"You have that three-day conference." Callie takes the plate over to the island.

"You're right, I forgot," I have to go to the cybersecurity conference in New York. "Want to come to NYC with me?"

She takes a bite of food, shaking her head as she chews it. "I'd just be a distraction."

"A sexy distraction." I wiggle my hips.

Her smile spreads on her lips, but doesn't light up her eyes. "Theo, I need to get the diner in order, and you have a business to look after. Don't worry about coming out for the next couple of weekends." I rush over to her, dropping to my knees beside her chair. "Callie, tell me what's wrong."

She places her hand on my head, rubs a circle on my scalp. It immediately makes me relax.

"You didn't do anything wrong. You're my perfect good boy."

Her words loosen the anxiety in my gut.

"But I need...with Daphne getting better and my plan thrown into pieces. I want to be with you." She says it softly.

I glance up, and she's staring into space.

"I want to be with you too, and if you need a pause-" I try not to choke on the word. "I can understand that."

"But I'm selfish. Because I still want my good morning texts and my good evening texts and my cock shots."

"Yes, Ma'am." Though panic is slithering through my body. She wants to go back to how we were at the beginning?

"I need to figure out what to do next."

"I understand." I want to gather her in my arms and tell her that we can figure it out together.

"This is good, thanks for breakfast." She pushes her plate away.

I stand, taking it to the sink.

Turning back to face Callie, I lean across the island and take her hands in mine.

"Callie, if you don't want this?"

"Boy, did I say I didn't want this?" Her tone is sharp, but her gaze stays on my face.

"No," I shook my head. "I think what you are saying is you just want to figure out what you do next."

"Yes, I will let you know."

"Okay." My mouth tastes like acid.

She gets up, comes around me, gives me a hug. "You're the best, Theo."

Her tone is one she'd use for a friend, and the distance makes me feel like screaming down the sun.

"Help me get my bags?"

"Of course."

I spend the next twenty minutes helping her pack, then I carry her bags down for her and load them in her car.

"Thanks for surprising me. I like that."

"You're welcome. I had a good time," she pats my face, brushes her lips against mine lightly.

I hold her door for her, then close it when she gets in.

She waves goodbye, and I wave back, my heart in my throat, wondering if it's the last time I'll see Callie.

26

CALLIE

MARCH 4TH

We are in that afternoon dip, past the lunch bustle, before the after school and dinner crowds.

I wonder what Theo is doing right now and if he is okay. I miss him so much I physically ache from it.

"That's not how I do it," Daphne yanks the silverware out of my hands, drops it on the table and unrolls it. "If you do it this way, it takes the customers longer to unwrap it."

"I do it how Grandpa did it. Nobody's complained." My voice is barely above a whisper.

I don't want to upset her.

But she hunches her shoulders and stares at the table, refusing to meet my eyes.

"It's one of the changes I made. If you had visited for more than two seconds when Shel's re-opened, you would have known that." Daphne brings the bin of silverware over to her and starts wrapping the napkins how she wants them.

She's still recovering.

It's something I tell myself daily. Daphne is making improvements. She's not driving yet, but this week, she worked four hours at the diner and went to Madison's basketball practice.

Her therapists and doctors are happy with her progress.

With her hair pulled back in her high ponytail, humming to herself as she works on the table settings, I'm transported to when Daphne just started taking over Shel's, and the memory roars in, playing like a movie.

I just finished my shift at the garage but drove to Rising Harbour because Uncle Henry was short staffed and slammed.

I stopped to get coffee.

"Don't you work a full day?" Daphne glanced up from her laptop.

"I'm done with my shift. Brenda, I'm here for Henry's coffee."

"Must be nice," Daphne said. "To work whenever you want."

That was one of the last times I had set foot in the diner.

Daphne likes things to be a certain way—who doesn't—and working as part of a team isn't something she's ever had to do, not really.

She's smart and friendly, people like her, and she's good at following rules.

Her movements are slow, but the look of determination on her face tells me to let her do what she wants to do.

"Callie, I don't like the menu changes you made. Seriously, who wants to come to a diner for lentil soup?" She says it as if I'm serving our customers filth on their shoes.

"It's Grandma's recipe, and customers have loved it! We serve it only on Thursdays, so it draws people in. That's the point of the specials."

"I know how this business works. I own seventy percent." Daphne slaps a set of cutlery down, glares at me.

"Daphne, what's wrong?" High spots of colour appear on her cheeks; her eyes are icy as she glares at me. It's her *I'm pissed off*, look.

But the only thing she does with her anger is make passive-aggressive comments.

"I got an email from a lawyer." She finally glances at me, her lip turning up in a snarl.

"Noel. I told you that Theo's brother was going to look at the sale of the building for us."

I say it as gently as I can, in case she has forgotten.

My pulse spikes, recalling the cute smile on Theo's face as I finally accepted the help he'd been offering.

I met with his brother Noel through a video call, and I can see the family resemblance, but Noel was all brisk and in charge, straight to the point.

"Who says I want to sell?" She pushes back her chair, stands up and strides to the back of the restaurant, looking at her mural.

"What?" I'm so confused, I don't know where to start.

My sister is upset, and I don't know if that's because of pain or brain fog or because she's just picking petty fights and wants an argument that I'm *not* going to give her.

It's ironic that Daphne has such strong opinions about me being a Domme.

Between the two of us, I'm not the one who would be pegged—scoff—as someone who could be in charge.

But I want the people I care about to be happy.

That's what Theo and I have in common.

My way of ensuring peace is not to give them fuel for their fire.

You want to throw a tantrum and trash the place? Okay, go ahead.

I'm not going to help, but I'm not going to stop you.

"It's nice to be asked, Callie. Nobody asked me whether I wanted to sell or buy the building. Nobody asked me if I wanted to have lentils on the menu!"

She turns, her hands on her hips, and I cover my mouth, stifling a smile because this is ridiculous.

We're not arguing about the price of lentils, because she knows as well as I do how damn cheap they are.

I'm not sure why she's upset, but I don't know if I want to tiptoe around her feelings when it's not going to get us anywhere.

"Daphne, I came back and tried to help. I know I do things differently than you, but if you look at the books, you'll see that what I have done—along with Uncle Henry, Brenda and Ryan's help—we increased profits. Tell me what you want, but I am not going to sit here to listen to you being petty with me."

We glare at each other, just like we did when we were kids and she blamed me for getting a stain on her favourite blouse, even though orange wasn't ever my colour.

The bell chimes, and fortunately Brenda is back from making a deposit at the bank.

"Hi girls! Rain is coming down pretty hard out there! I'm going to get soup on for the afternoon crowd."

"Thanks, Brenda, I'm going upstairs."

She raises an eyebrow at me, looks at Daphne's turned back, tilts her head, then makes a *shooing* gesture.

"Go ahead, Daphne, and I've got this, don't we? And Anna should be here any moment. I saw her getting her kids off the bus."

The door chimes again. "Hi!" our cheerful server calls out. "Here, Daphne, I got these for you." Anna gives Daphne a bouquet.

Daphne's face loses all the anger. She takes the bundled flowers and gives them a sniff. "Thanks, Anna."

"See you later," I call as I escape.

I leave them talking about where to put the flowers and if old Mr. Mallery is going to come in for his afternoon lunch late today and wave to our kitchen staff and Ryan.

But once I'm out of Shel's, rain pelts my skin, cold and insistent, each drop a jolt that cuts through the emotional fog. I lean against the door, closing my eyes.

I don't know what I did wrong or why Daphne always has this animosity towards me.

Our whole life, I tried to do what she wanted. I covered for her, I worked to make her life easier.

When she fell short on her first year of college tuition, I paid her fees before her scholarships came in.

Inside my cozy little apartment, I flop down on the couch, reaching for my phone.

There is only one person I want to text, and because I'm selfish, I do it.

> Hey Wolfie.

Even as I press send, tears gather at the corners of my eyes. I have to make a decision, and I don't know what to do.

> Hi Callista!

I don't want to leave him hanging.

I feel hollow inside, and I know it's unfair to him.

Since our night at Club Shivers, I've kept our interactions quick, almost brisk.

He came by one weekend after that night, and we spent most of it going over legal stuff for the building.

We fucked quickly, then sat and watched a movie.

Don't get me wrong, I loved cuddle time, with his head in between my legs, my legs over his shoulders, where I rubbed little circles on his head and Theo made those adorable sounds.

But I know I have pulled back emotionally, and that's not fair to him.

At least the timing works in my favour as I try to sort out my head.

Theo's been busy with his brothers as Evan is getting married soon.

> What's your self-care today?

My boy knows me so well.

Even if I haven't communicated to him why I have pulled back, he knows something is on my mind.

He hasn't asked, trusting me to tell him what's going on when I'm comfortable, and I appreciate that because my head is cloudy.

I'm feeling pulled between my obligations to my family and looking after my own self-interest.

> Going to take Morris for a ride.

> I'm so damn jealous of Morris.

I howl. The laughter eases the tension from the encounter with my sister, and I wish Theo were here.

> I'll send you pics.

> Have a good ride.

Feeling better than I had all day, I throw on my wet gear. I don't care if I look ridiculous in my lime green kit, I want to be visible to the cars on the road, and I want to take Morris on the highway.

***

An hour later, I'm loading Morris back into storage at Uncle Henry's, when the light in the main bay flips on.

"Hello?" I know Uncle Henry and Aunt Millie are out-of-town today and all the staff has long gone home.

"It's me, Callie."

"Hi, Grady."

He runs his hand through his beard, yawns. "How did Morris do?"

"Morris is always great." I chuck off the rest of my wetsuit, leave it to dry and lock the storage gate.

"What's wrong?" I stop in front of him. I see the worry on his face, and my heart's in my throat. "Are the kids okay? Daphne?"

"Everything's fine. Daphne wants to talk to you at Shel's." Grady runs a hand over his beard. The man is tired.

"Just hear her out, Callie, okay?" Grady's brown eyes are serious, and my stomach tightens in a ball.

"I'm always willing to listen."

"Give you a ride over?"

"Sure." I hop in Grady's truck, my heart in my throat, thinking this is just like Daphne.

Instead of texting me or coming over to the shop herself, she sent Grady.

But I chew the inside of my cheek and tell myself to be patient.

Using screens still gives my sister a headache, and she likes getting her husband to do things for her.

Daphne *really* should read one of my female-dominant books; she might be surprised.

"Your man is here."

My pulse jumps as I see Theo in front of Shel's, and my heart gives that ridiculous flutter. I hadn't dared to hope that he would come and see me without my asking him to.

I know I left things between us in a kind of limbo state, and guilt twists in a hard knot in my belly.

But I can't help the startle laugh that escapes my lips. "That's a surprise."

"Callie, I'm happy for you. You deserve to have someone to love."

"Thanks." I already have my seatbelt off, the door closing behind me and stopping myself from running to him and throwing my arms around him because this isn't a Hallmark movie.

"Hi Callista." Theo strides to me, leans towards me, and I know he wants to kiss me.

"Hey, Mr. Sexypants."

Did I say it just to see him blush? Maybe.

Yes, absolutely, I did. I wrap my arms around him, pulling him close, and he nuzzles against my neck. And he smells so good and feels so good in my arms, I never want to let go.

"When you texted me you were...?"

"On the way." Theo grins and pulls me close to him. "I couldn't stay away any longer."

The stupid wide grin on my face tells him everything I need to.

He opens the door for me, and I'm surprised to see Uncle Henry at the counter, Aunt Millie pouring coffee into mugs. "Everyone's here! Hi Theo, nice to see you again."

"Hi everyone," Theo strides over to shake hands with my uncle. Leaning over the counter, he gives my aunt a kiss on the cheek.

I stare at the mural as Uncle Henry offers Theo a drink. It's a piece that needs to be finished.

"Daphne, I want you to finish the mural."

"No. That was the old me. New me can't," she loops her hand through my arm and, just like always, any animosity for her fades away.

She's my little sister. I'll take care of her always.

Theo comes over to us, handing me a coffee with the handle of the mug turned out. "Thank you."

"Please sit down," Grady says.

"If this is a family meeting, I should wait upstairs," Theo says.

"I want you to stay." I reach for his hand, and I don't care that my family is watching.

I slant my lips against his in a quick, gentle kiss that lingers just long enough to make his breath catch, and then give him my hand. He takes it, lacing his fingers through mine, and I swallow past the lump in my throat.

He's here. He showed up for me.

"Sit, everyone," Grady says.

We file into the large corner booth.

Theo next to me, Uncle Henry and Aunt Millie across from us.

Grady brings over a chair for him and Daphne, so they're at the head of the table.

"I can't wait to see why I was summoned." Uncle Henry says.

"I just came in with Morris."

Theo squeezes my hand. The smell of his spicy aftershave tickles my nose, and I want to snuggle him and kiss him until he begs for mercy, but we have to get through this ambush first.

Uncle Henry raises a bushy eyebrow. "You took Morris out on the wet roads?"

"Yeah, there was lots of grip. I only went up to Edge's Valley and back."

"Lucky girl. I wanted to take out Church, but someone stopped me," he elbows Aunt Millie playfully.

"Your age stopped you, dear," Aunt Millie shakes her head, smiling endearingly.

"You know who doesn't own a motorcycle?" Daphne points to her chest.

"Do you want one?" I ask, and I can't stop the snarky smile that's on my lips.

"Obviously not!" Daphne rolls her eyes.

"Don't want you to feel left out." I give her a cheeky grin, and she sticks out her tongue at me.

Theo presses his leg against mine, and I exhale softly, wanting my heart to stop beating in double time.

"That's the point," Daphne says. She stares down at the table. "I'm sorry I've been a drag to all of you over the last few months."

"Honey, no!" Aunt Millie reaches across the table and grabs Daphne's hand.

"Daphne, we're happy that you are recovering," Uncle Henry adds.

"Babe, you're not a burden," Grady drapes his arm over her shoulders, which she shrinks out of.

"I mean, you are still a pain in my ass." I reach across the table and offer her a fist bump.

Daphne glances up, her tear-streaked cheeks shiny, and meets my gaze. She returns my fist bump.

"Thanks, Callie, for coming home and looking after my kids and Shel's."

"Yeah, no problem." I'm blinking back tears myself.

"I'm not the same. The brain injury has changed me."

"We still love you, honey!" Aunt Millie sniffs back tears of her own.

"Daphne, if there's anything you need–" Uncle Henry says.

"I know you love me, and I'm lucky to have an amazing family. I never left Rising Harbour because I didn't think I could."

Uncle Henry shifts in his seat, staring intently at Daphne.

Something deep in my chest aches.

I didn't know.

But now, looking at her hunched shoulders, her teary face, running through all the past remarks my sister made to me, it was so obvious I can't believe I missed it.

"Are you saying you wanted to leave?" The question, gently asked, as if he's curious, comes from Theo.

"Yeah. I had dreams, too. But Grady got a job here and there was Shel's and people who wanted to hire me when I finished school," Daphne says and shrugs. "I don't regret any of it. Maybe Shel's."

"You don't want to run the diner?" I can't keep the surprise out of my voice, even as Aunt Millie shushes me.

"No. And honestly, I can't right now, and I'm not going to ask Callie to do it. Noel, Theo's brother, has helped us with the town council. He's also approached the Hops family about selling the building." Daphne says and suddenly stops.

"You're doing great, babe," Grady says, squeezing her shoulder.

"After several conversations with Noel...your brother is very smart," Daphne says to Theo.

"He's pretty good at what he does," Theo agrees.

"They've decided to sell it to us." Daphne says and grins. She looks so pleased with herself.

I'm so startled by the news, I laugh.

"That's amazing, honey." Aunt Millie beams.

"Wow. I didn't think they'd ever sell," Uncle Henry says.

"Me neither," I say.

"Even spite runs its course," Grady says.

"So this building is ours, mine and Grady's. But I want to sell my shares in Shel's."

My head is spinning so fast, I don't know how to process this. I'm wondering why Noel didn't tell me this after all our conversations, but I guess he kept it confidential between Daphne and Grady.

"Okay," Uncle Henry says. "And do what?"

"We're going to live with Grady's parents. I want to teach riding classes."

"Daphne..." I can't get out more than her name. This is radically different for my sister.

"I'm not asking you to pick up my shares, Callie. What you guys want to do with Shel's is your business. Noel thinks we are underutilizing our tourism attraction power. He thinks I was on the right track with events, but he wants me to play up the diner experience even more. Your brother loves to give advice," she says to Theo.

"Yes, he does," Theo says.

"And we're grateful," Grady says. "So, you three need to talk about it yourselves if you want to buy our shares before we put them on the market. But Daphne and I are out."

"Wait, you're taking the kids from us?" Aunt Millie's voice breaks, and she looks heartbroken.

"We'll visit lots," Daphne says.

"Let them go," Uncle Henry says. He cocks an eyebrow at me. "They always come back."

"Not to make a hasty exit, but I'm going to take my wife through the drive-thru before we relieve the sitter. The kids are going to finish out the school year here, but we're going to list our house next week."

Grady stands, stretches out his hand for Daphne, and she smiles at him. A true, beautiful, with her whole heart smile.

"See you!" She giggles as they leave the table.

Uncle Henry slides out of the booth and goes to lock the door behind them. "First thoughts?"

"I don't know, Henry. You and I can't run the place. We could sell it as a turnkey."

"I don't know what I want to do." I hate voicing that.

Because I should know exactly what I want to do, and really this news changes nothing for me. Because it's still a choice between going back to being a mechanic or running Shel's.

Standing from the table, Theo takes my hand, pulling me out of the booth gently. "You don't have to decide tonight."

"I know." I'm so glad he's here beside me, my heart is bursting.

"Callie, take your time about this. No pressure," Auntie Millie says.

"Do what's right for you, Callie. Shel was a great man. The diner isn't the only way to remember him." Uncle Henry is right that we don't need the diner to remember Shel.

"I'm proud of Daphne. I didn't think she'd ever leave." My aunt says.

"You knew she wanted out?" My legs feel suddenly wobbly. I lean against Theo.

"Oh yes! She applied only to one university in the province on purpose. But Grady got the job here before she could give an acceptance."

"I didn't know."

"Callie, she wanted to do what you did. Go on adventures. Have fun," Uncle Henry says.

I let out a hollow laugh. "She had a funny way of showing it. Talk to you guys tomorrow." I hug my aunt and uncle, and we say goodnight. The wave of emotions coursing through me feels like it's strong enough to knock me off my feet, and I don't know what to do with it all; part of me wants to curl up in the fetal position and stay there.

But, this hot, delicious man showed up. My boy is here.

As soon as we are upstairs, I push him against my front door and kiss him.

I kiss him with a low throaty growl, pressing my nails into his ass through his pants. I kiss him until I am dizzy, leaning my head against his chest.

"Thank you. For showing up."

"You're welcome, Ma'am."

Theo heads to the kitchen, takes out a pan and starts making me a snack. I don't even realize I'm hungry until he's set the omelette in front of me.

"Thank you."

"Got to look after my Callista." His gray eyes are intent and smoky as he leans down, asking for a kiss.

I slant my lips against him, the feel of stubble tickling my cheeks.

"This is nice." I'm not fighting him.

Theo showed up. He wants to take care of me, and I'm going to allow myself to bask in his show of love.

He tidies up the kitchen, then drapes his arm over my shoulders. "Bath or bed?"

"Bed. I want to snuggle."

He rubs his nose against my ear. "Perfect."

In the bedroom, he drops to his knees, and slowly takes off my jeans, dropping sweet little kisses down my thighs.

Every brush of his lips against my skin makes me shiver, and I play with his soft, wavy strands of hair, twirling my fingers through them.

He takes off my shirt, my sports bra, then brushes kisses over my breasts, between my cleavage, then up to my collarbone.

"There's nowhere else I want to be than here." He sits back on his heels, and my heart clenches.

I want to give this man everything he is seeking, but I don't know if I can.

Can this be the first relationship I don't run from?

He stands, taking my hand in his, and leads me over to the bed, pulling the sheets down. I get in, my eyes immediately close as soon as my head hits the pillow. I hear Theo taking off his clothes, and I open my eyes to drink in the sight of his body.

Usually when we are together, I'm the big spoon, with my arms wrapped around him, my front to his back.

Tonight, he slides in behind me, and I shuffle over to make room.

He wraps his arms around me.

I love how his wall of muscles feels against my back.

"Good night, Callista."

"Good night, boy."

Everything in my world might be up in the air, but this boy behind me is solid, and I cling to that as I drift off to a dreamless sleep.

27

THEO

MARCH 5TH

Soft, warm lips trace my collarbone, stirring me from my sleep, then teeth graze lightly where those lips were, making my breath hitch.

"Good morning, Wolfie." Her hot mouth presses against my throat. I groan, wanting to kiss her.

"Good morning, Ma'am," I go to brush my fingers through her hair but she grasps them in hers, kissing my knuckles.

"I want you to keep your hands at your sides. You move your hands, and I stop."

My cock twitches, anticipation rolling through me. "Yes, Ma'am."

She leans in, her hair brushing my lips, as she kisses my nipple, drawing it into her hot mouth, she flicks her tongue against it. It makes me squirm, my hips rise off the bed but my hands stay at my sides with willpower that could light up the country because I don't want her to stop.

Callista lifts her head off. Her eyes glowing, she moves over to my other nipple, gives it a long suck that has me bucking off the bed.

Her fingers twirl through my chest hair with a light, teasing touch, then she drags her lips down my stomach, stopping an inch away from my balls, close enough that I can feel her hot breath.

"Please, Ma'am." I grunt out the words. Struggling for control is making it hard to think.

"This is so frustrating, isn't it, Wolfie?" She presses down on my balls, massaging them with firm pressure, giving me the sexiest smile that drives me wild, and I squirm as I feel her fingers stretch, pressing down on my taint.

Fuck, she has stolen my breath, and the only thing I want is what she can give me.

Yearning so strong my hands come up like a rocket and I'm reaching for her, needing her touch, wanting that release.

"Please, Ma'am!"

"I said, keep your hands by your side," her tone all cool command that makes me salivate as a hot blaze of desire licks up my spine.

"Sorry, Ma'am!" I want to run my hands through her hair. I want to cup her face to tell her I'm sorry, but my hands are exactly where she told me to put them again.

She taps my dick hard enough to make me cry out, making me draw my legs up. Damn, that fucking hurt.

But the way she licks her lips makes me want more.

"Shall I continue?" Her gaze softens as her palm grips my cock. She's intently studying my face, checking in with me.

"Please, Ma'am. I'm green." I grit out the words, needing her to continue, even though I burn where she slapped me and I'm fighting not to make another sound.

She massages my balls, slowly at first and I hiss as she increases the pressure, all while locking her gaze to mine and then she shifts, still with my cock in her hand, gives it a tug that makes me feel like I'm going to be consumed in that blaze of desperate need.

"Ma'am!" My voice breaks with need, and the holding on to my control is taking everything from me, and I feel like I am burning with how much I want her to let me have this release.

"Good boy, Wolfie," she coos and kneels back on her heels, glides her thumb over my tip, circles her fingers and slides them over the head of my cock and the sight of her playing with me has me so hard I could break cement and turns up the fire that's ready to engulf me to the next level.

Leaning forward, she touches her nose to my balls, then with the lightest touch, skims her lips against my sac, so lightly it makes me growl.

It's hot torture and the perfect way to wake up.

I'm making a fist, pressing my arm against my body, keeping myself still because she told me to.

"I need lube."

I swallow, but can't take my eyes off of her as she rummages through the drawer, takes out a bottle, squirts some on her hands, then holds up a finger.

"Where do you think I'm going to put this, Wolfie?" Her eyebrows arch. The slow, seductive smile that spreads across her lips has me moaning.

"Up... my ass." Somehow got the words out through the haze of need.

"Hmm, I'm thinking about it. Beg me to finger your ass." Her tone is all stern command that sends me into pure desperation. A long wail escapes my lips as my hips buck off the bed.

"Please finger my ass, Ma'am! I want to take your finger. I'll do anything if you finger my ass, please, Ma'am!"

She slides to her knees, presses her mouth against my balls while nudging my thighs apart with her body.

Her hot breath on my balls makes my dick throb, almost painfully.

I want her to touch it, to kiss it, to suck it.

She moves her lips from my balls and kisses me, close to my cock, but not on it.

"Ma'am!" The cry is a shriek of neediness, and I don't care how pitiful I sound.

Her mouth near my dick is making me unravel.

Sweat flows from my brow.

But in my head, I'm chanting, yes, yes, yes.

Her finger teases at my entrance, slow and deliberate, and I'm already trembling before she even slides in.

A low, guttural moan rips from deep in my throat as she slides in deep.

My body shudders, unable to control the reaction as she holds me there, making me hers.

Each swipe of her tongue burns and makes me ache for more.

The electricity builds inside me, sparking through my body in jolts of heat and desperate need.

I gasp, hips bucking involuntarily, but she doesn't stop.

I'm at her mercy, every nerve laid bare and screaming for more.

"Yes, please!" She hits my P-spot, and the wave of pleasure takes my voice away. The pressure is so damn good I am drunk on it. I want to come so badly. I'm desperate.

My hands lift, reaching for her.

"Bad Wolfie." Her finger slides away from my prostate, wipes it on my leg, then grabs my steel-hard cock and pulls it down, releases it, slaps her palm against it, enough for me to cry out.

"Sorry, Ma'am. You're driving me wild, making me lose control."

"Am I?" The grin in her voice makes my pulse beat. She leans down, takes my cock in her hands, then licks the underside slowly.

"Yes, you are!" I pant. I can barely form words. I'm thrusting, wanting to drive my cock into her sweet hot mouth but pumping nothing but air.

"Don't move those hands, boy." She takes my cock deep into her mouth, sucking it so far back I can feel her throat close around me, causing my eyes to roll back into my head.

My hands are fisting the sheets, and I'm not going to let go, not until she says.

"You're so good to me, Ma'am." My voice catches as she swallows deeply on my cock.

This unexpected wake-up eases the doubt that I had since Valentine's Day.

I know Callie pulled away.

She's scared of commitment.

Her instinct is to run; told me that from the first time we were together.

But I know I make her laugh.

I hope I give her enough of what she needs so that I can make her stay.

Because my heart is open to this gorgeous woman, wanting her to claim me as her own.

Not for another one-night stand or a scrappy weekend.

Forever.

I want forever with her, and I'll do anything she asks of me.

Does that make me selfish?

I don't care. I want to take care of her in all the ways she'll allow it, and I want to be her soft place to land.

Her safe place to rest.

That's why I came... to tell her that I love her.

My breath hitches as I think about it, my hands wanting to drop the fabric, but I don't.

She takes me even deeper, sucks me harder, and my eyes roll back in my head, and I close them tightly, desperately trying to hold off the storm that wants to consume me. "I'm going to come!"

I bite down on my tongue, holding back because I need her to tell me.

"Open your eyes, boy." Her voice is laced with hot sweetness, and it compels me to obey.

"Ma'am, I'm trying!" I grit out the words through a grunt that's raw and primal.

She holds up a hand, then puts her thumb down and then her tongue is on the underside of my cock, gliding along the length, her body rocking with my cock in her mouth the sight is so erotic I have to look away or I'm going to burst.

But I know what she wants, what her gesture means.

"Count? Ma'am! I don't know if I can!"

She slaps my thigh so hard the sound echoes in the room and grabs my attention.

"Fuck yes, I can!" I pant out the words, filled with the desperation that she knows I am going to try. For her, I will obey.

Or scream myself dry trying.

She pinches my inner thigh, hard and sharp, and it's the bite of pain I need as she sucks me even deeper, the hot heat of her mouth making me fight, to hold it off, even longer.

Slurping noisily, that makes my balls burn and ache.

Her mouth laves back up to the tip, her tongue flicking so hard it sets off new shivers of need.

She puts down another finger.

I moan loudly and desperately, needing to come.

The desperation makes my hips come off the bed.

Her hands slide up my inner thighs.

She squeezes, one, two, three.

I've made it this far, I can make it further, even through the exploding fire at the base of my spine and the growling noises that aren't stopping because it's my desperate pleas echoing around the room.

"Callista! Please, please let me come!" I don't care how often this woman wants me to beg for her.

I'll do it every moment of every day if it pleases her.

My thoughts are thick. I'm totally taken with the need to come.

She sucks my cock, laving my slit, sending agony rocking through me.

I physically hurt with the force of holding back.

All I want to do is touch her hair, caress her face, but I'm keeping my eyes open, my hands at my side, knowing I have to if I want relief.

She mumbles something around my cock, setting off new vibrations, raising the heat to magma levels. My heart is going to burst out of my chest.

I'm staring at her fingers, *needing* her to put another one down.

Her head lifts up slightly; she slows down her hot pulls, her tongue rolling against my shaft.

The change of pace drives my desperation. Teases my resolve even further.

All I can think about is whether she's going to allow me to come, to release in her hot mouth.

Another finger goes down, and a growl is ripped from my throat.

Her mouth, her tongue, is pure bliss, pure torture, pure everything that I have wanted for so long.

Everything I didn't think I'd ever have.

I know I will serve this woman with every cell of my body. I will give her whatever she demands.

Sweat is drenching my back, so I shift off the bed.

"Please, please, Ma'am, please let me come! I need you to let me come!"

She takes every inch of me, deep into her warm wet mouth, tightening her mouth around me, swallowing on me hard.

"Fuck!" I shout as she squeezes my balls, and I'm fighting to keep my eyes open to still hold back, because that's what she wants from me.

Finally, she holds up her fingers, making a circle, a zero shape.

Letting out a frustrated growl, my hips come off the bed as I give in to the orgasm, shouting so loud it echoes off the walls, making the bed shake.

I'm emptying my cum down her hot lustful throat, moaning with the ache of release, until I am completely empty.

"Thank you, Ma'am." My head is buzzing with the rush of endorphins, the high of the release, and I flop back against the pillows, trying to catch my breath.

"Good boy, I didn't think you were going to hold out," Callie plays with my nipples, making me shift, opening my eyes.

"I will always do what you ask, Ma'am. Or expire trying to!" I waggle my eyebrows at her, and she leans over, runs a hand through my stubble.

"Your efforts are always appreciated." Her expression softens, and how she feels for me is written in her gaze. She doesn't have to say it back to me, and I know she might not, but that doesn't matter; I love her without condition.

She makes me want to kneel with my head bowed, offering up my devotion, my obedience, my love.

"I guess we have to get up." She nuzzles against my chest. I pull her close, dropping a kiss on her forehead.

"We could stay here."

"I've got to check on the diner. I suspect you have to check in with your teams. I spotted your laptop open."

"My phone went off with an alert at 2am. Nothing major, but I had to take care of it." I thread my fingers through her hair, loving how bright her eyes are right now and the small smile that curves around her mouth.

"Do you have any ideas of what to do today?"

She asks it softly, but it gives me pause.

It's always up to her what we do, where we go.

"I know last night was a lot, Callista. Anything I can do to help, I'm here. I'd love to plan our day."

"Yeah? What if you borrow Church and I take Morris and we hit the roads?" She's teasing, and I kiss her nose.

"I don't have a motorcycle license." I twirl a piece of hair around her finger. "Hunter wanted me to get mine when he got his years ago."

"Why didn't you?" She slides her hand over to my other nipple, and I hiss between my teeth.

"Because I'm a scaredy cat."

Callie laughs, throwing her head back, and I grin, pleased to ease her stress.

"We leave in twenty. Is that enough time to plan something?"

"I think I can manage." I turn my mouth so it's inches from hers, and she rewards me with a sweeping kiss that makes me groan.

"Time to hit the showers," she scurries off the bed, grabs my hand, and pulls me to my feet. "I'll let you do whatever you want today, boy, but the nighttime? That's all my call."

"You got it, Ma'am!" I waggle my eyebrows, knowing it will make her laugh, and I grin as her peal of laughter makes her look carefree.

"Boy, I'm so lucky to have you," she brushes her lips against mine, then pulls me up, marching me into the shower.

***

My shirt is sticking to me. It's hot and humid, and I'd take a boardroom meeting over this field trip any day.

I swat away insects.

I know something is in my shoe.

But the hour it took to hike up here?

For how Callie's face is glowing, I'd do it again.

She looks athletic and strong. In her hiking boots and the way her trek pants cling to her ass, I could admire her all day.

"You're not looking at the view," she says over her shoulder.

"Oh, I most definitely am," I take a step so that I'm behind her. She grabs my arms, pulls them around my waist.

"This is exactly what I needed, Wolfie. Thank you."

Her praise makes me beam as I sniff her hair, the smell of the slightly damp earth and growing things mingling in my nostrils with her shampoo.

"The waterfall is gorgeous. I see how it's your favourite lookout." The horsetail waterfall flows, dropping to a steep slope.

"I wish I had my camera with me," Callie turns in my arms. "Was it worth the hike?"

Staring into her blue eyes, I know I don't ever want to let this woman go, but I want her to feel as if we can make it work, even through circumstance.

No matter what Callie decides to do next, I want her to know I am going to be here for her.

"I'll go on a thousand hikes if it makes you happy," I press a gentle kiss to her forehead.

Rising onto her tiptoes, she glides her hands up my back to my shoulders, cupping my neck as she pulls me down into a passionate, greedy kiss.

"I know you have my back, Wolfie. Is there a picnic in your pack?" She flicks the strap of my backpack with a smirk.

"Maaaybe." I lace my fingers with hers, and we go to the picnic table that's off the path slightly.

Whistling, I place my pack on the table, unzip it and take out an insulated bag and two travel carriages. "Coffe."

"Yes!" Callie claps her hands together. "What else?"

"Go ahead and open it."

Her delight in taking out the food boxes, the chocolate-covered strawberries, and the place settings makes me happy.

I want this woman to be happy, and if a picnic will do it, then I'll bring her a picnic basket every single day.

"How did you do this?" Callie opens the food box, revealing her favourite panini sandwich.

"Brenda. I saw in the Rising Harbour community group that she had a side business of making picnic lunches."

"I didn't know that! I bet these are her famous pickles!" Callie picks up a container.

"She assured me you'd like them. Told me to make sure you had a good time." She sits on the bench, and I slide in across from her.

"Brenda's always cheered for me," Callie looks wistful. She passes me a plate, holding a sandwich out to me. "Take a bite."

"Oh my God," I say around the mouth of the food. The softest bread, tender meat with a sauce that's tangy and bright.

"Even when I was traveling the world with my team, I thought of Ryan's food."

I raise my eyebrows, unable to hide my smirk.

She swats me with a napkin. "It's true! Okay, maybe I was homesick. Theo, I don't know what to do. I know I'm supposed to be confident and in charge, but inside I still feel like a mess. I feel like my brain hasn't moved on since I found out about Daphne's accident."

"Callista, the accident changed Daphne's life. It impacted yours in huge ways."

She concentrates on her food, and slowly I finish mine, letting her have space to sort her thoughts.

"Don't you think I should be over it by now?" Callie says, glancing away from me.

"No. You are in charge. You are also generous and kind. You don't have to be confident all the time. I need you to put me on my knees in the bedroom, not tell me what to wear every day."

"But that could be fun?" The way she gazes at me with that sexy sly smile on her face makes my dick take notice.

In so many ways, Callie is confident and sure of herself in such an effortless way that it makes my admiration for her constantly bloom.

Her life is a mess, often chaotic, but she *owns* it. And that kind of confidence is damn sexy.

But I also know the amount of pressure she's been under and how hard she's on herself.

"Since that night at Club Shivers...Theo, I don't want to hurt you and I don't know what I'm going to do with my life right now. If I went back to the motocross team, I'd be traveling a lot. If I stay in Rising Harbour, we're still four hours away from each other."

The hollowness in her voice makes my stomach clench, and I want to reassure her.

"We can figure it out. I like to travel, and I can work from anywhere." She shakes her head no, the breeze whipping her hair in front of her face. "You have to meet with your team and give presentations to CEOs. That's a big part of your job."

"Yeah, but I don't have to do that every second of the day." I brush my fingertips against the top of her hand, stroking her gently until she meets my eyes.

"If you want to make it work, I'm in. Whatever it takes."

She starts packing up the bag. "We haven't even spent that much time together, not really."

My heart plummets to my toes. Is she breaking up with me? I'll respect her choice if that's what she wants, but I know she and I are good together.

I know that I want to belong to this woman, in whatever way she'll have me.

"Callie, what do you need?" I heft the backpack back on my shoulders and slide my arm around her waist. "I'm here for you."

She sighs in my arms, tilts her head up, and her lips meet mine. It's a soft, gentle kiss but still sends shivers down my back.

"Maybe I need a Dom to make the decision for me."

The dimples flash in her smile. I chuckle, kissing the top of her head. "Should we start our way down?"

"Yeah, Brenda has an afternoon appointment, so I told her I'd fill in for her. I want to spend more time with you, Theo. The kids are on a school break next week, and I'm going to help out. Daphne's getting there but still needs lots of support."

Disappointment slithers through my gut, but I push it away.

Is this an excuse for her not wanting to commit?

But it's not like she's lying to me about needing to be there for her family.

Needing to show her that I mean what I say, I loop my arm through hers, spin her gently towards me, and then sink to the grass on my knees.

"Callista, you make me feel like I'm on top of the world, even when I'm on my knees for you. You've patched my heart back together. I didn't think I'd ever surrender to another Domme again.

"Take all the time you need figuring out what your next step is, but I'm not going anywhere unless you tell me to."

I bow my head, staring at the ground, determined not to move, even when an insect starts climbing up my hand.

"Wolfie," her voice breaks. "You've patched me back together too, I...I-"

Her phone buzzes in her pocket.

I exhale as she cups the back of my neck. "Aunt Millie, you sound upset. What is it?" Her face takes on that cool expression she wears with her family. "You're breaking up. I can't hear you."

Standing, I brush off the dirt on my pants, take her hand and we climb down the track.

"See? I can let you take steps with me," she says, after she gave up on her phone call. "Thanks, boy," she grabs a fistful of my shirt and kisses me, a passionate sloppy kiss, that has my cock pressing against my zipper. "Whatever happens next, I'm here, Callista."

28

CALLIE

Aunt Millie is waiting for us at Shel's, fluttering behind the counter, and wiping it down over and over, the rhythmic swipe of her cloth against the wood mingling with the faint scent of fresh coffee.

"What's wrong?" My family members have a way of telling me only bad news, and until they stop that, I'm going to be on high alert.

"Daphne's in-laws want us to visit them over spring break! Isn't that great!" Aunt Millie claps her hands together, her face all flushed.

That off-balance sensation that I have had ever since I returned to Rising Harbour threatens to choke me.

Grabbing Theo's arm, because I want to feel something solid, I ease into a seat, watching my aunt's face closely because for someone who complained about not having time with the kids, she looks happy.

"I thought I was going to hang out with them during the break."

"Callie, we don't need you. Think of all the time you can spend with Theo!" Aunt Millie looks him up and down, hides her mouth behind

her hand, laughing. "You can take her on all kinds of dates in the city."
Ridiculously, I feel my face blush, but I'm happy to see my aunt in
good spirits. "If you can really spare me."

"I got you, kiddo!" Brenda says, waltzing in from the kitchen. "I hear
there are shares that might be up for sale, and nobody asked Ryan and
me if we wanted in?"

So maybe it's true what my sister says, that I'm a control freak. And
maybe it's true what Theo said, that I don't need to take on all the
decisions for all the people in my life.

"I didn't know if you wanted... I still don't know what I want to do."
My head is sent spinning with too many thoughts crowding in all at
once.

"Take the week and think about it," Aunt Millie says. "Brenda and
Ryan don't want the whole thing. Uncle Henry and I still want our
shares, and I want to be here when I can. Callie, you've done an
amazing job here, and I'm so grateful you were there for us when we
needed you. Dealing with the town made my blood pressure rise. But
if you don't want to run the diner, we understand."

"Yeah, we got each other, Callie. Just like always," Brenda says, her
smile warm.

"I guess I could spend a week in the city?" I stare into Theo's deep grey
eyes. The slow, sultry smile that spreads across his face makes my pulse
jump with hot need, and there is nothing more than I want to do than
spend the week with my boy.

"Oh! Time to open!" Brenda says, racing to the door. Aunt Millie gives
my shoulder a squeeze as she passes me.

"Yes, Ma'am, you could spend a week in the city with me." Theo leans
down, his hot breath brushes against my ear, sending a shiver down
my spine. "I want to ask you something."

His tone turns so serious that I'm clenching my jaw.

I know what he's going to say... at least, I suspect.

"Ask me anything, boy." My heart is beating harder than a thoroughbred.

Still holding my hand, Theo slides into the booth across from me.

"I told you that I am not going anywhere. Whatever you want between us, I am here for it. I think I have proven to you that this isn't a transactional relationship. Callista, I care about you." He presses the back of my hand to his mouth. "I want you to be happy. I want to spend these five days together, and I want you to see if you can be happy with me, living with me, seeing each other every day."

The intensity of his words is stabbing me deep in my heart.

I know what's coming, and every cell of mine suddenly feels like it's in overdrive, telling me to bolt.

"Theo, I want to see you every day." I get the words out and wish I hadn't because he's looking at me as if he wants to take my hand and run through the streets.

As if he wants to give me everything he has.

My pulse galloped, a desperate mix of yearning and dread knotting my stomach.

There's a part of me that wants to gag him at this moment, to keep him from saying the words that are clear in his serious, grey eyes.

No matter how much I long to hear them.

He glances away, back to my face, and I see the hope clearly on his expression.

"Callista, I love you. I want more with you. Give me these five days to see if you do too."

My mouth is bone-dry. I can't form words.

He *loves me*.

It makes my head swim with emotion so strong it feels like I am being ripped apart.

I choke back a sob while my heart is soaring because he loves me. I know he loves me.

"Theo, I care about you and I-" Taking his hands in mine, I squeeze them.

He dips his head, staring at our hands, then meets my eyes.

The love I see there stabs me in the gut and makes me want to roar at the world because this man is mine.

"At the end of the week, tell me where you want us to go. If that's just casual play partners or if you want to carry on as we are or if you want to end things," he blinks back tears.

"Theo, I don't even know what I'm going to do-" I squeeze his hand, because I don't want to hurt him.

At this moment, I don't have it in me to reciprocate with those three little words.

"I know. I'm not asking you to decide everything. Just at the end of five days, if you can see a future with me, however it shakes out that you throw it on the table. Tell me how I can support you."

"You've been so patient. You deserve to know what I want from a relationship." The diner is filling up, bustling around me. I take one look at this man, with his hopeful expression, his heart on the table, and my heart yawns open through my walls.

"I know I want you. I need you. You make me breathe easier."

"There isn't a single thing I wouldn't do to make your life easier, Callista." He leans toward me, touching his lips to mine, and I want to hold him close, whisper to him that he's mine, and take all that he's offering... but I can't.

"Callie!" Aunt Millie waves me over to a table, and I'm thankful for the distraction because I'm afraid if I say anything to Theo, I will cry. And I hate crying.

As I lose myself in helping around the diner, a plan starts to form in my mind.

I can't walk away from him right now, and I don't want to.

And five days with my boy in the city, five hot delicious nights? I need to say yes.

"Let's go pack, boy." I say when the diner has calmed down.

The grin on his face makes me feel like a cherished prize.

"Yes, Ma'am." He waits until I walk in front of him, and then holds the door open for me as we exit Shel's.

Upstairs in the apartment, Theo helps me pack my bags.

"We're doing this, boy." I whisper the words against his mouth.

"Thank you, Callista."

We check that we have everything, pack the car and, next thing I know, I'm driving out of my small town.

Halfway there, we take a break for coffee and to stretch our legs, and I let Theo drive the rest of the way.

We take turns driving to the city.

And when we get to Theo's gorgeous apartment, we're so tired that we do nothing other than snuggle in bed.

When his breathing turns to that deep sleep, I stare at him, softly tracing the curve of his shoulder, the line of his neck, the set of his jaw.

I love this man. Even if I can't tell how he fits into my future, I know I don't want to be without him.

I wake up to the smell of coffee, the sight of Theo wearing nothing but a shirt on a video conference, and a plate of French toast waiting for me.

After he finishes his meetings, he tells me to pack my camera gear and get dressed in hiking clothes, and he surprises me by taking me to the bird sanctuary.

The whole thing took my breath away, but every time I glance at Theo, my heart skips and my body swarms with warmth.

This man is a part of me.

That scares me because I don't want to run away from him. I can't.

"Thank you for taking me to the bird sanctuary today." The smile lights up his face.

"You're welcome, Ma'am."

We eat dinner at a Thai place, and the minute we get back to the apartment, I cage Theo against the door, the way I love, pressing my breasts against his chest, crashing my lips against his, in a hungry desperate kiss.

His ragged breath against my mouth fires my adrenaline.

"Strip boy. I want your face under that new queening chair in five seconds."

"Oooh! We get to try out the new toy I bought for you! Yes please." He waggles his eyebrows, making me laugh.

I watch him strip, staying with my back to the door, stalling my thoughts.

The trip to the sanctuary? Nobody has ever done something as kind as that for me, taken me on a trip just so I could spend time taking photographs.

In the kitchen, I pour myself a glass of red wine and take a deep sip.

I want to tease him, play with him and show him how much I appreciated today's outing.

Coming back into the room, I see Theo is positioned under the Queening chair.

The new toy he bought me. A wave of giddiness rises up from my centre, and I have to bite my lip to keep from giggling, but power drums through my veins.

"I'm going to tie this cock up tight." I set the wine down on the little nightstand next to the chair, letting the anticipation thicken between us, and I slowly sink to the ground, glide my hands up his strong legs, feeling him flex under my touch.

Taking his cock in my hand, I palm it. "I love your long, girthy dick, boy."

Wrapping my fingers around his half-hard cock, I stroke him slowly, coaxing him to full harness.

He exhales through his nose, trying to stay still, but his hips twitch against my touch.

"Ask me, boy. Ask me to tie your cock and balls."

He whines and I pull on his cock, sliding it through my fingers, playing with his slit.

"Please Ma'am. Tie up my cock and balls. Please, I want to know what it feels like when you tie my balls and pull on the rope."

Heat flames my cheeks. I swallow because I want to give this boy everything he asked so nicely for.

"Stay right there, boy." I chuckle as he groans, and I rummage in my bag to find the rope I want.

I ditch my socks, my pants, and come back to Theo.

I claim his skin with hard kisses just above his stomach, loving the salty taste of his skin, and move my hands along his waist.

His abs tighten under my mouth as I trail kisses lower, slow, unhurried, down his torso until I reach his erect cock.

I take his length in my mouth, swallowing him deep, dragging a low moan from his throat.

His musky taste hits the back of my throat, making me salivate and sparking a desperate hunger for him. His hips bucking, wanting more, makes my pulse race.

I need to command him.

To control him.

Slowly, I suck his cock, then I take my time, letting my tongue dip into the slit, taking my time, as he squirms and whimpers under me, crying out for more.

He cries out, his fingertips grabbing my shoulders. I let go, reaching for the rope.

"My cock is so pretty, boy." Coming back with the rope, I stroke his cock in my hand, gliding it up and down, tugging, pulling.

He groans at my touch, his legs quivering.

Leaning down, letting the key on my neck key brush against the tip of his penis, I give it a little lick.

He arches his hips towards my mouth, and I pull away.

I squeeze his sac gently, massaging his balls, then I take a length of the thin gold rope and tie it at the base of his cock.

"Oh, it's so pretty."

"Ma'am! I need more touch!"

"I know, Wolfie. I'll take care of you. Not yet, but I will." I bring the rope around under his sac and wrap each ball, pulling tight, but loose enough to fit a finger through, then I bring the rope around the back of his penis, wrapping him from his base to his tip and tie it off, tightening the knot.

Taking that length, I attach it to a sturdy cotton braided rope and spend a moment, tying it to his wrist, skimming my lips up his arm while I do, laughing softly as every time he moves his arm, his cock moves and pulls in the ropes.

"There. All tied up. Colour, Wolfie?"

This is mild cock and balls torture but had been on his limit list.

The smile on his face tells me how he's feeling before he even says it.

"Green, Ma'am."

"Perfect. Now, get to work while I relax." I take my seat on the queening chair, opening my iPad.

I take a sip of wine and sigh.

This day? Exactly what my soul needed.

"Make it good, Wolfie."

He mumbles and I laugh.

"Is Wolfie tired? I can barely feel your tongue." I press my foot against his ribcage, chuckling as he increases his licking.

I do my best to ignore the sensation, sitting back against the leather cushion of the chair, scrolling through the photos I took.

"I love this picture of the black-crowned night heron I got in flight. We should go back there again." I don't know how I get the words out, as his tongue is working me up to a storm that's ready to break.

My skin is heated, tingles dance low in my belly.

But I want to play with my boy, give him the impression that I don't care too much about what he's doing with his mouth, even though his talented tongue working my pussy is impossible to ignore and I know I can't keep him in this rope for long.

I pick up the glass of wine and take a sip, but it doesn't stall the heat or the gathering storm.

Smiling with pure satisfaction, I reach down and pull on the rope.

He moves his wrist, putting tension on the tie leading to his balls.

"Yes boy, just like that." I try to keep still, but my hips roll forward as his tongue swipes around my clit.

His desperate cry sends shivers of delight through me.

My boy's trust is a valued gift, something I don't take for granted.

Theo's talented tongue keeps working, picking up the pace, and I set my device aside, take the glass of red from the side table, and sip.

My hands tremble as I hold the wine glass, my body quenching with the effort trying to hold back my orgasm. *Who is teasing whom?*

Pleasure starts to rise through my body, so strong I rock forward.

"Nothing to say? Maybe you preferred the Red-breasted Nuthatch?"

I slide my foot on the top of his leg, settling back against the seat.

A muffled reply comes from under me and just in time, I set the wine back down because the way his tongue circles my clit makes me tense, gasping and I would have spilled the wine all over my body - but the thought of having Wolfie clean it up, has me gripping the wine again, tipping it so droplets fall on his cock.

"Did I make a mess? Guess I'm going to have to clean that up later. Maybe."

The flick of his tongue hit my sweet spot.

The room spins on me, euphoria stems through my cells, ripping the cry from my throat.

Theo sucks on my clit as if he's trying to eat all of me, like he's intent on taking every part of me into his mouth.

"Fuck yes, Wolfie!" I grip the padded leather of the chair, ripples of pleasure exploding, sending me higher and higher with every motion of this mouth.

Damn.

And I had to doubt that this boy was good for me?

A laugh erupts from my mouth, then I can't stop laughing, not till tears are flowing down my face and I'm gasping for breath.

I press my foot against his ribcage, with soft pressure, loving how he wiggles under me.

He stops, and I tilt my head back against the red rest, staring at the beautiful recessed scaling of Theo's apartment, not wanting to be anywhere else in the entire world.

I'm so damn lucky that he didn't run out on me when I wavered, that he's given us this week.

Lifting off the chair, still slick between my legs, I slither between Theo's legs, bend down and drag my hair along his torso.

"Good boy, Wolfie, that was three orgasms." I lean down between his thighs and nip him, not enough to break skin but enough to mark my boy.

He cries out, his fingertips reach for me, his head lifts from the hammock.

I tap his dick, so he jerks. "Patience, boy."

Sitting back on my heels, I wait until his head is back in the hammock of the queening chair, then I reward him.

Because he's a good boy and I need to show him how grateful I am that we are here together, in his apartment, for the next five days.

Cupping his balls, I press my nails along his sensitive warm flesh.

He jerks in my hands, his cock twitches in its rope cage.

"It's so pretty all tied up like this." Bending, I pressed a kiss between the rings of rope, sliding my lips over his hardened cock, lapping up the spilled wine.

His cock is velvety soft, and leaking pre-cum.

I scoop a gob of pre-cum up with my fingers, walk my other hand up his chest, then press my cum-covered finger to his mouth.

"Who's a good boy?" His mouth closes around my digit with a moan, a pitch cry torn from his lips, the drowsy gaze in his eyes.

I withdraw my fingers, wiping them on his nipples.

"Too bad I have to undo the rope. I love how it looks. It reminds me of the cage."

His hips jerk off the floor as I circle it with my fingers, then give it another kiss.

I swirl my tongue over the tip, slow and indulgent, teasing him while my fingers work the rope harness off.

He's all muscle and restraint, his need simmering just beneath the surface, but his desire to please me is clear as he follows my every movement, waiting on me to command.

That power thrums through me, thick and heady, curling low in my belly.

"There, you're freed. Until the cage goes on tonight," I blow a warm breath over his balls.

"Yes, Ma'am!" he cries, the plea in his tone wrapping itself around my heart, making me feel so powerful and in control.

I want him inside me now, so I sweep my hands along his nipples, teasing and pulling, then I climb on top of him.

His head turns to the side, his hands come around my back, sliding down to my waist.

"I want to ride you until I have another orgasm. You're going to let me take that, aren't you, Wolfie? I want to fuck you so hard I empty your balls. You need to be soft for the cage."

His sweet whimper, as I straddle him, goes right to the depths of my soul.

I didn't think I'd ever let myself play with another submissive.

My past kept getting in my way, making me think it was my fault.

That I chose the wrong man.

But ever since Theo entered my life, my confidence as a Domme has been restored.

His submission has grown my dominance.

Even if nothing else, if at the end of the week we part ways, I'll always be grateful to him for that.

Your heart will be broken.

I push away the thought, and keep the words I'm not ready to speak locked up as tight as I'm going to lock up this cock when I'm done with it.

Inch by inch, I lower myself on his iron cock.

"Your cock inside me is hitting me just right, Wolfie." I rock my hips, loving how his dick reaches the spot, sending a ripple of bliss down my spine.

Thrusting my hips fast and deep, he lets out a cry. "Please Ma'am, please."

"You can control it even more, boy." My nipples tighten as he grips my hips.

I rock my hips, riding him so fast I'm bouncing up and down on his cock, wanting him deeper.

Brushing my lips against his, I tease him, and then he takes my lips in his, kisses me with a desperate, wet, hungry kiss that makes my pussy clench hard around his cock.

"You. Feel. Amazing." I pant as I ride him, his cock sinking even deeper, my thighs shaking from the force.

His hips rise to meet mine, and we are lost in moans, yips of pleasure, caught tangled in this web where the only thing that matters is the two of us.

Out there, he's a CEO, responsible for the security of multiple international high-profile companies.

But here, under me, this man is my *boy*.

And he's being a good boy, holding back, though I feel his legs tremble underneath me, his fists are clenched and his face is all scrunched.

Slowing my pace, I grab his hand, shove his fingers into my pussy. "Finger me. Get me closer, Wolfie."

He goes to work, staring with the tension to hold off his pleasure, his fingers circle my clit, making me moan.

I grind harder on his cock, taking him even deeper, until I can't hold it back.

"Come with me, Wolfie, fuck! That's so good!" The crest breaks.

He screams my name, opening his eyes as his release is deep inside me. It sends me over, and I'm falling into the wave of pleasure that's so intense it leaves me shuddering.

My body is tingly, my pussy is gasping, as if it wants even more.

"Thank you, Ma'am!" Theo brings his arms around me, and I let myself go, lost in his embrace. Lying on his chest, I hear the drum of his heartbeat, and there's nowhere else in the entire Universe I want to be.

"You're welcome, Wolfie."

We stay there, snuggled, until our breathing turns to normal.

It's late.

Theo has a meeting at five in the morning.

And I don't know what I am going to do with my stretch of time during the day, but I know these next nights belong to us.

"I'm sorry I can't spend every second of every day with you." He says, as if reading my mind.

"We have the nights," I rub my cheek against his stubble.

"Thank you for agreeing to spend the week here, Callista. It means the world to me. I'm going to prove to you that we can work."

"I know we can." I press a palm against his chest. "I...it's me, Wolfie. I have too many old wounds that are making me hesitant."

"Leap anyway. I'll catch you." His tone is all vulnerability, and I don't deserve it.

"Speaking of catching, I have this cock and I want it in its cage." I say it coolly, needing to take the focus off where I am emotionally.

"Yes, Ma'am," he slides against me, his muscles rippling under his smooth skin. He grinds against me, and I gasp but pull back.

"Don't start that or we'll have to do all that over again," I wave at the queening chair in the corner.

Theo waggles his eyebrows at me. "I can deal with that."

"Shower, boy, go." I roll my eyes.

He untangles himself from me, making me cold from the absence of his body heat. "If you insist."

I stand, give his ass a slap, and a little push.

"Okay, okay, I'm going." He shakes his cute bum at me, and I snort, covering my face in horror. My cheeks are burning bright.

He glances over his shoulder at me, gives me a grin like he just lit up the universe, and my heart melts even more.

I don't know how I'm going to keep the words locked away inside me for the next five days, but I don't want to hurt my boy.

29

THEO

MARCH 19th

Hot shivers raise every nerve ending across my skin in a sizzling arc, as Callie's warm, wet lips suck on my nipple.

The pinch of her teeth grazing my sensitive flesh makes me squirm as she switches sides and laps my other one.

"Stay still." She slaps my thigh with her open palm, hard.

My Ma'am is in a mood to play rough tonight, and I'm here for it.

Behind the silk blindfold, tears leak from my eyes. The quick vibrations from the prostate are driving me to distraction, and the spreader bar between my legs means I can't do much about it.

It's kind of exquisite hell.

Between the vibrations coursing through me, Callie's hot lips and tongue sucking and nipping me, I don't know how long I can wait before my balls explode.

But I waited all yesterday till I was home with her at night and, just like yesterday, she inspected the cage, made sure I was locked up before she sent me off to work for the day.

"I know you're struggling for me, Wolfie. I like it."

I jerk in the cuffs that are on my wrists. Heat swirls in my veins, desperate for release.

Only this woman has made me feel like this, like I can give her this raw vulnerability, and she isn't going to throw it back in my face.

The bed dips as she shifts her weight, leaning over my bent legs above the bar.

Her silken strands tickle my thigh, and when her teeth meet my inner thigh, I yell.

Hot, blissful pain racks through me.

"Still." She sinks her teeth in further, the bite painful as she sucks it, swirling her tongue over her mark.

"I'm trying, Ma'am." I cry out, my voice breaking.

"Oh, I love how you try for me, Wolfie." Her fingers grip my cock, feels damn good.

"Fuck!" The vibrations slam into me, turned up to a higher setting.

The powerful tingles shooting through my ass have me screaming.

I'm heaving, fighting with everything I have to hold back, but I know I will not last.

Callie's cool fingertips brush across my brow, her touch doing nothing to calm me. "I love how you're trying your best to hold off for me. I'm going to help you out."

She chuckles as the strong pulses rip through me, and I'm gasping for breath.

My ass feels like it's being slammed by miniature earthquakes.

Each vibration leaving me wanting more.

As the weight of the bed eases, I hear something rattle, then Callie skims her lips over my ribcage, following the path to my inner thighs, tracing the bite mark.

"Cold!" I gasp.

Callie's warm lips ease the discomfort of the cold ice cube, but I can't breathe.

I'm seeing black dots behind my blindfold.

My muscles are tense, trying to hold back the storm that is buzzing through me.

The ice hits my sac, the cold so searingly cold it freezes my balls.

"Ma'am!"

"This is what bad boys get," she says teasingly, and because I know she's teasing, I can laugh.

The laughter makes me super aware of the tingles and vibration in my ass until she slips more of that cold cube along my cock.

But just as fast as it's there, her warm mouth is back, soothing, sucking, tugging through, the vibrations are cranked up even more, as the block of ice is pressed against the tip of my cock.

"Ma'am! I need to come!"

In answer, she takes my steel-hard cock into her mouth, sucks me so far down I can feel the entrance to her throat.

Heat encases my cock, and I'm needy, desperate, coming apart.

The vibrations are shredding me into pieces.

My hips are bucking off the bed, my limbs pushing against the restraints.

"Fuck! Sorry, Ma'am!" I scream it as I pump into her throat deeper and deeper, until finally I can't stop the force that's intent on ripping me into pieces and giving in.

I release my hot cum down her throat in one long spurt, and it goes on until I lie panting, my ass so sore from the vibrations.

My mind is under a deep, heavy blanket of satisfaction and acceptance, my eyelids heavy. Only my Ma'am has ever made me feel this way.

"That's my boy, Wolfie." Finally, the vibrations stop. Callie removes the bar from between my legs and rubs them furiously, encouraging circulation.

She uncuffs my wrists, rubbing little circles on the side of my arm to get the blood flowing again.

I let out a whimper as her cool hands remove the blindfold, and I blink in the light.

"Sorry, Ma'am. I couldn't hold out any longer." I reach for her, but she shoves off my touch and gently removes the vibrator before I know what she's doing.

My body gasps, wanting the intrusion back.

Can I take another night of this?

Yes. Hell, yes.

I'll take every night that she gives me, gladly go through whatever game she's set up because the peace that flows through my mind as she puts me through her sweet torture is worth it.

"You were a bad boy." She slants her lips against mine, kissing me in a slow, meandering kiss.

"But you rewarded me." That dopey smile is back on my face.

"Couldn't help myself, Mr. Sexypants. You did well, Wolfie." Her hand slides down to my cock, now softening, and she pulls gently on my balls, making me squirm against her. A low whine escapes my lips.

"Thank you, Ma'am." I wrap my arm around her as she lays her head against my chest, knowing I'd give everything I had up to keep my goddess here with me forever.

***

The smell of something delicious teases my nostrils when I open the bathroom door, fresh out of my shower.

"Good morning, Ma'am."

"You look so damn hot wearing nothing but that golden cage," with a smirk, she strides over to me, rolling her hips. Callie is wearing flared jeans and a black t-shirt that hugs her breasts just right, with her hair swept up in a messy bun.

"You look gorgeous, my goddess." I meet her lips, and we kiss in a slow, languishing kiss that makes me groan against her mouth, wanting more, but she breaks it off.

"Eat, Wolfie. I did wake you up in the middle of the night," Callista cocks an eyebrow with a sly smile. She gestures to the table where there are breakfast sandwiches.

"That cafe beside your apartment is so cute with its glass sculptures."

"Yeah, and their pastries are yum. I loved how you woke me up." There's a huge-ass grin on my face because she woke me up by smothering my face with her pussy.

After she rode my face and I made her come three times, she locked me up and ordered me to sleep.

Sleeping with the cage on, next to her, is no hardship now that I've had time to get accustomed to it.

The cage is a weighted symbol of my submission, something that is physical.

I love how it makes me feel so eager and ready to please her.

Before sitting down, I pour us coffee and carry it to the table. "You are spoiling me so much."

"I like spoiling you." Her tone turns serious, and she glances down at her plate. "Theo."

My blood pressure rises, but I exhale, placing my hand on the top of the leg. "Callista?"

"I didn't ask you to skip the briefing yesterday." She takes a sip of coffee, but I hear how unsettled she is in her tone.

"You didn't." I run my hand up and down her thigh, trying to reassure her.

"But you did." She sets her coffee down, not meeting my eyes.

"Callista, I'm a CEO. I make decisions that are best for my company every day. This was an excellent decision."

"Did I influence you?" The wobble in her voice tears out my heart.

I scramble off my chair, sinking to my knees on my cold tile floor in front of her.

"Yes, you did. That's not a bad thing, Callista. Being with you has made me realize how much I used work to escape. I was pushing myself to take all the press conferences, all the briefings, even though I didn't have to."

"I don't like it." Callie sends me a look that's so stricken with fear, I sit back on my heels.

"You've gotta let me make decisions, even if you don't like them. My brothers have told me for the past two years that I don't need to take every public-facing event. Did you know Jayden has a degree in journalism as well as computer science? She worked as a radio host before switching careers."

A small smile tugs at her lips.

"True story. You can call her and ask." I waggle my eyebrows at her, wanting her to laugh.

"You have someone on your team who has the skill set to take the part of your job you hate... the one that leaves you wrecked for hours and you decide to make life harder?" She ruffles my hair.

"Well, you might not know this," I press my palms to the top of my thighs. "But I'm a bit of a masochist."

Callie laughs until her face turns bright red. I move behind her chair, draping my arms around her.

"We both knew we had baggage to work through. Callista, if we are going to use this week to test taking our relationship to a more permanent place, I didn't want to miss a thing. My surprise went well."

"I can't believe they liked me," Callie mumbles. She turns her face to mine, and our lips meet in a crushing kiss that takes my breath away.

"Of course they liked you," I say, stroking her hair, amazed as usual that someone so confident can be so insecure at the same time.

She hands me my coffee, gestures for me to sit.

"I liked them too. Your brother is kind, like you, and Mara is so sweet."

"I knew he'd make you feel welcome. I like Mara."

Callie walks her fingertips up my arm, igniting little shivers of want through me. "You didn't have to surprise me with them. I would have met them."

I cock an eyebrow, smiling at the determination in her voice. "I know you would have been anxious about it, and I didn't want you to stress. Evan called me and asked if I had time for a midday lunch. I told him perfect timing because you were in the city."

"Okay," Callie grins, tapping her nail against her mug. "You got me there. I would have freaked out about it."

Yesterday, after I told Jayden that she was taking the briefing with the emergency protection company, she looked at me as if I had two heads.

"You sure, Boss?"

"Yes. You are capable. I have a hundred percent confidence in you." I say the words, and I mean them.

Jayden deserves this chance. Her background as a radio host gives her the public speaking skills that I never had.

"Okay! I will not let you down, boss."

"I know. Now let's go over the notes. There's one reporter who always likes to spin something wild."

"I got it!" She pulls up her notes on her tablet and shows them to me.

"Yep, way better than I could have done. Good luck out there." I pick up my briefcase, checking that my system is closed for the night.

"You're leaving?" Jayden says.

"I have a woman I'm taking on a lunch date." My stomach forms a knot, wondering if Callie will be upset with me over the surprise meet.

"Are you sure you're okay? Not coming down with anything?" Jayden teases.

"I could stay if you prefer…"

"No, go! We're good!"

I arranged for a car to pick Callie up from my place, then we met Mara and Evan at Evan's favourite Greek restaurant and the conversation flowed between us.

"Mara invited me to drop by her studio. Think I'll do that." Callie squeezes my shoulder.

"Her creations are kind of exceptional," I rub a tiny circle along the webbing of her index finger and thumb.

Mara is a floral designer, and he makes sculptures and art pieces that are stunning.

"People told Mara that she shouldn't be a floral designer," I shrug, saying it as nonchalantly as I can.

"Get dressed, boy, before you keep saying things," Callie shakes her head, but her eyes are alight with amusement.

"Yes, Ma'am."

"I picked out a shirt for you. It's on the closet door."

My heart gives a leap. "Thank you!" I tidy up our breakfast things, then give her a kiss.

"Not that you needed any more reminders of me," Callie sweeps her hand down, cupping my cage.

Her fingers slide through the bars on the cage, then press firmly against my balls. I squirm under her exploratory touch and love how she smiles at me, all pleased.

"I'll take all the reminders of you I can get. It makes me more productive."

"Yeah?" Callie tips her head to me, brushes her lips against mine.

"Definitely. Makes me feel all subby and happy and more focused on my work."

"Does that mean you'll be home sooner?" She lifts her hand from the cage, thankfully, because it was hard for me to form sentences.

"I have two meetings today, then I'm all free. I was thinking we could go to the aquarium."

"Perfect. I can get used to this."

My heart gives a leap of hope because I want her to get used to this. I want to show her we can work, not just for the weekend or a rushed midweek drop-in, but for always.

"I sent you the number of the car service. Please use it, Callista. Mara's studio is a bit of a trek."

"Thank you for looking after me, Wolfie," Callie follows me into the bedroom, watching me as I get dressed.

The heat in her gaze makes my mouth water, my cock stir, pressing against the cage, and I want to stay in this moment, with her looking happy and oozing dominance. It's a sexy combination that's making me throb.

"You're making me want to stay home."

"Good," Callie flashes me a flirty smile, squeezing my arm. "But go, I have plans, boy."

"Yes, Ma'am."

She walks me to the door. I slide my loafers on, pick up my briefcase and give her a hug.

"Have a good day, Wolfie."

"I don't want to leave you."

"We'll have tonight." She pats my cheek. "Now go on and do CEO things."

"Yes, Ma'am." She kisses me with a quick, brief kiss that stabs my tongue but leaves my mouth tingling.

I can't wait for whatever plan Ma'am has tonight.

30

CALLIE

"Being here feels like being on a vacation." I shift back on the leather armchair that cushions my body like a supportive pillow.

"Is that a bad thing?" Theo tilts his head, that adorable smile spreading wide across his dimpled face.

I stretch my foot against his palm. "Hey, you're supposed to be working here."

"Yes, Ma'am." He rubs the top of my foot. The warmth from his strong hands penetrates my sore muscles, and the oil is slick.

The butterflies take off in rapid flight, deep in my belly because I'm about to say something that's going to make me feel sliced open.

But this man has proven to me over and over that I can trust him and that he accepts me as I am.

I couldn't ask for a better submissive.

Even in my wildest dreams, I couldn't have come up with someone as kind, generous and deeply submissive as Theo.

So why are you so afraid of taking the leap and committing?

The answer is obvious, but to recap: I get scared of commitment and I run. I'm always the peacemaker, and I'm afraid of doing something for myself.

"It's like I can't believe that life can be this... easy. Not stressful. That I can wake up every day feeling happy, not walking around expecting an anvil to fall on my head."

"No anvil is in sight, Ma'am, only me here with you," he rubs the side of my foot, his thumbs pressing into my sole so deeply it makes me moan in pleasure.

His touch eases my ache and makes me want to curl up like a cat finding a spot of sunlight.

This boy has given me this. That comfy feeling like an old pair of socks. I close my mouth on the fit of giggles that threatens to spill over.

"What's so funny, Ma'am?"

I can't help it. I giggle uncontrollably, kicking my foot out of Theo's hand, bringing my legs up to my chest on the chair.

Tears are streaming down my face, and I let out a horrifying snort, but it still doesn't stop my giggle fit.

"Sorry...I just thought like-" I cover my mouth, unable to stop the stream of giggles tumbling out of my lips.

The adorable grin on his face is making me feel worse as he calmly wipes his hands off on a towel and moves the bowl of oil to the coffee table.

"Yes?" He shuffles closer to me, so his head is on my knees.

"That you were an old pair of socks!" I'm gasping for air, waving a hand in front of my face, but I can't stop this fit of giggles.

Theo rolls his eyes in the most adorable way, gets up, disappears into the kitchen and a moment later he returns with a glass of water.

"Thanks. Sorry. You are not old." At thirty-four, Theo is only two years older than I am.

"Nope," Theo helps steady my grip on the glass.

"And you are definitely not a pair of socks. I just feel...cozy and comfortable and relaxed with you. I was trying to think of the last time I had felt like that."

He touches his forehead to mine. "That's how I want you to feel. I also want you to feel cherished. And loved." He lifts my hand to his mouth and kisses my knuckles.

Pleasure rolls through me, the start of a slow-building storm, and I know with full certainty that I want to let this man into my chaos, into my mess, into my life, if I can have this kind of night with him.

"With you, boy, I do." I stroke his hair, rub lightly biting his ears.

"Before you got called home. When you were on the beach. That's the last time...before us that you felt like that?"

I trace his jawline. He dips his lips to brush against the top of my thighs, making me lift off the chair as that storm rises up again.

My clit starts to throb, hungry for attention.

I push his face down, spread my legs and my boy needs no further instruction.

His lips close around my sensitive skin.

He moves over to my seam, slowly starts to lap and lavish.

A rising wave of pleasure buckles through, making me moan.

But my mind wanders back to that beach.

Hanging out with my girls, being part of the team, I had always longed for something like that.

I love that motocross team, and I'll always be grateful for that experience.

But with Theo? He makes me feel free, yes, but in a different way that I have ever had before. Unlike other guys, I don't feel that he'd ever hold me back from what I wanted to do.

He was the first guy who didn't flinch when I said I was a mechanic. And instead of running, when he knew I had responsibilities, he stayed by my side.

I could do what I wanted to do out there, but when it's him and me, I could steal his socks or leave my jeans on the floor, and he wouldn't care.

"It's a different kind of feeling. My team didn't do *this*." I open my legs wider, cup the back of his neck, and start to thrust up into his mouth. His lips close around my clit, sucking my clit so hard his cheeks hollow and he makes wet, noisy sounds that make me hum with a heat that sets every part of me aflame with intense arousal. I feel like I'm going to shatter.

My legs start to shake, the bliss overtakes me, the storm stirs to life, zeroing my focus on how he kneels before me.

The beauty of his submission is something so precious and dear to me. It makes me want to protect him, to savour what we have between each other.

Euphoric waves crash, drawing up from my legs to my lower body. The storm takes me, spins me higher and even higher—almost there.

"Keep going, boy!" I command breathlessly. "Your mouth feels amazing. Do not stop!"

He obeys my command with a feverish effort.

Deeper tongue strokes, eating me out as if I'm his favourite meal and he is consuming me whole, like he strives to show me every day, this man has made it clear he'll take whatever I give him.

"Theo!" I cry out, coming in one long gush, my wetness exploding. My body is shaking.

The storm breaks, and I can't stop screaming his name as the storm crashes over me, the orgasm spinning me into an ecstasy so intense I tremble through the aftermath.

He keeps licking me during the aftershocks, slowly down as I trail my fingers through his hair.

My hand drops from his hair. I lay back, my eyes closed, buzzing with the orgasm, not wanting to move.

"Thank you for that, boy." I open my arms, and he scoots up and lies across the arms of the chair, so his weight isn't on me.

I kiss him sweetly, slowly, tasting myself on his lips.

Taking his nipple between my fingers, I flick it, gently playing with it as I stare into his grey eyes.

"Where would we live?"

He scrunches his face as I pull and tug on his sensitive nipples.

"Wherever you want, Callie. If you want to keep a day-to-day hand in Shel's, I'd—" Theo gasps and I give the boy a break, pulling his head to my breast, cradling him in my lap.

My heart has no doubt that we can work.

It's in my head that I can't convince this is something real, something I can count on.

"We could buy ourselves a house in Rising Harbour," Theo continues. "I want to come into the office once a week at least, but that's for right now. I can cut back on that."

"And you fly out to Toronto once a month." The words are stark in this post-orgasmic bubble, and I regret saying them, but he glances up at me, shakes his head.

"Yeah. I don't care where we live, Callista, if we're together."

"But you have so much here. I don't want to ask you to give it all up."

"You're not asking me to do anything... at least nothing I don't want to do. You know I want to spend every minute of every day and night that I can with you, Ma'am. Every moment you'll allow me to."

I grab his chin, tilt him up to me and kiss him, deeply and slowly. My body floods with the endorphins that only this man has given me, telling me it's okay to rest here, with him.

That I can trust him with my heart.

That we can build a life together, one that I don't want to run from.

"Trust, Callista. I know it's scary," he kisses me again, this time more desperate, and my hand slides to his hardening cock.

Lightly, I stroke his cock, wrapping my fingers around the shaft.

He jerks in my hand, his hips bouncing off my legs.

I tease his bottom lip, nipping it gently.

He whimpers, which makes me tug and pull on his lip even more, while rubbing my palm up and down his penis.

I slow my stroke, pushing my fingers into his balls, making him gasp.

"Ma'am! I am so close!" His head tips back, his body tenses, and I love how gorgeous he looks right now.

"Good boy, I love how you're taking this."

He is my good boy. And he definitely deserves this orgasm.

Moving from his balls, I stroke him up and down, my veins heady with the control I feel over this man, the responsibility I feel for him. It sends a bolt of ice through my vines, but I keep touching him, stroking him.

He closes his eyes, his brows furrow. His penis is iron hard in my palm.

I stroke him faster, rubbing my thumb in a circle on the tip of his cockhead, pre-cum soaking the pad of my thumb.

If I ordered him to stop right now, I know he would.

If I told him to get off my lap, he would.

"Open your eyes. Kiss me, Wolfie."

Electricity dances on my tongue as he meets my lips, and we spin together, crashing, both wanting more. His body arches towards my touch, and I give him more, wanting him to lose the control he's fighting to maintain.

I stroke him quicker, faster, harder and he kisses me, like he's trying to plow into my soul.

"I'm coming! Ma'am!" He shouts against my mouth; the vibration of his words tingles on my lips.

His hot cum explodes all over my hand, dripping down to my wrist.

"Callista!" My name tears from his throat, boomerangs around us.

I rub some of his mess off on his leg, bring my hand to his mouth.

"Please, Ma'am," Theo opens instantly, and I stick my cum-covered fingers in his mouth, running them along his tongue.

He turns his head away from me, as if he has a moment of fighting off the post orgasmic clarity but then his eyes lock with mine and I see steely determination light them up.

His lips close over my fingers, sucking them greedily into my mouth, lapping them clean, making mewling sounds that cause my nipples to tighten.

I don't deserve this beautiful submissive, but I will do everything I can to protect him.

"Good boy." I hold him until we both get our breath back, and order him to the shower.

With the hot water flowing, he uses my favourite sponge and lathers it with my body wash. He gently turns me around and washes my back. But I don't want to be gentle, not right now.

I bat away his hands, turn to face him. "Fuck me, boy. Hard and fast."

He drops the sponge, his muscles ripple as he lifts me up, and I laugh against his mouth, wrapping my legs around him.

I kiss him, digging my nails into his back, wanting to feel his strength, his acceptance.

"I want to mark you so hard and deep that you can never rinse me off. Never get bored of me."

"Callista! I love you! I'll never get bored of you. Hurt me, if that's what you need."

The yell of exhilaration I let out shocks us both, but his grip doesn't falter.

I want to imprint myself on him, and in this one moment, I want to feel like I am being claimed by him.

Our kisses are sloppy and wet open; we're exchanging breaths; ravenous hunger fills me as I push my tongue as far as I can down his throat, loving how he groans.

My clit is throbbing, awake and ready, wanting him to fill me up.

"More," I say against his ear, tracing his shell with my tongue

The heat of his body sinks into every inch of me, a consuming burn that licks along my nerves. I can't tell where my limbs begin and where his start. All I know is I am aching, needing more.

"Yes, get your cock in me and fuck me, boy!" My voice is gravely, like I am not me but someone who wants to be free of control.

I want to surrender in this moment. To this strong man and all his glorious masculinity.

"Right there!" His cock fits into me so well. In one single thrust, we join together, and my thoughts are spinning as our mouths are sealed against each other. I can feel his heartbeat against mine, our cries of pleasure chasing each other.

I grind against him with all the hot desperation and uncertainty that I feel, but he kisses away my doubts, rocks his hips, making my thoughts halt.

My skin tingles, needing him.

Wanting his cock to go even further, deeper inside me. I want to be split apart by him and put back together.

My hands slide down to his ass, the heat of his skin searing my palms as I pinch and squeeze the firm muscle, feeling it flex under my grip with every powerful thrust. He groans into my mouth, a sharp cry of pain as I dig my nails, slicing his skin, scoring him.

He grunts, thrusts even deeper and nibbles at the base of my throat, skimming his teeth along my skin.

Our skin slaps against each other's, our pants and moans matching each other's as his cock plows into me, faster, harder, so hard that I struggle to hold on to his wet skin, so hard the shelf on the shower rattles.

"Fuck yes!"

He drives into me, forcing my pleasure to rise. The orgasm rips from my body so hard I'm left shaking, stupid tears streaming down my face.

"Shush, Ma'am, I got you," he cradles me against him. We're still joined, and he somehow gets us back under the spray.

He wipes away my tears, doesn't comment on them, and I'm trembling.

Still holding me, he washes me gently.

Turning off the shower, he helps me out.

I wanted to come apart, and I did, but I hate that I am crying.

"One moment." He's dripping wet, but he wraps me in the softest, fluffiest towel, dries my body, then takes another towel and gently dries my hair.

"I needed that, Wolfie."

"I like to serve, Callista." His lips slant against mine. It's a sweet kiss filled with promise and hope, and it leaves my lips tingling.

Lacing my hand through his, I let him take me to bed. He tucks me in, and then I pat the bed next to me. "Time to lock up that cock."

"Yes, Ma'am, please lock me up." Theo's voice is throaty, and the glassy look in his eyes makes me purr.

I shuffle up to watch him put the cage on, then I gesture for him to come closer. I take the key from the nightstand and lock it, dipping my fingers under the bar, over his soft penis, making him flinch in the sexiest way.

"Night night." I pressed a kiss against his soft dick through the cage, making him shudder. He climbs into bed next to me, and I wrap my arms around him, pressing my head against his shoulder blades.

"Good night, Ma'am."

"Night Wolfie."

Drifting off to sleep a moment later, tears leak down my cheeks.

What he gave me tonight was exactly what I needed.

He didn't tell me that I was the one who was supposed to be in charge—-he understood what I needed was what I asked for.

No, my boy simply served me.

There's no way I can walk away from this man, and nothing terrifies me more.

31

THEO

MARCH 20TH

"Are you ready, Wolfie?" Callie squeezes my ass as she brings me closer.

Her tongue pokes out between her lips. She gives the base of my throat a lick, and it makes me shudder.

"Thank you, Ma'am. You look gorgeous." My gaze drops to her boots.

She's wearing those burgundy boots I love, and they make her almost at eye level.

The boots shine.

I cleaned them myself this afternoon.

"I'm ready for this. Are you, Callista?" I stare into her blue eyes, searching for confirmation.

Ever since this morning, she'd been a little off, like she was nervous or stressed. But I sent her to the spa with Amy to get ready for tonight, while I stayed in our room at the Hugo Hotel and cleaned her boots.

"I haven't seen some of them in a while. Before the accident. I feel like I'm going to show up as a different person." She squeezes my hand. "But I think we'll have too much fun for me to worry about that."

"Guess it's time to get our birthday party on." I run my hands down the crotchless shorts she asked if I'd wear. "Do I pass the inspection?"

"Let me see you. Hands behind your back, boy." Her eyes are lit with pleasure, a pleased smile that makes her glow, and I move to obey her command.

My hands are behind my back, my feet shoulder width apart. Callie walks around me in a slow circle, making a tsking noise, in the bedroom of our hotel room.

I keep my eyes downcast, focusing on her booted feet as she circles me.

Shudders tumble through my body as she presses against my back, cupping my cock cage. "You're comfortable, boy?"

"Yes, Ma'am." I swallow and wonder if I can actually pull this off.

But when I heard that the dress code for tonight was the subs naked or mostly naked, I wanted to join in.

So, the crotchless hot pants went on.

"You look hot as fuck, boy."

She slips a finger through my cage, poking and prodding with light feather touches that make me groan.

"I love that this is going to be on display. Kiss me."

I turn my head, and our lips meet in a slow, needy kiss. Callie grinds herself against my cage while squeezing my nipples.

"Keep doing that, and I don't think I'll be able to walk."

"You can crawl, boy." Callie chuckles.

The slap of her palm across my ass surprises me, making me jump. "I love this silky black shirt on you."

"I like the look, too."

"If I know Amy, I know tonight is going to be wild. You're okay with playing in public?"

"Yes, Ma'am. I want to join in. Maybe not the service line."

"Definitely not the service line," Callie yanks my hair, pulling my head down to kiss me. "Though maybe I'll have you service me while I eat, what about that, Wolfie?"

Heat pumps through my veins, going right to my cock, my dick wanting to expand but the constrictive device not making it possible. "It's going to be a great night, Ma'am."

"Carry my toy bag, please."

I pick up the bag, Callie grabs the present she got for Amy, and I lock the door of our room.

We make our way down the hall to the elevator.

I'm not worried about passing any of the guests because I know these two floors have been blocked off for Amy's party tonight.

"Callie!" A blonde Domme, wearing a sparkling cowboy hat and cowboy boots, waves to us.

"Sam!" Callie's whole face lights up. The two women embrace each other, and the man beside Sam nods at me. He's naked except for his collar and leash.

"Good to see you, honey! Who is this beautiful boy?"

"This is Theo," Callie says.

The elevator doors open, and we step inside.

"Hi." My face is beet red.

"Why, hello! I would love to have him service me." Sam ogles me, and it's making me uncomfortable.

"He's not in the line, Sam. I don't share my sub." Callie cups her hand against my jaw, easing my anxiety.

"Such a pity," Sam winks at me. "Lucky I have Derrick here."

"Yes, you do," Derrick grins, and Sam takes his face in her hands, and their faces are locked together the whole way.

The short elevator ride feels like forever, but finally the doors open and we step out.

There's a line of about twenty people waiting to go through security before entering the restaurant. Callie keeps a hand on my ass the whole time, her fingers squeezing and pulling, brushing against my cock change, making my skin tingle with every touch.

Every person we pass hugs Callie, talks to her, tells her how happy they are to see her out tonight.

Seeing my Ma'am light up, the set of her shoulders pulled back further, her head held higher makes me stir with pride, my pulse quicken.

The air is thick with sexually charged energy that's electric, and the anticipation makes my belly clench with my usual nerves when it comes to crowded spaces.

All the tables are along the perimeter of the room, the glass tops glowing, in the centre of the room, there is a stage, with play stations, two spanking benches, a queening chair, a bondage table, an x cross and a pommel horse contraption.

At the front of the room, to our left as we enter, on another stage, Amy sits on a throne, with Clive kneeling at her feet, her legs propped up on him. Clive's face is in a bowl of something sticky.

"Happy birthday!" Callie leans down and gives Amy a hug. "I love your crown."

"I love that you're here!" Amy says.

"Wouldn't miss it," Callie says. "Is Clive okay there?"

"He's fine. Wait until I tie him up and throw cake at him later. I can't wait. You take your boy and go play, darling. I can't wait to watch. At every table, there is whipped cream, strawberries, chocolate, and honey. Do what you will with that!" Amy yanks on Clive's leash. "Come here!" Clive does, his face covered in whipped cream. Amy pulls him to her and starts licking his face.

A shudder rolls through my body. I'm not sure if I like the idea or find it...horrible.

Callie slaps my ass. "Boy, I told you to go to the stage! I want to play now."

"Yes, Ma'am."

Callie reaches up, ruffles my hair. "Isn't this the best?"

This scene, where everyone is engaged in some sexual activity, from the subs with their faces in their Domme's pussy, to the guy on the cross whose being worked over with an electric wand, the subs kneeling and eating food off the plate is not my scene.

It's not something I'd choose to do, but because I'm here with Callie, I don't care. I'm only focused on how her hand feels in mine as she pulls me through the crowd.

Stopping at every second person to say hello.

Warmth spreads through my chest. I'm so proud of my Ma'am. She doesn't get how much people love her. How they all flock to her and want to see her.

It makes so fucking proud of her.

"On that table, head down, ass up," she pinches my nipple, cupping the back of my head. I moan into her mouth as she teases me with her teeth and tongue, and I want more.

Whatever will make her happy tonight, I want her to do it to me.

"Yes Ma'am. Whatever you want to do to me tonight, I'm game." The adrenaline surges through my veins as I say the words.

I mean it.

Maybe I'm trying to prove to her that I can be whatever she needs me to be.

Maybe I want to prove to her that no matter what she wants me to do or what she needs from me, I'll give it.

Maybe it's the first kinky birthday party I've ever been to, and I want to let go.

"What if I want you to do that?" Callie turns me to the left, where a male sub is wearing a hood while licking off something from his Domme's boots.

"Fuck yes." My penis throbs painfully at the sight. My mouth salivates. I lean towards her, wanting more of her touch.

"Wolfie, look at me." Her tone is grave.

I meet her startling blue eyes. "Yes, Ma'am?"

"Humiliation is one of your hard limits. You want to lick my boots clean?" Her gaze is heated, intense and makes me squirm with how closely she's studying my face.

"Service," I croak out the word, though it comes from the depths of my soul as the realization sparks through me that is exactly what I want to give.

What I need to give.

Her face dawns with understanding, but I think she's going to argue.

Like she's going to tell me I don't have to prove myself to her.

"What if I want to tie you to that bondage table and fuck your ass with my cock?" She threads her hand through my hair, and I let out a soft whimper at her forceful touch.

Oh damn. Heat slithers, pulse deep in my balls at the base. I lick my lips, craving her to fuck me like she wants to.

"Yes Ma'am. Please."

Callie pulls me by the waistband, squeezes my balls through the cage, sending a fresh wave of need pulsating at the base of my spine. "Drop those shorts."

Trembling with anticipation, standing in the middle of the stage, my mouth bone-dry, I push the shorts off.

With a quick grab, she takes off my shirt and throws it to the floor.

She grabs me above my elbow, takes me over to the bondage table. "I'm going to tie you up, then change."

"Yes, Ma'am."

Scenes are happening around us while she's talking to me.

I don't care that the guy beside me is eating out his Domme while she uses an electric wand on him, or the guy on the cross is being paddled by two Dommes, shouting 'Yikes!' every time the impact lands on his ass.

The only thing I care about is pleasing my Ma'am, obeying her direction.

I climb up onto the padded bondage table and lay back, staring at the high ceiling with chandeliers hanging overhead.

Callie grabs my wrists and cuffs them to the table. Memories of our night at Club Shivers roll through my head.

My stomach tightens into a ball, but I want this so much. My blood is searing with arousal and need.

"Ohhh! Isn't this a nice specimen!" A Domme with a purple braid over her shoulder pauses by me.

"He is, isn't he?" Callie purrs.

"Are you up to playing with us?" The Domme jerks on her leash, and a woman with short hair rises to her feet.

"Not today," Callie says.

"Shame," the Domme says as she moves on.

As she tightens the strap to my wrist, she runs her fingers along my inner thighs, lightly grazing the skin, teasing with just the right pressure.

"You're so beautifully exposed for me," she whispers in my ear, her voice low and sultry.

And I'm halfway gone into that sweet altered state of consciousness, where I only want to wait on her command, fulfill her needs. The mix of arousal and anticipation flames through me, stealing my breath.

"Your eyes are all glassy. I love that look when I know you're halfway to subspace. My perfect boy," Callie presses a sweet kiss to my mouth, runs her hands down my chest.

She turns from me, reaching for something, turns back, holding a strawberry, then she pops it into her mouth, her lips closing around the red fruit, then she takes it out, showing it to me.

Strawberries are the only food I now want to eat, forevermore.

Callie sweeps her hand through, runs her hand down my arm and puts something silicone in my hand, closing my fingers around it.

"I'll be right back. If you're uncomfortable, squeeze that toy. There is a dungeon monitor right here," Callie gestures to her left. "And I'll be super quick. You stay here and don't move... not that you could. Hold this in your mouth. Don't drop it or swallow it until I get back. Open."

"Yes, Ma'am," I say, my voice thick with all the need that's coursing through me.

She presses the strawberry to my mouth. The pleased smile on her face makes me feel all gooey.

I seal my lips around it, feeling the flesh of the strawberry against my tongue, the soft sweetness making my taste buds tingle, but all I can focus on is the sensation of being completely at her mercy

Heat slithers across my body, burns low in my balls, my mouth is salivating on overdrive. I don't know if I can hold this piece of fruit for much longer, but she cups my face in her warm palm.

"Good boy," and then she drums her fingertips against my cock cage, giving me a wink. "I'll be back."

Yeah, I can do this. I can do anything she asks of me.

The waiting is delicious torture.

Hearing what's going on around me, the cries of pleasure, the slaps of flesh, the laughter, the background atmosphere noises of a party in full motion, makes me feel like I have a blanket over me, muffling everything.

I can't capture what's happening, can't make out what's going on, even though I can hear.

After what feels like an eternity, Callie's soft hands are sliding up my neck.

"There's my Wolfie." She takes the squeaker toy out of my hand. "That strawberry is still intact?" Her sultry purr as she said it makes me want to burst out of the cage, the need and hot yearning for her dialing up.

I mumble around the half-softened fruit in reply.

She plucks it out of my mouth, then crams it right back in, while sealing her lips over mine.

Her bruising kiss makes my cock throb. The invisible electric connection between us flares to life, and the only thing that fills my senses is her.

The smell of her perfume, the whiff of shampoo I love, as she climbs on the table.

She's wearing the black harness, the thick curved, and she looks hot as fuck.

Callie's hot tongue is on my nipples, licking, sucking them so hard I whimper, my hips jerk, even though I don't have full range of motion.

"Stop that," she slaps my ass.

I force myself to be still.

"Good. Eyes on me, boy." Her gaze drinks me in, steadies me, makes me smiles languidly, then takes both my nipples in her fists and yanks them.

It takes me a second to realize the scream is mine. She leans down, kisses my nipples, her tongue lapping away the hurt.

"Good boy. I want to hear you yell over and over again. You can't see behind me, but we have an audience. I'm going to fuck you with my cock until I'm satisfied."

"Yes, Ma'am." My voice is hoarse.

My entire body is a live wire. One kiss from her, one brush of her fingertips along my arms is enough to have me writhe as much as I can in the bounds.

She lowers herself until she's lined up with me, but she inserts a finger into my hole without warning.

"Ma'am!" Red-hot pinpricks grip me, making me pant with need so pure, I'm practically crying.

"At least it's lubed up." She circles me, moving her finger back and forth. My nerve endings wake up, my cock pressing against the cage, wanting release.

Pulling her finger out, she wipes it against my thigh.

"I'm going to go so deep. Does that scare you?"

"Nothing you do scares me, Callista," I croak out the words. It's true.

I know this woman will take care of me.

She won't harm me.

Callie closes her eyes, and I drink in how her long eyelashes curve, her high cheekbones with the right shade of blush make her look strong and fierce.

She's mine.

As much as I am hers, this woman, with all her insecurities and fierce confidence, is mine.

"What's this?" Her voice is low, teasing, as she leans closer. "Are you all dripping for me?"

Her fingers slip through the cock cage, brushing against my sensitive skin, making me jump.

She gathers up the pre-cum, her touch searing hot and deliberate.

Callie pulls my bottom, rubbing her fingers across it, and the taste of myself mixes with the fruitiness of the strawberry, spiking my blood with more desperate need.

The pleased smile she gives me is pure reward.

"Yes, I am so hard for you, Ma'am."

"Yeah, but it's my cock that's going to take you, isn't it, boy?" The gravelly pitch of her voice vibrates right to the base of her spine.

I whimper in answer, trying to spread my legs more, but the restraints trap me.

The tip of the dildo slides in, pressing against me, making me cry out at the first pass of the intrusion.

My body wants to expel it, then as she thrusts, accept it.

She thrusts again, her hips bouncing against me.

"Deeper!" someone from the audience cries out.

They're shushed, I hear whispers and talking and murmurs of approval flirt to my ears.

But all that matters is Callie is riding me hard, thrusting slow, deep.

Even deeper.

"Callista!" I cry out her name, my voice desperate and hungry.

I'm so damn needy, I know I'm going to explode, even as she thrusts deeper, so hard, it feels like I'm going to be split apart.

But I need more, want her to take more from me, need her to push me closer to the edge, right now.

She rocks on the table, thrusting, panting, the pleasure etched across her face, making her look gorgeous, a fierce warrior claiming her prey.

"That's a good boy. You're taking this fucking like a perfect submissive. You're my perfect submissive."

"Lucky you", I hear someone say, my awareness drifting back to the crowd.

Callie's mouth set in a determined line, she thrusts forward, leans closer to me, eats up the space between us.

"Oh!" The sound slips out of my lips. The stretch, the slight burn, feels so damn good. I have never been so dominated before.

"My cock is fucking your ass, boy!" Her tone is primal and reaches right into my soul, dominating every part of me.

"Thank you Ma'am, for fucking my ass..." the words are so thick I don't know if I made sense, but she pants, scratches me with her long nails and digs into my skin, her touch flaying me and exactly what I need.

I want her to bite me, and maybe I said it because she leans down, kisses me with an open mouth sloppy kiss as she grinds against my ass, so deep I'm going to come apart, then sinks her teeth into my shoulder.

"Callista! Fuck! That hurts good!"

She holds on, her hips grinding with a rhythm that vibrates through every single one of my cells.

"Ma'am! Callista!" My voice screams her name. My throat is raw.

My penis is throbbing, trying to escape the cage, wanting relief, wanting that orgasm that's denied to me.

"Poor Wolfie, so helpless," Callista whispers against my ear.

She thrusts harder and deeper. My arousal surges, and suddenly I'm aware of the creaking of the table, the sweat above her cleavage.

The harsh lights above grow brighter, and the noise from the room splits my head apart.

Fire builds from my caged cock, to behind my dick, and my legs start shaking.

My penis feels is tingling, aching with the need to rise but it can't.

My whole body is shaking on the table, pleasure zips through me, so hard and fast I can't see anything in front of my eyes except black spots dancing behind my eyelids, I'm screaming her name again, and half-sobbing, my mind feels pulled into a swampy warmth and I float, nothing mattering except for the immense ecstasy that is flinging me higher.

"Shhh. You're a good boy, Wolfie," Callista says beside me. I don't know when she got off the table, or when she unrestrained me.

But her head pressed to my chest, she's rubbing my arms, soothing me.

"More, I want more." I tell her.

"Boy you're so far gone. Stay right here for another moment." She holds me and I feel tears slide down my face. that scene was so intense, my mind is fuzzy with the aftermaths.

"You were so good. My good boy." She lifts her head from my chest and cups my face with her hands. "Are you okay to move?"

"Yes," It's all I can do to get the word out.

"Stay here."

She gets up, grabs a wipe, cleans me off and then using another wipe, cleans the table. My head is floaty and all the noise in the room feels very far away.

"Boy you're so far gone. Come with me."

Taking me by the hand, she leads me to the bar and orders me a sports drink and then holds it to my lips.

I sip it and give her a huge smile. "Thanks."

She leads us to a table with bench seating, to a bench, pushes me down and then sits down, and pulls my head into her lap.

"Wolfie, how are you feeling?" She rubs a circle on my scalp, making me lean into her touch.

Every part of me feels electrified. I am jazzed up and want to do more.

"That was amazing, thank you, Ma'am."

"I love playing with my boy."

We join some of her friends at the table, and she feeds me bites of cake, fruit from her hand, and then we watch the line of subs who are servicing Amy, until the whole place shakes from her screams.

But the only thing I really notice is Callie.

Her smile, the crinkle of her eyes as she talks to other Dommes, the touch of her fingers through my hair.

The feeling of her skin on my tongue as she hand-feeds me another piece of fruit.

Her palm is warm as I mouth the food from it, slithers of need crawling along my skin.

"Down, Wolfie," she says.

I kneel on the floor, close enough to still feel the heat of her leg, to taste her skin if I wanted to swipe my tongue along her leg.

"Here you go, boy, you've earned your dessert." A plate is put down on the floor and then a piece of cake, then her booted foot stomps the cake.

A garbled cry escapes my lips. I'm licking her boot, not tasting the cake but working to clean it for her because she set it down in front of me.

Because she commanded me to.

Because she's my Ma'am and I'd do anything to make her happy, to see that she is fulfilled and happy.

Her fingers entwine in my hair. She pulls my head up and down. Laughter spins around me, and I don't care.

I'm servicing her, and that's making me so damn horny I'm going to break out of this cage, but I can't because she holds the key.

I drag my tongue slowly along the curve of her boot, the sugar residue sticky and humbling, making me whine as arousal slams into my cock.

The leather is warm, I can taste the polish, and I am lost in the task of making her boot clean for her again, my whole body crouched bent to the task, until she pulls back my shoulder, commanding me to stop.

"Good boy. Up."

I stand wobbly on my feet. She pushes me into a chair and gives me a drink of water and then she has my head back in her lap.

People come over to us, talk to her, she laughs, she smiles, she shows someone something from her bag.

Her fingers circle my lips, trail down my nipples, to my ass, and I'm lost in how she feels.

I want to crawl into her skin and stay there. I want to never leave her lap.

The rest of the night passes in a blur. There's cake and candles and singing, and then we are back in the elevator, except I'm naked and she's carrying the bag.

We're in our hotel room, and she's furiously kissing me, a long passionate kiss that I don't want to end, a kiss that's sending me spinning into a new orbit.

I love this woman.

"You were a very good boy, Wolfie." She's pressing my head between her thighs, and I'm so happy.

I bury my nose in her crotch, inhale her sweet smell and lick her, suck on her clit the way she likes me to.

The phone rings, but I keep going, needing to wring out every drop of pleasure I can, until her legs are shaking against my cheeks and she's panting above me, then she's crying out my name.

"Oh, fuck, boy. You are so damn good at eating my pussy. I could make you do that all night." Her throaty tone makes me shiver with pleasure that I've pleased her.

I let out a piercing mewl. She laughs and pushes me on the bed and slides in next to me and lays her head on my chest.

This was the best night of my life, and I need to tell her.

"I love you, Callista."

"I know," she slants her lips over mine, kisses me until I'm breathless and my heart slows down.

A phone rings again, and she pulls a blanket over me.

"You are my very good boy. I'll be right back."

32

CALLIE

"Hello?" I see the number on my screen, but I answer anyway.

Even though all I want to do is stand under a hot shower, cry, wipe my tears, and hug my Wolfie close to me.

This night?

The *best* ever.

Fucking my boy in the middle of my best friend's birthday party, with an audience of Dommes behind me, made me feel bad-ass, hot, and powerful, and my veins surged with a confidence I hadn't had in forever.

It's almost the same way I felt when Amy first took me to Club Shivers, and I had my first scene as a Domme.

The pure power of being in charge, knowing my boy was there to serve me, gave me an intense high.

"Hey babes! How's it going?" Gianna's voice is as breezy and carefree as ever.

"How do you know you didn't wake me up?" I grab a bottle of water from the mini-fridge, uncapping it as I walk into the washroom.

"How do you know I wasn't going to leave a message?" Gianna quips back.

"What can I do for you, Gianna?" I grab a make-up remover pad and swipe it across my face.

My fingers tremble, but I keep going, swiping so hard the cotton pad flakes.

The adrenaline high from tonight is definitely tapering off.

"Get your arse on a plane and join your team. We need you, Callie."

Yeah, her words hit me like a punch to the gut.

Meeting Gianna and the motocross team saved me.

It gave me a break from the grueling repetitiveness of working in a garage. It took me out of Rising Harbour and fulfilled my dream of seeing the world.

Gianna gave me a new purpose, made me feel part of a team.

It was exciting, giving me the thrill I craved and the freedom I longed for, every day.

There's a huge part of me that wants to chase that again.

I want to get on that plane, go join the team and resume exactly where I left off.

But the part that speaks through my fear knows I belong with the submissive man who said, "I love you," tonight and makes my heart sing in a different way.

Running away from problems is what I do, if you ask my sister.

It's a habit I can't quite give up, because chasing the thing that makes me feel powerful and in control and free will always be on my agenda.

You felt free tonight.

One amazing night.

Not one, but four amazing nights.

After weeks of my Wolfie showing me he is who he says he is, that he's not going to love me and leave me.

Weeks of him showing me that he wants more from me than a glammed-up kink dispenser, acting like the perfect gentleman, and the most beautiful submissive I could have ever dreamed of.

"Gianna, I'll see you soon."

"Yippee! The girls will be so happy to see you."

I hang up, peel off my clothes, and toss them on the floor.

My heart twists because I know Theo will pick up those clothes.

He'll pack them away in a dirty clothes bag that he has in his suitcase, and he won't even comment on how I'm a slob.

As the hot water pounds my back, the emotion I tried so hard not to give in to slams into me like a tsunami.

I crouch in the shower, wrapping my arms around myself, tears streaming down my face.

I *hate* crying.

This can't be happening.

I can't walk away from Theo.

I don't want to hurt him.

But I don't want to hurt him next month or next year.

I want him to have a woman he can count on, and I don't know if I can deliver on all my promises.

Grief ripples through my veins, and I am suddenly homesick for Rising Harbour.

For the sounds of the diner in the morning, seeing Brenda's warm smile, and whatever interesting colour of eyeshadow she had chosen to wear that day.

I want to see my sister, now that she's better, and tell her that I'm sorry I snapped at her.

It wasn't her fault, what my ex did to me.

She was just trying to look out for me.

I want to hug my nieces and nephew.

Still shaky, I feel more resolved now and stand.

I squirt conditioner in my hair, and run it through, just so I can stay in the shower longer.

I want Aunt Millie to teach me her butter tart recipe and listen to Uncle Henry explain why the 86-90 Volvo 240s is his favourite car to work on.

Then, I want to argue with him that my favourite, the '84 Mazda RX-7, is the better vehicle to play around with.

Stepping out of the shower, I wrap myself in a towel, stare into the mirror.

Most of all, I want to be sure that I am making the right decision.

I don't want anyone to hate me.

I don't want to let the people I care about down.

Maybe I should have made this decision before now, that would have been fair to all the parties involved.

It's hard being a peacekeeper.

You can't please everyone, and you overcompensate to try to please everyone all at once.

But at some point, I have to do what's best for me.

Right now, I need to get out. I need to drink in the air and be alone with my thoughts.

Tiptoeing back into the bedroom, I grab a pair of yoga pants and a sweater from my bag.

Theo stirs in his sleep, a dopey smile curling on his lips.

My gorgeous, perfect boy.

I wipe a tear from my face, grab my phone and step out of the hotel room.

Waiting for the elevator, I scroll through my phone, looking up flight times.

Alone in the elevator car, I'm cold, my skin clammy, and my head is kind of foggy.

Downstairs, the lobby is quiet other than a man reading by the fireplace and a couple checking in.

The hotel lounge is closed at this hour, so I take a seat in an armchair by the fireplace.

"Callie?" The voice isn't Theo's but resembles his rich timbre.

"Evan. I don't have my bags." My words come out muffled. "To leave."

I cover my face with my hands, biting down hard on my tongue.

"Hey, we can get your bags if you want to leave."

I pull my hands away from my face, sniffling. My stomach lurches, and I wish I could disappear because I hate people seeing me cry, *even* more than crying.

Evan crouches down beside me, his dark eyes full of concern. "Come with me, Callie."

He offers me a hand, and I take it, thankful he did because I'm not steady on my feet, my head woozy.

Glancing down, I see my feet are in the thongs I bought in case we use the hotel's pool.

Evan guides us down a hallway behind the receptionist desk, to an elevator.

I grab the wall, suddenly feeling queasy. My head spins, as if every sensation is too much to process.

The lobby outside Sinful Bites is dark, with no security guards in sight.

From the wild atmosphere earlier to this quiet space, it feels abandoned.

Evan swipes a card through the lock; the doors click, then he pushes them open.

The restaurant is dark and empty. He hits the light.

"Ow." I put a hand up to shield my eyes.

"Sorry, one sec." The lights are lowered to an acceptable dim.

"Better, thanks. This looks very different from the last time I saw it."
Gone were the throne and the stages and the bowls of desserts and the
decorations.

"We clean up fast," Evan says. "We're going to the kitchen." He walks
a step in front of me, glancing back over his shoulder to make sure I'm
okay.

In the kitchen, he gestures to a table off to the side, and I pull out a
chair, still feeling wobbly, and sit.

"Coffee, tea or energy drink?"

"Energy drink. I like the coconut one if you have it."

"Coming right up."

I hug myself, drawing my knees up under me.

My thoughts are heavy and spinning around.

I don't know what to do right now.

Evan places the drink in front of me, along with some cold cuts and a
croissant.

Taking a sip of the drink, I realize how thirsty I was, drinking nearly
half the bottle in one gulp.

I tear off a piece of the croissant, roll up a piece of salami.

Chew. Swallow.

"Thank you."

"Better?" Evan casts an observing glance over me.

"I forgot what top drop was like." I take another sip of the energy
drink, guilt settling over me like a mist and as soon as I say it, I realize
that it's the aftermath of the scene that my body and brain are trying
to process and the guilt rises up from the dark corners of my mind.
That's part of it too, for me.

I pushed Theo too hard last night, asked too much of him.

"Spare me the details, but the party was good?" Evan says. His dimples crinkle like his brother's, causing my heart to squeeze.

"Amy's dream fiftieth came true." This croissant is airy and buttery, and I could eat a dozen.

"Glad to hear it. Were you leaving, Callie?" There's no judgement in his tone.

"I'm trying to make a decision. I'm supposed to be the confident one."

"From what I hear, you flew in like a superhero, kept your family together all these months and kept a business that's been in your family for generations up and running. And you didn't let the council close you down when they wanted to."

"I hate bullies," I mutter.

"These aren't the actions of someone who isn't confident," Evan says, his tone gentle.

"Then why can't I make a decision?" I finish the energy drink, tilt my head up to the ceiling.

"Maybe you don't have to. You know, being a Dom isn't about making all the decisions or being confident all the time. We're people before dynamics."

Theo told me the exact same thing, but the way Evan says it cements it for me.

Theo makes a million decisions for his company every day.

He makes them in nanoseconds, and people rely on him for his expertise to keep their business safe.

I don't think he's less of a submissive because he's the boss outside of our relationship, and I don't think he's any less of a man because I'm the boss inside our relationship.

"I don't want to hurt him," I spin the drink in a circle.

Could I actually have it all? I can't have it all at once, but could I have a hand in Shel's, pursue wildlife photography, and be part of my motocross team?

I shake my head, answering my own question.

My success with the motocross team was because it was the first time someone had chosen me.

They didn't use me. They valued my skills and what I could do for them, and they included me and made me feel part of the team.

Being a racing mechanic is high pressure and as exciting as it is, it can be draining physically.

I want to see my family, and even with Daphne moving, I'd see her more often here.

"Good. As his older brother, I appreciate that. I see how he looks at you, Callie." Evan cocks an eyebrow at me.

"Yeah, that's hard not to notice." I blink back tears, determined not to let them fall.

"I've also noticed how you look at him," Evan says with a grin, showing me his perfectly straight teeth. "It's like jumping off a cliff."

"And hoping you land," I push my chair back, certain of what I want to do. "Thanks, Evan."

"I'll have Mara call you and set up a time to have you guys over for dinner."

"Sounds good," I say over my shoulder. But my heart is skipping a beat. All I want to do is get back upstairs and see my boy.

Leaving Sinful Bites, I stab the elevator button, impatient wanting it to get here. Once on our floor, I have to stop myself from running to our door.

But as soon as the light turns from red to green on the card reader, the door opens and my boy is standing there in a shirt and shorts.

"Callista?" He takes a step forward, but I push him back with a gentle hand on his chest.

And like so many times before, because it's one of my favourite things to do, when the door clicks behind me, I push him against it, caging him with my body.

I press my breasts against his wall of muscles, pull his face down to mine and I kiss him.

A long, passionate kiss, where I groan into his mouth, tease his tongue with mine, a kiss where I stand on my toes so I can get a deeper angle. I kiss this man like I own him and never want to let him go.

He's grinding against me when I finally break the kiss, stare into his precious grey eyes. "I need you, Wolfie."

"I need you too, Ma'am." He leans into me, nuzzling my neck, awakening tingling sensations all over my body.

My throat closes with tears, I take his hand in mine and lead him back to the bedroom, where I push him down on the bed.

Placing my hands on both cheeks, I study his face, and the love in his gaze reflecting back to me makes me feel loved, like I have never felt before, and suddenly, I am very, very sure.

"No, I need you...after we said goodnight, Gianna called me."

"You're leaving?" Theo's brows furrow. He sits up, so we're at eye level.

"Her phone call made me think about it, to be honest... it's the thrill of the chase, you know? But then I realized that team chose me. That's the feeling I wanted."

"I understand," Theo glances down at his hands, avoiding my gaze.

"Boy..." my voice catches. "*Theo*, look at me."

He slowly brings his head up to me, slides his hand down my arm to mine, and I lace my fingers through his, feeling the charge of electric heat jump between us, our connection pulsating and consuming... with room to grow.

"You make me feel like that. Like I'm *chosen*. Like I mean something to you."

"Someone. You're someone. You're my *someone,* Callista." His voice is barely above a whisper, as if he can't dare to hope.

"You're mine, Theo. You're my someone. And you're my *very* good boy. I love you."

33

THEO

Tears gather in my eyes, slowly fall down my cheeks, and I can't move to wipe them away.

I'm zeroed in on how she's reaching for me, how her body is turning toward mine, the air crackling with heat.

I had hoped...even though I told myself it was fine if she didn't say those three words.

If she couldn't say them or didn't want to commit or if she was scared, it was fine because I'd take her anyway she'd let me have her.

"I love you, Callista."

Ripping my shirt from my shoulders, she throws it onto the floor.

She squeezes my ass, pulls my shorts down my legs, dropping kisses on my collarbone, then brushing her lips down my chest, over to my nipple and flicks it with her hot tongue.

My fists clench at my sides, struggling to maintain control.

"I know. Come." Her voice is low, commanding.

She grabs me by the cage, her fingers digging into my soft cock as she leads me toward the bedroom.

My dick throbs for her touch, and I want to pull her against me, kiss her, take her, show her that I love her with long caresses and sweet kisses, but she drums her fingers on my sac, making me yelp and stop. I suck in a breath and follow her.

Because I will follow this woman, no matter where she leads me or how.

"On the bed."

"Yes, Ma'am." Even as I am stepping toward the bed, she pushes me down, her cool palms against my chest, and climbs on me, kissing my collarbone, my throat, my lips.

"You please me so much boy," she nips at my neck, sending my hands to her waist, pulling her down tighter to me because I want to lick every inch of her skin, but tears are still leaking from my eyes, my heart bursting with love for her.

"Ma'am! I need you." I tangle my fingers in her hair. She tilts her face to me, and her eyes are also shiny with tears.

"Sush, you're my good boy. I'm going to fuck you and take every drop of your cum and then I'm going to slap that cage back on and not let you out for three weeks."

A fiery mix of need, want, and pure, submissive longing shoots through my body, making me gasp.

"Yes, Ma'am."

She throws off her clothes, kicks off her thongs and dives on the bed, tackling me with a yelp of joy, causing me to bounce near the edge of the bed, my head practically dangling over the edge.

Callie laughs, a whole-body laugh that makes her skin glow and her eyes glimmer.

"I love you." She yanks on my arm, bringing me back squarely on the bed.

"I've wanted to hear you say that for so long. I was afraid...that you were..."

"Going to leave?" She caresses my cheek, and I press into her hand, wanting more of her touch.

"Yes."

"It was close. Thought about it. I realized everything I want and need-" She kisses my forehead. "Everything that I have ever wished for, I found with you."

Sobs break out from my throat, and I can't hold them back.

She leans down and kisses me hard, her hair teasing my nostrils.

I return her kiss, hungry, insistent, wanting more, needing to taste her, wanting to cement her every molecule into my being.

This woman makes me feel like I am on top of the world, even when I'm on my knees for her to allow me to release.

"I'm going to sit on your face. You're going to make me cum."

My breath hitches in my throat as she lowers herself on my face, her seam at my nose, my hands roaming over her hips, guiding her down.

Her tangy perfume teases the back of my throat as I open my mouth, my lips close on her soft silky flesh.

Above me, she moans, sliding her open fingers over my nipples.

"Suck me good, boy."

I whimper, her tone sends my cock throbbing. I circle her swollen, wet clit with my tongue, flicking back and forth, then suck it as hard as I can, taking it into my mouth. Her legs quake against my cheeks, her neck strains as her gaze lifts to the ceiling.

"Yes! More."

I obey with my whole jaw, mouth working against her hard clit. I want to give her pleasure. I want to make my Domme fall apart.

Lost in her saltiness, I press my mouth against her clit, sucking, swallowing as hard as I can on the sensitive bud.

She makes a fist on my chest, brings it down on my skin, beats me in rhythm to my sucking. Around her pussy, I cry out, as her taste anchors me further to her, even as she keeps bringing her closed fist down on my chest.

I don't dare let go. I know she's close.

"Yes! Good boy, that's it!" She grinds her hips, her movements become frantic, pressing down against my mouth with a force so overwhelming, I can barely draw a breath.

My chest tightens, my throat swells with a panicky thrill. I need to move.

But just as my hands are going to tap on her, beg her for release, she moves, shifting the pressure. I inhale deeply through my nostrils, her craveable scent flooding the air.

Her hips continue to grind, slower now, each roll of her body making me want to please her.

Keeping my mouth on her hot pussy, I suck, feeling her clit grow even harder, swollen, ready to burst on my tongue.

"I am coming!" And she does, her muscles contract, her legs press against my face and she's coming, grabbing my nipples in between her fingers, pinching and pulling them as she does.

Watching her body rack with the pleasure I lavish on her gives me a buzz, sends me searching for my own high.

Knowing I can't get it because the key is around her neck and I'm locked up.

Finally, she moves off my face.

"Good boy," she traces my lips, wet with her juice, with her index finger. "Open."

I do and clean her finger, greedily sucking off the taste of her, my cock throbbing with frantic want.

"Your tongue is so damn talented, Wolfie."

"I love how you taste." I offer her my lips to kiss, and she takes them, lifting herself up, all flushed and beautiful, still catching her breath.

She licks my bottom lip, then kisses me with a roar that vibrates down to my toes.

"Off the bed, boy."

I scramble up, even as she's sitting there, her head lifted to the ceiling as if she's thinking.

Her gorgeous smile spreads across her face, lighting her up.

"Get my toy bag."

I scurry off to the main sitting room, from where it was left last night, and bring it to her.

She rummages through it, and my heart stills as she pulls out the collar and leash she used on me at Club Shivers.

"This stays on while we play. I want to get you something more permanent later." She says words, her voice low and thready, like she's trying to hold back emotion.

She settles the leather band around my neck, the coolness of the material sending a shiver down my spine.

My breath hitches.

A sob escapes me.

The pressure of the leather against my throat, combined with the weight of her touch, overwhelms me, because she's giving me exactly what I've longed for, claiming me permanently as her own.

"You're mine, Wolfie. I love you."

She kisses me with the authority of the woman who owns me, her tongue sweeping the edge of mine, with slow, quick strokes before her lips slant against mine, kissing with so much force a shockwave of pleasure rips through my body. Our combined moans echo around us, desperate, primal, needy sounds echoing each other's.

There is nowhere else I want to be.

Callie breaks off the kiss, glides her palm against my cheek.

"I love you, boy."

"Love you, Ma'am."

Callie lifts my chin to her shimmering gaze, then glides her hand down between my legs, sinking to her knees.

"This comes off when I want it to. I want to play with my cock now." She slips the key off her neck, unlocks the cage.

"Thank you, Ma'am!" I want to palm my cock, to feel it, but I wait.

Callie gives me a sly smile and takes my shaft in her hand. "Stand up, Wolfie."

With all my blood rushing in my ears, I do. The sight of my Domme on her knees, staring at me with that sexy smile on her face, is enough to make me come undone. She pulls my cock and I groan.

"Someone is so sensitive," she thumbs my slit and I jump, flinch, my cock eager to feel every sensation.

I let out a groan as she leans down and takes my cock into her wet hot mouth.

"I love the feel of your mouth on my cock, thank you, Ma'am!"

It's hot nirvana. It hurts to breathe. The pleasure she's giving me is so intense, it is taking everything I have to remain standing.

She sucks, taking me even deeper, licking the base of my cock, then her tongue flicks to my balls.

"You're beautiful, Callista. I want to come in your mouth. Please let me come in your mouth!" I can't help jerking my hips forward, thrusting but she picks up the leash, gives me two sharp pulls and I get the hint and stay still, as her mouth is sending a new wave of hot buzzing pleasure that's makes me groan out her name.

My thoughts are still, the only thing I want is release. I'm desperate.

"Boy, up now." Her tone is a sharp slice through the building pleasure, the need to spill.

"Yes, Ma'am," the words come out like a cry.

Callie laughs, tossing her head back. She stands, grabs my hardening cock, and slants her mouth over mine in a greedy, wet kiss.

Kissing her is my favourite thing to do.

My cock jerks in her hand, desperation slithers through me, but the feel of her lips on mine is something I want till the end of time. I don't care about anything else.

She breaks off the kiss, slings her arms around my neck, pulls me close, she presses against me. "Mine."

Hearing the certainty in her tone fills my eyes with tears. Again.

She reaches up, grabs a fistful of hair, and pulls my head up.

"My beautiful boy. Stay." Callie drags her hand down my chest, gives my cock one more tug before sauntering over to the bed.

She lies down, slowly spreads her legs wide open, and drags a finger down her stomach to her pussy.

"Come fuck me, Mr. Sexypants."

As if she'd pressed a button that revs me up to top speed, I jump on the bed, startling a laugh from her lips.

Diving in between her legs, she lets out a high-pitched shriek, and joy drums through my veins to match it.

I rub my cheek against her inner thighs, skim my lips over her soft, silky skin, before throwing her legs over my shoulders.

"Kiss me!" A tug on the leash makes me shuffle, and my lips meet hers. There is nothing that tastes better.

She deepens the kiss, her heel drums on my shoulder.

"Slowly, boy. Get that dick in me, inch by inch."

Electricity races up my spine, shooting me back between her legs. I line my dripping cock up with her entrance. I've barely touched her when the leash pulls on me.

"Slower." The smile on her face is pure amusement.

"Yes Ma'am," And so slowly, I don't even think I'm going to get seated with her, I enter her pussy.

Her sweet heat coats my cock, and I want to move in her, but my muscles tense, waiting for her command.

"Give me that cock, boy."

I plunge right to the hilt, and cry out, my cock in her sweet pussy exactly where I want to be.

"That's a boy," she pulls on the leash. "More. I want that cock. Don't stop."

"Ma'am! I won't! Hold on!"

She grips my hips, then traces her claw marks from last night, pressing her finger pads into them, setting off stabs of delicious pain. Her pussy clenches around me and, fuck, I don't want to move from here, ever.

I thrust, rocking my hips, plunging deep, wanting more, wanting to see her fall apart.

She digs her fingernails into my biceps, and the bite of pain spurs on my thrust as I go even deeper, rocking in her wetness, her pussy gripping my cock in a perfect fit.

We move together, the world falls away from us, and our moans and throaty breaths, our raw primal growls, are the only sounds that matter.

Her eyes light up as I thrust, hitting the right spot, her pussy gripping even more, taking me all the way in. She stares into my eyes, and I know I am exactly where I am supposed to be.

"Theo, more!" Her plea startles me out of my sensual, weighted thoughts, and I rock even deeper.

"Yes, Ma'am!"

Even more, I pound into her pussy, driving deeper, wanting to wring out more cries from her, even though I am drenched in sweat.

I love every unguarded sound she makes, the way her lips are swollen from our kisses.

She grabs a fistful of my hair, yanking the strands enough to make me cry.

"I better come in the next two minutes." It's a sharp, cool command.

I crash my mouth against hers, swallowing her laugh, as I grind against her, my cock thrusting into her sweet hot pussy.

Her nails catch me around my nipples, zip down my back, my skin feels like it's being flayed open.

With a roar, I plow into her, her pussy spasms like a vise around me, and I grind on her, my hands sliding underneath her because I want to stare into her beautiful eyes as she allows me this divine treat.

"I love you." My voice is shaky, her hips roll against me, urging me to penetrate her even harder.

I rock hard into her, so deep and fast we're bouncing on the bed.

Our cries echo, making us both vibrate. The room smells of sex and heat and passion. I want to give this woman everything I have.

"So close, Wolfie!" She pulls the leash, keeping my head right here as I grind into her, rocking her, taking us even deeper and further into our abyss.

Here, right now, it's just my gorgeous Ma'am and me.

I am hers to command, so when she slaps my ass and tells me, "Slow." I somehow pull back the momentum, even though it strains every single muscle.

"You have one more minute, boy, to give your Ma'am what she wants."

Anticipation and a twinge of fear races up my spine, I pound into her, my hands under hips, lifting her up, so we are merged together, her skin is shiny with sweat too and I lick it as I thrust, the salty taste of her skin makes my balls heat, close to explosion.

Her legs come around me, I go even further, rocking harder, loving her little cries and her scream as I hit the spot makes me grin through my sweat.

"Yes! Now! You better come right now, boy!" Her pussy clenches so hard my cock can barely move.

But her heat feels so good, and my balls are finally free to burst.

I come so damn hard I'm trembling, groaning like a wild animal.

Thank fuck.

"Thank you, Ma'am!" I cry out, into her neck, our bodies pressing together as I release deep into her, shuddering with the euphoria of the orgasm.

She wraps her arms around me. "I love you."

"I love you, too. Now clean me up." Pure velvet dominance in her tone compels me to obey even though I feel the come down of post-orgasm bliss.

I get between her legs, put my face right in her pussy and lap up our combined juices.

"You're a very good boy," Callie rubs a circle on the top of my head, and I let out a soft growl against her stickiness.

She unhooks my leash from the collar and sets it on the nightstand.

"Shower."

"If you insist."

She grabs my balls, gives them a tug. The pressure makes me jump.

"I do." The grin on her face is so slyly beautiful, I can't help but laugh, she laces her hand through mine.

She picks up the cock cage on the way to the bathroom. Making sure I see what she's doing, in the washroom she cleans it out before she turns on the shower.

"In, boy, hands against the wall."

The warm water sluices between my shoulder blades as Callie holds the shower head above me. Her cool fingers pull apart my ass, and she sprays the nozzle in between my cheeks.

I'm panting, my mind heavy and floaty from the sex, but I know what I want, and it's whatever this woman wants to do to me.

"I'm going to have to clean you better later." I hear the smile in her voice as she slips a finger between my ass cheeks, curling my hole, sending a shooting shiver of pleasure through my entire body.

"Callista! Yes, Ma'am." The water turns off, a soft sponge is on my back and Callie starts to circle it, washing my back, my ass, the back of my legs.

Her touch is sure, confident, quick.

"Come here."

Lifting off the wall, I turn to face her.

She slowly draws the sponge around my nipples, down my stomach, around my cock.

"There. This is ready to be put back in its cage." She rinses me off, grinning at me.

"Whatever Ma'am wants," I lean down and kiss her lips, gently and slow.

"Out."

I obey, stepping out of the shower and watch as Callie washes her breasts, pulling her nipple, teasing me with it.

She spreads her legs and washes her pussy, making me grind my molars with the effort of standing still.

I want this woman.

Not just for tonight or tomorrow but forever.

Callie stops the water. I hold open a towel, wrap her up in it and start drying her off.

"We need food. Desperately." Callie walks through to the sitting room. I reach for the phone, but there's something more than food I want right now.

I put my hands on her shoulders. She lifts her head, curiosity in her eyes.

"Stay right here, please?"

"I'm not going anywhere," she kisses my cheek.

Nerves flutter and grip me, but I push through.

There is only one thing I want, and it's so close I can taste it.

In the washroom, I pick up the cock cage, checking to make sure it's dry.

"Boy?" She glances over her shoulder, turning to me as I stop in front of her, sinking to my knees.

"I need you, Callista. I want you. Everything I have is yours, forever. I love you."

I take her hand gently, pressing the cock cage into her palm.

"Will you allow me to be your husband?"

Her eyes immediately fill with tears. She lets out a strangled sob, holding the cage like it's a precious gem.

"Oh, Wolfie. Mine. Yes." She wipes away her tears furiously, and she sinks down to join me on the floor.

Her lips slant against mine, and she kisses me, a hot, furious kiss that speaks of promises and control and flowing desire.

Our love pulsates between us, and hot tears splash down my cheeks.

Callie brushes them away with the pads of her thumbs. She opens the cock cage. I let out a whimper.

"Your submission is so damn hot and precious and I love you," she kisses my cheeks, drags her lips against mine, stopping my cries.

"I love you, Ma'am." My voice cracks. The weight of the cage in my hand now feels light and the most natural thing in the world.

"Lock up what's mine for me, boy." She slips the key off her neck, placing it in my hand.

My hands tremble as I slide the key into the lock and close it.

A deep, knowing sense of peace settles in my being as Callie holds me close. "I love you. I can't wait to marry you," Callie skims her lips over my cheeks, her eyes ablaze with the same deep love I feel for her. "And I can't wait to play again later tonight."

"All my nights belong to you, Ma'am. I love you."

Her lips meet mine, and she kisses me so fiercely I feel it down my spine, to the depths of my soul.

I love this woman, and I'll spend the rest of my nights showing her exactly how, tonight and forever.

***

If you enjoyed Callie and Theo's story, please leave a review!
Start the Sinful Delights Series from the beginning with Five Days of Christmas Spicand Five Days to Be Mine
The last book in the series is coming soon!

Acknowledgements

To my readers, you are the **best!**

Thank you for hanging with me and for asking for more books and sliding into my DMs to tell me how much you loved them. You all sure know how to keep an author writing. I'm so grateful!

Thanks goes to Cecil (for the motocross intel), Lane (for the "a day in the diner" rundown) and the real Clive (for giving Callie and Theo's story an early read and bringing that male submissive perspective) and Fern (for answering all my brain injury questions).

To my incredible beta team: Laura, Taira, Roxanne, Kayla: I'm one lucky author to have you read my stuff.

Many thanks to my ARC Readers! I couldn't do this without your wonderful support.

To my co-host and SSMWC: your friendship makes this writing thing so much better — *thank you!*

Much thanks to Rune. Your support and care, your attention to detail and your talented skillset, made this book a thousand times better.

Deepest appreciation also goes to raga.muffin.design for graphics and the gorgeous cover. Thank you for taking this on! Love it so much.

Thank you, to my dearest for all the things.

Thank you to my lucky stars and my Mate, for all that you do for me that allows me to do this... love you more.

www.ingramcontent.com/pod-product-compliance
Lightning Source LLC
Chambersburg PA
CBHW021845010726
47493CB00005B/1554